BETH BALL

FEATHER & FLAME
BOOK ONE

Published by Grove Guardian Press

Edited by Kat Betts of Element Editing Services

Cover design by Mibl Art

Second Revised Edition 2025

Paperback ISBN 978-1-952609-41-1

Hardcover ISBN 978-1-952609-42-8

Ebook ISBN 978-1-952609-40-4

groveguardianpress.com

ALSO BY BETH BALL

Feather & Flame

Phoenix Rising

From the Ashes (forthcoming)

Age of Azuria

Buried Heroes

Hadvarian Heist

Amber Queen

Forest Deep

Shadows Beneath

Heir of Lilith Trilogy

Phantom

Pain (forthcoming)

Novellas and Short Stories

Hexblade, a *Feather & Flame* novella

"Awakened Flame," an *Age of Azuria* story

Aurora, an *Age of Azuria* novella

Song of Parting, an *Age of Azuria* novella

Story Magic, an *Age of Azuria* novella

Stormborn, a standalone *Tree of Silver* novella

Promise, an *Heir of Lilith* novella

*To my sister, Rachel, who sees change agents where others see
only dreamers*

DUR'FOR
HALLOWED HILLS
BASTI
VERITA
THE GLADE OF SHADOWS
SCOURGE

NORTHLANDS
FAER HAVEN
VESTIGE
SANCTUARY
MERIDIENNE MOUNTAINS
RESPITE
THE GREEN MOUNTAINS
MAEN
THE EMERAUDE
CLE
PALAIS
BEACON
THE WORLD OF ELDURA

Let me tell you the story of heroes of old,
Whose adventures, now forgotten, were once
　　widely told.
Let me tell you the story of how the old world
　　fell,
Of those who fought to save it, and who
　　fought well.

CHAPTER ONE

TALI

SANCTUARY

Tali raced down the narrow stone stairs, breath short within her chest. In the courtyard below, Candace and Olivier, twin champions, she a wielder of flame and he of water, faced off against one of Alessandra's dragon-servants, fearsome creatures blessed in ancient times with elemental magic and might. The twins whirled their swords and scimitars, Candace pure rage, Olivier measured grace and power. The bloody remains of half a dozen soldiers lay scattered across the courtyard around them. The mutilated corpses were all that was left of their allies assigned to the upper ramparts. Sanctuary's forces, though well trained, were no match for a dragon.

Briznexi swirled above the twins, her wings and tail propelling her through the smoke-filled air of the courtyard, while the twins battled her from the ground.

"Hold on!" Tali shouted down to them, her voice lost

within the clamor of battle. The twins were beyond her encouragement anyway, and if she did not hurry, their bodies would join the piles of the dead.

She had to do something. Now.

Steeling herself, Tali rose on tiptoes to peer over the railing—Sanctuary had not been designed for dwarves—angling herself so that her arm could stretch over the stone wall. Tali set her teeth, clenching her will, and sent a beam of pure light into Briznexi's side. She had tried to maintain the element of surprise as long as possible, but Candace and Olivier could no longer wait for her aid. The twins would have been lost to the dragon had not Ilona, her titan, called Tali away from the battlefront at the gates to this surprise attack from the skies. If Briznexi were successful in gaining the towers, Sanctuary's troops would be routed before the third day of battle had truly begun. The city would fall to Alessandra's might, and all the souls trapped inside would be hers.

Eldura itself—not to mention the tenuous alliances of the Cities United—couldn't withstand losing one of their own to Alessandra. And so rapid a defeat as this one might be, the others could fall in quick succession.

Tali channeled her desperation into the beam, willing it to shatter the dragon's scales, impale her side. The pure light energy rippled beneath the swirling shadows that clung to Briznexi's scales before the rays dissipated to nothing.

She jumped as the dragon's voice echoed inside her mind. *"Your every strike strengthens me, lightbringer. Do you think my mistress retains no control over Ilona's light?"*

Tali cried out, stumbling back away from the wall.

Heresy. To claim that Alessandra could access even a drop of Ilona's elemental power—the titan would never allow it. "Liar!" Tali shouted.

The dragon chuckled in reply, her laugh rollicking flame and sizzling ember. *"You would do well to surrender now and save your friends, Champion of Light."* Briznexi's tail lashed the ground between the twins. They each dove to the side, away from one another.

Tali resumed her sprint down the winding tower stairs.

Briznexi was separating them, singling them out.

"Stay together," Tali shouted from the base of the stairs. Candace nodded. Olivier groaned as he extricated himself from the rubble.

Briznexi seized her chance. She pirouetted through the air and swept down toward Olivier. He cried out as she broke through his watery shield.

With a solid snap of her jaws and a scream from the elf, the dragon veered away. Blood splashed onto the broken stone of the tower, raining down with the dragon's saliva. Briznexi released Olivier's severed leg from her maw. It fell onto the courtyard's stones with a sickening *squelch*, the first sound Tali registered, so deafening were Olivier's screams.

Blood rushed from his wound, an effect of Briznexi's poison.

"Join my lady, and I will leave one alive," the dragon growled in Tali's mind. *"Choose. Quickly."*

"Olivier!" Candace climbed onto the pile of rubble separating her from her twin brother. Motes of flame rained down from her shortswords, each blade wreathed in fire. The fire droplets sizzled onto the crumbled stones on one side of the crevasse Briznexi's tail had created, a divide as deep at least as the elf was tall.

"I will never join you," Tali shouted back.

With two powerful beats of her wings, the shadow-clad dragon thrust herself away from the courtyard. Their one advantage might come if a regiment from the Luz spied Briznexi above the swirling smoke of Sanctuary. Tali's height prevented her from watching what transpired below. She shot a burst of light into the air, flashing ahead of the dragon's path, hoping someone below might see.

It was the lone chance the three champions might have.

Beneath the battering of Briznexi's wingbeats, Candace stumbled in her scramble across the rocks. She tumbled backward, losing the ground she had gained, and had to run again at the wall of rubble Briznexi had erected between her and her twin. Centuries of craftsmanship, smashed in a moment by the dragon's tail.

Olivier's screams had ceased.

Tali ducked beneath a toppled cart in the center of the courtyard. She stretched out her hand and sent a healing spell to Olivier's side, but still the elf's hands slackened around his severed thigh. The pale limestone beneath him turned red as the porous rocks slurped up the fresh blood.

Time slowed as Briznexi reared back. She pivoted, angling her neck down toward the twins, the one moment she might be vulnerable.

Candace's arms shook as she pushed herself over the

wall of rock. She stumbled to Olivier's side. The elf fell to her knees and pulled her brother's head onto her lap.

"No!" Tali yelled. She had been wrong to tell them to stay together. With a final roar, Tali raised her axe over-head and flung it at the flapping beast, desperate to drive her from the sky.

The dragon's words echoed in her mind, the impossibility that she might not only be immune to Ilona's light, but made more powerful by it, rather than the shadows that braced her hide . . . Tali stopped herself from casting a spell of light upon the axe as it flew, a great *whoosh* as it turned end over end, arcing straight for the base of the dragon's throat, where her poison brewed.

Briznexi thumped her wings against the air and dodged out of the way, sending a scatter of rocks across the courtyard as the wind she caused shifted course. "No!" Tali shouted again, her axe missing by inches. Another impossibility, her aim had been perfect. The axe crashed against a failing roof on the opposite side of the square, disappearing in a rain of shingles and tumbling stones.

Briznexi's foul yellow eyes fixed upon Tali amidst the smoke of the battlefield. *"I'll leave you to wonder why you were spared,"* the dragon snarled. She lowered her head and exhaled a bright purple stream over the twins.

Candace screamed and leaned closer over her brother, shielding him from the blast.

Tali's lips parted, her own screams dying upon her lips as the elf's skin, hair, and armor melted. Candace crumpled, a yellow-green husk of rotten flesh with her brother's ruined legs jutting out beneath her.

"Unity is weakness, Tali Silversword," Briznexi called back within Tali's mind as she flapped away. *"Remember that, until we meet again."*

Tali fled the castle of Sanctuary after Briznexi's departure from the ramparts, the dragon's words ringing in her ears, Candace and Olivier's ruined bodies burned across her vision. The fallen bodies of the Luz and their allies choked the hallways. She saved those she could and emerged into the smoky chaos at the base of the castle supporting a battalion soldier beneath the arm. The man collapsed as soon as they reached the edge of the field from where they'd staged their attack.

A stallion's shrill whinny broke through the dragon's echo, and Tali's eyes shot up to the black-plumed helmet of one of their allies' commanders from Vestige. "They need healers back at the camp," the woman shouted. But something about Tali made her stop.

The commander slipped off her helmet and gave a small tug on the reins. Tali stared up at the two of them. Had Candace and Olivier been stationed in Vestige before they all met to train on the outskirts of Respite?

Thick black braids wound around the woman's head. She stared down at Tali and blinked smoke out of red-rimmed brown eyes. "You've seen something, haven't you?"

Tali shook her head and the woman's eyes narrowed. She had never excelled at falsehoods.

"I feel it. Here." The woman placed her middle finger

between her eyebrows. "There's a seer in my camp. She can help you."

"N-no," Tali answered. "They need me here."

The commander nodded. "I will tell her to expect you, though she likely does already." The woman bowed her head, met Tali's gaze, and clicked her tongue to her horse. The two cantered away down the battle lines.

Had the dragon cursed her and written her doom, the doom of all Eldura, clearly upon her face? That couldn't be. She was a lightbringer, one blessed by the power of Ilona. Even a dragon's curse couldn't break her bond with the titan.

Tali hurried back to the side of the man she'd helped. His leg was bleeding profusely from a wound upon his thigh. Though not as great a torrent as Olivier's wound had been, the soldier wouldn't survive if she didn't act soon. Orange-brown irises blurred and focused on her face, and his head swayed.

"Shh," Tali urged, "lie back." As gently as she could with hands that would not stop shaking, she pushed his shoulders back toward the ground.

"You saved me," the man murmured in a thick mountain accent. He winced as she tightened a second tourniquet around the top of his leg. "You saved me," he murmured again. His eyes rolled back in his head, and he lay still.

CHAPTER TWO
TALI

The blood of the man she'd tried to save still clung to Tali's skin as she picked her way through the dark indigo tents of the soldiers from Vestige. The distant, muted cries from an unseen healer's tent echoed out into the night. Some shuddered at the sounds. Others failed to react, lost within the lingering roar of battle.

The sun necklace hanging proudly upon the center of Tali's chest was enough for the guards on watch to let her pass without question. She should have asked them where she might find the seer, but she had drawn enough attention to herself already.

Given how the day had gone, the rigors of the fighting and the vast extent of the losses, it was likely that rumors were already beginning of the failure of the champion of light, the one too weak to save those she should have worked hardest to protect—her fellow bearers of the elemental titans' will.

They were growing fewer and fewer, their numbers

shrinking with each passing week of warfare. Soon they, like the three titans who had already abandoned Eldura, would be little more than a memory.

The rustling tinkle of glass beads caught Tali's attention, reminding her of her purpose. She straightened and brushed her hair back over her shoulder. Tali wasn't given to such superstitions as fortune telling. Ilona held the will of all within her hands.

But she had seen her light, the force of Ilona's blessing, a physical manifestation of the titan's smile, fade into nothingness upon Briznexi's hide. The blast should have carved through the dragon's magical protections and then her flesh. How had Ilona's gift become a source of mockery, even humiliation?

Tali's hand lingered in her hair, smoothing it back. She wore three braids, each woven with the colors of the sun, the highest honor among the ranks of Beacon, her home. The other titans had favored cities of their own, those the titans had sworn to protect, but they spread their gifts across the world of Eldura. Not so with Ilona. Her champions always came from Beacon. Even the traitor Alessandra, a former, fallen champion of light.

Tali shuddered as she stood outside the tent that could only belong to the seer. Thin tendrils of pale smoke curled out of the purple beaded curtain that hung across the entryway. Tali inhaled and then coughed. *Sage.* The herb had never sat well with her. Beacon's priests preferred resins and sacred oils for the honoring of the titan of light and the few deities who had secured Ilona's trust and blessing. In Tali's home, they left the burning of herbs to the fickle witches of the Emeraude, those too cowardly to stand against Alessandra and defend their world from the press of darkness.

A low, scratchy voice called out to Tali from inside the tent. "You come seeking peace and bring a mind of war instead, Tali Silversword." Beyond the curtain, the dry *clack* of bone sounded across a wooden bowl.

Tali shut her eyes. What was she doing here? She'd find no help or sense from a seer.

"Step inside and choose your fate, Champion of Light."

Tali ground her teeth, her jaw still sore from battle, and considered the seer's invitation. Whatever had transpired with Briznexi had been easily visible to the dark-plumed commander. Was she dragon-marked, now?

She had peered into a mirror in her own tent, but her face appeared the same. Tan skin, broad brow, blond hair. The paint of Ilona smeared by dust and blood.

Melodic laughter rippled out from the seer behind the hanging strands of beads. "Would you prefer to be always wondering, or would you chance knowledge outside your usual realm?"

The dwarf rolled her eyes open and shook her head. She would need all the resolve she could possibly muster before facing a seer in her own domain. For reassurance, she clasped her sun amulet, reminding herself of Ilona's eyes upon her. To be a champion of light was to dwell always within the titan's gaze.

Tali glanced over her shoulder, but no one stirred through the dark rows of the camp. She pushed aside the beaded curtain and stepped into the seer's tent.

Knots of drying herbs hung from the ceiling, and

colored glass bottles and wooden bowls covered the round table in the center and the two shelves that ran along the side. One shelf held thick, leather-bound tomes and large crystals. The light within the tent flickered from tapered indigo candles that dripped dark blue wax onto iron bases.

Tali picked her way around the table and found a woman with thick, onyx hair perched on a purple floor pillow with legs crossed before a crystal orb. A gasp flared to life in her throat, but she stifled the urge to grasp her solar pendant and back away from the woman. Such divinatory practices were forbidden in the city of Beacon. Ilona and the sun god knew all. It was only the faithless who were uncertain about the future and tricked themselves into believing that such things might be changed with knowledge rather than prayers.

The voice in the back of Tali's mind sneered at her hypocrisy. *Then why are you here?* She ignored the twist of doubt in her gut and met the seer's stare.

A slow smile spread across the bronze features of the seated woman. "You bring such turmoil to my abode, Champion of Light. It hangs around you like a cloud of gnats. The question one might ask is whether you prefer to bear your burdens alone or are brave enough to ask for my help?"

Tali frowned at the image of gnats swarming about her head. Such pests gathered over the bodies of the dead upon the battlefields of Eldura. Countless times, Tali had carefully sifted through broken, bleeding bodies lying jumbled together, searching for signs of life that might be restored. What would a seer know of such trials? "There are few who would question the honor of a champion of light."

The woman's dark eyes danced as she stared up at Tali. She gestured to the cerulean cushion across from her on the other side of the orb. "I questioned whether you were brave enough to imagine guiding spirits outside the few you know. It is you who believes that questioning impugns honor."

Tali considered this for a moment. It had been a commander who had suggested she come here. If nothing else, she had to find out about the dragon's curse, if such a thing existed, however distasteful and dubious she found the seer.

Her presence here might serve to soothe uneasy relations later, if the armies from Vestige resisted the wisdom of those of Beacon and the Army of Light.

With a nod, Tali stomped over the few feet that remained between her and the seer and lowered herself onto the cushions. Her long dwarven torso, stretched as tall as she could make herself, brought her to the chest-height of the seer across from her.

The woman had grace enough to bow her head as Tali settled onto the cushions. Only the soldiers from Vestige would bring a seer with them to the battlefield. What was next, a saudad muster performing as the front guard of an army? Tali scoffed at the thought. Why had she come here? Was she truly so terrified of Briznexi's pronouncements that she had abandoned sense and reason?

It was true that she had neglected to write the letters to Candace and Olivier's family. One of the lower-ranking members of the Luz did it for her, and she had signed it before coming here. She hadn't even read the letter announcing the deaths of two who had served beside her for almost a year.

One thought repeated over and over in her head, circling above like the dragon had in her flight, lingering long after the dragon's wake of wind had passed—*Why had Briznexi spared her?*

"You know as well as any how common such questions are after we lose someone we care about." It took a moment for Tali to realize the voice was coming from without rather than within. She raised her gaze to the seer's who was staring at her intently, challenge and curiosity flaring bright behind her obsidian-rimmed irises. Like many of the residents of Vestige, the seer lined her eyes with a dark powder made from the crushed stones that covered their realm's northern beaches. *Tasine*, Tali thought it was called.

The dwarf squinted her eyes shut and opened them again. She needed to focus. "Who told you about their deaths?" Her voice was clipped and low. She had been right about the rumors.

The seer shook her head. "You wear them as a cloak about your shoulders and a mask upon your face, light-bringer."

"Fine," Tali huffed. The swindler before her had probably picked up the news from one of the many soldiers from Vestige who had shared the castle-front with the Luz, maybe even the commander in some sort of trick intended to intimidate Tali into altering her battle plans. The other commanders were constantly posturing in their attempts to secure the best, most advantageous field positions, only looking after their own units rather than the needs and cohesion of the whole. Tali's jaw flared as she clenched her teeth again. The other cities treated the soldiers of the Luz as disposable, tried to take advantage of their piety.

She wasn't going to let inferior armies order her or her troops around.

The seer's irritating smile returned. Her full lips hid her teeth, and the expression remained small, but Tali couldn't shake the sense that the seer was laughing at her. Mockery had been a common occurrence when she was a young dwarf, but it had ceased the moment Ilona had chosen her from among the countless children of Beacon.

"You are not actually here about the deaths of your companions." The seer spoke in a low chant, like the lulling cadence of the sea, her gaze growing more distant, pretending to stare beyond the realm of the living world.

"Then why have I come here?" Tali snapped. "Were you planning to offer me a chance to speak to their souls before they pass on to the plane of stars?"

"No." The seer's smile fell from her lips. "They rest already in Izadra's waiting arms."

Tali rolled her eyes at the heresy. How much was she expected to endure today? Everyone knew that champions' souls returned to their titans upon death, even the titans who held themselves more removed than Ilona, including the three who had left. Izadra, supposedly the titan of space back at the dawn of the world, was a myth the storytellers used to explain the three planes of life to children. There were only six true titans, one for each of the sacred elements.

"But they did speak to me before they left."

Of course they did.

The dwarf plastered a false smile across her lips and hoped that a spark of danger flashed behind her eyes. "Is that so? Then, please, enlighten me, seer. What did they say?"

"My name is Camelia." She reached forward and lifted the teacup that rested beside the crystal orb to her lips. Tiny purple flowers floated on the fawn-colored liquid's surface. She lowered the cup to her lap. "They asked that you turn from your current path. They said it will bring only ruination."

"What?" Tali spat out the word. Camelia went too far, disrespecting the souls of her friends, accusing a champion of light of treachery. The red of battle returned to Tali's eyes.

"It is not too late," Camelia soothed. "Do not take the dragon's words to heart. Briznexi does not see all. It was not Alessandra who asked that you be spared today but fate herself."

"What did you say?"

The seer frowned. "I spoke of the appointing of fate—"

Tali shook her head. Before she was aware of springing away from the seer she was on her feet, balancing upon her toes. "How do you know the drag-on's name?" Tali screamed down at the seer.

Camelia's placid expression, as though she knew and

accepted what Tali would next do, enraged her just as much as the seer's words. "Is she who you're truly working for?"

Camelia's mouth fell open, and she leaned away from the screaming dwarf.

But Tali knew the truth. Camelia was the real traitor. It was the likeliest of two possible explanations. The other hovered over her, an unspoken shadow, separating her from the light of Ilona, brought fully into being by Camelia's words. Alessandra had asked the dragon to spare Tali. The betrayer goddess had slaughtered the champions of light who came after her without compunction. Alessandra must have seen a shred of darkness in Tali's heart that she could manipulate or a way to twist Tali to her own ends.

The golden dagger was in her hand before she was certain what she wished to protect herself from—an agent of Alessandra or further accusations of her own treachery. They would parade her through the streets before they executed her, withdraw her magic to preserve it, and then shatter her. Never again would she look upon the sun-kissed towers of Beacon, the city she had fought so hard to protect.

She wouldn't allow a false fortune teller to take her legacy from her.

Tali raised the blade. Candlelight flickered across its gold plating. Before her, Camelia cried out and scrambled away, but the seer wasn't quick enough.

It was simple enough to stab her in the back between her ribs, a wound Tali had inflicted countless times when an enemy had no choice but to retreat from her attacks.

Camelia fell to the ground like the rest. The seer knocked loose a table covered in the odds and ends of her false magic. Her baubles fell to the floor—crystals, wooden bowls, incense.

The smell of the burning candle caught in Tali's nostrils as she reached the tent's beaded curtain. Her mind whirled as it had that afternoon. Each breath, each heartbeat urged her on. *Survive. Live. Fight.* Again and again.

She glanced back over her shoulder. The pillows where they had sat, where Camelia had revealed her treachery, caught flame from the toppled taper. The seer lay still. She was dead, then.

There would be fewer questions about what had transpired if they had only a charred skeleton to investigate. Tali shoved through the beads and dashed away into the night, back toward the white tents of the Luz.

By morning, she expected word to reach her that a small fire had broken out in the Vestige camp but had been quickly extinguished.

Instead, an entire row of tents had been caught in the inferno. Fifteen had perished, and several others, including the commander, were on the brink. The soldiers of the Luz had already dispatched healers to the camp. They would do what they could.

Tali heard the words through a dense fog. The scout before her cried out as Tali's legs gave way. He called for aid and caught the great champion before she fell.

After the funerary ceremonies, the Luz whispered among themselves about the great honor their champion displayed for the lightless soldiers from the north. She sat still and pale as sand through the ceremony of the passing of souls. Her brown eyes were wide for the burning of the two bodies that remained, the commander and her aide, a young elven woman the ranks of Vestige had hoped might one day be a champion herself.

YVAYNE

The burning of the soldiers' bodies upon a pyre was not the first such ceremony Yvayne had witnessed. In her homeland in the Shadowlands, those who chose the fire for their passing were transmuted into starlight and became part of the unending dance of story constellations that graced the nighttime sky.

Over millennia, the sacredness of such rituals had ebbed and flowed in her mind. Eldura was waxing into a time of greater death and turmoil, she could feel it. She had seen such signs before—increased secrecy, mistrust between factions, preemptive measures of war disguised as protectors of peace.

She brushed a thick, feather-laden braid back over her shoulder, her head strangely light without her antlered headpiece.

The key to her current mission was to observe rather than be observed. And the inferno caused by the champion of light had nearly robbed her of anonymity.

From beside Camelia, the seer whom Silversword had tried to slaughter, the fortune-teller's face hidden beneath a cowl, Yvayne straightened to have a better view of the dwarf who was studying the flames. Had no one asked about the tug of guilt about her mouth? Such secrets would devour one and metastisize given time and opportunity without release.

The dwarf ignored the two pyres with visible bodies and focused on the ceremonial pyre instead, the one that represented the fifteen who had fallen in the fire. Their bones were all that remained, and they had already been laid to rest.

Yvayne laid her hand gently upon Camelia's shuddering shoulder. Though the fortune-teller had narrowly survived Tali's assault, the flames of its aftermath had claimed the life of her partner, the commander of the ranks of Vestige. "We've seen enough," she whispered. Yvayne's lavender-hued eyes flashed in the dwarf's direction.

The risk of detection grew with each step Silversword made from guilt to blame. Whatever had happened within the walls of Sanctuary that had claimed the lives of two champions, what Camelia had sensed and what had pulled Tali inexorably toward the seer's tent was darker even than the inferno Tali's fear had caused.

At Yvayne's urging, Camelia rose and slipped away from the pyre that laid her lover to rest.

For herself, the fae had learned long ago that cause rarely mattered, if it was past the point of preventing. There was only effect—and she would not sacrifice Camelia or risk revealing her presence here for the sake of curiosity.

This was one secret the lorekeepers would not learn

the truth of, not for some time anyway. But part of their long-term survival, their ascension beyond the factions fracturing across Eldura—the Cities United finding greater and greater cause to perceive aggression and enmity by the professed neutrality of the disparate collections of natural magic users, from the witches of the Emeraude to the dryads of the Glade of Shadows and, above all, to the Pentacle, the leaders of the Academia Magica and rulers of all of Lis-Maen.

The drive of the Cities toward war was strong, and the professed desires of the Five Faces of the Pentacle, particularly the Sorceress among them, diverged from their intentions. Even now she was waiting to hear from the Oracle, one of the Faces who had turned toward the lorekeepers' cause. They had a secret project all their own that would soon need help coming to fruition deep within the forest wilds of Lis-Maen.

It was time to depart and leave the Cities to their own devices, at least until she knew more. Chaos followed the dwarven champion of light, of that she was certain. But what that chaos *meant* in the larger game for their world, the one she and the lorekeepers had waged in secret, with Alessandra as their true opponent, would have to wait longer for revelation.

The lesson of patience and taking the long-view had been hard won, but it was not a mantle she would throw off now that she had the scars to bear it.

Yvayne turned away from the pyres and followed Camelia. She and the seer still had much to discuss, and Camelia would soon need to return to her people.

As they passed through the shadows of the tents,

winding away from the pyres, Yvayne allowed her gaze to soften and revisited what she had seen.

An intuition she hadn't been able to name had led her onto the ramparts of Sanctuary that final afternoon of the battle, a sense that the Cities were playing precisely into Briznexi's hand. It was the latest in a series of signs that murmured to her, whispering that the Eldura they knew was about to fall.

Gods it irked her when the lingering Sight she'd inherited from her mother proved correct.

The dwarf had frozen upon the castle walls, gaze locked with that of the dragon. Yvayne could hardly believe her eyes when Tali's beam of light failed to injure Briznexi. She was far enough away that Tali couldn't hear her scramble down the battle-scarred rocks of Sanctuary's crumbling walls. And shadows curse her, Yvayne was also too far away to save the two stranded champions whose protective forces had abandoned them. What failure of strategy had left three champions to face Briznexi alone?

Yvayne knew the answer in her gut, even though she didn't want to admit it. The truth shone in the funeral pyres, reflected back in the dark brown eyes of the lone surviving champion of the battles.

The champion whose treachery had made itself known the night of her failure. The seer from Vestige had called Yvayne to her tent as darkness fell. Her visions of death had grown worse in the battle's aftermath. *Something foul is amiss*, her missive had read. *We lost more than the city of Sanctuary this day.*

Yvayne had crouched in the shadows as the champion of light approached Camelia's tent. She had clenched her hands into fists, restraining her magic when Tali raised her voice toward the seer—one of the saudad blessed with Sight from the goddess Cassandra. Again she doubted the threads of fate and wondered whether it was possible that Tali would be the hand of death Camelia had foreseen.

Could so great a transgression fall upon the shoulders of a champion of light?

Yvayne darted for the edge of the tent the moment Camelia screamed. The incense-thickened smoke obscured the fae's slash in the tent's side and prevented the frightened dwarf from perceiving Camelia's rescuer in her flight from the tent.

Yvayne dragged the seer to safety, but she failed to account for Camelia's tent's proximity to the stores of liquor and alchemist's fire kept by the soldiers from Vestige.

The inferno raged to deadly heights before she could intervene, and Yvayne couldn't risk exposing her own magic with Briznexi so near, especially not with so powerful a working as countering the alchemist's fire would entail.

The dragon would eradicate the whole of the army to capture a great-granddaughter of Verdigris, even one as alienated from her true potential as Yvayne.

"I can't believe she's gone," Camelia sobbed, thinking of the commander of Vestige, her partner who had fallen in the fire while trying to save her. The saudad lowered her head into her hands.

Yvayne's shoulders tensed, remembering, and she

checked behind them to make sure they'd slipped away from the burning pyres unseen. Camelia's hood paired with her veil passed for the traditional mourning garb in Vestige and had gone unnoticed thus far.

With great pain, Yvayne had ensured that the saudad's name had been recorded among the dead. It was Camelia's only hope of survival.

She closed her eyes, trying to draw from a well of patience that remained dry. Yvayne glanced at Camelia in their hidden position on the edge of Vestige's camp. The saudad needed more time to recover from Tali's attack and its aftermath, but their timeglass was running out. "Tell me again exactly what transpired as you remember it." She wanted to check the saudad's memory against her own.

Camelia repeated her midnight conversation with the dwarf. Tears lined her eyes as she reached the end of the tale. Yvayne knew Camelia blamed herself for the death of her lover, the commander. Arabelle had plunged into the depths of the flames trying to find and free Camelia, unaware that Yvayne had already rescued her body and that the fae was scouring the camp for the commander to prevent precisely what had happened.

"We leave at first light," she said when Camelia had finished her retelling. "Your muster will be waiting for us in the Emeraude. One of the matrons there will grant us counsel."

"But I don't understand," Camelia answered. "What of Arabelle? Of the others who perished in the fire. Is there to be no justice for the one who stabbed me?" Her voice rose with her questions so that she was almost screaming by the end. Camelia caught her breath, hand pressed against her side where her wound had been.

Yvayne had healed it herself as soon as she'd pulled the seer to safety, forgetting the danger of discovery such an action might provoke in close proximity to Briznexi. Dragons had a gift for sensing magic, part of their innate hungering to enhance their own might.

"Shh." Yvayne leaned closer. "There will be justice, I swear to you. But it must come at the proper time. We are still few, and our influence is limited. For now, we watch and wait."

Over the last two years, Yvayne had interrogated a score of scouts captured from Alessandra's forces. From each testimony, she gained a clearer picture of the dark goddess's plans. Alessandra was not idle in Scourge as she plotted her next moves against the Cities. But from all Yvayne could gather, the goddess planned for the ultimate downfall of the Cities United to come from within.

Tali's treachery, even if it had been accidental, was the first sign Yvayne had found of such an eventuality coming into fruition.

From there, her plan had quickly fallen into place. She'd requested the aid of an old ally who had fought faithfully in the wars leading up to the Fall of the First Age, Vaxis, who would meet her in the Emeraude. They would request shelter for Camelia and her muster and together, they would make their case to the grand matron before they attempted the same with the Pentacle in Lis-Maen.

Yvayne had hoped her secret order, the lorekeepers, could wait before revealing themselves, but the defeat in

Sanctuary had forced their hand. She and the other lore-keepers, working alongside small bands of independent spies sworn to the service of Lilith, called the Order of Verdigris, had set themselves the task of convincing the independent natural powers of their world to commit to a side. They need not align themselves with the Cities, but if they did not stand against Alessandra, Yvayne knew it in her bones, their world would fall.

She was one of few old enough to have seen it before, to have witnessed the Shifting, when Eldura had been one land before the continents had been driven apart, just as the three planes of life had been one world before the Fall of the First Age, when Alessandra had relinquished her position as the first champion of light, betrayed her fellow champions, and risen to a position of godhood. As always with Alessandra, her schemes meant division.

Their world wouldn't survive further separation, and Yvayne would do everything in her power to prevent such devastation from taking place.

"We'll find aid in the Emeraude," she promised Camelia and, secretly, herself. The scheme she and the Oracle had been working on, one that would recall a soul to their world, a soul destined to save, to *become*, depended upon the dwindling magic of a pair of witches within the Emeraude, those blessed and cursed with the magic of souls—spirit-witches.

CHAPTER THREE
TALI

RESPITE, THREE DAYS LATER

It was with haste that Tali made her way back to the fortress at the heart of Respite. With the loss of Sanctuary, the union of the Cities was more tenuous than ever.

She knelt before her altar, bowing her head and begging Ilona's forgiveness for the lives of those accidentally taken. For failing to save Candace and Olivier.

Her throat swelled as she awaited the titan's answer, some sign that Ilona had heard her, and that it had been the titan who had spared Tali, not the enemy's dragon lieutenant.

When the silence persisted, Tali allowed a sliver of doubt to float out over the city's ramparts, a pink dawn warming the rooftops below. "Why was your light unable to pierce the dragon's hide? I know Briznexi's words were untrue—the betrayer goddess does not wield your light—"

Tali winced at what she was asking of her titan, the accusation she had just made. It was a manipulation of Ilona's light that had been the foundation of the war that had consumed their world for generations. Alessandra, the first champion of light, had gathered her fellow champions to her side. She had manipulated her gift from Ilona and used it to destroy the other champions. When she imbibed their power, she ascended to godhood, becoming the betrayer goddess, bent on the destruction of the titans' worlds.

Weaker generations of champions had followed. Tali bowed her head, acknowledging that painful reality. If only Ilona had waited to bestow her gifts, had appointed Tali as her first champion—but it was not for her to question Ilona's will, only to see it carried out.

"I will do whatever you ask of me," Tali swore to the titan. "Whatever I can to make this right."

As Tali placed her small hands upon the rim of her altar to help herself up, the rumors she had heard in a recent alchemists' report floated back to her. It had been the retrieval of this information and the punishment for its escape that had led to the all-out attack against Sanctuary in the first place.

The information from behind their enemy's lines had been costly but invaluable. The souls of a city, condensed into a single military strategy, a secret of Alessandra's far-reaching plans.

It was what the betrayer goddess did to champions who fell into her hands.

What Briznexi might have done to Tali had the

dragon not spared her *by Ilona's will,* she forced herself to add.

Tali's breath caught in her chest as she pushed herself up, lingering before the altar. Was this Ilona's answer? A shift in their own strategy?

A city weaker than they had been before, more extreme measures had to be taken.

But the question remained, did the Secret Council have the strength to see such steps brought into being? Would they be willing to alter the course of Eldura's future to protect the fate of their world?

"Thank you, Ilona," Tali whispered, steeling herself in the resolve her morning prayer session had given her.

Less than a week had passed since Briznexi had killed Candace and Olivier. By the grace of Ilona, Tali would see that the dragon was never in such a position of power again. Could never again besmirch Ilona's name or pretend to spare Tali from Alessandra's wrath.

Her fate was in the hands of Ilona, the titan of light, not the betrayer goddess.

She would have to be careful, Tali reminded herself as she prepared for the meeting with the council. She painted her features with ash for mourning and gulped down a scalding cup of water to accentuate the effects of the smoke from battle upon her voice. Champions healed more quickly than those unblessed with the titans' magic. Let the council fill in for themselves how harrowing the encounter with Briznexi had been.

Her honor guard led her through the upper halls of the Palace of Respite, standing watch at the door as Tali presented herself and her plan to the will of the council.

With gravel in her voice, Tali gave her report to the Secret Council, the combined military and political advisory board of Respite, the newly appointed commander of the troops from Vestige, and the ministers of the Luz, Ilona's Army of Light alongside a few representatives of Bastion. "It was my proximity to Candace and Olivier that spelled their doom. The foul dragon could not help but brag at having sensed the combination of our powers." Tali shook her head, breaking her gaze from the council members as though tears filled her eyes. "I can only ask myself what might have happened had we not pooled together. Not only would they still be alive, but we might have saved the city as well."

The council members looked between themselves, confusion knotting their brows. "What exactly are you proposing, lightbringer?" their speaker asked.

Tali inhaled deeply, carefully maintaining the air of dignity she'd spent years cultivating as she rose through the ranks. It was this sense that had faltered in the battle for Sanctuary. She would not allow panic to get the best of her again. "I know as well as the rest of you how much our cities, our armies, depend upon an ever-dwindling supply of elemental magic, distilled from the titans themselves into the very fabric of our world. In their absence, we face a difficult choice: adapt and alter our way of life to more closely resemble that of the primitive civilizations—the whole of Lis-Maen, the witches of the Emeraude, the various clans of the Glade of Shadows."

One of the commanders from Verita chuckled at the mention of the dryads' ancient forest and crumbling civilization. Tali smirked—it was only a matter of time before the forest fell. So near to Scourge and so determined to retain their independence, she doubted they would be able to withstand Alessandra's assaults for much longer, even with the rumored Sapphire Circle secreted away within their midst. It would take more than a handful of druids to stand against the betrayer goddess's forces.

With good humor restored among the various leaders, Tali resumed her speech, "Or, we continue on as before, not reverting to the past but looking instead to the future. We take advantage of the gifts the titans have left in their wake, the embodied magic of the champions themselves."

A startled silence followed Tali's declaration. The choice between the two options was perfectly clear. It was only a matter of awakening the council's courage for them to see it. If the generals of Beacon and Respite agreed to her terms, the rest would fall into line. They had little other choice.

"What exactly are you suggesting, Commandant?" one of the elves from Bastion asked, a Mistress Darkstrider.

Tali grinned. Her moment had arrived. And after she secured the Cities' future, there would be no question of why she had survived when the twins hadn't, no impugning of her reputation for being near the site of the fire outside Sanctuary's walls that had taken the lives of several of Vestige's soldiers including one of a similar rank to herself though not a champion. All would go on as before. As she and Ilona intended.

"There is a theory developed by alchemists stolen

from among our ranks and forced into servitude to the betrayer goddess. One of the ancient magics, set at the foundation of the world, the magic of souls." Tali took a deep breath and tucked her arms behind her back, clasping them lightly. Standing before the council, she was the same height as those seated before her, but that hardly mattered when she held the way forward for them all. "It's said to be a derivation of the very same magic Alessandra used to subdue her fellow champions when she rose to become the betrayer goddess at the beginning of this age."

Tali began to pace before them. There was no need to specify that the great price that had been paid was the lives of Candace and Olivier and the entire city of Sanctuary, trapped within the walls by Alessandra's overwhelming forces. As she paced, she settled into the rhythm of her speech. The method before them was simple—the champions would go into hiding and become yet another rumored magic of this world. Concealing their whereabouts would make it more difficult for Alessandra's forces to identify them on the battlefield, especially when they gathered together, uniting their forces as the champions of old had done.

Yes, it was true, some champions would be condemned through her proposal of secrecy, those who refused to go into hiding or made themselves known, drawing danger to all nearby. However, by revealing themselves, these champions would have singled themselves out as those whose desire for fame and recognition would see them risk the lives of selfless champions like herself, not to mention those who followed the champions into battle. Moving forward, the council had to act decisively and prioritize those who had an eye to the future and protecting the collective good, not those too blind to follow orders.

Tali laid out what Ilona had explained to her in the darkness, how soul might be severed from body, leaving behind, in the champions' cases, an energetic reservoir that could be broken into shards and repurposed. "The life of a single champion might be extended one thousandfold," Tali proclaimed, her mind racing ahead with the possibilities for warfare and progress such sacrifices might unleash. She was single-handedly solving the Cities' dwindling supply of elemental magic. "The possibilities are even greater as our alchemists learn to adapt the uses of the shards."

The council stared at her in stunned silence. A few of them gazed off into the distance, their faces alternately troubled and bright. The bonds between champions and the Cities ran deep, for it was the champions who had served the Cities' armies for generations. Children learned their names, adopted their identities on the festival days celebrating the elements and the titans throughout the year. She could see how some might see her suggestion as treasonous, but Ilona had given her the strategy. It was Tali's duty to see it through.

And anyone who resisted would prove themselves an enemy of Ilona, the titans, and the Cities themselves.

One of the generals from Verita wetted his lips. "With all due respect, Commandant, aren't these measures . . . extreme?"

Tali angled herself toward the political leader whose

faith was flagging. She would not label him a traitor of Ilona, not yet. Before she replied, she met each of their cowardly gazes in turn. "These are extreme times," Tali answered simply.

Ilona help me, am I the only one with the strength to do what must be done?

"We have lost one city," Tali added. "With the fall of Sanctuary, a momentous choice is before us. We can continue on as before, increasingly forced to quarrel amongst ourselves, wondering which city will fall next." She waited for the weight of this inevitability to settle over their shoulders. The battle for Sanctuary had made one thing abundantly clear to Tali and each of the representatives in this room—they were losing the war.

It didn't take long for their expressions to shift. They leaned forward, waiting hungrily for her to remove the guillotine dangling over their necks. "*Or,*" she said as the chamber held its breath, "we change tactics, hide the remaining champions from enemy forces, and punish those who prove their disloyalty in their refusal to adapt to our new regime."

Tali clacked her heels together, the sound of her metal-covered boots making several of the representatives jump. "Take more time to decide if you must. I for one am already settled on the matter. The souls of Sanctuary will not have been pulled into Alessandra's embrace in vain. Not while I still draw breath."

She turned to leave.

"Wait, Commandant." The general who had questioned her most fervently held out his hand. "You're suggesting this new punishment only to those champions who would reveal themselves following an order of secrecy."

Tali tilted her head to the side, allowing her grin from before to return to her features. "Of course." She met the gazes of the the gathered council. "I'm not a monster. Given the new ability of Alessandra's field commanders we discovered in Sanctuary, the rapidity with which they can sniff out champions, especially champions gathered together, these are figures who will be marked for death regardless." She clasped her hands before her hips. "All I'm suggesting is that their deaths serve our purposes, respond to our needs, rather than the ravenous maw of Alessandra."

With a bob of her chin, Tali spun on her heel and marched out of the chamber. The late afternoon sun glinted upon her silver armor as she strode along the ramparts, gazing down upon the glories of Respite. True, it was no Beacon, but given its many towers, the open-air markets, the airships drifting overhead, she could see the argument many made for Respite being the greatest of the Cities United.

The collection of generals, councillors, and military strategists would come to the right decision, Tali felt sure of it.

Not a monster, she repeated to herself as she waited for the news from the council.

Not a traitor either, the small voice in the back of her mind added.

She didn't have to wait long for them to present her with a draft of their proposal, needing her approval and, if she was willing, her name.

As the sun set over Respite, painting the pale tan of the city's towers gold, Tali unfurled the drafted scroll that had been brought by official messenger to her quarters within the city.

---

*A*nd *it was thus, following the brave testimony of Tali Silversword, that we, the Secret Ministers of the Cities United, declare that all champions shall henceforth remain unknown to one another to protect both them and ourselves from destruction. The future of Eldura depends upon our secrecy.*

Those outside our sacred order should be led to believe that the titans have withdrawn the blessings of their magic from individuals and have instead chosen to bestow their gifts upon the vast armies that protect our world. Henceforward, anyone beyond our number must believe that the champions are no more.

The champions who are known should be separated from one another and hidden among the ranks of our extensive forces. We, the Secret Ministers, will retain the only record of their names and locations, just as we will be the sole keepers of the names and identities of any new champions who arise in our time of need.

Any champion found to be in violation of the Order of Secrecy will find their life forfeit, their magic stripped, and their gifting from the titans reapportioned.

So shall it be, and so shall it be done.

Tali sighed as she looked up from the scroll. *So it*

begins, Ilona, exactly as you wished. Find me ever faithful, Titan of Light.

But just as before, Ilona was silent.

The champion of light tightened her jaw. Perhaps creating the law wasn't enough. Maybe Ilona was waiting to see whether or not she was dedicated enough to carry it out.

CHAPTER FOUR

ROWAN

WILLOW GLEN, LIS-MAEN.
TWENTY YEARS AFTER THE FALL
OF SANCTUARY AND THE
PASSING OF THE ORDER OF
SECRECY

Almost. There. Rowan's arms strained as she pulled herself up the series of vine ladders that wound along the strongest boughs of the forest canopy. Sweat beaded her brow. She gulped a chest-full of air until finally—her head breached the dense layering of delicate leaves and blossoms that covered the treetops over the Willow Glen conclave in early summer.

Rowan closed her eyes, turning her face to the sun like the buds in her cultivation patch angled themselves toward the aging light orbs she'd scavenged from the conclave's repurposing orders. The chill of the conclave's settlement in the understory faded from the long, pointed tips of her elven ears. She had twisted her hair into a low knot, worn at the base of her neck; one of her rituals for canopy days.

She took a final deep breath, enjoying the moment before turning her attention to the task before her—attending to the orbs of light for the refractory. The orbs charged in the treetops before being dispersed throughout the conclave. The forest community had been founded by druids in generations past but, given the mix of magics across Lis-Maen, the central continent of Eldura surrounded by the Circle Sea, the conclave's populace had altered as well.

It had been with an eye to adversity that her paupa had first invented the orbs. While other forest communities had to relocate from the druids' founding settlements, the conclave of Willow Glen had been able to remain without thinning the trees they depended upon. "This way, we grow *with* the forest," Paupa had told her countless times.

Her world was simpler up here. Just herself, the orbs, and the sleeping phoenix hidden away in the back of her mind.

In years past, Rowan had raged against this simplicity, the way the conclave's council had ousted her father, shunted him to the side, and replaced his leadership. Then they took him for granted and, after his passing, did the same to her. "Where would we be without Paupa's inventions?" she had screamed at one notable council meeting—the last she had attended several years before.

The orbs glimmered in the warm, burnished gold of sunrise. Rowan smiled at them, remembering Paupa's delicate forming of each one, a process that had taken her years to learn while working at his side.

She was like the orbs now—taken for granted to the point of invisibility. Rowan just didn't mind as much as she once had. Though the orbs meant little to the rest of the conclave, they were one of her last remaining connections to her paupa's handiwork, and that was enough. The garden patch in the sagging corner of her home in the refractory was the other.

Very few members of the conclave shared Rowan's propensity for climbing into the treetops in order to experience the fullness of direct sunlight for themselves. Fewer still appreciated the soothing light of the moons, particularly because the wyverns combed the treetops at night.

After the brush of dawn light condensed the sweat at her temples to salt and her pulse returned to its low, steady beat, Rowan took stock of the vine-rows of light orbs glittering along the canopy before her. Once a week, Rowan dared her system of rope ladders to check on the orbs' resting places in the light.

From the refractory—located at a higher elevation than most of the rest of the conclave to support the intricate rails that guided the orbs on their circular path from canopy to conclave and back, she could engage the release mechanisms that would recall the orbs and distribute their light across the conclave. Paupa had designed the orbs' rail network inspired by the steamtrain rail in Delmoir, the capital of Lis-Maen, with one third of the orbs spread along the understory where the conclave resided, another third recharging in the sun, and the final third resting in the refractory before being sent into the canopy. Paupa's web of light, as he called it, had allowed the few remaining druids of their number—Rowan being one of the last—to remain within the ancient grove of their ancestors even though the trees' growth had long since overshadowed what most would deem an adequate degree of light for maintaining their settlement.

Rowan sighed, trying not to think of those below while within the sanctity of the upper branches. Here, there was only her and Paupa's orbs of light.

Under her careful eye, the orbs glowed brighter with the warming dawn. He'd patterned the glass after faery wings and protected their fragile surfaces with thin strips of living vines to pad the glass as the orbs rolled along the railings. Paupa had delighted in telling her how it had been his genius in designing the network of light and his insistence upon engaging her mother's help in bringing it to life that had won Mamaun's heart for him, long before Rowan's birth.

Being in the canopy often made Rowan think of her mother, someone she had no memory of. Her mother had died shortly after bringing Rowan into the world nineteen years ago but, when she and Paupa were in the canopy together, he would tell her stories about her mother.

Paupa's death had been slower—half of him laid to rest with his wife, the other half shimmering on, with Rowan bobbing at his side, through the first decade of her life.

Rowan clenched her jaw. The council had seen an

end to that, hadn't they? She shook her head, wishing it were as easy to dispel the council from her thoughts as placing her face in the sunlight and melting away their darkness just as the light orbs did. That had been Mamaun's gift to the orbs' engineering, alongside the delicate strands of vine to protect the glass.

Her mother had understood the duality of light and darkness—the orbs needed both energies, ebbing and flowing together, to illuminate the conclave each day.

As the years passed, the conclave had abandoned such teachings, surrendering their beliefs in the sanctity of the six elements in favor of more immediate, lesser powers, namely the ruling magical order of the Pentacle in Delmoir. Rowan's stomach twisted. The Pentacle claimed to represent the five schools of magic across the whole of Lis-Maen equally—the Sorceress, Oracle, Creatrix, Healer, and Druidess sharing the leadership of and looking out for the interests of the peoples of Lis-Maen.

In practice, the Sorceress and the Oracle centralized power and influence to themselves. They'd slowly extracted the magical teachings of those on the margins like the conclave of Willow Glen and placed sympathizers into council positions the continent over.

The Pentacle's meddling was why she had climbed into the treetops outside her regular schedule. A hummingbird had appeared outside her door yesterday, a missive from the council attached to its tiny pink foot. They needed her to ensure all was well with the orbs before the visit of the Pentacle's agent the following afternoon, just a few hours from now. *The future of the conclave depends on it*, they'd written.

We'll see about that, Rowan had longed to reply.

But in honor of Paupa's memory, she did as they asked instead, adjusting her routines to check on the orbs this morning before dispersing them to light the understory below.

Scanning the orbs' rows, all remained in order save one that had developed cracks along its glass surface. Such compromised orbs could, on occasion, explode, singeing the delicate vines that carried the orbs along the conclave's railings and creating more work for Rowan to fix them.

Rowan exhaled her frustration at the lone orb all the way across the rows on the opposite side of the patch. She glanced about and then, remembering where she was, chuckled at herself. There was no one here to see.

She extended her hand toward the ball of light. "*Pssh, pssh, pssh,*" Rowan called to the cracked orb, urging it toward herself like she would a dracat that had wandered too far from its nest and needed to be shown the way home again.

The orb rocked along its axis, pirouetting back and forth but otherwise resisted Rowan's invitation.

Miscreant, her nickname for Paupa's tortoiseshell dracat, Majestyk, would never allow herself to be lured so easily either.

Would you like to help? Rowan asked the slumbering phoenix who dwelled in the back of her mind. It had fallen dormant over the nine years Rowan had tended to the refractory all on her own, the demands of carrying on

Paupa's work by herself preventing her from engaging in the magical training that kept her phoenix fed and energized.

Against Rowan's wishes, her mentor and the last living friend of her parents, Athenza, had asked the council to appoint an assistant to help Rowan with the light network so that Rowan might continue her magical training as her father had wished. "He never would have chosen his invention over your future," the aged elf had said more times than Rowan could count.

The council had seen the matter differently. There was little need for magical cultivation within their own number now that the Pentacle had extended their goodwill to the outlying conclaves such as theirs. There was an annual visit from ministers of the Sorceress to attend to magical needs of import, a seasonal trek made by apprentices of the Healer, and a biannual delivery of crops and herbs blessed by the Druidess.

The conclave's dependence upon the Pentacle and surrendering of their own individual magical giftings was the inevitable conclusion that her paupa had foreseen all those years ago. He'd lost the goodwill of the council in trying to prevent precisely what had happened.

In her parents' youth, five or so decades before, the Druidess had joined the centralized powers in the capital of Delmoir, transforming the Quadrate into the Pentacle as she did so. That had been the first warning stroke in the demise of an independently magical Lis-Maen. And after the fall of Sanctuary, one of the grandest holdings of the Cities United, in the year before Rowan's birth, the

Pentacle had seen fit to recruit all those with magical potential from the outer conclaves to train in the Academia Magica in the heart of the Pentacle's grounds in Delmoir.

The druids like her paupa they left in peace.

Her father had been the last naysaying voice that advocated for self-reliance among the conclave, believing that the Sorceress, in particular, was too hungry for the attentions of both the Cities United and Alessandra to choose a wise, peaceful path forward for the peoples of Lis-Maen. Though it had not yet come to open war with either the Cities or Alessandra, with each passing cycle of the moons, rumors grew and darkened overhead. It was only a matter of time until someone's patience wore out and either the Cities or the dark goddess forced the forest peoples of Lis-Maen to choose a side in the larger conflict for Eldura.

The phoenix clacked its beak but remained unmoving. She'd have to summon the orb on her own.

Fine. Rowan tightened her hold on the branch, angled herself further out of the treetops, and narrowed her gaze to the orb. A few years before, she would have easily been able to will the flickering ball of light to her palm, but her hold over the elements, especially those beyond water and earth, was slipping.

Athenza's magic was dimming too. Rumors held that it was occurring to all of the druids across Lis-Maen who dwelled outside of Delmoir.

Rowan allowed everything else to fall away, narrowing her focus to the floundering flicker within the orb. She softened her gaze and willed the ebbing darkness and growing light within the orb to quicken their pace, renew their energetic ties.

With a fizzle of sparks that made Rowan jump, the tendrils of gold within the orb crackled to life, spiraling tighter in their threads, and the swirling smoke of elemental darkness compressed in the center of the orb, gathering itself into an indigo cloud.

"That's it," Rowan murmured. She stretched her hand out further. The energy should be enough for the orb to float away from the others and into her grasp. "Come here."

The orb raised as Rowan asked, shivering with the pulsating energy growing within itself. A puff of indigo cloud expanded into the spools of gold, obscuring one of the threads from sight.

"No," Rowan corrected. She bit her lower lip between her teeth, harnessing her will to redirect the energy. They needed to exist *together*, not be at war amongst themselves.

The tendrils of light fought back against the cloud of darkness, poking at its edges and singeing the darkness where they touched. Inky scabs swelled to life along the cloud, which compressed further onto itself. The strand of light it had captured squealed and shook.

As the ball lifted away from the others, it vibrated and spun. Rowan tightened her jaw. She could control it. With just the right amount of focus . . .

The shaking worsened, and the orbs beneath the levitating ball began to quake as well.

Titans be—if it shattered, it would take the rest of the orbs with it.

"Come. On," Rowan said through clenched teeth.

A pair of golden eyes joined the focused beam of her peridot gaze. Rowan's breath caught. Her phoenix had awakened.

The bird fixed the orb in its stare, and the elements within froze in place. It squawked a single, low note.

The orb shot toward Rowan. She cried out as it slammed into her waiting hands, knocking her backward onto the needle-thin branches and spangle of blossoms behind her.

Twigs snapped, and the branches groaned and gave way. With one arm around the orb, Rowan flailed, trying to catch her balance. With a snap, the branch she'd been holding broke from the limb and plunged her below. It swung down and thrust Rowan into a heavy branch beneath, knocking her breath from her chest.

Overhead, the orbs tinkled as they jostled into one another, but her railings held, as did the branch she now clung to.

Rowan coughed, catching her breath, and checked on the orb she'd seized. It shone brighter than any of the rest, golden light and thick shadow, trapped within glass.

She smirked at the brilliantly shining orb and released the branch covered in pale, pink flowers. It plummeted into the tangles of branches below, raining petals as it fell.

You woke up, she thought to the phoenix. *And enhanced the power of the orbs tenfold.*

But it had already curled back into itself and resumed its slumber.

Rowan shook her head and tucked the shimmering orb into the leather pouch at her side. She'd add it above her garden patch in the refractory and hope no one asked her about its brightness.

"They cannot know about your phoenix," Paupa had warned. "They say they don't want our magic, but they will want you."

She rolled her shoulders and began her climb down to the refractory with just enough time to transition the freshened orbs into their positions around the conclave, casting their light upon the dreaded agent sent by the Pentacle, come to insist upon new ways of deepening their dependence on the outside magic no doubt.

CHAPTER FIVE
ROWAN

A few hours later, Athenza adjusted the set of the spectacles at the end of her long, delicate nose, making her bright, azure eyes even larger than normal. "Did Majestyk get to you this morning, child?" she asked, leaning forward with a squint to better see the scratches along Rowan's face and arms from her tumble in the canopy.

"Not yet, but we shouldn't put it past her." Rowan grimaced as she forced herself to stretch, tugging on the scabs that had formed after her plunge through the trees following her phoenix's intervention. The scrapes she could do little about, but she could prevent her muscles from seizing.

Athenza had eyed the glowing orb shining down upon Rowan's indoor garden patch, but the aging druid had simply raised an eyebrow, not commenting further. She'd made herself at home in her favorite wicker chair, the dracat perched on the chair's back, her scales catching in the light, while Rowan worked the refractory levers and exchanged the lights illuminating the whole of the conclave.

The whirring of the orbs overhead made conversation during the transition impossible.

Rowan relished the rushing glow—like elemental light charging through water—and the noise drowned out the sense of dread that had begun to wash over her with the visit of the Pentacle's agent.

Her final task completed, Rowan excused herself from Athenza's inspection of her injuries and began rummaging through the canisters arranged above her cooking cabinet. There had to be additional chamomile leaves here somewhere—she'd grown extras and dried them specifically for instances like these scrapes so she wouldn't have to visit one of the trainees for the Healer. "Do we have any word yet on when the agent will be here?" Rowan asked, trying to keep her voice even.

Fennel, sage, cinnamon, bay leaf. Powdered lavender. Where was the chamomile for the salve?

The habitual tasks of the refractory and the intervention of her phoenix had changed Rowan's mind about the agent's visit. Maybe it was time for her to have a more direct understanding of what was transpiring around her. To see if the Pentacle was playing a role in the shifting magic of the conclave.

From her comfortable position atop her wicker chair, Athenza reached back absentmindedly to stroke her fingertips along Majestyk's delicate scales. "Absolutely. She's here now, about to make her speech before the council. Announcing something bold and new, if the gossips are to be believed."

"Now?" Rowan straightened and whirled to face the druid. "Then what are we still doing here?" She gestured to the empty cup on the low table before Athenza. "Having tea?"

Her mentor chuckled to herself, slowly raising to her feet and snatching her walking cane from where it leaned against the wall beside her. "Here I was, thinking you wouldn't want to go."

"Of course I don't want to go," Rowan snapped. How much of the agent's meeting with the council had they already missed, and how much more would transpire by the time she and Athenza actually made it to the meeting? There might be clues hidden within the requests the agent made, the contributions the Pentacle demanded from the conclave in exchange for the academy's help and protection. "That doesn't mean we won't go." What Rowan *wanted* had long since faded from the considerations that motivated her decisions.

She hurriedly returned the canister she'd withdrawn onto the shelf, clacking it against the others beside it, and rushed to the refractory door, bouncing onto her tiptoes while she waited for the druid's steady, deliberate steps across the bent boards of the refractory's aging floor.

Rowan restrained herself by plunging her nails into her palms and keeping her shoulders clenched as she accompanied Athenza down the trails that wound through the understory of Willow Glen, taking as direct a route as possible toward the central reaches of the council tree. If she hadn't had to transition the orbs ahead of schedule, she and Athenza might have had tea in Athenza's hut at its lower elevation, though the druid's home was nearly as far from the central council chambers as Rowan's.

As they neared the great willow oak from which the conclave had gotten its name, Rowan slowed, adopting her friend's measured pace. Years had passed since Rowan had last crossed the threshold of the oak, the one whose boughs she had spent so much time beneath in her childhood, before Paupa had lost the council's favor and his position. Aside from the few instances in which her thwarting of conclave guidelines regarding the private practice of magic had brought her before a disciplinary hearing, the only way Rowan trespassed the boundaries of the sweeping oak's branches was through the light orbs sent from her refractory.

The design of the council chambers had been set back in ancient times, inspired by the Brightlands fae. At its center, a wide, flat branch housed the sitting area for the council members themselves and a stage for whoever had been given the right of voice before the conclave.

In tiered rows stretching in wider and wider heights above this central branch were positions of honor for those of high standing within the community. And on a second wide, sloped branch just off the rounded center, was the gathering area for everyone else.

The chamber had always inspired a strange mix of calm and dread in the center of Rowan's being, as though she had been born to stand within such a space and yet desired to be anywhere else. Likely an ancient, residual energy that the lingering shadows hadn't yet displaced.

She dismissed such recollections now. There were

too many gathered too tightly for her to pick up on the latent energies anyway. The conclave members each carried buzzing auras of their own.

"Pardon us," Rowan murmured to the conclave members gathered at the outer edges of the sloped platform, weaving her way through them toward the toadstools nearer to the front. Someone there would yield their place for Athenza, even though the aging druid was even more unpopular than Rowan herself among the conclave's loyalists.

Below them, the Pentacle's agent stood before the conclave council, clad in the white robe and emerald ties signaling her connection to the Druidess, the least despicable of the Five Faces. Before Unity—when the Quadrate became the Pentacle and the druid conclaves yielded their independence to Lis-Maen—the ancient line of Druidesses had been spiritual leaders for the conclaves, connecting them back to the ancient roots of the world through the Undying Grove.

The elf sent on behalf of the Pentacle nodded to herself as she spoke, as though modeling for the rest of the conclave how they ought to respond. The beams from the orbs of light overhead flashed in her golden hair. "This invitation marks a new era of unity for all of Lis-Maen, a sharing of blessings as Verdigris herself intended."

Rowan hissed under her breath at the Pentacle's agent invoking the titan of nature. By their very existence, the Pentacle and their allies had forsaken Verdigris's true mission—the balance of the six elements—in favor of a more distant, tamer magic, presided over by the Five Faces. It was a betrayal of the druids' wild magic. Maybe she shouldn't have come.

Athenza squeezed Rowan's elbow, sensing her distress.

"Almost there," Rowan whispered back to her mentor. There were only a few others between her and an open toadstool where Athenza might be seated. "Excuse us," Rowan said, pressing upon the arm of a conclave member who stood directly in her path.

The elf stiffened instead, thin muscles tightening beneath the thin wraps of his garments. He whirled about and scowled down at Rowan.

It was a figure she recognized from childhood, Vraise. They had been friends before her father lost his seat on the council, and she hadn't seen him since. One of his fathers had taken up Paupa's position after he was ousted.

"We're just trying to get over there," Rowan explained, indicating the area reserved for those with infants, the elderly, and the infirm. Athenza was too proud to admit she could have qualified for either of the latter categories, but the sickness that had claimed Paupa's life had left Athenza's leg muscles permanently weakened.

Rather than moving, Vraise sneered as Rowan tried to angle past him, blocking her way with his shoulder, as though he could force her to bear witness to the conclave sacrificing the last vestiges of their independence to the centralized powers in Delmoir by prolonging her time here.

Such a surrender would be the final unraveling of her father's work.

"I'm surprised to find the daughter of traitors at a meeting such as this one," Vraise said, his upper lip curling. "Don't you have little orbs of light to tend?"

Slow exhale through your nose. Don't rise to such needling bait.

Rowan raised her gaze overhead and opened her palm to face the canopy above them, indicating the glowing orbs that hung upon their tracks over the council chambers. The freshly revived orbs had completed their journey down to the conclave a couple hours before.

From behind Rowan and Vraise, her mentor snorted, overhearing their exchange. Others standing nearby shushed the three of them for disrupting the agent's speech.

"Why should my presence here be a surprise?" Rowan challenged when Vraise still refused to budge from her path. "I am a member of the conclave after all."

"Maybe I'm shocked that you would deign to answer an invitation from the council after all these years." His smirk deepened. "Assuming you received one, of course."

Rowan forced another calming exhale. This was why she so studiously avoided trespassing the central reaches and passed the orbs from the tainted areas through a cleansing smoke first. Anger and resentment lingered. Without the smoke, the choking energies would gather within the refractory, contaminating the one place beneath the treetops that felt like home.

Turning from Vraise, Rowan took in the gathering of

her conclave. Memory flickered over the present, filling in her father's tall, stately form in place of one of the council members. Rowan gasped, her entire body going rigid.

It was never worthwhile to come back here. All her returns did was unearth long-buried memories. Even if the rumors of coming warfare had finally gotten the better of her and brought her here.

"Tell her what the agent's asking for or move," Athenza spat.

Vraise stiffened at her tone but made a show of rolling his eyes as though he wasn't afraid of someone with the druid's reputation.

The body holds the truth, doesn't it?

There had been a time when Rowan would have made such observations to her phoenix but, aside from its intervention that morning, saving the very orbs Vraise had failed to notice overhead, it had grown dormant over the last few years. The magic embedded with the conclave's trees and earth was growing too faint, and the bird was losing heart. Or getting bored with her.

Rowan pushed away the stinging thought. It had saved her that morning. More than anyone here aside from Athenza would have done.

"Well enough," Vraise said, straightening his spine and adjusting the set of his coat to affect the ease Rowan knew he didn't feel, "but only because I am possessed of a degree of loyalty you'll never understand." He nodded toward the agent from the Pentacle, opening his body so his back was no longer to the agent and Athenza could pass. "They're under increasing pressure from the Cities, so if we want to remain an independent state free of their military drafts and mandatory stationing of troops, the Pentacle needs help from the margins."

Rowan narrowed her gaze at the agent who continued her smiling speech two-dozen paces away. "What kind of help?" The margins, as the Pentacle called conclaves such as theirs, already contributed from their stores of food and any and all goods they created to sustain themselves. In exchange, the Pentacle provided magical protectors who guarded the conclave's borders and who, if needed, would summon the Pentacle's military to shield the conclave from either the Cities or Alessandra, whoever's threats against Lis-Maen came to fruition first.

Vraise ran his tongue over his teeth, not bothering to disguise his impatience with Rowan's questions after he was the one to interpose himself into her way. "They're here to recruit anyone with magical potential to be part of a new research division."

"Ha!" Rowan couldn't help the outburst—the gall of the Pentacle truly knew no bounds. Had this been their plan, decades ago when they incorporated the Druidess—

A new round of shushing erupted around them, glares seeking to silence Rowan in particular. The elven woman in white glanced toward her and Vraise but didn't falter in her speech. "In return for your gifted ones and their time and abilities, the Five Faces are prepared to give..."

Rowan stopped listening to the visitor's empty

promises. "They ask that we make the same sacrifice to them the Cities would ask of us," Rowan shot at Vraise.

Past the pair of them now, Athenza bobbed her head before wobbling over to her seat. "And at least the Cities have the decency to call it a draft. What fancy obfuscation is the Pentacle using?" Unlike Rowan, Athenza hadn't bothered to lower her voice to a whisper. All eyes of the gathering were upon them now.

"An offering," the voice from the center of the council platform declared. While everyone else stared at Athenza, the agent's gaze fixed on Rowan. "An offering from the wilds in exchange for our aid, which grows more necessary by the day."

The council members beyond the agent had flushed, anger tightening the line of their mouths.

"Aid from ills brought on by empty politicking and failed negotiations," Athenza cast back, inciting more ire among those gathered. She settled onto the rounded top of her toadstool as though it was a throne.

Others nearby edged away from Athenza, trying to distance themselves.

The hairs along the back of Rowan's neck stood on end, alerting her to something.

Her phoenix's golden gaze joined her own. *What was it noticing?*

Unlike the rest of the conclave, the agent seemed intrigued by Athenza's goading. The light from the orbs sparkling overhead caught in her dark irises. "Perhaps." Her expression flattened into a mask. She glided toward the edge of the platform, closing the distance between herself, Rowan, Athenza, and Vraise. "Let's say your accusation is correct."

Athenza rested her walking cane across her lap and poked out her upper lip, waiting for the agent to astound her.

Instead, the agent turned back to Rowan. "Tell me, what distinction do you think the Cities would make between your conclave and the rest of Lis-Maen if they deemed a violent reprisal of one kind or another were in order." The added weight of the question went unspoken by all gathered—the Cities knew of no other kind of reprisal. The ruins of countless, now-destroyed societies could attest as much.

Rowan wetted her lips, not wanting to speak the obvious.

The agent clasped her hands in front of her hips.

"None," Rowan finally said.

The elf's mask cracked, and the agent smirked. "Then why insist upon a distinction among those of your own kind?" She spread her arms wide and twisted away, preparing to continue her speech, confident in her belief that Rowan and Athenza had been conquered.

Beside Rowan, Vraise released a slow sigh.

"Because we are not the same."

A collective gasp rippled across the conclave, sharp as an autumn wind before a storm.

Rowan sucked in her breath as she realized she'd voiced aloud the lesson Paupa had taught her so long ago.

"Is that so?" The agent spun back. Holding Rowan's gaze, she swirled her hands over one another. The energy that had risen along the back of Rowan's neck spread in goosepimples down her arms. Rowan shivered.

With a crackle of sparks, a ball of flame roared to life between the agent's hands. She tilted her head to the side. "Are we not?" she cried. And with her proclamation made, her gaze darted over to Athenza, and she hurled the ball of flame at Rowan's mentor, the last of Paupa's living allies.

Rowan shouted and dove forward, throwing herself between the aging druid and the ball of fire. She set her teeth and ripped the flames off their path, daring a burn across her chest as she pulled the shimmering energy toward herself. Rowan's momentum carried her in a rolling tumble through the toadstools that creaked upon their bases. A few thumped to the side.

Rowan came to rest on her back. The ball of living fire swirled, hot and bright between her palms. Her pulse echoed the roiling rhythm of the flames.

As she had felt the phoenix do that morning, Rowan eased the flame's energy, soothing the rough edges of the raw magic. Its swirling steadied. Rowan pressed her elbow onto one of the toadstools and pushed up to her feet. She willed the ball of fire to hover between her hands.

The crackle of the fire was the sole sound of the captivated conclave, the attention of all caught by the swirling flames in Rowan's palms.

Fire had been the first of the elements to leave them. The most difficult to control.

For a flash of a moment, Rowan's phoenix trilled its delight in the back of her mind. With golden eyes squinted in pleasure, the bird tossed its head toward the agent, willing Rowan to throw the flames back, knocking the agent from her smug position in the center of the council's branch and sending her plunging to the forest below.

A true offering.

No, Rowan thought back. They would only lock her away. Instead, Rowan marveled at the fire in her hands. Had the agent truly produced it from nothing? Could she teach Rowan to do the same?

Rowan met the agent's stare. The elf smiled openly now, her greedy gaze unrelenting as it took in Rowan and the spell she'd intercepted. Her eyebrow crooked as Rowan tightened her grasp on the flames, willing them to reveal their secret, especially how they had come into being.

She knew how to renew the orbs of light that graced the canopy around them and made their homes within the treetops possible. Her phoenix had soothed the discord between light and darkness. But to do the same with fire . . . her mind raced ahead with what such an ability might mean.

The agent bobbed her chin toward Rowan, disrupting the silence. "This one counts as three," she called. "Two more, and your quota to the Pentacle will be fulfilled."

Discordant conversations broke out across the conclave. The meeting had concluded.

The agent sprang over the gap between the council's branch and the sloped terrace where Rowan, Vraise, and Athenza had watched her speech. She sauntered up to

Rowan's side. "You're more than I'd dared hope for," the woman said, dark eyes a swirl of emotion in the glow of the fire between Rowan's palms. She cupped her hands together and bowed her head over them. "I'm Samara, first handmaiden of the Druidess. And it would be my delight to escort you to the Pentacle."

Rowan frowned and shoved the ball of fire back at Samara. The *last* place in the world she was going was the heart of Delmoir. "Keep it," she seethed. It was the Pentacle whose interference had taken Paupa from her, their slowly closing grasp choking the final remnants of joy from his life so that when his sickness took hold, his will to fight it had ebbed away.

Samara gasped as the flames returned to her hands. She winced as though the spell she'd cast had burned her. The elf's jaw tightened, her arm muscles strained, and she clapped her hands together, compressing the flames into an ember, which she stashed in a leather pouch upon her hip.

Titans, what a trick. With practice, could she uncover how to condense fire in that way? No. It didn't matter.

Rowan met Samara's surprised stare. "Find your three elsewhere." And with that, Rowan stormed away.

CHAPTER SIX

MARCON

RESPITE

Marcon stared down at the dispatch scroll he'd received from Commander Rezza. *The generals have ordered a counterattack to reclaim Sanctuary from enemy hands. Briznexi has retreated from leadership of the city.*

"It's our best chance in twenty years," the elven commander had said with a nod as she placed the scroll into Marcon's hands. "I know of your ambitions. There will be few opportunities more promising than this one."

His mouth had gone dry at that promise, and his heart had yet to return to its steady, normal rate.

Captain Colabra—his pulse spiked again. If he could prove himself in this battle, that's who he would be.

Marcon held his head higher, saluting to the wardens overseeing the ingress and egress between the Outer Ring and the communal outskirts where he and Lorieannan had built their home.

We'll be moving to the Outer Ring, he imagined announcing to her upon his return to Respite, victorious, the ash and blood of battle still clinging to his armor, a fresh captain's eagle affixed to his epaulets. *Ah, don't bother to pack. The Battalion*—he would wait for her gasp of delight at his promotion into such elevated ranks, a finer caliber of warrior than even the elite troops of the Army of Light—*has promised to furnish our new residence. Everything you could possibly desire is there already.*

With a glorious future elevating his shoulders, Marcon rounded the bend of his and Lorieannan's street.

Fat droplets of water plinked onto his head from above, like lavender rain mingled with dirt. Marcon grimaced, wiping his brow. With so many residents packed into such a small space, it was difficult for the washing to be fully clean.

He darted out of the way just in time as a trio of scrawny children hurried past, kicking up dirt that rose in tiny, foul clouds behind their scurrying feet. Marcon shook his head. The spacious lots of the Inner Ring— where he would relocate them after a few years on a captain's salary—allowed play areas for the residents' children. There was no need for them to dart over filthy puddles and evade aging mechoburros tethered outside the more prosperous of the residences. The burros' lowing cries and occasional burst gaskets disrupted the twilight hours, groaning out their own tiredness along- side that of their masters.

The apartment door creaked on its hinges as he opened it—when Abbot had time, they might see about mending it. With a captaincy illuminating his future, his chest failed to swell with pride as it had when he and Lorieannan first moved from the vineyard orphanage where they'd grown up to the apartment outside the city's walls.

All those years of training, dreaming, and drills were about to pay off.

"Lorie?" Marcon called as he stepped into their apartment. He closed the door slowly, allowing his eyes time to adjust to the dimness of the interior. The two square windows carved into the front of the apartment cast light upon the kitchen cabinet and washing bowl, but left the curtained bedroom and chair by the furnace in darkness.

A fragmented fire crystal abandoned by the apartment's former residents flickered half-heartedly behind the furnace's screen. Marcon's first attempt at mending it had left blisters along the fingers and palm of his sword arm so swollen he couldn't train for a week.

Vateri, a fellow lieutenant, had been sympathetic to his plight, but Cole had mocked him mercilessly, asking after the other tasks he found difficult in his home-keeping duties.

"Lorie?" Cole's mockery still stung, even if Vateri said that their friend teased out of jealousy that Marcon had managed to find a partner and build a home away from the barracks.

As difficult as such a feat had been, Marcon wasn't so sure.

Perhaps she was out and working for the herbalist or with the nursery today.

A sniffling sound echoed out from behind their

bedchamber curtain. Marcon slid deeper into the apartment. What was she doing still in bed in the high afternoon hours?

"Oh, you're back." A soft, hoarse voice drowned out the sniffling. Fabric rustled—a rough-spun woolen quilt scratching over linen—and Lorieannan slunk out from behind the bedroom curtain they'd erected to separate the narrow bed from the rest of the dwelling.

She rubbed the corner of her wrist beneath each of her eyes.

Marcon squinted to better see her—eyes swollen, nose red.

Lorieannan sniffled for good measure.

"Why are you still in bed? Are you ill?"

She jolted back as though stung. "I'm simply resting between shifts. Did you need something?" *You're an imposition*, her tone said.

Marcon tried to roll the tension from his shoulders. It had been growing since he stepped beyond the walls, he realized now. And it would only continue to do so unless he could avoid the brewing fight.

"I have good news." Marcon forced a grin. "We're being deployed to Sanctuary. The dragon has departed from the ramparts, and the generals believe it will be our best chance to recapture the city." He stood taller as he remembered his commander's words. "Rezza believes this will be my best chance to make a name for myself, achieve the captain's rank I've been working toward for so long."

Finally he met her gaze again. She'd been there since the beginning, had been the first person he confided his dream of becoming a captain to. Like his parents. She'd share his sense of pride—

Lorieannan's lower lip began to quiver, and Marcon's entire body clenched.

Not again. Not now.

"Everyone's talking about it." The quivering increased, and thick tears began to form in the base of Lorieannan's eyes. Her voice took on a warbling quality. "They're sending you into what's bound to be a slaughter, and I'll never see you again."

If she had produced a blade and stabbed him, Marcon would have been less shocked.

"Of course that isn't what's happening," he cried.

Lorieannan gasped, her eyes wide at his tone.

Marcon squeezed his fist and forced a slow exhale, the same kind he had practiced as a soldier's aide in his earliest years of training. Why would she put so much stock in others' gossip? When had he ever misled her?

He tried again. "That is not how this attack is going to be. Your sources are mistaken."

"You're right," Lorieannan wailed. "It'll be even worse! You'll never come home."

"How can you say that?" Marcon stared at Lorieannan, his mouth agape. "The generals would not be so foolhardy as to send us into an impossible battle to recapture Sanctuary. Have you so little faith in me—"

"How could you possibly see my questioning of them as a questioning of you?" Lorieannan shot back. "You're a foot soldier. They're military strategists and commanders. Your life, our lives, aren't important to them." She reached out toward him, the wrinkles in her dress showing as she neared the light. She truly had spent the entire day in bed, the whole time he'd been training.

Marcon sprang away from her, hands upraised by his shoulders. He didn't have to listen to this. Didn't have to stay in the apartment he had worked so hard to afford for the pair of them only to hear himself and his fellow soldiers disparaged for fools. If he wanted to hear talk like that, he'd sit in one of countless tavern counters across Respite and belittle the sacrifices and bravery of the very souls who protected those who thought so little of them.

Lorieannan shook her head at his rejection of her comforting gesture, hugging her hands around her waist instead. The well of tears began to drip down her cheeks.

An all-too-familiar sight lately. When had she last passed a day without melancholy? In her eyes, he was a constant disappointment. And it was exhausting. "Does all I've worked for truly mean so little to you?"

"I have stood by your side through *all* of this!" she shouted back. "All the training, all the pointless ambitions and plans."

Marcon's jaw tightened.

"I just thought you would have grown out of your desire to play soldier by now."

The words landed as a physical blow. The dream he'd spent his life trying to achieve, the heroic deeds he knew he could perform for their city, the renown that would follow his name—it meant nothing to her. *He* meant nothing to her.

He lowered his voice. There was no use shouting, not

if this was where matters had settled between them. "Maybe the thing I've outgrown is you."

Lorieannan whimpered in reply, the tears coming fast now. She rushed past him to retreat to the opposite corner of the apartment and folded herself into the chair by the furnace.

Marcon punched the threadbare curtain aside and snatched his belongings from the basket at the foot of their bed. He needed a drink, and he needed to sleep somewhere he wasn't despised before his ride out into his first true battle.

He hadn't spent over a decade in military training only to throw it all away when an opportunity to affect Respite—and all of Eldura—for the better arose.

The forces of the Luz and the Blazing Battalion were going to storm the gates of Sanctuary and drive back the enemy's forces.

Sanctuary would be brought back into the glorious fold of the Cities United. And Lorieannan and all the other disloyalists across Respite who doubted them would be sorry.

When he emerged, Lorieannan sat huddled in the chair in the corner with her face in her hands.

The worn curtain whispered back into place behind him. Motes of dust sparkled in the low-slanting sunlight that struggled against the interior's shadows. *Pathetic excuse for a space, a home*, Marcon thought to himself. No wonder she's unhappy. But it was the best he'd been able to afford on his foot soldier's salary.

All of that was about to change, he reminded himself.

During this battle, he'd earn his promotion. Then she would see.

Marcon forced his jaw to unclench as he glared over at her. There were practical matters to attend to after all. "The apartment is paid for the next two months. Send word to the barracks if you need more. We should be back by then."

Lorieannan's work as a nursery and gardener's aide didn't pay enough for her to live on her own. He'd support her until she found other accommodations. It was the honorable thing to do.

Without another word passed between them, Marcon swung open the apartment door, tensing at its familiar squeak. He swung his pack onto his shoulder and returned the way he'd come.

Cole and Vateri would be celebrating their upcoming deployment in Cole's favorite tavern, the Dracat's Grin.

For once, he'd be able to join them.

CHAPTER SEVEN
ROWAN

Less than an hour passed before a knock sounded at the refractory door. Rowan sighed. She'd known Athenza would want to talk over the agent's demands with her. Come to think of it, she should have gone straight there, saved the druid the extra climb.

"I was expecting you," Rowan said as she swung open the refractory door, careful to not jostle its crooked position upon its sagging vine hinges. Without Paupa to help her manage the repairs, Rowan had to prioritize the orbs over the refractory itself.

She jolted back at finding not only Athenza outside but Vraise and Samara too. "Why would you bring them here?" she asked Athenza.

"You know we can hear you, right?" Vraise said, his shoulders tight by his ears.

"Of course she knows that," Athenza spat back on Rowan's behalf. "She's just in too confused a state to care."

Rowan's lips thinned into a line. Trust her mentor to reveal more than necessary while trying to defend Rowan at the same time.

Athenza brushed Rowan back and heaved herself up the refractory stairs into the tall, interior chamber of Rowan's home. Shortly after Paupa's death, she and Athenza had fought, and she'd attempted to bar Athenza's entry into the refractory by not inviting her in. "You were not even a glimmer in your mamaun's imagination when I helped your paupa lay these floorboards. Do you truly believe their space belongs more to you than me?" Wisdom had taught her to avoid arguments with Athenza ever since.

"I suppose the two of you can come in as well," Rowan said before following after Athenza to ensure she was seated comfortably. She needn't have bothered—Athenza had already settled into her favorite corner, the one with the best view of the orbs arranged along their vine tracks awaiting their turn in the canopy above.

Majestyk had already slunk out of her spot on the windowsill and was pacing across Athenza's lap, purring and rubbing her scaled head against the druid's attentive hands.

Rowan turned back in time to catch the Pentacle's agent, Samara, let down her guard enough to allow her jaw to drop upon seeing the refractory's interior for the first time. The elf stared overhead at the sparkling orbs, swirls of inky purple undulating within them. As the dappled light from outside caught upon the series of mirrors Paupa had installed to soothe the orbs and illuminate the refractory's interior, the mottled glass of the orbs' surfaces cast soft, rainbow-hued lights all along the walls, rippling like the refractory was underwater.

Rowan's chest swelled. *You're still astounding people, Paupa.*

Gathering herself, Samara re-clasped her hands before her hips and turned to Rowan. "I believe we may not have had the most ideal first introduction. I should not have tested your abilities in so overt a manner."

"I would have been ready," Athenza quipped from the corner of the refractory. Majestyk cooed her agreement, unfolding her reddish-gold wings so the druid could scratch at their base by her shoulders. It was a great symbol of trust, for a dracat to extend their wings while at rest.

"Undoubtedly," Samara agreed, bowing her head in Athenza's direction. "May I?" she indicated an open stool by Rowan's stores of herbs, nodding politely at the cultivating corner with the cracked orbs hanging over it.

Rowan assented.

"You clearly have a gift with the element of earth," Samara said, retrieving a pair of spectacles from her pocket and studying the delicate flowers of the cultivation patch.

Rowan tightened the set of her jaw to prevent herself from calling out that Samara should be careful near something so delicate. The agent was moving with an ease that spoke to her understanding of the flowers' and the orbs' fragility.

She turned from the cultivation corner and settled onto the stool. "I was impressed by your aptitude with the element of fire today. It has proven by far the most difficult of the six for our offerings to master. Perhaps we will start there with you."

From the opposite corner of the refractory, Athenza cleared her throat but, when asked, proclaimed it was nothing. "Some tea would be excellent."

Rowan busied herself with preparing a soothing blend for Athenza while Samara explained the Pentacle's plan—given the lack of success with their offerings plucked from the finest mages across Delmoir, they had turned their eyes outward, offering mutually beneficial positions to those from the margins whose fate, it had to be admitted, was intimately tied with the Pentacle's own. It was in everyone's best interest, surely Rowan must see, for the collective power of Lis-Maen to work toward this goal of combining the six elements across a troupe of casters.

She had heard similar aims before, though from a very different elf with markedly different aims. Combining the six elements was a dream her paupa had shared with her, one of the most profound ways in which she might help revive Verdigris, the vanished titan of nature.

Samara continued on, oblivious to the memories struggling upon Rowan's heart, a kaleidoscope of butterflies with rain-sodden wings. "With such power at our hands, the troupe will be able to ensure a peaceful future for Lis-Maen. We won't be at the mercy of the Cities and their hidden champions, should such beings resurface, nor will we be vulnerable to Alessandra and her elemental attacks." Samara sighed. "The troupe will be the perfect peacekeeping force."

Rowan blew over her lavender tea, savoring the spritz of lemon she'd squeezed over the scalding liquid. Her senses were not so clouded that she was unable to perceive the dangerous assumptions and obfuscations of Samara's presentation—a clarity she did not trust Vraise to bring to the situation—but the agent's points did pique her curiosity, especially the possibility of the champions resurfacing.

"Has something happened, in the Cities? Does the Pentacle have reason to believe the champions are returning? Or coming out of hiding?" She pictured the map of their world that she'd seen years ago—in the south, a dark continent representing Alessandra's strongholds and forces, its gloom leaking across its former borders into the Glade of Shadows. Above the Glade and spiraling north and east were the Cities' holdings, a series of great settlements said to be almost unimaginably impressive for those from the forest reaches where populations were smaller and "civilization" less grand. In the center of all of these, either exposed or enclosed, depending on how one looked at it, was Lis-Maen itself, increasingly alone in its desire to remain removed from the ever-escalating war between the Cities and Alessandra. Only the Emeraude to the east supported Lis-Maen on their quest, the covens' matrons aligning themselves to the will of the Pentacle.

A contingency of soldiers stationed in Lis-Maen was the closest the Cities had come to keeping troops within the forest's borders and pressing their expressed vows of neutrality. Negotiations for their work across the small island continent had fallen apart shortly before Rowan's birth, after the fall of Sanctuary.

"Not to my knowledge, no," Samara replied. "But the Oracle urges the other Faces to remain vigilant should such a shift occur. We are not guaranteed peaceful dealings, particularly given the strain their armies have been under of late."

Rowan asked over the particulars of the peacekeeping force the Pentacle was recruiting. Would they be required to settle permanently in Delmoir, or would they have the freedom to go wherever in Lis-Maen they chose, perhaps even opting to travel?

Samara drained her teacup and placed it upon Rowan's hewn wooden counter. "I'm afraid these specifics are beyond my purview. This force remains hypothetical, especially given the volatility of the magics involved."

Rowan frowned at that. It was the most nervous Samara had been in their conversation thus far. "What happened to the first round of offerings?" she asked softly, stealing a glance at Vraise as she did so.

The agent dropped her gaze, scanning the chaos of jars and drying herbs scattered along the back wall that Rowan used as a kitchen and for orb repair. "They have . . . retired from the trials. When our success seemed questionable, the Faces saw fit that we pause the attempts and reassess." She cleared her throat and straightened. "Nothing for you to worry about, though. We have learned a great deal through the first trials. Made several improvements to the processes. It's only barely dangerous now."

Athenza's gaze met Rowan's. They both knew a partial truth when they encountered one. It would be one of the first things she worked to discover when she arrived in Delmoir.

"And why did *you* come here?" Rowan tossed at Vraise over the agent's shoulder. He stood off to the side, hands clenched, watching the three of them.

"I'm to be one of the other two offerings, if you agree." Vraise straightened, waiting for her to insult the council's choice in his appointment. "I have learned a lot the past few years. Samara believes I have potential." He flinched as the agent met his gaze. "Not like yours," he mumbled.

Samara smoothed her robes and smiled at Rowan. "I do hope you'll consider the program. Why don't you and your, erm, friend talk it over while I attend to a few of Vraise's questions."

Rowan would have preferred the two strangers to have vacated her house altogether, but she took the opportunity to confer with Athenza in private.

"Go ahead," Rowan said, sinking onto the footstool beside the druid's chair. "Tell me what a bad idea you think it is."

"I'm actually quite intrigued by the possibility. It's why I brought them here." The elf smiled sadly. "It's no hearttree, but I think this is the sort of opportunity your paupa would have wanted you to avail yourself of."

Rowan shook her head, unable to believe what she was hearing. "My Paupa is dead because of the Pentacle's insistence upon rooting out any and all naysayers who protested their extension of their rule to the outskirts, not to mention their disdain for anyone who would rather follow apocryphal teachings of Lilith on how to revive Verdigris than bow the knee to their centralized power."

Athenza simply shrugged, used to Rowan's outbursts. "Then show them what can be done by those who wield the six united rather than their five." It was something her father had often told her—she was destined to bear the six elements, joined together in one, and in so doing, help to restore Verdigris.

In a moment of weakness following his death, Rowan had accidentally confessed Paupa's directive to someone outside his circle of friends and like-minded allies. With condescension dripping from their voice, the conclave member had assured Rowan that, according to the expertise of the Pentacle, such an objective was not possible. The combination of multiple elements in one being would in and of itself be a miraculous occurrence, the purview of a gifted mage, not the child of druids from the margins.

"The union of the six is the mission Samara invites you to," Athenza said, "even if she used different words."

The druid leaned closer, for once lowering her voice. "The degree of loyalty you bear and to whom is and will always be your choice." She shook her head. "Do not turn up your nose at such a chance to grow your magic for the sake of the dead. It cannot bring them back. And you have exceeded the skill of any around you. Including me," Athenza added quickly before Rowan could protest.

Her phoenix stirred at Athenza's words. From the back of Athenza's armchair, Majestyk chirruped her agreement, causing Vraise and Samara to jump. The dracat took the added attention as an invitation to leap off the chair and scurry about the refractory.

Rowan ran her tongue over her teeth, her throat struggling to form the words. She swallowed down her retorts. Years had passed since Paupa's death, and though the hole in the center of her being seemed only to widen rather than heal, Athenza was right—she needed a change. Needed a chance to grow.

Until she could prove herself worthy of approaching the hearttree, there was nothing left for her here.

Rowan turned her focus inward, seeking the phoenix. With the Pentacle's resources at hand, she might be able to awaken the phoenix to its true power. *Do you remember our trip to the hearttree?* she asked the mystical bird, her hand outstretched toward its sleeping form.

They had met when she and Paupa traveled to the hearttree. Her proximity to such concentrated, sacred magic had granted her the phoenix, awakened her magic into this internal form.

But there was another set of domesticated hearttrees kept by the Pentacle. So near to the Undying Grove, what might she and the bird discover?

Rowan rose, brushed a stray clump of hair back into the knot at the base of her neck, and crossed the room to stand before the Pentacle's agent. She leveled her gaze with Samara's. "I will accept your assignment, but there is a condition."

The agent's eyebrow rose. She had expected as much.

"I want an oath from each of the Five Faces that you will protect Willow Glen, no matter what."

"The Pentacle has already—"

Rowan shook her head. "A promise of aid is not the same thing as a blood oath." She paused, letting her demand sink in. "This is in addition to the oath they've made with the council. One they make with me."

During her conversation with Athenza, Rowan had been trying to work out how best to ascertain the value the Pentacle placed upon this training program they were inviting her and Vraise to. That she counted as an offering of three said she was valuable, but what was the Pentacle's investment beyond that?

If she was going to betray Paupa's memory, she would protect his true purpose. Willow Glen was the final defense between the rest of Eldura and the heart-tree. Whatever happened elsewhere in the margins, her conclave had to stand.

Samara inclined her head. "This is not a promise I can make on their behalf, but for my part, I can swear to bring you and your request before them."

Rowan met Athenza's gaze, ensuring there was nothing she had missed.

Her mentor was smiling, leaning upon her cane just behind Rowan. "It will be an interesting journey for us all."

"What are you—"

"I convinced Samara here on our way over." Athenza was beaming, delighted with herself for having concealed the secret through the entirety of the exchange. "She rightly thought it would be best for you to have someone watching over you, given your history. And being magically inclined myself, I volunteered."

"*History* is a bit of an overstatement, don't you think?"

Vraise and Athenza both chortled at that.

"Were it not for the refractory, I'm not sure they would have allowed you to stay," Athenza added, smiling.

Rowan crossed her arms over her chest. "It was just a few magical accidents."

"You set fire to a dozen homes across an ancient oak before you were twelve," Vraise pointed out unhelpfully.

Her phoenix released twin curls of smoke out of its nostrils at the reminder.

Rowan glanced at Samara, certain the agent was going to rescind her invitation. "Like I said, it was an accident." Her anger had known no boundaries in the wake of Paupa's death, and her phoenix had resorted to fire to express their displeasure at the scrubbing of his records from the council histories. "But we're not discussing me." She glanced at Athenza. "We're discussing *you* joining the so-called offerings for the Pentacle."

"That is what they are called," Samara said dryly.

Rowan looked between Vraise and the agent who were both watching her closely in turn. With the open curiosity in their gazes, Rowan realized their mistake. "I believe the two of you may have miscalculated which of us is the true fire risk." She glanced back at Athenza. "If you think she'll allow me to talk her out of whatever she's set her mind to, you have grossly overestimated my abilities."

Athenza bowed her head over her walking cane, her

pleasant smile deepening the wrinkles beside her eyes. "It is too late now," she added cheerfully.

Samara had the good sense to pale as she reevaluated the three of them. Whether the agent was more uncertain after Rowan's demands or in light of Athenza's determination, Rowan wasn't sure. "We leave at first light," the agent said. "Pack well. Our project will last months, perhaps longer."

She bade Rowan and Athenza farewell until the morrow.

"Was what you said before the council true?" Vraise asked Samara on the way out. "The Pentacle is stealing back from the Cities the elemental powers they stole from us?"

Rowan met Athenza's gaze, her lips parted.

Her mentor gave a tiny shake of the head, bidding Rowan to wait.

"One of the Pentacle's most sacred tasks in maintaining our neutrality in the Cities' warmongering is being able to defend ourselves, especially given the Cities' insistence upon hopeless causes like reclaiming Sanctuary," the agent answered as they climbed down the refractory steps and wound their way along the curving treetop paths.

"What was that about?" Rowan demanded the moment the pair had passed out of earshot. "Elemental magic is a gift. How could it be stolen?"

Her mentor was slowly crossing back to the fraying wicker armchair. Athenza settled herself onto the worn cushion with a sigh. The chair groaned alongside her,

Majestyk's signal to hurry over and claim her position on the druid's lap.

"You will have to get used to such professions," Athenza said, tilting her head back to study the refractory tracks overhead. The next evening, Rowan would need to release the levies holding the charging orbs to return them to the understory and propel those shining about the conclave's treetops to the refractory before sending them to the canopy to recharge.

"It is easier for most to believe another is at fault than to hold up a mirror to themselves and accept the responsibility, especially for so fickle and valuable a resource as magic," Athenza continued. "One of the Pentacle's newer arguments in their struggle to maintain independence from the Cities simultaneously allows them to blame the Cities for the waning magic felt across our lands. Rather than finding a fault amongst themselves, they claim that the Cities have stolen stores of ancient magic that rightly belong to the Pentacle."

The druid shrugged. "Without new champions to lead the Cities' armies and with their own dwindling magic, the Cities have done little to deny such claims. In actuality, the truth is more complicated than the stories being woven around it, as your father would say."

Rowan nodded, only half-listening to the druid's warning and the lesson hiding behind it. Stolen magic or no, there were reserves of power in the Pentacle. Some in the form of knowledge, others of invention, like whatever magical secret had allowed Samara to produce a ball of fire from a stone.

With similar abilities at her command, Rowan could

present herself to the hearttree and become a protector of the deep forest alongside the two great wolves her paupa had told her about, Grandmother Wolf and Schaeza. Rowan stared down at her palms, imagining balancing the flames there. It might be enough. If Paupa was right and she could indeed wield the six, such an achievement might truly prove her and her phoenix worthy.

"Ouch," Athenza called, scowling at Majestyk who had just accidentally pricked the druid with her claws when her balance slipped. "Of course you're coming too. Rowan was just about to pack your bedding."

Rowan spun back toward the pair of them, a sudden smile threatening to overcome her features. It was finally happening, the change in fate she'd awaited for so long.

CHAPTER EIGHT

MARCON

Marcon's trek through the Outer Ring saw him weaving in and out of a stream of workers on their return from their positions in the city's interior to the outskirts beyond the wall and on the edges of the Outer Ring.

Before Sanctuary's fall, when Alessandra's armies had pressed along the outskirts of the region, the residences of the Middle Ring had grown even more valuable as the city moved those who weren't of noble birth or part of the upper echelons of the military out of the Inner Ring to make more room for training and to increase the fortifications. Those unable to remain in the Middle Ring had relocated to the Outer Ring, with only a single wall protecting them from the wilds of Eldura and Alessandra's armies, if they were to route the Cities' forces, but such an attack had never occurred.

As the years passed and Alessandra's forces seemed content to remain within Sanctuary's walls—having renamed the city Reckoning—the fears of an attack against the outskirts beyond the walls abated further.

Refugees from other regions settled within the outskirts. Farms like the vineyard where he and Lorieannan had grown up employed workers from all across Eldura. The city became a refuge, the toast of their world.

He showed his papers to the wardens who guarded the passageways into the Middle Ring, where his friends would be waiting for him. Tucked away among the artisans' residences and shops, built into the wall of the Inner Ring itself, the somber music and loud conversation of the Dracat's Grin welcomed him into its embrace.

Even before the dinner hour, the tavern was packed. Many soldiers came here straight after their sparring and drills—sweat and other personal odors mingled with the tavern's heady hops, but warm and inundated with soldiers hot from a day's work, the Dracat remained a favorite with Respite's soldiers for its proximity to the barracks' location and its scent of indoor training rings.

"There he is," a familiar voice called from the bar. Marcon's friend Cole balanced against the footrail to raise himself over the crowd and wave Marcon over. "Thank you, love," he said with a grin that was not returned by the barkeep. "Oh, and one for my friend too," he added. The woman's eyes warmed at spying Marcon and she slid away to fill a tankard for him as well.

"I swear, the moment you arrive, you steal all the lasses from me," Cole complained. "Over a year I've been trying to woo her to no effect, and you saunter in with your dark hair and stormy eyes and win her affection immediately." An affected twinge of hurt lingered in Cole's voice. "He's taken, love, just think on that," Cole said to the barkeep as she returned.

The corner of her lip upturned, and she winked at Marcon before sauntering away again.

"Unbelievable," Cole cried. "Welp." He slung his arm over Marcon's shoulders and angled him toward a small, raised table by the window where Vateri waited, kicking her feet from atop the tall stool where she'd perched.

Her grin faltered as she spied Marcon approaching with Cole's arm around his shoulder. They'd been friends since the earliest days of their infantry training, notable to their instructors for their inseparability from one another's sides—Marcon with his broad shoulders and quick reflexes was the natural sword-wielder in their ranks. Vateri, shy and quick of foot, her light brown hair shorn on level with her chin, was the archer among them, and Cole, a human like Marcon who in other settings appeared lanky and awkward, was adept with both lance and pike.

Vateri eyed Marcon as he approached, calculation furrowing her brow. "What a pair the two of you make. To what do we owe such an occasion?"

Cole answered before Marcon could speak. "He's come to celebrate his first deployment with the lowly likes of us, of course."

Guilt twisted low in Marcon's gut. He shoved it aside. Lorieannan was the one who should feel guilty for disparaging everything Marcon stood for, all he'd worked for, especially on the cusp of achieving all he'd hoped for and more.

Marcon repeated the words he'd been chanting to himself on his hour's walk here. Joining the Army of Light was the best thing that had ever happened to him. He was following in his parents' footsteps.

Parents who'd perished in the First Battle of Sanctuary.

He would avenge them in the Second.

"Uh oh," Vateri said, her scowl deepening. The elf narrowed her eyes at Marcon and Cole as they sauntered over to the table. Marcon carried the tankard he'd received free of charge from the taverness and a fresh glass of wine for Vateri. She crossed her arms over her chest, on her an expression of consternation more than Lorieannan's of self-protection. "What did you do?"

"Nothing."

Vateri dropped her chin, heightening the gold-flecked glow of her hazel stare. "Liar. Try again."

Cole shifted his weight back on his stool, smiling at his two best friends. He took a deep swig of ale, immediately acquiring a mustache of foam across his upper lip.

Vateri had been trying to keep the two of them in line since they'd met a decade ago in the junior ranks of Respite's standing army before working their way up to join the city's division of the Army of Light.

This deployment would be their first where they were part of the fighting ranks of the larger Luz. The Blazing Battalion was riding up from Beacon—the elite military unit Marcon had dreamed of joining from his earliest memories, ever since Joane and Abbot had tended to a wounded soldier from among their ranks in the vineyard when he was just a boy.

It was rumored that Field Commander Silversword might even lead the forces in the battle to reclaim Sanctuary. Marcon's chest swelled at the thought—to be in the ranks of one of the last true champions, one blessed by the titans' might before Sanctuary's fall. No new champions had been appointed by the titans since.

Lorieannan was not going to take this opportunity away from him.

Beneath the prickling discomfort of Vateri's stare, Marcon sighed and confessed the argument in its entirety. "We've been fighting for months, ever since she started working at the nursery." He downed a gulp of ale. "Why would I sacrifice all I've worked for to settle down as an apprentice somewhere in the city? Especially after how hard I've worked to be among the city's defenders. It wouldn't be right. There are plenty who are unable to serve."

Marcon shook his head, thinking of his favorite blacksmith, Garreth Stozdak, a half-orc who'd been injured in the First Battle of Sanctuary. His son had joined the ranks of the Army of Light a few years behind Marcon in what had become a sore spot between father and son. He soothed matters as he was able. "We couldn't afford the children she is so desperate for us to have then," Marcon admitted.

The other alternative—that upon his promotion, they marry and start a family—was unthinkable.

Marcon wouldn't risk a child of his growing up on Abbot and Joane's farm, an orphan like him. He'd never voiced such a concern to Lorieannan, but they had talked around such matters growing up together, slowly falling into, and now out of, love.

Lorieannan had no desire to serve in the military, but if matters worsened and the pressure around the Cities grew, she wouldn't have a choice. The bravery of people like his parents didn't guarantee the safety of those less willing to put their lives on the line for others' protection.

It took people like himself, like Cole and Vateri, to stem the tides of darkness that would see their great city overwhelmed.

Cole shrugged. "The two of you have been together for a while. Maybe it's better that you find out now. Make a clean break before we're all promoted and start our tour of the realms." The boozy gleam of their brilliant future within the Army of Light shone in Cole's eyes.

Vateri stared at him in disbelief. After shaking her head, she turned back to Marcon. "Please don't listen to *him*." A thunk sounded under the table.

Cole jolted to sit up straighter. "Hey! She kicked me!"

The elf grinned, a small sense of justice returning to her carefully ordered world. "Marcon is too smart to take into account the perspective of someone whose only romantic relationships have been ones *purchased. By. The. Hour.* Not even the night." Vateri returned her scowl to Cole. "So he understands that a relationship is more than a matter of exchange." She tucked a stray lock of hair back behind her pointed ears—a favorite movement, particularly when she believed she'd won an argument.

Vateri had often joined Cole on his tours of the pleasure houses, occasionally soliciting the services of the women and men who worked there, but only on the occasion that they proved to be "stunning conversationalists" first.

She always returned from such visits happier than Cole.

Vateri sipped her white wine, its contents the same color as the flecks of gold in her eyes. She tilted her head, frowning out the window onto the darkening street. "Maybe she's just scared about you being deployed for the first time."

Always the wisest of the group, Vateri's words had a sobering effect upon the three of them. She frowned and leaned toward the center of the table. "What do you think it will be like?"

Marcon and Cole followed suit, drawing their heads near Vateri's so they could hear one another more clearly over the shouted conversations of the increasingly intoxicated tavern-goers. So near to the barracks, this was a soldiers' bar, and they weren't the only ones on edge about the upcoming battle.

"Chaotic," Marcon said, answering truthfully this time. "They've had twenty years to entrench their forces."

A castle in the center of the city with tall ramparts that spiraled outward—in theory making the city simpler to defend and harder to take because the walls hemmed in attackers.

Marcon had questioned almost every survivor he'd found about the battle, trying to understand the fight that had claimed the lives of his parents and left him an orphan at a vineyard.

Two years after the battle, at the mature age of five, Abbot had agreed that Marcon might appeal to join the training ranks that took in soldiers' children, allowing them the chance of avenging what their enemy took from them.

He'd been preparing for precisely this deployment ever since.

Marcon thought over what they'd learned from Commander Rezza. The generals of Respite had ordered the attack as word reached them that the dragon, Briznexi, who had turned the tide of battle two decades before, had left the city. Lesser evils ruled over the teeming ranks of the vultura—the undead remnants of the former residents of Sanctuary, now fallen into mindless servitors of the enemy's will. "Dragon or no, it will be difficult."

A lieutenant from a partner unit strolled by their table, noticing the three of them conferring. "Vateri," he purred.

The elf's expression didn't change.

The soldier paled. "Vateri's friends," he added with a nod. Before moving away, he thumped his open palm onto the table, causing Cole to jump. "Don't look so glum, young ones." He forced a smile despite his horror at Vateri's blatant rejection. "Probably at least one of the three of you will survive."

They stared after the lieutenant, temporarily in shock.

Cole turned back to face Marcon and Vateri. "If you sleep with him, will you be able to pass his death wish on us back onto him?"

Vateri lifted her chin. "I wouldn't give him the satisfaction."

Marcon knew her well enough to catch the tremor of fear in her voice.

"Here." Vateri dipped her fingertips into her glass of wine, murmured a few nonsensical words in Elvish, and flicked the wine dripping from her fingers toward the lieutenant's fleeing back.

Marcon and Cole glanced at one another before turning to stare into their drinks.

"What?" she asked.

Marcon raised his mug to hide the smile he couldn't suppress. Only Vateri would handle a proposed romantic entanglement and subsequent twist of luck in such a manner.

"Oh you two," Vateri huffed after Cole chortled into his ale and emerged from his own mug, coughing. "So it's probably not a curse-canceling charm rooted in the inherent magic of Lis-Maen," Vateri sighed. Lis-Maen had always intrigued Vateri. It was where she'd been born. Her parents died when she was a toddler, at which point Vateri had been relocated to the Cities. The rehoming project was one of several failed peacemaking campaigns between the Pentacle and the Cities United, but their shared experience as orphans had brought the trio closer together.

Vateri was better off for it, he and Cole both thought. Why grow up in a veritable wilderness when she could live in the greatest city of the age? "And with such friends," Cole often added when the homesickness for a land she barely remembered returned to hang over her.

"Well if it wasn't before, I'm sure it is now," Marcon assured her.

The lieutenant's warning hung over their merrymaking. Cole surprised them all by being the first to suggest that they finish their drinks and return to the barracks.

Marcon had a single stop to make first before following his friends. "I'll join you shortly," he assured Vateri and Cole who nodded, knowing where he was headed.

His feet carried him to the blacksmith's forge within the Middle Ring of Respite, the walk so familiar he had little to occupy himself beyond the fuzziness of the ale and his circling thoughts, cawing overhead like crows over a battlefield. Marcon shook off the thought—such meditations were unbefitting of a soldier. Not even crows picked over the vultura, and those were the only corpses he wanted to imagine right now.

Garreth Stozdak had been among the soldiers who located Marcon after the First Battle of Sanctuary, those who helped the young orphan find a new family on Abbot and Joane's vineyard. As a child, he'd been frightened of the half-orc when they first met. Garreth had returned from the battle with a severe injury to his leg, one the medicos hadn't been able to fully mend due to its magical nature. The broad-shouldered man had filled the whole of the doorway, his face twisted in a grimace of pain, eyes full of sorrow.

With his career as a soldier behind him following the battle, Garreth had turned to blacksmithing, a position that allowed him to retain his proximity to those he'd served with—the few who'd survived, anyway—and, as rumors occasionally suggested, also opened doors for the smith to circulate among those who disapproved of the leadership of the Cities United, particularly the one many held responsible for the failure of the First Battle of Sanctuary, Commandant, now Field Commander Tali Silversword.

Marcon squashed these rumors whenever they cropped up in his hearing. Citizens of Respite had the freedom to speak their minds, within reason, but Garreth's disapproval of the field commander's methods and outright sedition were far from equivalent.

Their relationship had deepened over the years, particularly as Marcon worked his way up the ranks of the Luz. He turned to Abbot for advice when he could and tried to put his adoptive father's lessons into practice for his comportment, but when it came to military matters and, increasingly, his daily concerns, Garreth was the one he sought out.

The blacksmith lived alone after the passing of his wife in rooms behind the forge itself. Marcon's shoulders eased as he strode within sight of the forge and Garreth's home. The warm glow of interior lanterns shone out onto the street and—Marcon quickened his pace—raised voices rang out from within.

He rushed the rest of the way down the street, breaking from a jog into a run at the noise. Marcon butted his shoulder into the cracked door and found Garreth glowering from his kitchen, his knuckles white against the counter, and his son, Patrick, preparing to storm out the door.

Patrick stopped short before barreling into Marcon.

"Makes sense you'd be here," he snapped, shoving past Marcon and into the street. "Don't expect a runner upon my safe return," Patrick shot back over his shoulder before storming back the way Marcon had come. "You can learn of our victory like everyone else."

A different pain than the one Garreth had worn upon their first meeting hung in the shadows beneath the half-orc's eyes as he stared after Patrick and took in Marcon's arrival.

"I . . ."

"Come in, son." Garreth waved him inside.

The half-orc refilled his glass of wine with a bottle of chilled red from the icebox, his favorite. Marcon waved his hand at Garreth's offer of a glass of his own. He was plenty tipsy from the tavern, though encountering Patrick in such a state had a sobering effect.

Marcon perched on the edge of the narrow couch beneath Garreth's front window, opposite the smith's favorite armchair. "I apologize for my timing."

Garreth shook his head as he trudged over to his chair. Despite his limp, the half-orc's every movement suggested strength. "Nothing for *you* to apologize for there."

He nodded, taking the smith's meaning. Field Commander Silversword had been a sore spot in Garreth and Patrick's relationship since Patrick's promotion.

"I doubt he's what's brought you to my door so late, though he acts as though I should be glad of hearing from my own son before his deployment." Garreth waved his hand, staving off Marcon's intervention into their quarrel. "Just as I doubt you're afraid of what's to come." The corners of Garreth's eyes crinkled as he peered across at Marcon, deep green creases that spoke of his concern.

The jagged fragments that had twisted in Marcon's chest during his fight with Lorieannan finally settled a little. A deep breath further smoothed his unease. "It's a fight I've had with Lorieannan," Marcon said, telling the blacksmith about their argument, her dissatisfaction with the life they'd worked so hard to build, his many shortcomings that she so often reminded him of, her desire for children that he couldn't see his way to answering.

Garreth listened through all of it, sipping at his wine and nodding. His steady presence didn't ask Marcon to hurry, didn't rise to interject in Marcon's defense as Cole had.

"Before her passing, my wife and I didn't always agree," Garreth said when Marcon's story was through. "But when it came to the core things, even if we weren't eye-to-eye, we held one another's gazes true."

Marcon considered this, easing back against the floral cushions of Garreth's couch.

"I'm not saying you need to decide, forever, right now, especially with so momentous a battle before you. And what I'd not have you do is let your argument scramble your focus as you'll need every scrap of that to survive." The smith scowled, the gravity of his words making his posture rigid. "But if she's showing you that it's time to let her go, time for you both to find your own way, you might see about letting that be less frightening than it is right now."

Garreth smirked, catching Marcon off-guard, though it wasn't an uncommon expression when he spoke of the wife he'd lost and still bore a lantern for. "You wouldn't be remiss in allowing yourself to start anew. No need to carry on in one direction simply because you've started down the path and walked far enough you're familiar with the way."

The smirk deepened, and Marcon knew the smith was thinking fondly of his wife, the sort of memories that didn't bear sharing as they couldn't exactly be understood outside the confines of the relationship itself. "If she's trying to let herself change, you'd do well to allow yourself the same, lad. Let yourself venture down a new path and see what—and who—lies in store for you."

Marcon wetted his lips before he spoke. For a moment, the vision of the sort of life Lorieannan wanted for herself filled him with a flare of anger. He imagined a merchant caring for her, for their children— But just as quickly, the anger ebbed. Had he been too hasty in his retreat from their life together? He'd assumed responsibility over Lorieannan from an early age. Or was Garreth right that it wasn't one he needed to carry forward?

A single golden seed glimmered within the dark of the hollow, settling into his chest. There were still jagged branches around it, but also the promise of something new for himself. Someone who might smile as she said 'Captain Colabra.' Someone who would be proud of all he'd worked for.

A second flash—brilliant green and the *shing* of steel.

Someone who might fight at his side, as his parents had done for one another.

"Thank you," Marcon said, inclining his head to the smith. "You've given me a lot to think over, and I promise not to let it impede my judgement in battle."

"Glad I could be of service," Garreth said, the warm brown of his eyes an enveloping fondness Marcon's hadn't realized he'd been desperate for. "Now, as to your deployment—we've spoken of this before, and you know my stance where the field commander is concerned. Some dangers dwell outside our influence," Garreth advised, nodding as he spoke. In Marcon's experience, the smith was most at ease when he was dispensing wisdom to others. "City's been through war before and will again, so long as it survives." The smith's gaze grew distant, the far-off look of a battlefield twenty years in the past, a specter that continued to haunt its survivors.

Marcon would see that city in a few days' time. The one that had taken his parents' lives.

"Avoid those prone to worrying as best you can. They can't help you when the time comes. Your training can. The elf and the fool lad who love you will do the same. Trust that."

"I will," Marcon said, rising from his chair. He fetched the bottle from the icebox and refilled Garreth's glass without the smith asking or refusing the gesture. Garreth wasn't one to accept help if he didn't have to, but he allowed small tokens of returned affection. "Take care of yourself. I'll send word."

Marcon jolted at his last words to the smith, afraid of the sting he'd accidentally inflicted, only now remembering that Patrick had refused to send his father news upon his safe return.

Garreth simply nodded, taking Marcon's words as the kindness he'd meant. "Keep an eye on him, will you?" The half-orc's jaw tightened, like he was physically restraining what else he wanted to say. Patrick's recent appointment into Silversword's service remained a sore point between the two of them. It made sense for his friend to be even more worried now with the army's deployment.

There was one last question he had to ask to set his mind at ease. "You don't doubt us too, do you?" Marcon said. He shouldn't make this moment about himself and his own concerns, but his fight with Lorieannan, the revelation of her doubts, still pressed itself upon his judgement. He couldn't have Garreth questioning him too.

"Course not, lad," Garreth answered. He limped over to Marcon's side and clapped his heavy, calloused palm on his shoulder. "I've never doubted you for a moment. You've everything you need to see you through. Don't forget it."

He bowed his head in thanks and made his way back to where Vateri and Cole would be waiting for him.

Marcon had spent very little time within the barracks themselves. He'd helped Abbot and Joane at the vineyard for as long as his training allowed and then, a little before he could truly have afforded to, he rented an apartment for himself and Lorieannan that was nearer to the Outer Ring's gate, making it easier for him to attend extra training sessions in addition to those mandated by his rank.

Though he had only spent a few nights here over the last three years, Marcon quickly fell back into the pattern of life in the barracks. He bathed, refreshed his rations, sharpened his blades. Anything to keep his hands busy. His fight with Lorieannan and the nervous tension that hovered in the air of the soldiers' dorms made it impossible for him to access the same quiet for his mind.

As the others began to settle in for the night, Vateri showed Marcon an open bed where he could sleep.

A bed he'd be returning to after the battle. Indefinitely.

The buzz of the ale was fading from his senses. In its place, regret remained despite Garreth's reassurances. Was there time for him to return to Lorieannan and make his apology in the morning? Even as a soldier, the wardens wouldn't allow him through the gates, not without a writ of passage. If he woke at first light and sprinted to the outskirts, there might be enough time. Would she even hear him out, allow him in?

"Marcon?" Vateri's whisper sounded over the snores echoing around the room.

He turned toward her, the rickety cot creaking beneath his shifting weight.

"Are you scared?"

"Yes," he answered simply. "I think it would be foolish of us not to be."

Silence stretched for a few minutes, and he was just about to slip away into sleep when her whisper sang out again. "Do you think we'll die?"

Marcon smiled sadly. She was one of the kindest people he'd ever met, and she deserved a world different from the one she'd been sent into. "Not yet," he answered. "I won't let anything happen to you. You'll cover me from range. And Cole is too stubborn to let either of us go or to leave without us."

Vateri chuckled at that and settled deeper into the folds of her cot. Soon enough, her breathing deepened, and she fell into a fitful sleep.

Her question had awakened something inside of him, the yearning he'd long pursued and tried at times to fulfill, at other points to keep at bay.

He had far too much still to do, glory to heap onto his name and the greater honor of Respite. His parents had both been lieutenants. They'd died fighting side by side. He was going to make it to captain, maybe even one day, commander. He rolled back over, staring up at the stone ceiling and imagining it was the stars that had graced the vineyard of his childhood, those he'd watched with Lorieannan more times than he could count, imagining his future as a soldier of the Battalion. Death wasn't coming for him or his friends in this battle. "Not yet."

CHAPTER NINE
ROWAN

It would take three days for the party setting out from Willow Glen to reach Delmoir upon mounts, longer on foot. Rowan steeled herself as best she could for the journey. The last time she had embarked upon a multiday trek through the woods had been when Paupa took her to the outskirts of the hearttree's protectorate as a girl. Where one day, once she was worthy, she would return.

At Rowan's insistence, Athenza had agreed to the use of three cervidae from the conclave's herd so they might make better time en route to the Pentacle. The journey was further than Rowan believed reasonable for Athenza to attempt given the weakness of her ankles and frequent joint pain, but she avoided saying as much aloud lest the druid's stubbornness rebel at being coddled.

Rowan had always loved the mosses, flowers, and vines that grew about the cervidae's antlers, the swish of their long foxtails, and their delicate deer-like frames. Her cervidae frequently wrinkled the sharp end of her nose, testing the air before them as she clomped along the forest paths.

The cervidae had grown extinct beyond the wilds of Lis-Maen and the Emeraude, their population within the Glade of Shadows dwindling as Alessandra pressed her assault there, her armies burning hectares of forest as they went. Already the dark goddess's generals had ordered a redrawing of their own maps of the region— The Ashen Thicket they called it.

She couldn't let such a fate befall Willow Glen.

The days astride her cervidae were the longest she'd spent with someone besides Athenza and Majestyk since her childhood. Rowan quickly learned the limitations of her own conversation as well as the concerns she had missed in the wider world, consumed by her routines within the refractory.

Samara proved to be a great aid in this regard, Rowan's conversations with Vraise often leading to tensions that escalated into arguments between the two. The agent shook her head as she surveyed a shallow patch of forest, golden rays illuminating one face of the trees and casting the rest in shadow, making them appear dual-colored, much like the fading orbs of light Rowan tended. "Our scouts report that very soon, the Cities mean to attempt a counterassault to reclaim Reckoning, though the souls of what was once Sanctuary have long departed for Astralei."

Rowan tried not to think about the family appointed

to her home in her stead. A grandmother, a couple, and their two children—the conclave saw them as truly blessed in the size of their family, an auspicious sign for those who might spread the light across the conclave in Rowan's absence. Athenza had soothed her frustrations slightly, pointing out that the conclave had appointed five others to replace Rowan's daily tasks.

She turned her mind instead to Samara's report. If she were to leave Willow Glen and her memories of Paupa behind, she would need to understand the workings of the wider world.

"Why mount a counterassault now?" Vraise asked. "They lost Sanctuary when I was in my infancy. Rowan was not yet even born."

A flicker of surprise crossed Samara's expression, and she glanced at Rowan before continuing. "It seems the dragon who led the charge that took the city in the first place has departed from its walls. This is really the first opportunity they've had to return Sanctuary to their possession."

Rowan frowned at this revelation, not bothering to puzzle through Samara's inexplicable study of her for the moment. Why would her age in relation to the fall of Sanctuary matter? "Do they know why the dragon has departed? That is strange, is it not?"

The agent nodded. "Quite unusual, and a departure from Alessandra's traditional strategy. It is a mark of honor, especially among her dragon lieutenants, to hold rulership over one of the wasteland fortresses." Samara lowered her gaze. "Our informants also report the possibility of a change in leadership for the Glade of Shadows.

Braemorn rules it now, but Briznexi may yield her control of Reckoning in exchange for the forest ruins." The agent shook her head. "The dragons don't see it as anything more. They don't care about how powerful the ancient magics hidden beneath the glade's soil might be."

A heaviness settled over Rowan's heart, picturing the burning forests so like the home she knew but said to be even more vast. How could the dryad clans survive such assaults?

Rowan's jaw tightened. She knew the answer. Even as far from Delmoir as Willow Glen, word had reached them of the dryads, even the Sapphire Circle begging for aid from Lis-Maen and the Emeraude.

The Pentacle had refused, as had the central coven of the Emeraude witches. Resources were too scarce, they said.

And so the Pentacle allowed Alessandra's armies to advance upon their very borders instead.

She had to think of something else or the folly of such a tactic would scorch her from the inside out. "Who are these informants?" Such a position had to be more than dangerous—a special magic would need to be involved. Alessandra was no fool, and those with access to the inner workings of her military would have to magically conceal their intentions while simultaneously conceal such magical workings. Her mind raced ahead with the possibilities. Would such magic be within her grasp in her studies at the Pentacle's Academia Magica?

The corner of Samara's lips twitched in the closest the agent had come to a smile through the entirety of their second day of travel. "Your questions are wise, Rowan." The agent sighed. "I am afraid that the answers are far beyond my purview."

Rowan inclined her head in thanks to Samara for her answer. Something about the agent's reply—the hesitation or the sense of regret—made Rowan believe that like the true fate of the first offerings, Samara was keeping the full breadth of the truth from Rowan or, failing that, the agent reasonably believed that the Cities were sprinting straight into a trap.

And just like herself, Vraise, and Athenza, it would be those the Cities saw as disposable, those pulled from the margins, who would be brought into the front lines and sacrificed.

T heir second day of travel, as the narrow forest trails and hours mounted upon her cervidae began to wear on Rowan's lower back and burn along her inner thighs, she extracted one of the three damaged orbs of light that she'd removed from the refractory. Since they could no longer be used to light the canopy of the conclave, the replacement family had given no objections.

She'd hidden away the orb brightened by her phoenix within her pack. The questions such a discovery might unleash were too dangerous for her to risk.

The Rowan of a few years before—the one given to magic-fueled spikes of rage that caught homes on fire—would have thought the new family was lucky that she didn't maim the tracks that ran along the conclave, permanently disabling the system until she returned. Then the council could see what they thought of her meager contributions to the whole and how valuable her paupa's work had truly been. But she could never have damaged something forged by his hands.

Allowing the sway of her hips to hold her balance upon the cervidae, named Gardenia for the delicate spray of fragrant white flowers that grew in drooping vines along her antlers, Rowan examined the inner workings of the first orb. If the Pentacle meant to have her, Vraise, and Athenza attempt to incorporate the elements into their beings through some new magical process, then she was going to use this travel time to her best advantage and practice with the elemental magics, starting with the element of water.

But before that, she would have to separate and then disperse the stores of light and darkness contained within the orb.

An hour later, Rowan's lower lip was raw—she'd worried it a few times too many trying to work out how to condense the light and darkness the way her phoenix had three days before.

"What are you working on?"

Rowan's jaw tightened as Samara and her mare fell into step beside her and Gardenia. "Separating and then dispersing the light and darkness from the orb."

Samara's eyes widened. "And this is a magic you can wield now?"

From behind Rowan, Athenza's chuckle bounded about the forest. "Of course she can. A few more days by her side, and you'll wonder why the Pentacle didn't send for her sooner." The druid winked at Rowan and clucked for her cervidae to carry her forward. It released its foxlike cry of glee and complied, leaving Rowan and Samara alone.

"It is an intriguing question," Samara added. "How is it that no one recruited you to join the Pentacle's ranks before now? Your baseline tolerance of the elements, not to mention your capacity to control more than one or two, marks you as a prime candidate for recruitment."

Samara's contemplation created a furrow in her brow, something Rowan had noticed when they made camp the evening before. Were Samara not an agent of the Pentacle and, therefore, someone never to be trusted, she would make for an intriguing romantic partner, something Rowan had only dabbled with among her peers in the conclave. Her reputation, as Vraise called it, kept most of the young elves away, and Rowan bore too much resentment toward those who had failed to defend her father to bother returning the interest of any of the older males and females among them.

"I'll be surprised if the different disciplines don't fight over you when we arrive," Samara added, oblivious to Rowan's study of the pleasing shapes of her features.

"Disciplines?" Rowan added.

"The Faces, I mean," Samara clarified. "Among the members of the academy, where there are so many practitioners, we refer to one another's magic as pertaining to one of a number of disciplines. This project is special in that regard." The agent smiled at Rowan. "It's one of the first unified efforts that's lasted beyond the planning phase in ages."

"The Pentacle isn't interested in druids from the margins," Rowan said without thinking. It was one of the few assurances upon which her paupa agreed with the other members of the conclave, one he'd given her growing up and that Athenza had repeated to her after he was gone.

Samara laughed in answer, the sound oddly pleasant despite the curl in Rowan's stomach that said the agent was only just shy of laughing at her. "Where do you imagine the recruits for the Druidess come from?"

Her bell-like laughter carried them up a rise to an overlook of the descent of their path undulating before them. "We should arrive about this time tomorrow," Samara called out to Vraise and Athenza ahead of them. "Follow the pentacles emblazoned into the trees. They won't lead you astray."

She returned her attention to Rowan. "Your observation reminded me of a curiosity I encountered before I departed from the academy." The attractive furrow in her brow returned alongside a slight pout in her lips. "This is my fifth year working the recruitment circuit and your conclave was one of a handful where the instructions were quite explicit, that only those above or below a certain age might be recruited to the Academia Magica's number and never for the Druidess." Samara shook her head. "I've never seen anything like it before."

Rowan frowned, wondering what Samara's discovery might mean.

Athenza was waiting for them at the bend in the path

and maneuvered her cervidae to ride beside Rowan, placing the two of them before Samara and her mare. "I hope you've been asking what sort of food we should expect in the city," Athenza said as she directed her cervidae forward again.

"There are a great many restaurants in Delmoir proper," Samara answered, the conversation between her and Rowan for the moment forgotten. "One of my favorites is by the docks, though they'll likely keep you and the other offerings near at hand for the first few weeks of your training."

"Near at hand?" Athenza repeated. "Whatever for?"

A chill darted down Rowan's spine at the rapid shift in Samara's demeanor.

"Observation." Her voice was flat, suddenly cold. The agent clacked her tongue and urged her mare forward without saying anything further.

Rowan and Athenza looked at one another.

"That doesn't sound promising," her mentor observed.

"No, it doesn't," Rowan agreed. The cryptic threat of close supervision settled uneasily beside the strange detail of there being limitations in who the Pentacle could recruit from their conclave and a handful of others. How would such a directive come about? And who had it been meant to protect?

Rowan bit her lower lip again, jolting at the soreness she'd forgotten in her conversation with Samara. The light and darkness remained on their separate sides of the orb in her hand, but neither had condensed enough to be extracted.

She sighed and returned the orb to her pack. The magical secrets that she had been trying to unravel were more pressing than her elemental magic practice, and she was too flustered to turn her thoughts to teasing out the elements anyway.

In the back of her mind, her phoenix ruffled its feathers, its face turned away from her.

CHAPTER TEN

MARCON

THE RUINS OF SANCTUARY

Four days' march brought Marcon, Vateri, and Cole to the ruins of Sanctuary, what had once been a proud member of the Cities United. The two decades of enemy rule had seen the verdant gardens and white stone towers decay, as though shadows had been made flesh and had seeped over the walls of the city, choking out even the memories of life within.

The entire company came to a halt upon the ridge on the outskirts of the city. They were part of a coordinated cordon between soldiers of Beacon, Bastion, and Respite. A field of ash marked the no-soldiers'-land between their cordon and the city walls.

This had been the domain ruled by Briznexi, who released her acid breath upon any who trespassed too near to the city.

In the dragon's absence, they would finally have a chance at reclaiming what had been theirs.

Cole and Vateri hovered close by Marcon's sides.

"Are we sure we want it back?" Cole muttered, frowning as he looked over the shadow-cloaked walls.

"Why would Briznexi leave?" Vateri added. "Was there an outbreak? Was she called elsewhere?"

Marcon held his questions. Their opinions on matters of tactics held no sway with their superiors, and the oaths they'd made bound them to follow orders.

Finally, he stood before the city that had forever altered his destiny. And it was just as dark as he had always imagined it would be. Swirls of impossibly black clouds twisted over it in a reverse spiral to the rounded spokes of the castle's curved walls.

Somewhere on the razed fields between where the forces of the Luz set up camp and the moldering parapets, his parents had fallen, fighting side by side. His lone comfort was the Luz's assurances that the bodies had been recovered and burned.

Though he could scarcely remember their faces, he didn't have to contemplate the nightmare that haunted many of his fellow soldiers, especially those senior enough to have fought in the first battle—they would be facing the undead remnants of those they'd lost before. Any body unrecovered was one easily brought into Alessandra's forces. The raised undead would have no memory of their life from before. Every drop of their spirit would have been bled away, replaced with an unrelenting urge to spread the enemy's death and destruction across the whole of Eldura.

He reminded himself of the promise proclaimed by the lone force remaining behind to protect Respite in their absence. "We'll watch over the walls," their captain had cried, his troops arranged behind him. "And we'll be at the lead of the crowd ready to welcome your return in victory."

His chest had swelled at the words, his footsteps lighter, bolstered by the assurance of success.

Seeing the ghostly ruins now, he was less certain.

One by one, the soldiers of their unit broke away from their survey of the city and returned to the area set aside for their camp to begin assembling tents, cook fires, and a station for the medicos and healers.

Vateri inched closer to him, a slight tremble to her hands as she surveyed the walls that would define their new era as soldiers of Respite. "I don't remember seeing those on the maps," Vateri said, pointing to the black siege towers poking out between the smoke-encrusted battlements.

"They must have added the towers during the occupation," Marcon answered. It seemed obvious now that Alessandra's forces would have increased the fortifications, adding towers between the outer edges of the spokes and the castle's towering heights.

For a moment, Marcon's faith faltered. Would their siege weapons be enough to assault the towers and the existing ramparts? "Do you think Briznexi used them?" he murmured, imagining a great black dragon landing atop one of the towers, its horrible screech echoing out over the battlefield before it took flight, spraying poison on anyone unfortunate enough to be in the creature's path.

The elf beside him nodded. "Sanctuary was once the birthplace of the dragons," she said, staring out at the city that had claimed his parents' lives, the walls that held in the hordes of undead who had once been living souls, like them, traversing the city's streets. "It was called Draykemire then, a kingdom, before the great cities centralized into the Cities United and renamed the reach of their domains."

"Something you picked up on your island?" Cole asked, his eyebrow raised as he glanced around Marcon to meet Vateri's gaze. His teasing tone reminded Marcon of their growing up together, how often the pair of them had teased Vateri about how much shorter she was than the two of them. It had taken a single test of combat skill in their early teens to put an end to the good-natured mockery—Vateri's arrows could skewer numerous combatants hundreds of feet away while Marcon and Cole were still waiting for them to charge within reach.

"Of course not," the elf scoffed. "It was part of our military history training. Of the many devastations losing Sanctuary cost the Cities, one of the worst was that we lost the record of the dragons' lineages—the meticulous accounts of their magical abilities and number."

Marcon frowned, finally intrigued enough to look away from the curls of stone before him. "Number?"

"Yes." Vateri brightened, leading them back toward the encampment slowly taking shape before them. "That's a key part of their lore as well. There were as many dragon eggs as abilities possessed by the goddess of dragons, Rasvana. Many elves have been named after her, the derivatives said to evoke wisdom and magic even in the goddess's absence."

"Absence? Like the titans?" Marcon asked. Three of the six had pulled away from their world entirely. The other three had restricted their magic, with no new champions being appointed in the two decades since the First Battle of Sanctuary.

Vateri nodded. "The wolf-god Fenrir taught her to create a people of her own, but after tricking him and resisting the love he bore toward her, Rasvana missed part of the creation ritual. Unlike Fenrir's offspring of the daimon or the Lycan, for each dragon she created, a drop of her magic fell away, gifted to her draconic offspring. When she created the last dragon, Rasvana ceased to be."

Cole raised his eyebrows, impressed by this strange story. They waited in line to receive their squares of canvas from the cart. Apprentice mechanomancers paced down the already settled rows, casting reserves of their magic into the tents to raise them from the earth and enchant their canvas to resist acid on the off chance Briznexi returned in the middle of the night.

The enemy had seen all settlements near Sanctuary destroyed. There was nowhere to shelter beyond the micro-fortifications they transported from Respite.

Marcon narrowed his eyes, looking over his shoulder to keep an eye on Vateri and the city at once. "That does sound more like Elvish folklore than the Cities' military history."

The elf beside him rolled onto her toes, no longer able to contain her enthusiasm for the subject at hand.

"Oh, that part is. I was too curious after the histories to not find out more." The gold flecks in her eyes brightened. "The military records rooms really are spectacular—"

"You three," a bark rose out from behind them, and a soldier with a glimmering sun pin upon his lapel jogged toward them.

Marcon thumped his fist against his chest in salute while his friends turned about and did the same. The flash of uncertainty that had sent a chill along his back dissipated as he recognized the soldier hurrying toward them. "Stozdak." He greeted Garreth's son with a nod, his thoughts immediately returning to the night before their deployment when he encountered Patrick outside his father's forge. That explained the lapel signifying a position in the ranks of the lightbearer, Field Commander Silversword. Only a few weeks ago, Patrick Stozdak had been appointed to her employ, much to his father's dismay.

"Colabra." Patrick's demeanor warmed only slightly at finding a familiar face before the ruins that had affected his family as well. He made no mention of their meeting back in Respite. Sometimes Marcon wondered if Patrick knew how lucky he was for his father to have survived the battle, even if he had been injured in the fighting. "You're actually just the people I was looking to see."

Vateri sighed, her shoulders slumping in relief. She more than Cole or himself feared doing something wrong in the eyes of her superiors.

Patrick slid closer to the trio so he could lower his

voice and be heard over the bustle of camp. "It's my understanding that the three of you will each be placed within different divisions tomorrow."

Beside Marcon, Cole fidgeted with his belt. The more experienced among their number had often said it was the wait before the battle that was the worst part.

"Field Commander Silversword has asked me and a few others of discretion to see about maintaining eyes and ears within the units."

Marcon tilted his head, studying his fellow soldier. Patrick couldn't mean—

"Are you asking us to spy on our own units and commanders?" Vateri asked, surprising the three of them by being the first to put the request into plain speech.

Patrick cleared his throat, the tips of his slightly pointed ears flushing a darker green. "Not spying, no." He straightened as though his posture might settle the matter of right and wrong in a time of war. A frown hovered between his brows as he added, "It's more a question of morale. This fight is personal, to those of us from Respite and the soldiers from Beacon. Colabra, you know this, as do I."

Marcon assented, though he was still concerned by Patrick's directive. Commander Rezza had been leading their unit for years, had the requisite experience, to judge for herself where best her soldiers might serve.

"Of course Field Commander Silversword trusts her units to follow orders," Patrick continued, "but with this being the first counterattack in some time, she'd like more of an ear to the ground, a chance for concerns to be voiced more quickly. That's all."

An uneasy silence hovered between them. Patrick fumbled with the buckle of his sword on his hip, avoiding eye contact before reasserting himself. "It's my first personal mission from Field Commander Silversword," he added quickly. "Since I know the three of you, I was hoping I might rely on you for assistance in this matter."

"Ah," Marcon added, trying to ease the tension. "Not so unusual a request I suppose."

Cole opened his mouth to speak, but Marcon bumped him with his shoulder, clearing his throat to disguise the sound. *Wait until he's gone.*

"How shall we report our findings of morale to you?" Vateri asked, sliding closer to Patrick.

The half-orc relaxed, pleased by her question. "I will come around on the morrow and confer with each of you, if that's agreeable." He smiled—one of the first times in recent memory Marcon had seen him this happy. Garreth had specifically asked him to keep an eye on his son. And for his part, Patrick was just as stern as his father, despite their differences.

"I can't tell you how greatly I appreciate it," Patrick added, almost beaming now. He leaned closer to the three of them. "You know, they're looking for standouts in this battle. There will be promotions, even transfers into the Blazing Battalion." Patrick nodded toward the rows of burgundy tents slithering up to full height in the center of the camp's formation. Unlike the smaller tents used by most of the Luz, the battalion's tents housed entire units, precisely the same setups they used in the fields in the most dangerous locations throughout Eldura.

Cole's eyes shone, staring over at the battalion. The soldiers were too distant to make out their individual heroes, living legends walking among them, but they might be stationed near the battalion units in the battle itself.

It had been both Marcon and Cole's ambitions to join the battalion since they'd entered the training ranks of the Luz in childhood. Vateri had slowly warmed to their shared dream, though other appointments bore equal interest for her.

"Do you really think so?" Marcon asked Patrick.

He bit his lips together and nodded. "I overheard it from Field Commander Silversword herself," he whispered.

Cole turned to Marcon. "Do you know what that would mean for us?"

Ever practical, Vateri laid her hands on each of their arms. "Let's focus on getting ourselves set up, resting, and being fresh for our first true battle tomorrow." Her voice quavered on "true."

Marcon understood that. They all straightened at her words.

"A wise sentiment," Patrick added, saluting to the three of them before making his departure.

They received their tents and followed the captains' directives for where they should set up camp. As they waited for the apprentice mechanomancers, Marcon wondered if it was time to bring his friends into the confidence that he'd learned from the smith in Respite.

Patrick's request for information on morale sat uneasily beside the accusations his father had leveled against the champion of light. "You'd know if you'd been there," Garreth had said, grimacing. "She's gone so far as to quash those who've tried to speak out about it since." He'd never seen the half-orc so grim as when Garreth had confided that Field Commander Tali Silversword was responsible for the failure of the First Battle of Sanctuary.

"Absolutely ridiculous," Cole burst as Marcon relayed some of the accusations he'd gleaned from the smith. He'd avoided telling them of Lorieannan's disdain for their efforts and position thus far and would avoid confessing as much unless absolutely necessary, just like he neglected to name where he'd uncovered these rumors, only that they were something he'd overheard away from the barracks before their departure.

While Cole and Vateri bickered over the various possible origins of these rumors and their underhanded motivations—each theory growing more unlikely than the last—Marcon extracted from his pocket the ribbon he'd found among his belongings, one belonging to Lorieannan that had accidentally fallen in with his pack.

He rubbed the gossamer threads between his fingers. What would change if he returned to the city victorious, a captain, even? Would she apologize?

In the corner of his heart, he'd banked the ashes of the connection they'd once shared, the one they'd both grown out of, he was starting to believe. But in the off chance that he was wrong, he couldn't ruin any chance of his friends considering Lorieannan a good match for him in the future. Not even Vateri would excuse the way she'd spoken about their work in the Army of Light.

Marcon clenched his jaw. In the days since he'd left their apartment, a realization had been yawning open in his gut. The worst part of their fight wasn't how they'd left things. It was that she'd felt such disdain for what mattered most to him and hadn't told him.

They had no future together, so long as his heart remained with the Luz, with the battalion. A lightness swelled in his chest looking over the battlefield, knowing the struggle and adventure yet to come.

The red pennants of Ignis flapped in the sharp wind over the tents of the battalion. One day, he'd stand beneath those pennants, a unit of his own under his command.

He smiled, thinking of what that might mean.

When that day came, he'd have someone—not waiting for him, but fighting by his side—someone who believed in the ferocious necessity of their cause.

There would not be another generation of orphans on his watch. Their enemy had to be defeated.

He'd make his first true strike against the forces of darkness at dawn.

His entire life had been leading to this moment. Marcon's chest swelled. He wasn't going to let the opportunity pass him by.

Marcon and his friends discovered shortly after setting up their camp that Patrick's information held true. Cole was to join the cavalry, Vateri the archers, and Marcon the infantry. Vateri had taken this news the hardest of the three of them, the distress still crinkling her features as they sat around the fire that evening.

"Oh just tell us already," Cole cried, unable to take her frowns and soft sighs a moment longer. From what Marcon had observed of the pair of them for a decade and a half, Cole's low tolerance for Vateri's bad moods came out of a place of deep affection for the elf, even if it didn't always seem that way to those outside their band or, almost as often, to Vateri herself.

The elf tensed, drawing away into the shadows of the fire.

"She's worried that our assignments are more dangerous than hers," Marcon said. Cole had been too excited at the prospect of riding one of the Luz's famed biomecho stallions into battle to have caught the horror on Vateri's face as one of the captains spelled out their assignments.

Cole whipped toward Vateri, leaning into the glow of the flames. "Is that true?"

She hugged her hands around her knees.

"Titans, Vateri!" Cole sprang out of his seat by the fire and began to pace behind it. "Do you think we *want* you to have a more dangerous position alongside us?"

"Of course not," she spat back.

Marcon held up a hand to steady Cole who grumbled before returning to his seat. He didn't like the idea of them being separated any more than the other two did, but it did make tactical sense. They would each be playing to their strengths on the battlefield.

"I think what Cole is trying to say," Marcon said, his voice low, "is that we actually feel more at ease in these placements than we would stationed by your side among the archers."

Cole opened and clamped shut his jaw, allowing Marcon to continue on his behalf. "To the untrained observer, a remove from the battle lines versus a position at the front or along one of the flanks may seem less dangerous, but we all know how cunning the enemy we face is."

They both nodded, watching him intently.

"Tomorrow, we fight as though we're by one another's sides. That's how we make it back here. Unhurt, with tales of glory to share. Agreed?"

"Agreed," his friends echoed.

The peace lasted a quarter hour until Vateri pressed for Cole to admit that he found archery equally as dangerous as the cavalry. Cole refused, their argument escalating, and the pair of them turned in for the night not speaking.

Alone with the embers of the fire for company, Marcon gazed at the constellations overhead, filling in the maps of the stars beyond the obscuring clouds that hung heavy above Sanctuary even now. The shifting winds of the afternoon hadn't diverted the cloud cover over Sanctuary. He doubted anything natural would— not until they'd uprooted Alessandra's forces entirely from the city and purged it of her evil for good.

Staring across the blighted fields between the army

and the fallen city, unease fluttered low in his gut. He could only hope his two best friends would be similarly bickering the next night and that he'd be here to witness it. Just like tonight, he wouldn't stop them. It was one of those things that he knew, eventually, he would lose— that was what happened with everything he hoped would never change.

CHAPTER ELEVEN

MARCON

Shortly after dawn, Marcon bid farewell to his friends. "Fight well," he told Cole. "Focus on your surroundings. We will find you at the day's end," he promised Vateri.

They embraced before departing, Cole running after Vateri and catching her hand, his fingertips lingering over hers before she joined the archers' ranks.

Marcon strapped his sword over his back, adjusted the belt of daggers at his waist, and grabbed his shield from the side of his tent before jogging over to the infantry division.

Commander Rezza would be leading his unit into battle. He forced down his ration, accelerant, and water. So many tasks he'd repeated countless times, now taking on new meaning as they led him inexorably toward war.

The camp was quiet in the gray morning. Like the others around him, Marcon's gaze kept drifting over to Sanctuary. Shadows moved along the decaying ramparts, archers gathered about the city's spires, blackened ivy hanging in thick strands from shattered windows.

At the base of the city's walls, clouds of ash drifted skyward from the shuffling steps of the entrenched army gathering. The army they'd face soon enough.

Commander Rezza pulled Marcon aside before their unit joined with the vast forces of the Luz waiting to hear Field Commander Silversword speak and give the order to send them into battle.

Rezza's dark skin and onyx negata horns spun through with gold looked even more at home upon the field of battle than in the training rings of Respite. Though many around them fidgeted nervously, some even retching up their breakfast ration, Rezza held firm, resolve glittering in her eyes of liquid gold.

"They will look to you today, Colabra," she said, her voice low and even. The same voice that had guided him through proper form with the longsword, that had demanded excellence in his footwork, that had pushed him to master weapons outside of his natural inclinations—adding daggers to swordplay, pikes to spears. "Just as your friends have looked to you for strength these many years." She thumped him on the shoulder. "Do not shrug off the mantle of leadership when others place it onto your shoulders." The corner of her lip upturned. "It's been meant for you all along. I only wish I could have told your parents as much, when I fought by their sides."

"*By* their sides?" The commander had told him that she'd been familiar with his parents before their passing, but to have been in the same unit with them, familiar with them—

Rezza inclined her head. "They would be proud to see you avenging them here. Follow your training. Your sword will hold true." And with that she departed to join the head of their company.

The fluttering in the base of Marcon's stomach abated slightly. For the tenth time that morning, he checked the fitting of his sheath along his back, the blades at his hips. A roll of his shoulders settled his pauldrons and twist of his wrists adjusted his gauntlets. *Ready*.

He joined Rezza's forces near a raised wooden platform where a dwarven woman clad in shining plate rimmed in gold stood before her company.

Tali Silversword. Field Commander of the united forces of the Luz, a lightbearer of Ilona. Marcon stared up at his childhood hero. What Garreth had said of her couldn't be true—he saw that now.

Those assembled held their peace, a collective inhale as they waited to see what their legendary field commander, one of the last true champions, had to say.

"Twenty years ago, we faced a debilitating defeat at the base of these very walls, one we have been struggling to rebuild from ever since," Silversword called out, her voice amplified by the alchemists' recreations of the windcallers' magic, echoing across the gathered armies. In the distance, the cavalry sat tall upon their mounts, the biomecho stallions' breath rising in bursts of steam from their nostrils.

"But with our patience, strategy, and preparation, we

have seen an end to that era of darkness. We stand here, forces of the Luz, ready to take back what is ours!"

A steady "hurrah" rose up from the clump of the battalion soldiers clad in black at the base of the field commander's tower. Marcon's heart thudded against the confines of his chest at their rallying call. *One day*, he promised himself. One day he would join their ranks. Lead them into battles like this one, the fate of Eldura, of the Cities United, secure upon his shoulders.

"This day, we will reclaim the blighted lands of Sanctuary for ourselves, for the forces of life. We will see stolen souls put to rest, and we will fortify the hearts of all the faithful across the Cities United."

The shadow memory of his parents flashed before Marcon's eyes at her words. He shouted in answer, joined by his fellow infantry soldiers, their cry echoed across the battalion and the other armies gathered at the base of the lightbringer's battle tower. The shouts rose in volume, with first Commander Rezza and then the rest of the infantry thumping the flats of their swords against the broad faces of their shields. The archers raised fists into the air, and the biomecho stallions whinnied.

"Forces of light and fire," the dwarf cried, "reclaim your birthright! To arms!"

With a bellow that emerged from the depths of his being, Marcon lifted his chin toward the sky. *I swear to avenge you*, he promised the souls of his parents where they resided in Astralei.

Rezza gave the signal, and his unit parted from the gathering and took their lines along the center of the rise.

A similar battle cry rose opposite along the city walls, the hiss and cackle of Alessandra's array of foul beasts, the screech of the vultura causing the hairs along the back of his neck to stand on end.

You've prepared for this, Marcon told himself, trying to ignore the chilling effect of the monsters' calls. Was that the last sound his parents had heard before their spirits departed from this world? Or had it been the other's dying breaths?

He ground his teeth, setting his jaw. It was precisely because of the creatures arranged against them that he would never know.

Today, for that, by the swing of his sword, they would pay.

His heart thumped in his chest, each pulse urging him forward. On the far side of the battlefield, the biomecho stallions stamped, raising dust clouds of their own.

The armies of the Luz awaited their signal, and the commanders gave it.

Rezza tilted her flag from high overhead toward Sanctuary. Marcon and his fellows screamed again, tearing forward across the field. His vow held true in his sprint, a mask pulled over his mouth to hold off the plumes of ash from his lungs as he helped lead the stampede toward the battlements his parents had died defending twenty years ago.

Marcon renewed his vow as his line met the advance forces of their enemy, a cry of delight escaping him as he sliced through the clacking jaws of vultura. For years he'd imagined a battle precisely like this—Alessandra's undead hordes, their skin dripping off like candle wax, falling to the swords of the Luz. His visions of glory had failed to account for the rusted armor the vultura wore—the same as when they'd defended the city from the very forces death had forced them to join.

Little matter, he reminded himself. We're here to free them now.

And then a shadow wraith overwhelmed one of the men he'd spent his entire life training beside.

The soldier's eyes turned liquid and melted down his face as blood poured forth from his nose and black ichor leaked from the corners of his mouth.

He swung to face Marcon who had slowed in horror, unable to believe what was transpiring before him.

"Please," the soldier gurgled, trying to speak around his swollen tongue. "Please," he begged again, falling to one knee. He coughed up a burble of black ichor. Its acid cast boils along the underside of his face, and the soldier screamed.

Head still arched back and spine held at an unnatural angle, the wraith's claws burst out of the soldier's fingers. In a matter of moments, the wraith would possess him fully, would turn him into one of their enemy's minions, his mind and body no longer his own.

Marcon set his jaw and swung his sword.

The soldier's head slid free from his neck, a burst of black blood spurting out of his spine.

A heartbeat passed, the second spurt shorter than the first.

The body toppled to the side and the wraith swept free of the corpse, screeching as it inhaled and gathered itself. Black orbs pooled toward the center of its face—the yawning chasms of a skull. With a second shriek, the wraith launched itself at Marcon's head, surrounding him in a dark cloud and obscuring his vision of the battlefield.

Trapped by the wraith, the screaming intensified. First the soldier he'd seen killed, then the souls it had taken in the first hours of battle.

Marcon slashed wildly, only remembering after his first strikes that he might hit an ally nearby, granting the wraith a second soul in a matter of moments.

"Fight wraiths with *fire*," the memory of Vateri's exasperated instructions echoed in his mind.

He patted along his side, trying to find the alchemists' flint he'd been issued before departing from Respite.

Along the edge of his vision, a diamond-shaped flame darted closer.

"Agh! Back, beast!" an unfamiliar voice cried.

The flames swooped toward Marcon's head, matched by a raven's caw.

With a shrill scream, the wraith swept away from Marcon's head, darting in a low slither along the battlefield away from the torch wielder.

Marcon doubled over, trying to catch his breath. "Thank you," he rasped, coughing away the smoky essence left in the wraith's wake.

"Anytime." It was the most melodic voice Marcon had ever heard.

He looked up, expecting to find a siren and discovered instead a woman clad in figure-hugging dark blue leathers, an unfamiliar insignia of a glowing hexagon with an inverted pentagram emblazoned upon her shoulder.

The raven he'd heard squawked again and flapped down to land upon the woman's raised arm. The woman smiled, a far brighter sight than belonged upon a battlefield, and Marcon realized he'd been staring openmouthed at the pair.

"Keep your flint handy," the woman advised, her alto voice lilting and tumbling over the notes of her warning like water along a mountain brook. She inclined her head to him, a soldier's salute, and sprinted through the bands of vultura to join the circle carved out by the Blazing Battalion, alchemists' fire bright upon their weapons, making their move toward the city walls.

The infantry rallied as they passed, redoubling their efforts to beat back the hordes. Apprentice medicos tended to the wounded while others saw to the fallen. Their bodies would be burned to prevent them from swelling the ranks of the undead.

With the battalion pressing ahead, the vultura stumbled. They clacked to one another, suddenly uncertain. Marcon joined a band of shielded warriors who pressed into the flank left in the battalion's wake, felling the vultura as the creatures tried to flee back to the lines of the city.

Marcon shrugged off the exhaustion of the battle. It was working. The tide was turning to their side.

And then a great battle horn sounded from behind the walls of Sanctuary.

Soldiers gathered together, splitting their attention

between the enemies on the ground and the cloud-covered skies overhead. Was this Briznexi's trap? Had she returned, ready to fell soldiers by the hundreds where they stood?

The sound returned the vultura to their unrelenting hunger.

Marcon darted back as groups of the undead creatures coordinated their efforts, leaping onto soldiers and knocking them from their feet. Falling one upon the next in a feeding frenzy.

From deep within the city, darkness pooled.

The wraiths, Marcon realized, without enough time to adjust his position on the field. "Fall back!" he shouted to anyone who would hear him. "Fall back!"

They were too late.

The wraiths pooled their foul energies together and shot across the fields of slaughter, felling dozens of soldiers at a time and sucking the lingering life force from the vultura as well, rending their victims to bones and ash.

Horns signaling retreat sounded as the wraiths' beams of darkness cut off the infantry and cavalry from one another. A different signal—one calling for rescue—sounded up ahead. The battalion soldiers had been stranded near the city walls, their front line decimated by the wraiths.

Marcon's breath caught in his chest as the afternoon sun drifted behind the clouds that hung heavy over Sanctuary. With the darkness, the armies of the Luz fell apart.

Field Commander Silversword's rousing speech

melted around him with each cry of pain from fellow soldiers, those overwhelmed by wraiths and worse. Those devoured by vultura. The hordes were unrelenting as they retreated toward the rear lines, trying to answer the summons of the horns.

A soldier he'd met in passing only the night before had flailed behind him, nearly slicing the back of his arm as he struggled against a vultura swarm that quickly overwhelmed him and pinned him to the ground.

Their shrieks of delight brought others of the scavengers nearer.

Marcon shuddered at the sound of flesh rent from bone, the greedy slurping of their decaying mouths and rotting teeth.

"Colabra, leave him," Commander Rezza's shout rang out from atop her horse.

The years of training came back to him—how had the specifics of vultura tactics never struck him with horror before? From the back of his mind, the even-voiced tacticians' lectures pooled over his consciousness —*When the creatures fell an ally, allow them to feast and swarm, thinning the herd. While they feed, pick off their stragglers from a five-point defensive positioning. Do not try to free the trapped soldier. Their sacrifice allows your life and our victory.*

Marcon tried to dull the noise of the battlefield, allowing the years of drills and training to guide his feet, his body. *Don't see it as real. Drift away and survive.*

His feet carried him to the right-most arm of the five-pointed star formation, four other fellow soldiers already positioned around the corpse and feeding frenzy.

Distantly, from the back of their lines, shouts for the alchemists and a jar of their fire extract rang out.

Marcon's shoulders tightened as the whizzing of a glass vial shot through the air.

"Away!" Rezza shouted.

Marcon dove, tucking his hands around his head.

The soldier and the vultura exploded in a rain of fire and gore.

A young medico appeared at Marcon's side, heavy towel in hand, and led him toward one of the fortified areas on the edge of the battlefield. The ringing in his ears blotted out the medico's words.

He waited, disoriented, at the edge of the tent while one of the apprentice medicos pressed a tiny cup of accelerant and a tankard of water into each soldier's hands.

The liquid swallowed—this one bearing the bitterness of the coffee grounds it had been condensed from but none of the earthiness to cut the flavor—Marcon's hearing came back. As did his dread—the screams and moans from inside the tent were worse than those upon the battlefield outside.

He backed out of the tent, determined to find Rezza, his unit.

A few hundred paces away, the Luz fought sword to sword against the hordes. The distress calls rang out again, fainter this time.

The horns of the battalion and the archers.

"Vateri!" Marcon sprinted for the front.

CHAPTER TWELVE

ROWAN

owan tried to find a few moments alone with Samara to ask after the recruitment guidelines for her conclave and what they meant, but the agent resisted all of Rowan's attempts to speak without the others overhearing.

The two days of constant travel were beginning to wear on Athenza, and Vraise surprised Rowan by helping her tend to the older elf's needs. He prepared a soothing tea that Rowan had made before they left while Rowan ground the base ingredients of an ointment that would ease the tension in Athenza's muscles.

"What do you think the academy will be like?" Vraise murmured to Rowan, kneeling beside the fire while he waited for Athenza's tea to steep.

She searched his features before she responded, so used to being ignored or mocked when dealing with one of the members of her conclave. Was this an openness that would last, or would it fade the moment there were other offerings for Vraise to associate with after they'd arrived at the academy? "I'm not sure. Samara mentioned that we're part of the first collaboration between the different divisions of their magic that's occurred in some time."

Vraise nodded thoughtfully. "I hope that sense of partnership plays in our favor. It's my understanding that the competition between the factions can be quite intense. And us being the second round of what in other instances I might call an experiment seems intense enough to contend with for me."

Though the outer conclaves had grown reliant upon the Pentacle for their magic, the sharp divisions, even rivalries of which Samara spoke hadn't leeched out of the walls of Delmoir and into the outlands.

Rowan tilted her head to the side, trying again to find artifice in the elf's features but coming up short. If he was willing to confide his questions to her, perhaps she might respond in kind, but there was a test he needed to pass first. "What made you want to be an offering?"

The look of disbelief on his face made them both laugh. Vraise carried Athenza's tea over to her and offered a cup to Rowan as well. She sipped it, savoring the familiarity, the connection to the refractory and the small life she'd lived there.

Finally, the chance to grow in her magic, to prove herself had come. She wasn't going to waste it.

Vraise's grin lingered as he returned and settled down beside her. "While I would question whether or not any of us *want* to be offerings as the Pentacle certainly could have chosen a more tempting name for this grand operation we're joining, I, well—" He rubbed the back of his neck. Twin spots of color blossomed onto the tops of his cheeks, their blush heightened by the firelight. "When Samara appointed *you*, the sudden swell of jealousy was more than I could stand."

He shook his head, his gaze contemplative. "I know how that must sound to you but, well, I've always admired your independence. So often, I fall into one of my fathers' shadows. This time, I wanted to do something for myself."

He bit his lips together, apprehensive of how she would take his confession.

Rowan gave a small smile in return. "Do you think they're proud of you? For stepping out of their shadow?"

Vraise's shoulders relaxed. He blew on his tea and settled onto the edge of his bedroll, his feet stretched out toward the heat of their small fire. "I hope so." He tipped his head back to stare at the branches overhead, the bright glimmer of stars winking through with the breeze. "Or if they aren't yet, that they will be."

She and Vraise talked over a few conclave matters as the exhaustion of the day's ride competed with their curiosity about what lay ahead.

A short while later, Athenza's snores echoed up toward the forest canopy, and Majestyk curled up in the crook of Rowan's arms, her head tucked into the circle of her feet and wings.

Vraise had been too conscientious to ask Rowan the question she most wanted to know the answer to— whether or not her paupa would be proud of her and the steps she was taking.

In her youth, he had railed against the Pentacle and

their indulgences, their deliberate weakening and silencing of the peoples of Lis-Maen. For reasons she had never been able to work out, he blamed them for her mother's death, just as Rowan blamed them for his. Was his reasoning as flimsy as hers had been, that they might have done more? Or that in doing what they had, they had squelched the very resources that might have saved one or both of her parents?

The conversation she'd overheard between Vraise and Samara about the Cities United stealing their magic drifted back to Rowan. The sense of blame and the lingering fear were familiar. She hadn't realized at the time how much their fears had sounded like Paupa's.

Are you afraid? Rowan asked her phoenix, imagining the great bird nestled down beside her and Majestyk. The dracat smacked her tiny lips on a yawn to heighten the effect of relaxed ease Rowan was trying to channel to her overactive mind.

But the phoenix slumbered beyond her reach—its thoughts and fears its own.

Morning came before Rowan was ready, her questions about what awaited with the Pentacle only just releasing her as dawn warmed the treetops.

Their camp was quiet as they packed up and remained so throughout the morning. As midday passed, Rowan was surprised to find Samara clucking her tongue and guiding her mare to ride alongside Rowan and

Gardenia. She had been planning trips through the countryside outside Delmoir and ways to take Gardenia on canters along the beach, the mysteries of the academy temporarily forgotten.

Samara gestured down the winding dirt path before them. "We'll be approaching Delmoir from the forest protectorate—one cordoned off for use by those attending the Academia Magica. We've passed their guards already."

Rowan frowned, turning back over her shoulder. She hadn't sensed anyone but, so far from Willow Glen, the latent song of this part of the forest was strange to her.

"After you're settled, someone will see to guiding you through Delmoir proper—the markets and the docks—but most of your time will be occupied with your studies and your work as offerings."

"It sounds worse each time she says it," Athenza murmured from just behind the pair of them.

Rowan agreed, though she kept the confirmation to herself, most of her thoughts occupied with seeing for the first time the place and institution that had played such a central role in the undoing of her early life. Those whose policies—and perhaps worse—had ousted Paupa from his council seat, those who had refused aid when the terrible sickness ravaged Willow Glen, sweeping Paupa away in its wake.

"Do you know what our days as offerings will be like?" Rowan asked Samara instead. "Can you tell us about your training?"

A small, sad smile crossed the agent's face. "I wasn't quite so lucky as to arrive in Delmoir with friends already, and so my first few months were rather lonely. My family was poor, and they'd needed me to work rather than hone my magic, so I had quite a bit to do in catching up to the others who had started their study as children." Samara caught Rowan's eye. "I think you will have the opposite problem, unless the magic you have shown me thus far is an anomaly—they'll envy you the vast reserves of magic you have. When they try to provoke you, remember that."

"Where would the other routes take us?" Rowan asked, unsure of how to respond to Samara's warning. The agent had grown more and more withdrawn as they approached the Academia Magica. Rowan couldn't tell whether Samara had grown tired of her three charges or if something about their travels had filled her with doubt.

"The few who come by sea pass through the docks and the central metropolis of Delmoir." Samara smiled at that. "Well, I suppose I should say it's a metropolis to us and will likely seem a vast cityscape to you, though the few who earn entry into the academy who originate from the great settlements of the Cities United are quick to point out Delmoir's relative smallness in comparison to Respite, Bastion, and Beacon."

"So nearly everything that can be a point of competition becomes one?" Rowan added, thinking of her and Vraise's conversation the evening before coupled with Samara's warning.

Their guide suddenly grew grave again. "To be sure. The competition between the Faces trickles down to their apprentices and adepts. They encourage a constant jockeying for favor among their ranks. It helps to solidify their hold."

Samara's second warning sat uneasily beside the first. Why would the Pentacle be so insecure within their position of power? If she could uncover at least a portion of their weakness before they arrived in Delmoir, she might be able to use it to her advantage as she demanded their vow to protect her forest in exchange for her service as an offering.

"We'll be arriving soon," Samara added. "The forest dampens the sounds of the city." That same, stoic look returned. "The academy grounds are usually quiet."

Athenza urged her mount forward to take Samara's place as she rode ahead to tell Vraise what she had just imparted to Rowan. "I must say, I cannot decide if this school you've gotten us into is going to be dangerous or boring."

"Me?" Rowan answered. "You mean *you*. You're the one who insisted upon coming along."

The old druid smiled. "I certainly wasn't going to remain back there without you." She reached over and patted Rowan on the shoulder. "I have a few promises to keep for your parents besides."

Rowan knew better than to ask what those promises were. For years Athenza had alluded to secret promises made between the three of them before Rowan was born. She'd kept her secret for over nineteen years now, and there was little hope of her caving anytime soon.

About an hour later, Vraise called back to the pair of them. "I think I see it!"

She straightened in her saddle and urged Gardenia forward.

At the edge of the trees was an archway made of branches and antlers, marking the exit to the forest. The dirt path continued ahead though it widened after departing from the forest with a row of stones marking its borders on either side.

Gardenia trotted forward, her steady rocking taking Rowan and Majestyk beneath the arch to the top of a hillside. Below them, the Academia Magica grounds stretched over the landscape. Peeking out from either side and over the tops of the walls beyond was the sprawl of Delmoir.

Rowan's lips parted, her breath catching as she took in her first glimpse of the academy proper.

"It's beautiful," Vraise murmured.

Gardenia trilled her agreement, and Rowan patted the sweat-coated fur along her cervidae's neck. Within the walls, a few clumps of forest dotted verdant fields with ordered pathways winding between five towers, each of which jutted up high above the protection of the walls. There were a few wild garden patches arranged between the structures alongside greenhouses, potting sheds, and large garden beds attended by figures wearing white robes accented with different colors.

"The realm of the Druidess," Samara explained, gesturing to a gray stone tower bearing the largest number of greenhouses, each of which was bordered by unruly garden patches. She caught Rowan's eye. "I have a feeling that's where you'll feel most at home."

Rowan couldn't keep from grinning at the sight

arranged before her. How strange would it be to be able to walk wherever one wished upon the forest floor without fear of bears or jaguars? She glanced overhead—there were no nets to prevent midnight attacks by wyverns. Perhaps the Pentacle had other ways of fending them off or they didn't roost this far north?

"Can we see the city itself before we travel inside?" Rowan hadn't expected to want to see the city more than the Academia Magica, but beyond the sprawling green grounds, the densely packed buildings with plaster and wood towers, pale blue shingles, and brightly colored flags called to her. Was there a festival today, or did the metropolis always raise flags in celebration of the every day?

She sniffed at the air, trying to see if she might be able to sense the seaside that she knew waited on the opposite end of the city's sprawl, only a few miles from where they had landed here at the forest's edge.

"I'm afraid that won't be possible today," Samara said. "We've an appointment to keep, and I'm sure you'll want to stop by your rooms before dinner tonight."

"Are other offerings arriving today too?" Rowan asked.

Samara shook her head. "The three of you are the last to appear. I sent a bird ahead as we were setting out, and she returned before first light this morning."

Without further delay, Samara led the three of them down the winding hillside trail to the towering stone walls of the Academia Magica itself. Each of the Faces kept her office at the top of one of the towers, Samara explained, and the students lived in dormitories along-side the Faces' apprentices and staff.

"Those who have not yet earned the individual attention of one of the Faces are called adepts. They are still honing their skills within one of the practices and have yet to determine their discipline." The colors upon the white robes indicated each adept's hopeful association, Samara added. Gray robes emblazoned with one of the Faces' symbols indicated an apprentice.

"What about those who aren't in robes?" Rowan asked as they rode past what she had taken, from a distance, to be oddly shaped garden patches. More than a dozen workers clad in brown from head to toe attended a series of mounds upon the hillside, just beneath the shadows of the academy's walls outside the safety of the structure.

Samara held herself stiffly, gaze fixed upon the path ahead. "Workers of various kinds," she said without glancing at the gardeners.

Rowan turned back before their path curved away from that shaded portion outside the wall. One of the workers lifted a silver pendant from their chest and kissed it before dropping the silver back to their chest, bowing to the earth, and stepping away.

She gasped as the realization hit her—they were not gardeners working within a vegetable patch. They were gravediggers adding the last few corpses to the field. Others in their number lingered beyond it, arranging stones in an expansion of the existing path.

The dozens and dozens of graves in a row weren't enough, even though at least six of them had been freshly dug. What sort of magical academy kept such an expansive graveyard or saw the death of so many of its residents at once?

Rowan's pulse spiked as she took a final glance toward the stone fence that curved beyond the tombs. How many more bodies were they expecting in the near future that they were preemptively expanding the cemetery into a new field?

What exactly had they agreed to?

"Hurry along, please," Samara said, stiffening upon her mount as she spurred the horse forward. "They're expecting us in the Grand Hall."

Rowan bit her lower lip, savoring the distant view of the outskirts of Delmoir before it too fell away—the brightly colored festival flags catching on the breeze, fluttering up as though bidding her farewell before the walls of the Academia Magica proper swallowed the travelers, blocking the flags from sight.

The grounds of the academy were different from any place she'd ever been. Shrubbery organized into rows, gravel pathways, trees carved into strangely curved shapes. Unlike the conclave where most of the residents remained out of doors at all hours unless they were sleeping, the academy was either largely unpopulated or kept its residents indoors, even on a fine summer day.

Such a possibility hadn't even occurred to Rowan. How stifling the students must find it, being trapped in stone buildings rather than roaming about the grounds.

Was she truly to join their ranks now? Rowan trailed her fingertips through the thick fur along Gardenia's neck, a small semblance of home returning to soothe her.

At the edge of the academy's grounds stood a clump of trees—beech, ash, willow, birch, maple, and oak. The copse was too small to feel like a forest, but she might be able to slip beneath its shade and, for a moment, return to her forest once more.

"The fungi stretch between the roots, joining the whole of Lis-Maen like one giant forest," Paupa had taught her before he died.

What remained unappreciated, even unseen below the soil, connected all the way back to her conclave, to her refractory.

She patted Majestyk on the head and, for once, the dracat obliged her without scowling. They had survived far worse than a temporary relocation, Rowan reminded herself. They'd find their way within this new environment soon enough.

CHAPTER THIRTEEN

MARCON

The chaos of the front lines was even worse than Marcon had imagined it being. Their enemy's forces had infiltrated the carefully organized lines of the Luz, driving a wedge between the more vulnerable archers along the right flank, the cavalry along the left, and separating the infantry along the center.

New hordes teemed out of the fortresses of Sanctuary, swelling the ranks before the city walls. Their greater numbers forced more and more vultura into the gap in the Luz's defenses.

If the infantry did not divide the vultura's ranks and carve out a route of retreat for the archers and riders, they would be lost.

"Soldiers from Vestige? Are they coming?" Marcon asked his commander, failing to keep the panic from his voice. They would need some sort of additional fortification for the battle to not be a disastrous slaughter.

Rezza shook her head. "They will not reach us in

time, and they sent only half the numbers the field commander requested."

"Bastion?"

"Their airships stalled in a storm over the Circle Sea. They had to turn back."

Marcon gritted his teeth. One of the keys to the Cities' strategy was the way in which each city could count on reinforcements from the others to protect them in times of vulnerability. If only the foresters of Lis-Maen were not so difficult to reason with—but such frustrations would have to wait.

Respite will be fine, he reminded himself. Marcon glared out at the battlefield, trying to see it with a strategist's eyes. *I'm not going home without Vateri and Cole.*

Rezza was one of a few commanders gathered among the thin, bewildered forces that stood between the vultura and the reserve forces that stood between Sanctuary and the fields and mountain passes that led to Respite.

Failing to hold back the ranks of the undead was not an option he could live with. They had all sworn to die rather than allow such a tragedy to take place.

"Commander," Marcon called, catching Rezza's attention from the waves of death washing over the Luz's battered forces as the divides between the ranks grew. Thinking of Vateri and Cole had reminded him of one of Cole's harebrained schemes. Something that just might work to turn the tides.

It had started as part of the rivalry between Cole and one of the young captains placed over them, a man who had little patience for Cole's determined sense of humor.

To prove he'd earned his place among the fighting forces of the Luz, Cole had set himself the task of outsmarting the captain and pioneering a new way of thinning undead forces.

In Cole's strategy, soldiers would work in concert together and carve out clumps of vultura a few at a time, dividing them from the rest, and then press forward again, restricting and surrounding a new group while other soldiers filled in behind them and eliminated the newly divided undead.

Though the idea had been born out of an immature rivalry, the strategist Cole had shown it to thought it might turn the tides when defeat pressed near.

That strategist had been separated from the main forces of the Luz with the archers who were taking heavy fire from the ramparts and were being driven back by the majority of the vultura.

"I know it's unorthodox," Marcon added as he explained the strategy to Rezza. In most cases, soldiers would do anything to prevent even a small group of the vultura to be able to surround them. That was how soldiers were eaten, like the man whose devouring had saved Marcon's life before.

He swallowed down bile. "Cole calls it a zigzag," Marcon repeated. Titans he wished his friend could see the look on Rezza's face as she contemplated the idea. The commander had taken it just as poorly at first as he and Vateri had, better than the captain Cole had bested with the strategist, and then the genius of the strategy slowly dawned on her, just like it had Cole's friends. "Get the signal to the cavalry," Marcon urged. "Cole will explain to his commanding officer. They'll be ready to meet us."

His commander nodded. "Gather your troops, Colabra. Let's get our forces back."

With Rezza's permission, Marcon recruited a clump of soldiers who were still able-bodied and of sound mind from the battle thus far. He walked them through the strategy, most importantly their own wedge formation that would allow them to funnel part of the vultura's line backward where Rezza's unit would be waiting to eliminate them, surging forward to regain part of the line.

"We save the archers first," Marcon added, his heart banging against the confines of his chest at having to choose one friend rather than the other.

The archers made the most strategic sense, and were their positions reversed, Cole would have chosen the same.

"Ready?" Marcon asked, his gaze dancing over the blood-spattered members of his new line.

They nodded their heads. "Ready," they answered as one.

Marcon tightened his jaw. *Here we go.*

As he had with his fellow recruits in adolescence, Marcon won over the new forces he'd recruited in a mix of fervent belief and excellent swordplay. He savored the whispered sigh of delight that echoed out behind him as in a trio of slashes he carved the heads from the three nearest vultura and threw himself into a gap in the horde.

The soldiers shouted, carving their way toward the position he fought to hold, surrounded on all sides by the undead. The moment they caught up to him, Marcon glanced back, Rezza's forces closing in the gap as promised. "Again!"

His commander had pulled in a chain of small groups to regain the field they'd occupied that morning and provide an exit strategy for the archers they sought to free from the vultura horde.

Five such presses took them near enough to see the whites of the archers' panicked eyes. Nearer to their lines, the battle was fiercer than it had appeared even from a distance.

They had arrived just in time and, even so, had proven to be too late for a great many of their brethren.

The energy among the soldiers he'd recruited began to flag around the fourth bisection of the vultura's ranks. Though they might not be fighting to rescue a dear friend like he was, they knew how necessary the ranged warriors were to their larger efforts.

As he cleaved yet another vultura head from its rotting body, he searched the lines of the archers, desperate for a glimpse of the thin elf fighting among them.

He found chaos and sprays of blood instead.

"VATERI!" Marcon shouted, terror gripping his throat as a tidal wave of vultura clambered over one another, their nails sharpened into claws digging into the earth, into each other, as they sought to overwhelm the line of archers.

Cole's plan was just as dangerous in practice as it had seemed when his friend first pitched the idea. This deep into their enemy's ranks, it was easier for them to press forward and divide the line but harder for those coming in behind them to sweep the way clear. Rather than a steady stream cutting through the horde, their formation was a series of rocks within a raging river. If one failed, the rest would be stranded and drown.

He shook his head, forcing himself to refocus upon the task at hand.

A vultura latched onto the top of his shield, throwing off his balance as he tried to slash at one of its fellows.

Beyond their immediate struggle, streams of arrows answered the vultura's assault, the bolts raining down upon the horde. Entire clumps of the undead creatures fell to the archers' attacks, but more were waiting beneath the scramble of bodies, and reinforcements continued to surge forward from the rear lines.

Fall back, Marcon shot a thought-arrow of his own to the archery commander. *You have to fall back.*

He dropped his struggle against the creature trying to climb over his shield and slammed his forehead against its own instead.

The vultura slumped back, stunned.

Beyond the archers, trapped between their narrow inlet and the shadowing walls of Sanctuary, the battalion fought for ever-diminishing ground.

The archers' efforts divided between protecting

themselves and the battalion soldiers trapped nearer to the wall.

It was a sound strategy in a stronger position, but in this moment, the attempt was akin to a slow death sentence for all involved.

Vateri, where are you?

The first line of the vultura met the single row of melee defenders stationed in front of the archers as a last-ditch precaution. Marcon had seen their ranks in the practice fields before the battle. To a soldier, their armor had been spotless and perfectly fitted.

Cole had scoffed as the three of them passed their immaculate tents where the soldiers lounged in chairs conveyed to the battlegrounds, bustling servants attending to their every need.

The spotless armor was now soaked in blood. Half of them lay dead and dying upon the fields. *Leave them*, Marcon urged, hating himself all the while.

He tightened his grip on his sword, the blood and gore from the vultura slicking the pommel and his gloves so he struggled to grasp it.

Another ten rows of enemy forces and they'd be there. "Twice more!" Marcon called back to his wedge soldiers. Several of them had fallen in their progression across the field, but they'd nearly made the archers.

"Grrah!" One of the vultura squealed as it launched itself toward Marcon's unguarded flank.

He spun about and crunched his elbow into the creature's face. Its hollowed skull cracked at the force behind his armor. Its breath made a scuttling noise as the monster fell backward, clawing at its face.

From the center of the archers' line, a familiar cry rang out.

There, among the burly silhouettes of the high-class infantry soldiers given what should have been a less dangerous job were the strategy of the day less flawed, a thin, agile figure held her own.

As he watched, Vateri shoved the point of an arrow into a vultura's eye and jabbed another through the throat, the enemy forces pressing so closely she couldn't loose a shot from her bow.

Marcon grinned, awed by his friend's tenacity. *The best of the three of us*, he and Cole liked to say, much to the elf's embarrassment.

If the next few moments of the battle could go their way—

An enemy arrow struck the archery commander in the throat. He crumpled to the ground.

"Fall back!" the second-in-command screamed, waving the archers toward herself. She snatched a horn from one of the bewildered infantry soldiers standing uselessly beside her and bellowed the cry of retreat.

The break in the chain of command sent a flurry of uncertainty along the vulnerable line of archers. They wavered, allowing the vultura several strides nearer to the archers trapped behind them. Several darted through the gaps, snarling as they launched themselves into the vulnerable holes in the archers' armor meant to allow them ease of movement in their ranged attacks.

They never should have been so near to the undead that the beasts could capitalize on such a weakness.

Seeing their line falter was the only catalyst Marcon

and his recruits needed. As one, they cried out and dove forward, redoubling their efforts to eliminate the hungry vultura before they could overwhelm the archers.

Marcon hacked and slashed, seeing nothing but his friend's struggle, desperate to reach her side.

Vateri's kind, familiar eyes widened in fear when one of her arrows snapped. She stumbled back away from a vultura and dug a dagger out from within her belt. As she stabbed it forward, a clawed vultura hand answered. It pierced through Vateri's arm, its claws emerging on either side of her elbow.

Her head reared back. Despite all the chaos of the battlefield, her scream echoed in Marcon's ears.

He dove forward and tackled the offending beast to the ground. Before it could right itself, Marcon dug the pommel of his sword into the cavity of its head. He pushed off the ground and stomped upon its ribcage. The monster would drown on its own fluids, the body too ruined to rise again no matter the necromancy wielded by their enemy's mages.

Marcon whirled about and caught the elf as she fell, careful to not jostle her injured arm. "I've got you," Marcon murmured, holding her between his shield and his chest as he shoved through their own line to pull her to safety.

Lorieannan had been right, Marcon thought as Vateri slumped against him, whimpering at the pain in her battered arm. The battle was hopeless. Lost before they'd even begun.

CHAPTER FOURTEEN

ROWAN

amara introduced the three newcomers to the guard waiting at the gates by the forest entrance to the academy's grounds. A handful of sentries paced upon the ramparts, and Rowan gathered that there were more waiting unseen within the small, tower-like structures interspersed along the walls.

She pointed out the other buildings as they rode into the Academia Magica proper. The five had been arranged in a pentacle formation, with great pains taken within the last fifty years to include the Druidess among what had been the Quadrate through the generations before. "The earthshapers sent by the Cities United made quick work of the necessary alterations," Samara added. "It was lucky that the shift in the Faces' number occurred during a time of collaboration." Samara held Rowan's gaze as she spoke, though her tone remained flat.

At the top of the pentacle, facing the Circle Sea and the city center of Delmoir was the Sorceress's tower, the grandest and oldest of the structures of the Academia

Magica. "Any servant of the Sorceress will be sure to remind you of such a claim to the rule of Delmoir," Samara added, "myself included."

The Oracle's tower pointed to the northeast, distantly facing Respite and what had been Sanctuary before its fall. Opposite the Oracle was the Healer, and the Creatrix held the position opposite the Druidess. "They're waiting for us in the receiving hall in the Sorceress's tower," Samara explained. Her eyes were wide, but her face remained pale.

Rowan kept waiting for their guide to seem more at ease now that she was home or to explain the waves of nervous energy rippling off her, but Samara did neither.

They passed a pen on the opposite end of the Druidess's holdings where they deposited the cervidae to the attendants. Gardenia snapped good-naturedly at one of the horse trainers who had reached toward a carrot rather than a skinned rabbit, her preferred treat.

The cervidae galloped after Rowan, sensing her unwillingness for the two of them to be parted.

Rowan climbed onto the railings to make herself tall enough to place her forehead against Gardenia's. "I'll find you soon," she murmured. "Take care of the others."

The cervidae's creaking bark said that she would.

As they crossed the academy grounds, Rowan took in the clumps of trainees gathered at different locations across the academy. Everyone seemed hard at work in their assigned task despite the dinnertime hour. Adepts whose robes bore green hems knelt in the gardens, tending the new summer growth for the Druidess.

Of even greater interest to both Rowan and Vraise,

adepts whose robes had dark blue hems—signaling an assignment with the Sorceress—battled one another across sand training pits. Some of them wielded magic, their hands glowing as they flung spells at one another. Others bore long sticks that they used atop balance beams while a third set of adepts simply sparred in hand-to-hand combat.

"When do we get to do *that*?" Vraise asked, his eyes dancing over the choreographed movements of the trainees.

"When you wake up too sore to be able to move and have hours' worth of chores to do, remember that you asked so enthusiastically," Samara cautioned.

Vraise's enthusiasm ebbed. "It won't be that bad, right?" he whispered to Rowan.

She bit her lower lip as one of the adepts struck another in the face with her fist. The target slumped backward, clearly unconscious. "Maybe let's wait and find out for ourselves," Rowan added, offering the lone comforting truth she could think of.

The breadth of the grounds kept Rowan in a state of constant amazement. Though the wonders of Delmoir pressed close against the far walls, the scattered copses of trees kept out the noise of the city. Were it not for the distant speck of airships whose unusual flight patterns made them easy to spot in contrast to the occasional arcing path of a bird nearer at hand, she might have forgotten that she was on the outskirts of a city at all.

It would have been impossible for her to forget that she was no longer in the outskirts, however. At the slightest noise, at least one of the three outlanders would flinch, glancing overhead where there was no tree covering. When one particularly delighted cry surprised the three of them, Samara kindly adjusted their route, leading them along the covered garden walkways instead of the open fields that crossed the academy. "I'm told you'll adjust in time," she assured them.

Rowan held her silence about her doubts on that front.

She caught her breath instead when their path curved around rows of greenhouses used by the Healer and revealed the full heights of the Sorceress's tower.

The tower was the oldest of the five structures that made up the academy grounds, originally the province of an empress who had ruled over the forests, fauna, and peoples of the small island continent. In the stories, the empress's tower was tall enough for her to gaze down upon the entirety of her realm at once so long as the fogs held back from the seas.

Rowan craned her neck to stare up to the tops of the highest tower, trying to imagine what she could glimpse from such a height. The thought created a pang in her heart, imagining being able to see the refractory from what was to be her new home for the next several months if not longer.

Even the middling ancestor trees of Willow Glen would have stretched far above the grandest heights of the Sorceress's tower. Rowan hurried to catch up with her companions who had continued on without stopping to stare up. Either the ancient bards had been exaggerating or—Rowan smiled to herself—the empress's people had learned to trust in homes that would one day outgrow those who sought to rule over them.

She clasped that reassurance tightly in hand and stepped beneath the long afternoon shadow of the varied towers. The chill slid beneath her skin and wrapped itself around her bones, resting uneasily beside the sudden speeding of her heart.

They were to appear before the Five Faces, and Rowan would make her counter-demand in exchange for her service as an offering—a blood vow that bound them to the protection of Willow Glen.

Guards waited before giant wooden doors propped open to a long, dark hallway. Samara urged them past a series of stained-glass windows that told the story of the Pentacle. The paint around the windows depicting the addition of the Druidess had yet to fade to match the panes for the other Faces. And in each of the windows, the five-pointed pentacle shone brightly—those portions had been added in place of the Quadrate that had come before.

Rowan trailed her fingertips along the rough pores of the stone walls, wondering what legend the empresses of old had told about themselves and their rule. Was it strange for the Sorceress, who had overseen the addition of the Druidess fifty years before, knowing that another such change in rule could occur—the Cities might grow tired of Lis-Maen's neutrality. Alessandra might turn her gaze from the Glade of Shadows and beset their forests instead. Would a dragon lieutenant maintain the window panes?

"Hurry along," Athenza called back to Rowan who adjusted the set of her shawl and slid in behind her friends. There was a small queue before a grand receiving hall with wide rows of partially filled benches. An aisle between the benches led up to a receiving area below a raised dais featuring a long table with five overly large chairs. Two of the chairs were empty, their padding and ornate carvings marking them as belonging to the Creatrix and the Healer. But the Sorceress, Oracle, and Druidess were there.

Rowan stood on tiptoes, using Vraise's shoulder to help her balance. He didn't push her off.

The deep sapphire, amethyst, and emerald of each of the three made plain which Face belonged to which discipline.

The Sorceress was just as severe-looking as Rowan had imagined her, with pointed features and dark hair pulled into a tight bun at the back of her head. The Oracle wore her curling blond hair short, falling just to the tops of her shoulders.

Of the three, the Druidess was the most striking. Her deep, gray-brown skin reminded Rowan of a forest caught in early morning light. Her large elven ears helped her to balance a golden ivy circlet atop her head where she'd shaved any trace of hair—the gold of the forest was the ornament she chose.

"The final offerings, presented by Agent Samara," the announcer called before them.

From the center of the table, the Sorceress raised her hand and beckoned them forward. Athenza strode forward first with Vraise close on her heels. The druid's cane clacked against the flagstone laid in an intricate pattern across the floor.

It was strange to walk toward such a lopsided receiving table, with one figure in the middle, two on one side, and two absent. To Rowan, it seemed as though they were being received by the Sorceress, with the other two as witnesses.

She made to follow after Vraise, but Samara caught her elbow.

The agent gripped her so tightly that Rowan winced. "Listen to me—"

Rowan tried to yank herself free. She had not planned to cause a scene with her arrival and certainly not due to a perceived inability to walk down an aisle. The entire assembly had turned back to watch, and her and Samara's struggle was drawing unwanted whispers Rowan's way.

The agent held firm. "I underestimated your potential, even seeing what you did when we met. For that, I apologize." Her voice was low and hurried. "But please, do not continue forward with your plan of asking the Faces to swear an oath. Their schemes are far-reaching."

The announcer cleared his throat and urged them forward.

Samara eased her hold on Rowan's elbow, her whisper falling softer still. "There's more that they didn't want me to tell you about why they wanted sacrifices from the margins—"

"Sacrifices?"

Samara nodded fervently. "The first offerings, they—"

"Ahem." The Sorceress had stood from her chair. She would have towered over those around her regardless, but was made even taller by her position on the dais. Her dark eyes gleamed as she stared, unwaveringly, at Samara. "You return with three offerings rather than five, agent."

Rowan searched the Sorceress's robes, finding a tilted wand embroidered into the shoulder of her garment with golden sparks shooting out of the end of it. Her breath caught. The figure was indeed the Sorceress. The leader of the Five Faces, though they denied centralized power. This was exactly who she needed to impress.

And here was Samara, choosing this moment to try to impart her final words, as though they wouldn't be able to see her after their grand reception.

The Sorceress met the gaze of each of the three offerings in turn. As her eyes locked upon Rowan's a flash of blue erupted behind her irises. Rowan stumbled back, bumping into Samara. She winced again as Majestyk dug her claws into Rowan's shoulder for balance.

Rowan shuddered as the bright blue faded, trying to rid herself of the distinct sense that she should cover herself like she would if a stranger was watching her bathe. "Welcome to the Academia Magica," the Sorceress said evenly. The corners of her mouth uplifted in a tiny gesture toward a smile that reached no further than her cheekbones. "I am the headmistress here. You likely know my reputation already as the Sorceress."

Vraise's pallor had increased under the Sorceress's scrutiny. His lips parted at finding she would be the headmistress over their training as well.

"My acolytes will guide you to your rooms." Her dark eyes flashed again at spying Majestyk on Rowan's shoulder. "And we can arrange accommodations for any . . . pets."

Rowan crossed her arms over her chest. "The cervidae can remain in the thicket yard—they'll adapt to their new herd. The dracat stays with me."

The suggestion of a smile faded entirely from the Sorceress's expression. "You will find that it is not usually the place of acolytes to make demands of even the adepts who oversee their training sessions, not to mention one such as myself." Her glare flickered over to Samara. "I hope your host has not given you a mistaken impression of your role here. Offerings are below acolytes still."

Athenza glanced at Rowan, her expression drawn, but there were too many other occurrences vying for her attention for Rowan to sort through what her mentor's look meant. The acolytes who had appeared at the end of the table to escort them stared at Rowan with wide eyes, appalled at her frankness with the headmistress.

But Rowan wasn't done surprising them.

However well-meaning Samara might have been, she had kept a great deal hidden. And Athenza was right. Rowan *needed* to train.

She would get the oath she'd vowed to obtain. "It's my understanding that you need offerings from the margins because your own mages proved unequal to the task of creating an elemental army capable of wielding the six elements reunited," Rowan said, loud enough for the entire assembly to hear.

The whole of the room held its breath.

"If that is not true," Rowan continued, her gaze never faltering from the pooling dark irises of the Sorceress who glared openly, "then we can return to Willow Glen and carry on as before. But I'll not part from a companion who's been by my side throughout my life at your whim." Rowan glanced again at the apprentices waiting for them, elves even younger than she was. She shook her head. The Sorceress was accustomed to dealing with children. She would not find Rowan so easy to control.

The headmistress inclined her head, a true smirk tugging at her lips now. "As you are just arrived, Rowan of Willow Glen, I will forgive this impertinence. *Once.* But be warned, I am not given to whims." She clapped her hands together, startling the apprentices at the edge of the dais.

"Escort our guests to their residence. Samara, remain here with me."

The agent brushed her hand against Rowan's arm but made no other move to restrict Rowan's following the Sorceress's orders.

"There is one other request I should like to make," Rowan added, trying to be more mindful of her tone this time.

Annoyance flickered in the Sorceress's gaze. Beside her, a puzzled frown shadowed the Oracle's face. The Druidess stared straight ahead, paying little heed to the events unfolding around her.

"I am not unaware of the dangers facing us as offerings." *Nor could anyone be given that you're calling us offer-*

ings she wanted to add but refrained. "To take such time away from home and dedicate myself, my magic, my being to your efforts, I would like a gesture in exchange."

The Sorceress openly scoffed. "This is not a gambling den. Make your bargain requests elsewhere."

Rowan forced her shoulders back, ignoring the currents of nerves rippling off Samara behind her. "I want a promise of protection for my forest. Whatever it is you're going to demand, it could cost us our lives." The room had fallen silent again. "I know that," Rowan added, trying to find the strength of her voice, the conviction that had guided her out of Willow Glen in the first place.

"All of Lis-Maen falls under our protection," the Oracle reminded her.

"For me to take your magic, I'd like to engage the ancient magic of binding," Rowan said, ignoring the Oracle's correction. If they weren't willing to offer the protection to the conclave and to the willow hearttree, then Rowan knew her path to proving herself worthy had to lie elsewhere.

Rowan kept her head high. She'd thought carefully over the wording of her request for an oath as they rode through the forest. "Swear a blood oath that whatever transpires here, you will protect Willow Glen, and I will serve you until your goal is realized."

"Hah," the Sorceress laughed. The sound spit out of her like the pitter-patter of raindrops, but it contained no true mirth.

Rowan clenched her jaw. There was no need for mockery. She could simply refuse.

But before Rowan could say as much, a low voice rose out of the shadows. "Surely you aren't feeling threatened by such a request, Sorceress?"

On top of the pressing silence, the entire room froze except for the three gathered before the dais. Rowan leaned forward, trying to see around the end of the long table, but she needn't have bothered.

A collective gasp rippled out across the gathering as her advocate paced into view.

A man, no, something else—seven—eight feet tall with impossibly long, bat-like wings gathered at each shoulder ambled into the audience chamber from an unseen position in the wings. He wore a dark tunic that gaped open across the chest, revealing gray planes of muscle and golden tattoos inked onto his skin, which was the shadowed gray of a cliffside. Close-fitting breeches hugged muscular legs atop pristine leather boots. The wings' talons pointed toward one another like a crown, further accentuating his height.

Rowan's breath caught as the figure's gaze met hers —golden eyes, not dissimilar from those of her phoenix —though that may have been the sheer sense of power radiating off him in waves.

"Lucien," the Sorceress greeted coldly.

Rowan jolted, her mouth falling ajar. Lucien as in one of the *guardians*—sworn protectors of the lands and peoples of Eldura, more powerful even than the Archfae who had departed from Lis-Maen long ago? Each of the seven guardians had been gifted a unique magic by the gods and placed as protectors over the three Planes of Life after the Fall of the First Age.

They all possessed shape-shifting abilities as well as wings, allowing them to adapt their forms as they saw fit. The ongoing war between the Cities and Alessandra had divided the guardians amongst themselves—some had sworn neutrality. Others had sided with the Cities.

And some, like Lucien, had yet to declare a side.

The guardian angled broad shoulders toward the Sorceress, casting a single glance back at Rowan before lifting his chin to address the mage before him. "Your Excellencies," the guardian cooed in a low, lilting voice.

Rowan wasn't alone in leaning closer, drawn irresistibly toward the figure before her. She clamped her hands upon the wooden audience rail they waited behind.

At her side, Athenza seized her wrist. Her palm was clammy where it touched Rowan's arm. Behind Rowan, Samara's breath was shallow.

"Pray tell," the Sorceress addressed the intruder, "what interest do you take in our proceedings? It is most unusual for you to stoop to observe the intake of, well—" She gestured toward them as though brushing away a fly. "Those who could barely be described as *adepts* despite their advanced years."

His low, answering chuckle was so soft Rowan could almost have convinced herself she had misheard. "You and I both know potential when we see it, Sorceress." He rolled his shoulders back and glanced about the gallery. "It's one of the reasons you keep me around."

The golden gaze met Rowan's. There was no flare of pale blue this time, but the corner of his lip twitched before he turned away to pace behind the table to the other side of the Faces. The entire gallery held its silence, the echo of his footfalls reverberating out to the corners of the room until he leaned against a pillar on the opposite wall, arms crossed over his chest. Once he was settled, flurries of whispers buzzed behind Rowan while the guardian's attention roved about the room.

Though the Sorceress and Oracle refused to follow his movements, the Druidess shot nervous glances in the guardian's direction. Apprentices holding stacks of paper Rowan now realized were representatives of the Healer and the Creatrix tiptoed away from him, withdrawing into the shadowy recesses behind the dais.

A sharp, rapping sound echoed out around the gallery as the Sorceress reached across the Oracle and banged the wooden gavel against the tabletop. Her rival Face, the Oracle, looked more amused than concerned by the Sorceress's flash of impatience.

"As I was saying," the Sorceress continued, "the matter of a blood oath is more complex than your casual demand admits, outlander. Were the five of us to make it to you, the vow would be as weak as the weakest of the five, and it would expire as soon as one of the Faces did."

Those gathered studiously avoided looking at the empty chairs where the Healer and the Creatrix would have sat. Even as far from Delmoir as Willow Glen, the rumors about the two figures said they were ancient. For Rowan's entire life, they had been hovering beneath the branches of the yew, waiting to be called into the afterlife. She wouldn't risk her forest on so flimsy a thread of life.

"I fear our prospective offering may underestimate

the very real danger before *her*, Sorceress," the Oracle added. She smirked as she looked Rowan over, her lip curling, unimpressed by what she found. "Your understanding of such promises and their inherent dangers is no doubt limited by your own narrow experiences." The Oracle glared at Samara. "Your agent should never have made such a promise on our behalf."

"Perhaps with more time to discuss—" the Sorceress began, preparing to dismiss them.

"Make me your arbiter, then," the guardian said, the low peal of his voice sparking a flurry of whispers across the hall.

"Excuse me?" the Sorceress asked, disbelief clouding her tone.

"It's a simple enough concept." The guardian straightened upon his wall. He never turned back toward Rowan but kept his attention fixed upon the Sorceress and the Oracle. "The two of you have spearheaded this newest attempt at imbuing the offerings with power. To balance the scale and ensure a sense of fairness, I'll uphold the vow's binding."

Athenza stumbled into the railing, her cane wavering beneath her. "Under no circumstances—"

"Silence!" the Sorceress screeched. Her dark eyes had turned into swirling pools as she looked between Rowan and Lucien, the predatory gleam so bright Rowan half expected her to lick the corners of her lips in anticipation.

"I hope you know what you're agreeing to, Outlander," the Sorceress said with a grin.

Beside her, the Oracle had reclaimed the gavel.

"Done." She banged it against the table and gestured to dismiss the three of them in the same motion.

"Take them to their rooms and then return to me," the Sorceress ordered Samara.

Their agent's hands were shaking as she led them out of the receiving hall.

CHAPTER FIFTEEN

MARCON

"Clear the way," Marcon shouted, glaring at the frightened archers and injured infantry defenders who were trying to fend off secondary waves of attackers while the flailing front lines struggled to hold their own.

The scrabbling vultura had kicked up clouds of dust in their wake, making it difficult for him to see deep enough into the lines to tell whether his plan of salvaging as many of their number from the impossible battle was working.

In an hour, perhaps two, they would know.

A soft cry from Vateri returned his focus to more immediate threats. Not five paces away, an archer caught an arrow glowing with a sickly green energy in the neck. He garbled as the arrow severed vocal cords and veins, falling to the ground.

"The green—" Vateri warned.

Marcon had already slid her behind him. He clasped his sword and lowered in his stance.

One heartbeat. Two.

The body began to shake.

Marcon sprinted over, the spell he'd feared having taken hold of the archer's body.

He leaped into the air as the archer's head reared up at an unnatural angle, the face marred by dirt and a monstrous snarl. The newly formed vultura tried to crawl to where Marcon had left Vateri.

Marcon landed upon its back instead, his sword sinking through the body and into the dirt after severing the spinal column.

The foul green glow faded from around the corpse and sank into the earth.

No wonder the surroundings of Sanctuary were nothing but ash.

He hurried back to Vateri's side and scooped her by the waist, angling their way back toward the small pocket of battle-medics assigned to field duty with the archers.

Vateri's shaking had worsened upon seeing the undead soldier rise in the place of someone who'd been fighting in such close proximity to her a short while before. It was one of the cruelest and most difficult parts of battling Alessandra's forces.

The commanders had warned them about precisely such an eventuality—that their own friends and allies would be raised as their foes, but their words hadn't fully captured the horror of cutting down a soldier dressed exactly like him, or landing atop an archer armed precisely like Vateri, who looked just as alive and covered in dirt save the green glow of the necromantic energy. Or, in the case of the infantry soldier he'd cut down fighting to get to Vateri, the teeth marks embedded into the stubble of the soldier's jawline.

The cries from the front lines pressed close, and a series of screams told Marcon that his plan was failing but, just as all hope seemed lost, the bugle of riders broke through the chaos.

All around Marcon and Vateri, the archers and medicos began to cheer.

Armored riders mounted upon biomechos whose armor grew along their hide like tortoise shells sprang to the archers' defense, spearing through vultura and driving back the hordes.

Vateri shouted, pointing behind him with her good arm as a familiar figure neared. Gore coated Cole's pike, and his shield was nearly beyond even Garreth's ability to repair, but he urged his mount, Stella, over to the pair of them.

They wouldn't have long, Marcon knew, especially as dusk approached. Their forces would have to retreat if not fall back entirely.

There was no use fighting the undead under cover of night.

The arrival of the cavalry had bought the archers a reprieve but, beyond them, the battalion's defenses looked even tighter, the area they defended growing smaller.

"She's hurt," Marcon shouted up to Cole, the slavering cries of the vultura and cries of pain from the medical tent drowning out his voice.

"I can fight," Vateri protested weakly. She didn't

resist when Marcon lifted her by the waist and placed her into Cole's care.

Cole's eyes were wide when his gaze met Marcon's. The horrors he'd witnessed in the cavalry unit had been emblazoned onto his expression. Whatever they'd gone through in the hours they'd been cut off from the chance of retreat, with more than half their forces falling to the hordes, his friend wouldn't soon forget.

Marcon reached up and grasped Cole's hand. "Get her to the medicos behind our lines," he ordered, the ring of command echoing in the low tones of his voice.

His friend gazed back toward their meager lines of defense.

"Soldier!" Marcon shouted.

Cole jolted and looked down at Marcon.

"Now."

The order in his tone snapped Cole back to himself. "See you on the other side, brother," he said with a nod, clasping his arm to his chest.

Cole clicked his teeth to his mount and tugged on the reins. The biomecho's internal gears whirred to life at its shoulders, and Stella cantered away, carrying his two closest friends to safety.

The interaction between himself and Cole earned Marcon the attention of a few other soldiers nearby. A few of the pike-bearing riders slid off their mounts and strode over to Marcon. They poured great gulps of water from nervous medicos straight into their mouths and oiled their horses' gears as they addressed Marcon. "We heard you were the one responsible for the zigzag formation that saved our tails," the taller of the two said.

His friend nodded over toward the shrinking territory occupied by the battalion soldiers. "Any idea how to save the pride of the Luz?"

The pride of the Luz. He liked the sound of that.

Marcon grinned, the shift in the winds of battle lifting his spirit. "I have been working on something."

"I've admired the Battalion all my life," one of the riders admitted to Marcon after he'd laid out his plan of staggered attack to carve out a route of egress for the surrounded forces. "Seeing them fight their way forward today—I've never been so impressed." The soldier laughed. "Well, until I saw your unit hacking your way upstream that is."

Marcon's renown as the soldier responsible for the archers' rescue quickly earned him an audience of eager soldiers who found themselves still hungry for striking their enemy's innards as part of the Army of Light, especially if that meant being part of rescuing such a valuable force as the Blazing Battalion.

Though he hadn't counted on swelling his numbers so quickly, the soldiers who had battled their way here had added recruits of their own—archers they'd saved, riders they knew. He had almost a fully realized military unit at his command.

After the archers' commander had been felled, they had fought on by rote, the few nobles among their ranks who had survived striving to protect the archers, many of whom had abandoned their bows and arrows for melee weapons.

With a new force organized around him, Marcon quickly fell into the signaling used across the Army of Light. He ordered those unfit for a press attack to defend their flanks and maintain their return route.

The most capable of the melee combatants, he rallied to himself. "We stay as a defended unit," Marcon explained. "Shields up, circle formation." He nodded toward the embattled battalion soldiers. "We're getting them out of there."

With each passing minute, the battalion's warriors lost ground.

They couldn't withstand the enemy's press for much longer.

But they wouldn't have to.

"Our way forward will not be easy," Marcon warned. "All who wish to attempt the Battalion's rescue should be of sound body. Wraiths and worse await us."

Judging by how the battle had gone through the afternoon, Marcon expected a large number of the soldiers to break away at his cautioning. Instead, their courage somehow swelled at the prospect. They raised a triumphant cry and thumped swords onto shields, pikes onto chest armor.

Their confidence bolstered his own. The forces of the Luz might emerge with a halting victory today or could at least depart from the fields of battle without the shame of utter defeat weighing their shoulders.

"We haven't far to fight," Marcon added, gesturing to

the base of the nearest watchtower at the foot of Sanctuary's walls. The battalion soldiers continued to hold their ground there, despite the aerial assault coming from the two nearest walls and the tower itself and the ground forces that had pinned them in. The city's defensive spiral, brought into being by a visionary of the royal line generations before, was truly performing its work—only in this instance, it worked against them rather than on their behalf.

They had no route of egress, no way of returning to the rest of the Luz.

Two dozen warriors at least.

Marcon wouldn't let this glorious stand be the end of their battle. Nor would those who had flocked to his side.

"Archers, at the ready!"

"Hoorah," they answered as one.

"Defenders, ready."

The melee defense Marcon had appointed to oversee the archers' protection clapped the broad sides of their swords against their shields, thumping a steady, thunderous heartbeat to the entire operation.

Marcon raised his sword high overhead and bellowed their rallying cry. "With me!"

His unit answered, and they charged forward against the enemy's ranks.

The soldiers yelled and fell in behind Marcon. They sprinted along the narrow line behind the Luz's archers, crashing as water upon rock against the pressing tide of the vultura hordes.

The battle was fiercer than he had yet faced, as though the forces of darkness were determined to blot out the defenders of light and of fire.

Midway toward the battalion's lines, the archers upon the ramparts of Sanctuary turned their fire upon Marcon and his forces. A soldier beside him screeched as an arrow pierced through his shoulder. Another caught a bolt upon her shield, saving Marcon from the arrow that would have pierced through his eye.

It was the turn of the defense's focus that won Marcon his next victory.

Seeing the army of the Luz rally to their aid, the battalion redoubled their efforts.

The woman in blue armor who had saved him earlier led the forces to meet Marcon and his soldiers, the vultura momentarily beaten back and the battalion lines fortified. "There's someone I want you to meet," she said, waving Marcon to the center of their lines.

His steps faltered as the figure she'd indicated turned.

The stars and flames upon his shoulder signified the rank of captain within the Blazing Battalion. The embodiment of Marcon's dream.

"Ah, the soldier you were telling me about," the captain said, his wide, ready smile catching Marcon off-guard.

Marcon was breathless, either from the fight to this moment or the encounter itself. He'd never spoken to a battalion captain before.

"Isadora was right to put her faith in you," the captain said, clapping Marcon on the shoulder. His gaze rarely left the woman in the blue leather armor and pale blue cape. The captain's smile brightened whenever she neared, the blood and ichor of the vultura splattered across her face.

She eyed the captain in precisely the same way—the pair were clearly attached.

"So, what's our rescuer's plan for getting us out of here?" Isadora challenged Marcon, a playful gleam in her eyes as though they weren't surrounded and vastly outnumbered by an undead force. The raven upon her shoulder stared at him with each of its dark eyes in turn, its suspicion emphasizing its mistress's surprising curiosity.

The soldiers who'd fought their way here by his side had been emboldened by their success, but the swell of pride would only last them for so long against so many enemy forces.

Marcon searched the meager defenses of the camp, his gaze alighting upon a single crate of alchemist's fire. "I've heard rumors about the strength of the battalion's shields and their ability to withstand dragon's fire."

"Guilty," the captain answered with a grin.

He nodded toward the crate. "Would you be opposed to burning your way out?"

The captain chuckled at that. "I'll take whatever heat the field commander wants to drop upon my wasteful-ness so long as my battalion still stands at the end of this." He shook his head. "But you should know—stores are low. It was never a full crate to begin with. They kept those behind the lines in case the dragon surfaced. We have five jars."

Marcon released a slow breath. Half of the stores he'd been hoping for. He narrowed his gaze. This was the battalion, for titans' sakes. They could fight their way out of anything. "Five is all we'll need."

Once again, the sounds of the battle raging around them faded away as Marcon outlined the plan of attack. In a bare swath of dirt miraculously free of pooling blood, he explained the alternating explosions that would drive back the vultura and allow the battalion's forces room to make their escape.

"We'll strike here, nearest to our lines first so they can gain ground on our behalf. Then, we'll use the second jar of alchemist's fire as near at hand as we can survive. Jars three and four will thin the center of their forces."

"And the last one?" Isadora asked.

"We toss behind us as we carve through to cut off their pursuit. Whatever we can do to prevent ourselves from being surrounded."

"It's the best plan I've heard all day," the captain said, nodding to Marcon before he strode away to deliver the orders to the rest of the soldiers.

CHAPTER SIXTEEN

ROWAN

"Keep your distance from that one," Athenza warned Rowan as soon as they stepped into the side hallway outside the gallery.

From behind Rowan's shoulder, Samara said nothing, only ushering them away from the dais. The agent stared straight ahead, her expression stricken.

"I don't care what vow he made or how you believe he's helping," Athenza continued as though the doors weren't open behind them. "He isn't."

If the guardian had heard her mentor, he gave no sign. He'd raised his taloned hand before his chest and studied his nails as they passed his pillar, his look of boredom belying the disruption he'd provoked within the gathering.

Majestyk crawled over Rowan's shoulder, balancing her squat hind legs on Rowan's elbow. The dracat let out a low hiss directed back toward the guardian.

Rowan followed the creature's displeasure before turning away from the open door.

Lucien's hand was still raised, but he no longer studied it. Instead, his golden gaze danced over her before he returned a disinterested stare to the leaders of the Pentacle. The air around the Sorceress shimmered as she struggled to contain her rage.

Though he looked away, Lucien smirked when she turned back.

Rowan's stomach tightened. Was he pleased at having caught her attention?

"Sapling," Athenza called, a shivering drip of fear in her voice. The nickname was one Rowan's father had gifted her, teasing her for her extremities growing more quickly than the rest of her, as he'd said, not to mention her penchant for slipping away into the trees.

Lucien's wings unfurled like the easy drift of a butterfly's wings when it landed upon a branch just as the thick wooden door swung shut behind Rowan, locking the Faces of the Pentacle in with the guardian.

"Th-that could have gone worse," Samara said, biting her lower lip as she looked over her three charges. "If you'll come with me, we'll find your rooms."

As they walked through the patterns of shadow and light from the archways overhead—a feature she was going to have to adjust to—Rowan repeated in her mind the way the golden eyes had met hers just before she turned to follow Athenza. *Try to stay away all you like*, the gleam ignited by his smirk seemed to say. *You'll still find your way back to me.*

Rowan pressed cold fingertips to the heat that had risen in her cheeks during the questioning. The Academia Magica was proving to be even more diverting than she'd dared hope.

Samara's confidence returned as she led the party through green-walled gardens and up a marble staircase to their dormitory within the Druidess's grounds.

"Athenza, you're there on the end." Samara pointed down the hall to a narrow wooden door impossibly close to the stone wall beside it. More promisingly, the stone wall perfectly framed a floor-to-ceiling window that cast its warm glow along the marble hallway.

Rowan grinned, glancing up overhead to find scarlet and gold trails of ivy weaving over the arched doorways and along the thick wooden molding lending its dark weight and warmth to the stone walls and plaster ceiling.

"Vraise, you're just here," Samara said, indicating a room on the opposite side of the hall. "And Rowan here." She rapped her knuckles against the arched wooden door of Rowan's room. "You and your roommate share a bathing chamber with Athenza and the pair of boarders in the room between the two of you."

"A roommate?" Rowan's smile faltered. She'd been on her own since Paupa's passing.

"*Enter,*" a low, alto voice chanted inside her mind.

Rowan's eyes widened. She smoothed her breeches, tucked a strand of hair behind her ear, and twisted the worn brass knob of the room that would be hers for the next months, possibly years of her time as an offering—however long it took for the Pentacle's experiments to succeed. And throughout that time, thanks in part to Lucien, her forest would be safe.

The door slid open, and Rowan caught her breath for the second time that hour.

A rich, blue-green gaze met hers, the eyes rimmed in a band of pure gold that matched the shimmering fur of her new companion save the burnished bronze of her paws and—as the clouds shifted outside—rich jade hue caught on the tips of her fur, most concentrated upon her green ears.

Rowan stood eye-to-eye with a giant wolf who—she audibly gasped—unfurled deep sea-green, eagle-like wings from her back before they disappeared again, fading into the shimmering pattern Rowan had glimpsed along the fur of her back.

"Viridian," Samara said from behind Rowan before introducing Rowan in turn.

Naming the wolf for the shade of green of her wings made sense—Rowan startled. Not a wolf. A daimon— the enchanted offspring of the wolf-god Fenrir. Great wolves blessed with magic across their lineage, exactly like the protectors of the willow hearttree.

"I see you are familiar with my people, Rowan-roommate."

From Rowan's shoulder, Majestyk trilled a greeting.

"Ah, and you have a furry companion already." The daimon padded over toward the window, granting Rowan enough space to enter their narrow, shared room. There would hardly be enough room for the pair of them to both maneuver at the same time, particularly given the length of Viridian's body. The daimon was over six feet tall when seated. *"You will have to excuse me from the keeping of a pet,"* Viridian added.

Rowan was already growing accustomed to the lilting rhythm of the wolf's voice in her mind.

"I find I shed enough all on my own." The daimon laughed at that, and Rowan smiled in return.

"You don't mind sharing a space, then?"

The daimon inclined her head. *"The scent of the forest is strong upon your shoulders, as is the warm, earthy tinge of the magic in your veins. You are a welcome addition, room-friend."*

Rowan adjusted her hold on Majestyk and stepped into the room, the excitement of the receiving hall, the Sorceress, the Oracle, and Lucien for the moment forgotten.

After depositing her belongings and swapping out her shawl from the road for the rough-spun jacket from her bag, Rowan stepped back out into the hall where Samara still lingered. Their agent conferred with an elf in her middling years, the dark, rootlike wrinkles of age just starting to crinkle the sides of her eyes. The second elf wore pale blue robes with dark blue seams, what Rowan gathered signaled her as an apprentice or even higher level in the service to the Sorceress.

"I'm sure that once you explain, she'll understand," the second elf was telling Samara.

"You didn't see her expression," Samara said, eyes downcast. "I fear what her punishment will be."

The two figures looked up as Rowan's door creaked.

The flash of fear across Samara's expression told Rowan that she'd overheard something she shouldn't have.

She broke the uncomfortable silence. "Samara, about earlier—"

The agent turned away from her companion, squeezing her forearm before hurrying over to Rowan's side. As she crossed the hall, she plastered a grin across her expression that looked more like a grimace. "That wasn't your fault. I should never have put you in such a difficult position at an already heightened time."

Then why did you? Rowan wanted to retort, but her insight into the disparity between her understanding of Samara's position and the agent's actual position within the academy made her hesitate. It seemed unlikely that Samara would answer any question she posed about the punishment that would be doled out as a consequence of Samara appearing with three offerings instead of five.

To the Sorceress, Rowan didn't count as three. She wasn't sure if that was welcome news or not. "Are the Faces always so . . . brusque?" Rowan ventured instead.

Samara's expression lost some of its rigidness, though the fear lingered. "For the most part, though they are sometimes less severe when you catch them on their own and not before each other or a crowd."

"Even the Sorceress?" Rowan asked before she could stop herself.

The agent laughed in reply though there was no mirth to the sound. "Unfortunately, no. In her case, the harshness remains constant."

Samara wetted her lips, glancing down at her dirt-speckled boots. "I . . . I don't know what you must think of me, working for them. Their position in Lis-Maen. But I do believe in what they're working toward." She met Rowan's gaze, a furtive hope lingering behind her eyes. "If you can find a way to adapt to their habits, I have no doubt that you will be a prime addition to their ranks."

She gave Rowan a hesitant smile. "Seeing you catch that ball of fire—that would have taken most mages I've met years to be able to wield. You did it so naturally. It was the most optimistic I've felt in a long while, especially after . . ."

"After the first offerings were sacrificed?" Rowan ventured, echoing Samara's warning when she'd called the first offerings "sacrifices."

"No, no," Samara answered too quickly. "I-I was nervous and chose my words poorly. The age has passed in which the Pentacle took part in actively sacrificing mages."

Rowan had no idea how to respond to such a confession. Should such a habit have *ever* been the case, she wanted to add. "Will the Sorceress be angry with you since there are just three of us?" She couldn't think of who else in Willow Glen Samara might have assigned. That she'd managed to recruit a mage as gifted as Athenza was the most impressive coup by far, and the Pentacle hadn't even noticed the druid's potential.

Samara nodded. "Yes, I'm afraid, though I will endeavor to help them understand."

Vraise's door burst open and her fellow offering hurried out into the hall, clad in entirely fresh attire, so new that it made even Rowan's carefully preserved jacket look as though she'd worn it through the ride here.

"What?" He frowned and checked the carefully pressed pleats of his woolen pants. "I want to make a good impression on our fellow offerings."

He donned a woolen cap with a flat bill, completing the ensemble.

Rowan pressed her fingers to her lips to restrain her mirth. At least someone was enjoying their arrival in the Academia Magica and was optimistic about what the evening's banquet held.

From the end of the hall, Athenza's door banged open. She strolled out, striking her cane so hard against the floor with each step it reminded Rowan of when tree frogs had invaded Athenza's hut.

The druid's method of dealing with the frogs had been decisive—she had impaled three upon the end of her cane despite Rowan's cry of dismay. Athenza then wielded the bodies before the others, taunting them that they would be next if they failed to leave.

In a haste-filled yet surprisingly orderly fashion, the frogs had hurriedly departed from the hut.

"Let's go make our grand appearance," Athenza muttered, looking just as road-weary as when they'd arrived in the dormitories, though Rowan noted she had opted to don her second-favorite shawl, one she'd helped Athenza to create shortly after Paupa's passing. The druid had never complained about Rowan's poor attempts at adding leaves to the scarf's design, though they more closely resembled discolored blobs than anything else.

"One moment, before you go," Samara said, gesturing to her friend. "I won't be able to accompany you to the dining hall within the Druidess's gardens, but you will have a guide to lead you there."

Once again she caught Rowan's elbow, this time pressing a slip of parchment into her hand. "The Oracle and Sorceress have agreed to your terms. You are to meet Their Excellencies and the guardian at the receiving hall at dusk." She shook her head. "Do *not* be late."

Her caution given, Samara released Rowan and stepped away from her, raising her hand in farewell to Vraise and Athenza. "Best of luck to you both," she called.

"Wait, will we not see you after this?" Vraise asked.

Samara bit her lower lip. "I believe it is unlikely, at least for a time. They'll be sending me out again quite soon."

"If you'll come with me," their new guide said, beckoning the three of them down the hall after her.

Rowan had opted to leave Majestyk behind with Viridian, in part because the dracat had curled onto her favorite quilt immediately upon arrival and had grumbled at Rowan's furtive attempt to shift her so she could prepare her bed for the evening to come.

Viridian also declined Rowan's offer for her to join them, though she promised to do so soon.

Rowan glanced back at Samara before following after the apprentice clad in shades of blue.

The agent stood rooted in place, her face pale, eyes unnaturally wide as she watched them go. Rowan couldn't help but think of the way Samara had stiffened when she met the Sorceress's unwavering stare.

Despite Samara confiding in her about the belief

she'd inspired, she had to believe there was a deeper reason Samara had offered to take Rowan in the place of three others from her conclave. The Sorceress's reaction made it seem as though that wasn't Samara's place, but why would the agent take such a risk for someone she didn't know?

Rowan played with the fraying ends of her sleeves as she thought it over. There was more they didn't know about the previous offerings, though without access to their one ally, Rowan wasn't sure how they would find out more in a timely fashion.

The slip of parchment crinkled in her hand. *Sorceress's Receiving Hall. Dusk.* She searched the back but it was blank.

"Were you able to learn anything further from the agent?" Athenza murmured as they traversed a stone path lined with low, puffy clouds of bright purple phlox. Vraise cheerfully chatted to their new Sorceress-appointed guide, either unfazed by their eerie reception or affecting ease to slough off suspicion.

She suspected the former.

"Very little. I overheard a threat of punishment that she didn't want me to know about."

Their new guide's path curved around the outside of the Druidess's intricately crafted wood-and-stone buildings toward the series of gardens where a large, ornate greenhouse waited at the top of a hill. Rowan's eyes widened—though much of the academy was even stranger and more unsettling than she'd been anticipating, the greenhouse was stunning. Intricate arbors marked the winding path through lush beds. Condensation clouded the windows, interrupted by the shadowy lines of vines along the panes.

Athenza had come to the same conclusion as Rowan, that Samara made an offer to the three of them that fell outside her purview.

The phlox had yielded to dark green ivy that interspersed the rocky path boundaries while climbing roses dripped down from the wooden arches, the mingled greens running freely over obstructions and flourishing, like water over river rocks.

"Maybe the Sorceress is displeased with our potential?" Rowan said under her breath.

Athenza shook her head. "That was a spell of recognition, that flash in her eyes. I should have seen it coming, shielded you better, something."

Her mentor's reaction was even more puzzling than Samara's. "Why?"

The druid was muttering to herself, clacking her walking cane upon the stone cobbles more loudly than was necessary. "That which lies concealed in you needs to stay that way for as long as possible." Athenza's lips thinned as she pressed them together. "What they'll do if they find it—I'd never forgive myself, and neither would your paupa, if I allow that to happen."

"Are you talking about—"

Athenza shushed her, catching Rowan's wrist and squeezing before she could mention the phoenix aloud. "Assume they are always listening," she muttered.

Their guide led the three of them around the side of the greenhouse where clumps of adepts—mostly elves— sat around low tables with moss-covered cushions around an outdoor dining hall. Flowering trees interspersed the spread of tables with small, glowing lanterns hanging from their boughs. They so closely resembled her father's light orbs from Willow Glen that Rowan stopped short, her chest tight.

"Rowan, come on. The food is this way," Vraise called, holding open a side door for her and Athenza.

She scanned the outdoor dining area once more before passing inside. Most of the robed elves were in white with green hems upon their sleeves, signaling their association with the Druidess.

Not having seen the Healer or Creatrix at the ceremony, Rowan considered asking those with the red-hemmed white robes whether the Healer normally attended such gatherings. She couldn't work out how to ask whether the Healer was as ancient as the rumors held.

She followed after Vraise into a circular glass dome where a rainbow of butterflies flitted overhead. There was a short line for trays of food, though Rowan couldn't tell who had prepared them. Near the rear entrance that led back out to the gardens, she spied a few additional tables. Their apprentice guide had drifted that direction upon their arrival. Most of those dotting these taller tables were fellow apprentices, the colors of their robes speaking of higher ranks.

By the back doors, an adept with gold-hemmed robes glided out into the gardens. Rowan wondered if the representative of the Creatrix felt as alone and singled out as Rowan and, she assumed, her companions from the outskirts did?

Those in line before them kept turning back to stare, not even caving to Vraise's confident greeting of them all.

When it was her turn, Rowan took one of the trays and glanced down at the heaped salad and round roll before following her friends outside. A cup of pale pink tea cast curls of steam up from the side of her tray.

"I wish Samara could have told us more of what we should expect once the training begins," Vraise said as he adjusted his seat onto the cushion at their table on the edge of the dining area. The unabashed stares had followed them all the way back outside, with conversation falling away the moment they neared. He'd turned his back to most of the diners, his sweater collar pulled closer to his neck.

Rowan smiled at their new outlander companion. He wasn't as used to being on the margins as she and Athenza were.

"I'm sure we'll be able to confer with her after the welcome banquet," Athenza assured him.

Vraise shook his head, his pallor remaining. "Her friend was just telling me on the way here—the Sorceress is sending her back out straightaway, on diplomatic mission to the Glade of Shadows." His hand shook as he raised his cup of tea to his mouth and took a hesitant sip. Vraise leaned closer. "The last known dryad copse fell this morning."

Rowan stared down at the wooden planks of the table, resisting the urge to pick at the soft flecks of lichen growing upon the worn wooden surface. "Do you think they were angry with her . . . because of me?"

Athenza held her peace and turned to Vraise who

wetted his lips and scratched the back of his neck. "If they were, that's not your fault." Vraise shrugged. "How were you to know how they would react to Samara's offer? And if Samara did and chose this path anyway, then that's her decision. Not yours."

He smiled as their gazes met. "You're a lot more worried about everyone around you than I thought you would be." He bit off a chunk of his roll, chewing contentedly. A quick flare of mischief brightened his eyes. "I hope that extends to me during these undoubtedly dangerous magic lessons they've prepared for us."

Rowan couldn't help but chuckle at his swell of optimism. "I'll do what I can."

The three of them settled into a comfortably quiet dinner. Rowan's thoughts kept bouncing between the guide who had led them to this point and her appointment with the Sorceress, Oracle, and Lucien that evening. The frequent worried glances she received from Athenza communicated that her mentor was also thinking about the blood oath but waiting for the right moment to speak to Rowan about it alone. What about their arrival in the Academia Magica had made Samara relent and want to tell Rowan the truth of what had happened to the first offerings? And what else had she concealed?

"I think I've waited as long as I can," Vraise declared. "We have to meet at least a few new people before we turn in."

Rowan sipped her now chilly tea, tugging herself out of her contemplation to focus on Vraise. "Everyone thinks we're odd or dangerous."

Vraise's lips parted as he prepared to argue with her but then thought better of it. "Well enough," he admitted, "that may be true, but that doesn't mean they need to *keep* thinking that's the case."

"And how do you suppose we change their minds?"

At that, her new companion laughed. "It's a simple matter of charming them and making ourselves the people to know."

Rowan glanced at Athenza who smiled to herself and leaned back, declining to get involved. She sighed. Her circle of friends in the conclave had joined her here—Athenza and Majestyk. Vraise deserved to feel similarly at ease, especially given the unspecified dangers of their impending "offering-hood." "How do we start such a . . . transformation?"

"I'm glad you asked," Vraise answered brightly. "Perhaps we can seek out other offerings? I'm sure they're equally as nervous as we are."

Rowan's instinct to avoid befriending other offerings was nearly as disconcerting as the name itself. Why befriend someone you would either be pitted against or would soon lose? She pressed her fingernails into her palms. That was precisely the reaction the Pentacle wanted them to have. One of the surest ways of thwarting it was to develop alliances amongst themselves. "That makes sense. How can we tell if someone else is an offering? They said we were the last to arrive."

Vraise adjusted the fold of his cream-hued collar. "It is my fervent hope that we are and will continue to be set apart by not wearing the robes."

She choked on her fruity tea and, as soon as she was

done coughing, laughed openly for the first time in days. "Is that what you're worried about? The robes?"

Her companion's eyes widened. "Aren't you?" He glanced about and leaned even closer, tipping off his cushion to better whisper to Rowan, "I mean, they aren't flattering *or* distinctive. Though I would never say as much to the Faces, of course."

Even Athenza chuckled at such an innocent concern in the face of so much uncertainty.

Cheered by his companions' encouragement, Vraise sauntered away to the nearest table of diners who weren't clad in robes.

Athenza took advantage of the opening to ask Rowan about her blood oath and her private conversation with Samara.

"She was trying to tell you something, was she not?" Athenza asked, her voice low in case any of the nearby diners might be listening.

Rowan nodded. "She didn't finish whatever the warning was before we met the Faces, but I think she lied to us about the first offerings."

Athenza frowned. "Lied in what way?"

Rowan shook her head. "I think they're dead." She had gone over the other possibilities of what the half-delivered warning might mean and could come to no other conclusion. "She called them sacrifices, though she later said she'd exaggerated." Rowan drummed her fingertips along the tabletop, weighing the possibilities for how they might uncover more. "Maybe I can find out when I speak to the two Faces and the guardian."

Her mentor went rigid at the mention of Lucien. "I

know I encouraged you before, but I think a blood oath is a mistake."

She had been giving it a great deal of thought as well. The piles of fresh dirt arranged as funereal mounds left few other possibilities beyond the fate of the first offerings. What might induce the Pentacle to be more careful this time around? To not sacrifice them but, instead, truly allow them to grow their magic, to do what Rowan had set out to accomplish?

She glanced at Athenza and sought out Vraise who was grinning on his way back to their table, a new acquaintance in tow. Would she find out quickly enough for the three of them to survive?

The new acquaintance was dressed similarly to Vraise, with a short, quilted jacket atop pressed trousers with wide legs. Rowan had noted her from a distance— the elf smiled while speaking to others but, outside of conversation, narrowed her eyes in close observation of her surroundings.

"Good news." Vraise grinned. "I *have* found another offering, one who's been here a couple days. Orella."

Her straight brown hair slipped out of its tuck behind her ears as she lowered to shake first Athenza's hand and then Rowan's as Vraise made their introduction.

At the mention of Rowan's name, Orella's expression soured. "The one with the special appointment with two of the Faces," Orella said, her mouth downturned as though she smelled something unpleasant. "Despite the fact that you just arrived *and* had your agent sent away all in one go."

Rowan resisted the urge to draw away from the offering. Was it possible she was jealous that Rowan's arrival had sparked a punishment for the person who recruited her and conflict between the Faces all at once?

Or was it something simpler? She hadn't had time to bathe after their arrival, and the musk and sweat of Gardenia likely still lingered about her person. Rowan bit her lower lip and sent a wave of affection toward the cervidae's pen. She would check on the cervidae as soon as time allowed the following day to ensure she was settling into the herd well.

"Orella was telling me that our lessons start tomorrow," Vraise said, his excitement bubbling over and seeking expression in the increased movement of his hands as he spoke.

The happier Vraise looked, the more sideways glares Rowan received from Orella. This was why she had avoided company outside of Athenza and Majestyk back at the conclave. With the two of them, Rowan knew where she stood. Vraise she was figuring out. The other offering seemed to dislike her immediately and however Rowan tried to participate in the conversation, Orella's impression of her wasn't improving.

But all of that would have to wait. For the present, she had an appointment with two powerful mages and a guardian to keep.

Rowan excused herself, taking a moment to squeeze Athenza's hand to reassure her before slipping across the grounds of the Academia Magica as the sky faded from orange to indigo.

CHAPTER SEVENTEEN
TALI

From the single rampart of Sanctuary the forces of the Luz had regained, Tali watched the shielded circle of soldiers march across the field of battle, vultura falling back in their wake. Five distinct explosions of alchemist's fire burst around them in a coordinated pattern, with forces from within their ranks quickly filing forward and establishing a new perimeter which those who had been on the outside sought to fill. The strategy was advanced yet simple—an old maneuver of the Blazing Battalion. One Tali hadn't seen them use in some time.

Part of the formation's success lay in the exchange of front and rear forces. The brief reprieve granted those who had been fighting sword to sword a chance to resettle their nerves before battling forward again.

"Do you see this one, Ilona?" Tali prayed to her silent titan. "Such bravery, at my service, and in your name."

All around her the screams of the dying members of

the Luz rang out, making it difficult for her to concentrate on her prayers.

She would burn her way out soon enough, the chaos of the battle shielding her from prying eyes that might wonder at the blazing white of her light since the First Battle of Sanctuary rather than the pale gold it had been before.

There had nearly been an upset in Beacon, but she had seen the priests who raised the alarm against her removed. They experienced the burn of her light firsthand.

She left the silhouettes of the blast on one of the sacred inner courtyard walls, the black a sharp contrast to the ivories and golds of Ilona's temple. No others had dared raise their voice since.

The attempt to retake the city had been an utter failure—that much was clear now. Given the opportunity again, would she have taken the risk?

Tali frowned down at her diminished forces. The true impact of the battle would be clearer after the return to Respite.

Some degree of treachery is necessary—inevitable—in so complex a war, Tali reminded herself. It was one of the truths Ilona had whispered to her in the darkness, one to which Tali held tightly.

For moments of doubt, she'd kept the missive sent to her by Respite's alchemists near at hand.

In the weeks between her scouts' reports of Briznexi's rumored departure from Sanctuary and the confirmation that the dragon would be absent, granting Tali and the Luz an opportunity for redemption in Ilona's eyes, there had been several attacks against the alchemists' hideouts scattered throughout Eldura.

The alchemists of fire in Respite had captured and tortured the aggressors against them, discovering a pair of individuals called "offerings" from deep within the Pentacle's secret workings.

We were not immediately able to make sense of the foresters' attack, they wrote. *Their assassins struck our outer camp in the dead of night. But with the news from across our network, for which we are most grateful to you, Field Commander, we have uncovered a pattern in the purpose of their disparate attacks. It seems to be motivated by an ancient belief, one maintained by the druids and other pre-urban cultures whose remnants linger in Lis-Maen. These beliefs revolve around a former, deceased titan by name of Verdigris and a figure said to be this titan's granddaughter, Lilia.*

The stories exist in only fragments now, and our scribes are still piecing through them. Our discoveries thus far have uncovered the suggestion of a preferential power or sacredness found within a balance between the elements, a union we have never, in our experiments, found possible or worthwhile. But according to these myths, the union of the six elements creates an undying—or re-living—being that can perpetuate itself and its elemental stores even after death.

A second branch of these fragments suggests a recurrence of souls, for lack of a better explanation. Some of the more apocryphal foresters believe that this Lilia will return to their woods and, when she does, she will make way for this elemental convergence.

Most pertinent to our purposes—if the forest mages successfully create one or more of these elemental warriors, they would have, in essence, a perfect weapon—one who united the elemental potential of a champion and the everlasting fortitude of the undead.

On a last, disturbing note, a third thread of the foresters' records indicates deliberate effort toward this end. Pursuit of this path would put the soldiers of Lis-Maen on near-equal footing with our elite fighting units. We leave it to you, Field Commander, to determine whether the pursuit of such a path is enough to name the peoples of Lis-Maen, particularly their leaders the Pentacle, the enemies you have warned the Secret Council they would become or whether such a determination could only be made after and if their experiments succeed.

Our recommendation, should such an event transpire, is to abandon all pretext of allowed neutrality on Lis-Maen's behalf and the immediate seizure of any and all of these elemental warriors for study and duplication before eliminating the enemy's perfect weapon soldier experiments.

Tali had forced her archivists through a series of sleepless nights in the interim, attempting to uncover any similar such attempts throughout history. One found a few scant records of blood experiments performed in Sanctuary before it had centralized as a great city-state, back when it had been called Draykemire.

She had the successful archivist put away for a time, at least until she was able to retrieve the records. The possible risk to their safety was of greater priority than the archivist's stated needs of independence and freedom of movement in their research.

If the Pentacle uncovered what she'd found, the delicate scale of their loyalty might tip into Alessandra's favor. Like the generals, Tali had no desire to side with the woodland mages, but like the Glade of Shadows which was burning even now, their land provided the perfect shield to protect the Cities, and their peoples could fuel Alessandra's bloodlust while the Cities prepared for a more decisive attack to drive back the dark goddess.

Tali smiled to herself as she weighed the particulars of the plan from the single reclaimed rampart, the forces of the Luz struggling valiantly below. It perfectly coincided with the claim the forest peoples often made, that the Cities would not treat them as equal allies.

Why should we, when you are so much weaker, so disposable in the grand scheme?

MARCON

The lingering energy of the alchemists' fire still flickered across Marcon's fingertips as he told Cole and Vateri about fighting his way out from behind their enemy's lines, a battalion captain and the soldier in blue by his side.

"Her armor sounds like she's somehow connected to Thalyssa," Vateri said, frowning at the possible connection to the Titan of Water. The healers had placed her arm in a sling that rested against her chest. "But I didn't think there were any waterweavers in the ranks of the Luz, much less connected to the battalion."

Marcon shrugged, reflecting upon the soldier's

connection to the battalion captain. They had each shone brighter in their proximity to one another. It seemed too private a detail to share with his friends even though it didn't involve him directly. He hadn't realized the ways in which he'd given up on that degree of attachment to another. *One day*, he told himself.

Through the dramatic events of the afternoon and evening, Cole and Vateri had taken a tentative step toward finding such fulfillment for themselves. Marcon doubted Vateri had noticed the way Cole kept casting worried glances in her direction, the extra care he took in addressing her, but she would in time.

He lowered his gaze, staring into the fire, granting the two of them the space he could without worrying Vateri by withdrawing early. Maybe something worthwhile would come out of this disastrous Second Battle after all.

The cavalry had not fared much better, Cole related to Marcon and Vateri after Marcon had finished his tale. A pall hung over the camps, with the cries of the wounded still echoing out from the medicos' tents. Others called out the names of the dead while those who had turned in early continued fighting the undead in their sleep.

Field Commander Silversword had punctuated the rescue of the Battalion by flying down from a secret position upon the ramparts, blasting rays of light from out of the side of a pale blue airship that had rested invisibly behind the lines of the Luz.

Her display of the might of the champions, though

she was but one, earned them all a greater assurance of rest for the night.

Unlike the evening before, there was little talk of the next day of the battle to come. Their numbers had been reduced by nearly half, and they had only just managed to maintain the initial ground they'd claimed outside the wasteland surrounding Sanctuary's ruins. The few who dared speak of the next day did so with grumbling trepidation.

Marcon could only hope the commanders had a wiser plan in place that might see less loss of life and more gains. Despite saving the battalion, a feat from which his chest still swelled, he struggled to see how they could possibly retake a city already so lost.

Rezza stopped by their campsite as she made her rounds. "You fought well today, Colabra," his commander said, balancing a damp cloth against the swollen side of her face where she'd nearly lost an eye in the battle. Rezza shook her head. "If the battalion's captain gets his way, they'll be promoting you away from me soon enough."

Cole and Vateri gasped, their side conversation utterly forgotten.

"My superiors are impressed with the lot of you," Rezza added before they could question her further. "As soon as we've made it back to Respite, expect to celebrate."

Despite the ache in his limbs, including a scratch along his back and a deep bruise of his knee that he couldn't remember receiving, Marcon couldn't sleep.

After working toward it for so long, finally, a position within the battalion might be his.

And for his friends to receive a promotion along with him . . . Marcon smiled, staring up at his tent overhead. Such a turn in fortune seemed nigh impossible.

He must have dozed off because in the middle of the night, a sharp bugle sounded, rousing them all from sleep.

"Are we under attack?" Vateri asked, rubbing her eyes with her free hand.

Cole hovered protectively behind her. "No—it's the wrong signal."

A messenger came darting back toward their section of camp. "It's Respite!" he cried. "The armies of the dead have routed us!"

Shouts of confusion and alarm rang out across their camp.

"What of the soldiers of Bastion, sent to protect the city in our absence?"

"Rezza said they faced storms at sea. They had to turn back."

Marcon's friends met his gaze, their expressions reflecting the horror that had sunk into his very bones.

"We're cut off," the scout added. "With no protectors, the city will be overrun." He sprinted away again to rouse others. Marcon grabbed his sword and shield and, Vateri and Cole at his side, went to find Rezza.

Forget the reclaiming of Sanctuary. They needed to return to Respite. Now.

CHAPTER EIGHTEEN
ROWAN

J ust before she stepped beyond the borders of the Druidess's holdings within the Academia Magica, where rambling roses stretched furtive tentacles into the middle ground of the shared central spaces, Rowan altered course. With Athenza's warning echoing in her mind, she doubled back to her room to check on Majestyk.

The dracat was still sleeping, her head curled into the circle she'd made of her paws.

Viridian looked up from a similarly curled posture upon her raised platform bed. *"I am certain your companions have already wished you caution, room-friend, but I should like to do the same. Wherever you are coming from, matters among the Pentacle are far from what they seem."*

Rowan accepted the daimon's warning with a soft smile of thanks. "I'll be back before midnight."

"That is well. You will need your rest before the dawn breaks."

As she left their chamber, Rowan tugged her woolen jacket tighter around her shoulders, grateful for once for its rough-spun edges, the warm smell of home caught within its fibers. The bright green of the cloth always reminded her of Paupa as it was the same shade he insisted upon for the vests he wore throughout the year. "When you have eyes like ours, sapling, it is your duty to show them off."

He tended to say as much with a tug upon one of her braids before sending her out on a scavenging mission of some kind. She'd return with mushrooms in her pocket or buttons in hand to find Paupa with red-rimmed eyes, their hue even brighter than usual.

As she grew older, she realized that he used such opportunities to grieve for her mother.

Rowan released an uneven sigh and hurried back the way Samara had led them that afternoon. It wasn't that she never longed for the sort of partnership her parents had shared, but the years alone had taught her to long for something better instead—the worthiness that would come from succeeding in her goal.

As she neared the Sorceress's steepled building, an adept was waiting for her at the base of the outside stairs. "This way," the young woman said, signaling that Rowan should follow after her through a side passageway.

"You will learn all the secret routes in time," Samara had assured Rowan and her companions as they remarked among themselves at the size of the Pentacle's holdings in Delmoir. Before leaving the conclave, she never could have imagined such a vast, settled territory *existing*, much less that so large a space was dedicated to the study and practice of magic.

She clutched the ends of her sleeves in her fists and did as the adept bid.

The hair along the back of Rowan's neck prickled. Two low voices echoed out along the shadowy corridors the adept navigated without pause.

"We made a vow all those years ago," the lower voice murmured. "Whatever it took to bring the Hexblade about, we would do. Whatever the cost."

"Sorceress, I recall, but you can't truly believe that she—"

The voices stopped abruptly as Rowan's guide slid to a stop and rapped her knuckles against the open door of the chamber. "The offering you requested," the adept said, keeping her gaze averted from the two mages standing in the center of the room, a clear crystal orb balanced upon a wooden pedestal between them.

"Excellent," the Sorceress said, barely glancing toward Rowan and the adept. "Be gone then." She waved her hand, dismissing her servitor.

The adept scurried to obey, leaving Rowan hovering in the entryway alone.

She was back where she'd arrived to see the Pentacle that morning, the winding passageway she'd left behind having deposited her near the front of the receiving hall.

Arriving suddenly at her destination, Rowan found herself lost for words. Athenza's whispered fears came drifting back to her. It was true that she didn't know the motivations of the two figures before her.

But she knew her own. *Whatever it takes*, she'd

promised herself. She would prove herself worthy of the hearttree and become one of its protectors.

"Oh good, you've all arrived," the low, melodic voice that hadn't entirely left her mind the whole of the afternoon drawled from the opposite end of the audience chamber as Lucien emerged from whichever side passageway he'd appeared through during Rowan's first audience before the Faces.

Unlike the Sorceress and the Oracle beside her, he fixed his gaze on Rowan. The guardian gave a small smirk, looking her over and beckoned her nearer.

It was like willing her feet to move as though they were disconnected from her body. How had Grandmother Wolf responded when a band of rogue maera had pressed close against the willow hearttree? Had she hesitated before transforming from fae to daimon, opting for claws instead of swords so she might rend her enemy from existence rather than see even one willow frond set aflame?

Rowan set her jaw and forced herself forward.

The Sorceress and Oracle glanced up at the sound of her footfall upon the stone of the chamber, and she nearly froze again at the dark gleam in the Sorceress's eyes.

To Rowan's relief, the guardian seemed determined to be less rude than those who had requested the audience with her. He continued past them to Rowan's side and spun about next to her, his elbow extended. "I won't make you false promises about the mages before you being without bite, little bird," Lucien purred.

A shiver rushed down Rowan's back as she took Lucien's arm. Did he know about her phoenix?

The gold in his gaze was both strange and familiar. It glinted, beckoning her deeper in as he led her across the room.

"What I *will* urge is that you remind them that you will bite back." His pace was almost languid, given his height, but his ease in movement masked Rowan's hesitation. The smirk from earlier returned as Rowan searched his features.

Why was he so keen to help her? Rowan stilled the urgent flapping of the question and nodded. A reminder of inner strength was precisely what Grandmother Wolf would have shown. What Schaeza would show. "I can do that."

His smirk twisted into a lopsided smile. "It is good that you have found your voice, little bird." Lucien inclined his head to her. "Remember that you don't bargain with them alone."

She doubted whether Athenza would find Lucien's reassurances comforting, but she'd deliberately come to this meeting without her mentor by her side. They were in a new place, with new rules, and she was entering into a blood vow with the two most powerful mages in all of Lis-Maen.

"You made quite an impression upon Samara," the Sorceress said as Rowan and Lucien neared the center of the room. "Before you allow that fact to take too firm a root within your mind, allow me to impart the truth of your position here—you are on equal footing with every other offering. Equally . . . valuable as the rest."

The way she said "valuable" implied that she found the offerings to be anything but.

Lucien lowered his arm as he deposited Rowan on one side of the pedestal, the Sorceress towering over her and the Oracle on the other.

Don't argue, Rowan reminded herself. *Don't rise to their baiting.* "Thank you for clarifying," Rowan answered, proud of herself for maintaining an evenness in her voice that was far calmer than what she felt. "I understand that Samara has already departed?"

The Sorceress's smile was cruel. "Do you want to spend the little time you have with the two of us speaking of the agent who brought you here? I assure you—there is little need for you to ever worry about her again."

Rowan frowned. The Sorceress's cold manner left up to chance whether Rowan believed the threat lingering behind her words was more directly tied to Samara or to herself and the other offerings.

"However," the Oracle interjected, "the pair of us have been discussing your demands, and we believe that we have worked out a way in which we can honor your request and see that you aren't receiving unfair treatment."

"What role does fairness play in our vow?" Rowan answered.

From just behind her elbow, Lucien cleared his throat.

"I mean—what arrangement did the two of you work out?" Rowan refrained from glancing back at Lucien to confirm whether she'd taken the right tack. She could not swallow the words once uttered.

The Sorceress clasped her arms behind her back and leveled her dark gaze with Rowan's. This time, no bolts of blue echoed out of the darkness. "The path before you and the other offerings is not an easy one," she explained. "Our first round of tests failed utterly, leading to the death of all save a few. For them, we shall see what the future holds." The Sorceress shrugged as though there was nothing unusual about such a declaration.

Rowan's mind reeled. The graves she'd seen on the way here—the ones Samara had avoided her questions about—those *had* been the first offerings. What she'd told Athenza had been true.

"As my supplicant told you," the Sorceress continued, "we've taken new precautions this time around." She pressed her lips together, preventing a smirk and creating a sharp pout instead. "There are other side projects in play which should help matters." She glanced at the Oracle.

"You needn't concern yourself with such measures," the Oracle supplied, her tone disengaged, almost bored. "And the caution the Sorceress bids should be heeded— it is unavoidable that some of the new offerings will die." She waved her hand, loss of life being a matter of course.

The back of Rowan's mouth dried. *Athenza. Vraise.* The others along their hall, their futures hidden behind closed doors, many of which opened onto graves . . .

"Alongside these new precautions, we have found ways of mitigating dangers. Incorporating stopgaps into our tests." She grinned. "So long as fortune favors you, you have little to fear."

Rowan's lips parted—coming from one gifted with Sight, was such a message a boon?

"But the other precaution taken was really the removal of an impediment from before. Put into place by my predecessor." At that, the deep purple of the Oracle's gaze flashed.

If Rowan remembered correctly, the Oracle's role was matrilineal, and so her mother was the predecessor of whom she was speaking. Within the outskirts, there were rumors about precisely what such a transition entailed. Some even whispered that the Oracle devoured her mother's eyes so that the visions might pass along to her, but she didn't want to believe such barbarousness was possible within the boundaries of Lis-Maen. Leave such deprivations to the Cities, to their armies and courts.

"It was one such impediment that kept you from our scouts' notice for so long, and that should be cheering news indeed."

Behind her, Lucien cleared his throat again. "Speak more plainly if you wish to honor the dictates of a blood vow."

"Fine," the Oracle huffed. She glared at Lucien before turning her attention back to Rowan. "There were efforts made before I came into power, attempts at reviving ancient magics the likes of which Lis-Maen has not seen for an age."

At this, her phoenix stirred.

"The margin enclaves that attempted such revivals

were left out of our initial recruitment for both adepts and offerings." She exhaled audibly again. "In short, if there are traces of success in these older efforts, they should likewise spell a greater probability of success in our new attempts."

Rowan's fingertips tingled. The revival of ancient magic like that of Verdigris was precisely the sacred work her parents had believed in, though it had cost them both their lives.

She rolled the set of her shoulders, pushing away the intruding memory of Athenza's fear from the corridor, her insistence that Rowan's phoenix had to stay hidden. "Are you saying there's a connection between the ancient magic they were trying to revive and the experiments you've recruited a new round of offerings for?"

The Oracle bobbed her head side to side as though see-sawing her answer within her mind before speaking it aloud. "More or less."

Rowan grinned. "So what you said when I arrived wasn't entirely true." She looked up at the Sorceress. "There *is* something special about me and the new offerings."

The dark eyes flashed. "Perhaps." She met Rowan's grin with a cruel smile of her own. "Do you have the fortitude to prove as much one way or another?"

The Sorceress withdrew a blade from within the sleeve of her robe. Blade and handle together were little longer than her hand. The sigils of the six elements had been carved into the wood of the handle.

Rowan reached out and took the proffered blade, careful to avoid touching her skin to the Sorceress's.

She couldn't have said what she was afraid of happening if they did touch, only that she wished to avoid it.

The two mages watched Rowan hungrily.

She stretched out her other hand over the orb with the ceremonial dagger balanced against her palm.

"I bind myself to you, to this orb, to the sacred task of uniting the six elements," Rowan said, casting the vow they'd demanded into her own words. "I will allow you to avail yourselves of my inherent magic in pursuit of the six in exchange for the protection of Willow Glen and its hearttree."

Rowan winced as she sliced into the center of her palm and formed it into a fist over the orb.

Blood dripped from her hand down upon its surface.

Watching it, she gasped. The blood pooled along the top before dripping within rather than pouring down the sides.

From behind her, the guardian reached out and clasped his hand around hers.

"Ready?" he murmured as his chest pressed against her back.

Rowan nodded and Lucien tightened his hold around her hand, quickening the flow of blood across the top of the orb.

Along the back of her hand, she felt the wet stickiness of blood. He'd cut his palm without the other two seeing. But why?

She stiffened, relaxing only slightly at the soft "shh," that sounded against the shell of her ear. "Trust me," he murmured so faintly that the Oracle and Sorceress couldn't hear, soft enough that Rowan wasn't sure whether she had imagined it or not.

Two heartbeats passed. "That's enough," Lucien said aloud, pulling Rowan's hand back from the orb and twisting her palm to face the ceiling. With a flourish, he withdrew a handkerchief from within his robe and wrapped it quickly around her hand.

He's covering over the blood he shed, Rowan realized as the guardian withdrew his own hand deeper into his sleeve.

The moment her training as an offering allowed, she would find the archives and research blood vows. There was clearly more at work here than she had initially allowed herself to believe.

With a shaking hand, Rowan held out the ceremonial blade to the Sorceress who accepted Rowan's vow and made one of her own, swearing the protection of Willow Glen so long as Rowan proved herself true and used her magic to strengthen the will of the Pentacle.

A soft touch at her back prevented her from protesting the twisting of words. She'd made her promise as carefully as she could and wasn't surprised the Sorceress would do the same.

The mage handed the bloodied blade to the Oracle who swore on what had been, what was, and what was yet to be. "By the blood of the ancients, the sacrifices of our predecessors, and by our own spirit-fire, we swear to the protection of Willow Glen so long as the offering's magic empowers our ends."

The Sorceress and Oracle met Rowan's gaze. "You may leave us now," the Sorceress said. "Guardian Lucien, would you do the honors?" She nodded toward the orb before them.

He reached out with both hands, and Rowan's eyes widened at finding his palm undamaged. "It would be my honor," he said with a slight bow.

Lucien lifted the black cloth from beneath the orb and wrapped it soundly before scooping it gently into his arms. The orb that would hold her vow looked strangely small in the guardian's hands. "I'll show you out, sparrow," he said, glancing at Rowan. "These two have more scheming to do."

The Oracle exhaled her protest, but his words only widened the Sorceress's smile. "Right you are, Guardian. We do."

"You did well," Lucien murmured as they reached the door of the audience chamber.

"Why did you—"

"Shh," he urged again, raising a taloned finger to his full, gray lips. "In time, sparrow. In time." He nodded back the way Rowan had come. "I'm sure your friends are anxious to hear of your experience." The gold of his eyes shimmered in the darkness. "Your survival here will depend upon knowing who you can trust."

Rowan lingered by his side. "Does that include you?"

The guardian's full smile flashed so quickly, she could almost have convinced herself she'd imagined such a sighting in the darkness. "I suppose we shall have to see, sparrow." With that, he spun on his heels and strode away.

Shadows pooled behind the flapping of the cloak that

stretched beneath his wings. They swarmed over him, obscuring the guardian from sight.

Rowan clutched her bandaged hand to her chest and hurried back to her dormitory where she knew Athenza would be waiting.

Viridian and Majestyk were there too, the dracat already overly familiar with Rowan's daimon room-friend. In Rowan's absence, she had decided to impress upon the giant wolf her scent and, as Rowan began her story, Majestyk paced back and forth along Viridian's paws, rubbing her head against Viridian's legs and the puffy sides of her fur.

The dracat's casual adaptation to their environment helped Rowan feel a little more settled within the academy, despite the jarring series of events following their arrival.

When she recounted her vow to Athenza and Viridian, she omitted the guardian's blood that had pressed against her palm, the way he'd bound an oath alongside hers.

Her mentor shook her head as Rowan spoke, alternately staring at the dark and mottled reflection of Rowan and Viridian's room through the window and running her tongue over her teeth, a sign Rowan had learned in childhood meant Athenza was barely restraining what she truly wanted to say.

As had been the case in her younger years and remained true now, the words eventually burst from Athenza, causing Viridian's ears to dart back in surprise. "I *told* you to be careful where the guardian was concerned,"

Athenza cried when Rowan revealed that Lucien had been present at the blood vow. "Why was he there? What sort of loyalty does he bear two of the Five Faces?"

"I don't know—"

"And you made the vow anyway!"

"What would you have had me do?" Rowan shot back.

Athenza's breath caught and she clenched her jaw.

Rowan winced and dropped her head. Fighting with Athenza never went well. In the moment, it felt like she was striving for space, for the chance to decide for herself when so much had already been decided for her, when so much had been taken away, and then she pushed away the one elf who had remained by her side and taken care of her. "I'm sorry," Rowan murmured.

Viridian laid her head on her paws, the tip of her tail flicking up occasionally from her bed, which occupied the whole of Majestyk's attention.

The tension in the room remained a taut rope. "I am trying to protect the hearttree, to keep my promise to Paupa, to you. The Pentacle—" Rowan stopped herself. She didn't want to tell Athenza about the offerings. Tomorrow, she would confess what she had learned to Athenza and Vraise, but for tonight, she could let their embers of hope continue to burn.

She tried again. "We aren't valuable to them," Rowan confessed, tightening her hands into fists. She understood Athenza's anger. Its current ran deep within her chest, embedded almost as solidly as her phoenix. "But I found a way to secure our leverage. Even if all it does is present a check against them discarding us, the risk is worth it."

Her mentor disagreed, as Rowan had suspected she would, but Athenza calmed enough to let Rowan walk her back to her room. The druid reached out and caught Rowan's hand after settling onto her narrow bunk. "If the only value they find is in the magic of your blood, sapling, then they are lacking even a thimble-full of wisdom."

Rowan returned to her room and bid goodnight to her room-friend. She lay awake long afterward, staring at the sloped stone of the ceiling overhead. It was strange to not find the familiar worn, wooden planks she'd known all her life there.

Stranger still to have the memory of dried blood from a silent vow crusted along the back of her hand, washed away but still felt. A vow whose parameters she did not know. Yet.

CHAPTER NINETEEN
ROWAN

The Oracle's confession of the fate of the first offerings still lingered in Rowan's mind as she rose before sunrise the next morning, her eyes scratchy from the lack of sleep.

Even so, her fingertips tingled. Today would be the first where they began their study of magic, where they ignited their attempts to carry the six elements united in one body.

Her daydreams of joining the daimon protectors of the hearttree had been joined by a new imagining—herself at the head of a force of mages, antlered head-dresses and woven crowns of ivy over braids or loose tresses. They didn't bother with the academy's cumbersome robes but each wore the armor of the forest—for herself she'd imagined an armor fashioned from leaves and bark, frightening and alluring all at once for that was what it meant to embody the revived magic of Verdigris. Soft wrappings fashioned from moss formed half-gloved gauntlets and padded the sheafs of bark at her shoulders.

What she and the mages in her vision strode toward, Rowan wasn't yet sure. She sensed fire in the distance, different from the occasional rain of ash from overhead where her phoenix flew openly above her, rather than hidden in the recesses of her mind.

She closed her eyes as she combed the tangles from her hair before deftly braiding it along the nape of her neck and tucking the ends back into the braid to hold it in place. Different elements glowed upon the hands of the mages she envisioned. Earth for herself, fire for Vraise, water for Athenza who joined their ranks with no need for her cane.

The vision was clearer than it had been when she conjured such images in the forest, anticipating what the transformation the Pentacle was preparing them for would be like.

A great shaking of fur from the bed beside hers tugged Rowan from her imagination and back into her cramped stone room, her room-friend, as Viridian called her, hopping down from the mattress and onto the stone floor.

"Will you be joining us this morning?" Rowan asked after she and Viridian exchanged pleasantries. Though she hadn't lived in close proximity to anyone in nearly a decade, the daimon made her feel at ease in their manner together.

"Perhaps I should have confessed as much to you yesterday, room-friend—though my position within the Academia Magica is similar to yours, I am not an offering and so cannot join your first lessons."

Rowan frowned at her misunderstanding. "Similar in what way, then?"

Before she answered, Viridian snuffled the air between them and then opened her mouth in an open pant. *"You smell of inner conflict with a lingering hint of blood,"* the great wolf said within Rowan's mind. *"I do not wish to add to your distress, nor do I wish to burden you with concerns not your own—I say my position is like yours in that I am a bargaining chip, kept here rather than in my home. Part of the 'magical enhancement' of the academy. Allow that to suffice for now."*

Her lips had already parted to protest, but the daimon shook her head. *"Do not be late to your first lesson. And do not underestimate the lengths to which they will go to meet their own ends, especially when the one they seek to harm causes them fear."* Viridian's deep teal gaze flashed, catching Rowan's.

She bit her lips together instead of arguing and turned to go, Viridian's words churning within her mind.

Rowan paused at the door. "Why would they fear me?" She looked back at the daimon whose expression softened and panting returned. "That is what you meant, isn't it?"

Viridian inclined her head. *"You carry the wild magic they fear, the heartbeat of Lis-Maen herself. If they cannot control you, they will seek to diminish you instead, precisely the way they have with this land you call home."*

Rowan drummed her fingertips against the wooden frame of their door before twisting the worn brass knob. "I'm glad they made us roommates," she confessed before sliding out into the hall.

"*As am I,*" the daimon added softly.

She shut the door gently behind her and hurried to rap against Athenza's door. A magic lesson awaited the pair of them. Rowan's pulse skipped ahead, visions of elemental sparks and intricate potions shimmering in her imagination.

"Coming, coming," Athenza grumbled from behind the faded oak of her door. The clicking of her cane sounded as the druid puttered back and forth across her room.

A pair of elves emerged from the door beside Vraise's, both of them with matching mops of curly brown hair. They glanced nervously at Rowan before hurrying the opposite way down the hall to the winding stair that led outside.

The question of what to tell Athenza about the blood oath from last night remained unanswered. Rowan had nearly resolved to tell her mentor nothing when the druid's door swung open and their gazes met. Dark shadows hung beneath Athenza's eyes, and Rowan's nerve faltered.

"Are you alright?" she asked instead.

"Fine," Athenza lied with a forced smile.

Rowan raised an eyebrow. They'd known one another too long for the druid to dismiss her that easily.

"Just struggling to adapt to these stone confines," Athenza admitted with a sigh.

"Go-od mor-ni-ing," Vraise's singsong greeting echoed out from behind Rowan, interrupting her conference with Athenza. "Are we ready to begin our magical lessons?" Vraise frowned. "Magic lessons?" He gasped, his gaze darting about the hallway in case someone else was there and had overheard him. "Gah, which is it? What did I say to Orella yesterday? She'll think I'm a dullard!"

"Vraise."

He jolted at Rowan's grounding tone and stopped his frantic questioning.

"You said you wanted to make friends among the offerings, right?"

With a slight pout to his lip, Vraise nodded.

"I think that will be easier if we remain calm."

She offered her arm to loop through his.

Majestyk's irritated cry resounded from behind her door as the dracat scratched at the wood.

Rowan shook her head. "She would have been very angry with me for keeping her outside all morning, and she will be just as irritated at being kept indoors."

"I find her quite agreeable," Vraise countered. "If we fail at our initial friend-making, perhaps we can dress her in a sweater, tiny scarf, and pair of spectacles and see if she can help round out our circle of acquaintances."

The elf was definitely making for more enjoyable company than she'd initially believed possible. So much so that she would only laugh a little at the scratching he would receive if he tried to dress Majestyk as an archivist.

Rowan could only hope the other offerings would prove to be as open as Vraise was. By banding together, they might stand a chance of survival.

The soft summer breeze brushed across Rowan's face, the scent of hyacinths catching in her nose as they crossed the Druidess's holdings to a domesticated pond with winding walking paths, small bridges, and six crystal pillars standing in homage to each of the elements.

Almost two-dozen fellow offerings, marked by their lack of robes and overabundance of nervous energy, waited on the far edge of the pond for their first lesson to begin. Rowan noted the twins who lived beside Vraise and the elf with brown hair who had not been thrilled to make Rowan's acquaintance the evening before.

This third elf, Orella, looked Rowan over again, her expression unmoving, but she waved when Vraise caught her eye.

Much better to befriend someone who's skilled at making friends, Rowan decided.

As they arrived at the edge of the pond, a fae with long, pointed ears and spring-green skin greeted the three of them, gesturing to a space directly before them on the grass. Rowan sensed the unsteady energy of her fellow offerings as it flitted across the pond's surface, bouncing between the elemental pillars, before finally drifting up into the boughs of a river oak tree whose branches stared down at their reflection in the pond below.

Rowan settled onto the cold, damp earth and closed her eyes, settling her own energetic flow. With her fellow offerings omitted from her sight, she took in the chirruping of birds hidden within the oak and the bright whiffs of wildflowers that lingered on the breeze.

She knew without looking that Athenza would be performing a similar grounding ritual—after all, it was she who had insisted Rowan take such steps before beginning any magical interaction after Paupa had passed.

Her internal landscape settled, Rowan sank deeper into her own mind and extended her thoughts toward the slumbering phoenix—

The instructor's voice drew her back before she could brush the bird's feathers. "I am Professor Tullemaien, energetic specialist, and most delighted to make the acquaintance of our newest recruits." They smiled at the gathered pupils, completely ignoring the unease around them.

Rowan wondered whether such pretending was a normal practice of whatever an "energetic specialist" was or if the professor, by design, was waiting for the offerings to regulate themselves.

She found the collective unease distracting, the energy feeding off itself.

"For your first lesson, the headmistress has deemed it advisable for each of you to begin to practice with your first element. At the end of the day, we will pay a brief visit to the imbuers so you have an idea of what the coming lessons will entail."

The fae withdrew a parchment scroll from within their draped vest—the design of which Rowan noted for herself for later when she sketched out her next knitted garment—the additional pockets would perfectly complement the bodice, draped sleeves, and breeches that she already preferred. Wearing one's pockets was much simpler than toting them about in a satchel, Athenza liked to say.

"Ahem," Tullemaien cleared their throat in what Rowan hoped would not be a continuing habit but more to do with the pollen hanging about. "Elemental assignments—the element of air—" Their professor named four offerings and pointed to the pillar depicting the sign of Atamos—a triangle with three straight bands rushing through it. Light and darkness garnered four more offerings each.

To Rowan's relief, Tullemaien referred to them as "students" rather than offerings. It was an optimistic gesture that she hoped would catch on across their numbers.

She hadn't considered that their elemental training would begin with a single element rather than the interactions between them. How were they to be separated?

The fae named four more students to the element of earth, sparking an internal peal of disappointment for Rowan.

With only fire and water left, their numbers were growing thin. Gazing out across the pond, Rowan noted the increased energetic ease among the offerings. They were introducing themselves, shaking hands, exchanging smiles.

This might work.

"Element of fire," Tullemaien said. "Orella, Rowan—"

"No."

Eight pairs of eyes turned to the figure who had

disrupted the professor's careful ordering of the offerings.

Tullemaien adjusted the round spectacles at the end of their nose and squinted at Athenza. "Beg pardon?"

The druid leaned upon her cane, her shoulders relaxed, posture fully at ease. "It's a mistake is all," Athenza said with a shrug.

Studiously, the druid avoided Rowan's gaze.

The fae stared down at their list and back at Athenza. "And why is that?"

"You're an elemental expert, aren't you?" She kept an airiness to her tone that Rowan knew meant Athenza wasn't telling the full truth.

With faltering forbearance, Tullemaien withdrew the spectacles from their nose and tucked them into a chest pocket on their vest. "I have just told you as much."

Athenza smirked, daring the scholar to cross her. "Then you already know the answer. And why she was assigned the fire in the first place."

Tullemaien fumbled for words before grumbling under their breath, rolling the scroll of parchment back into their pocket. They assigned Athenza in Rowan's place and sent Rowan to the pillar of water with Vraise, a young elf who couldn't be much older than seven named Forsythia, and a blond elf who introduced herself as Yatha.

"Excuse me, professor," Orella whined before following Athenza toward the pillar of fire. "Why isn't she obeying her assignment from the Sorceress?"

Rather than irritation at the continued discussion of a clearly uncomfortable subject, Tullemaien turned the flat force of their smile on the overeager elf. "Fire needs to be controlled, Orella, wouldn't you agree?"

"Yes, of course," she answered brightly.

"And would you rather control an inferno or a campfire?"

Orella frowned. "A campfire, I suppose."

Tullemaien's smile tightened at the edges. "Then you have your answer."

The professor went around the circle, doling out the same instructions to each group of four offerings. "Focus your energies on the pillar," Tullemaien said. Beside Vraise, Yatha kept wiping her palms along her thighs. Forsythia grinned up at Rowan, her dark hair framing iridescently clear eyes, saying nothing.

Rowan frowned at the fae's instructions. How were they supposed to withdraw water from a crystal pillar marked with an upside-down triangle and two beams shooting through it?

Yatha moved her lips silently as she worked. Vraise started by taking different postures in relation to the pillar—he stood with hip out, hand resting beneath his chin. With hands on hips. Arms crossed shaking his head.

Forsythia simply turned in a circle, humming to herself, fingertips holding the corners of her dress as she spun.

Rowan's gaze drifted toward Athenza and her position before the pillar of fire.

Had her mentor truly thought Rowan couldn't handle the flames, even after Rowan had proved herself before the whole of the conclave at Samara's test?

Across from Athenza, Orella focused intently on the pillar, both hands extended. Her hair had begun to stick to her brow with the sweat of her efforts.

What Tullemaien was asking for differed greatly from how Rowan had learned.

"The water is right there," she murmured to Vraise with a nod at the pond.

He shook his head, jaw set, trying to ignore her. He'd opted for a position similar to most of the other offerings with hands outstretched toward the pillar. One of the offerings assigned to the element of earth rested their hand against the pillar and stretched other parts of their body in opposition to it.

The youngest of the bunch, Rowan thought Forsythia was responding most reasonably to their task. She had given up her efforts and relocated to a patch of grass beside the pond, arranging daffodils into a small bouquet.

Rowan tried to do as Tullemaien asked, tried to call upon water from within a crystal pillar. But there was no answer when she sought out the element.

Instead, whispers rose behind her. Whispers from where the element waited in plain sight.

There was nothing for it.

Rowan turned her back on the pillar and focused on the energy of the pond. She closed her eyes, extending her hands out toward it.

Like her phoenix had taught her before it grew quiet, she became the water.

Across her surface, a gentle wind tickled her skin, causing ripples and divots. Along her depths, verdant plant fronds rooted between rocks. They fed her, puri-fied, and she cared for them in return.

Beyond the air, heat and light bathed her surface, stretching her, pulling infinitesimal molecules up and mingling her essence between the three. And at her greatest depths, below the covering of rock, she became the darkness.

"What is going on? Who is responsible for this?" A distant, screeching voice tried to disturb her.

But water is not easily bothered. It moves of its own accord. Fills the space within which it finds itself.

Shrinks. Expands. Rowan knew how to do those things too.

"Whoever it is, stop this right now. You're not ready!"

A warm hand at her elbow. A recently familiar voice calling to her. Murmuring her name. Shaking her shoulder. Turning her about.

One emerges where the six combine . . .

"Rowan."

A series of shouts echoed out across the training area, yanking Rowan from her reverie.

She opened her eyes, struggling to make sense of the sudden chaos surrounding them.

Vraise gripped her shoulders, his eyes wide in panic.

He'd been screaming her name, standing directly in front of her, holding her by the shoulders.

The hair along the back of her neck prickled, and she knew without turning that the pillar of water behind them glowed a perfectly bright, sapphire blue.

What she hadn't expected was the shared glowing of the other pillars.

The brilliant orange of the fire was so bright that three of the four offerings had stumbled back away from it, their hands shielding their eyes. Only Athenza remained before the glow, her skin reddening from the heat.

Voices rang out and fell silent around the pillar of darkness as a cloud of deep amethyst shot out, pooling around the four offerings encircling it.

"Contain, contain," Tullemaien screeched.

But they were too late.

The energy was out of balance between the six pillars, and one by one, they began trying to right their natural flow.

"I can fix it!" Orella cried, reasserting herself before the pillar of fire. She held out her hands and squinted tight her eyes.

Twin gouts of flame shot toward the two offerings who still cowered away from the pillar. Agonized screams filled the training yard as their clothes caught aflame.

Rowan shielded her eyes, one of the few, she hoped, who witnessed the shield the fire formed in front of Athenza—whether the fire element had protected Athenza of its own accord or the druid had shaped the flames into a shield mattered little. Either revelation might draw more attention to her mentor and Athenza's true power, heightening the danger they were already in.

Those nearest to the pillar of fire rushed to the two flaming offerings' aid.

The blond elf who'd been attempting to awaken the pillar of water rounded on Rowan. "What did you *do*?"

she yelled, fury blazing behind her eyes. "You careless, overconfident—"

The elf doubled over, retching an endless stream of water.

Vraise tugged Rowan away as the elf fell to her knees, the stream unending, more water than a person could contain flowing out of her.

"We have to do something!" Vraise shouted. "Tulle-maien! She'll drown!"

Across the courtyard, chaos reigned. Tullemaien was still trying to put out the two flaming offerings, waving their hands uselessly before them.

From the pillar of earth, a cry rang out and immediately fell silent. One of the offerings had been turned to stone.

The three others screamed and sprinted away.

The cloud surrounding the pillar of darkness spit out one of the offerings, sending their body with a bone-crunching snap into the trunk of the oak tree.

Two dark hollows hung skull-like in the center of their face. Hollows where their eyes had been.

A sharp cawing sound rose from the pillar of air. The offerings cowered at its base, their hands clasped over their heads. Their hair lifted into the air and tugged. Spurts of blood darted off their clothes as an invisible flock of predatory birds attacked them.

Vraise shouted in fear as the clear water pouring out of the blond elf turned pink then pure red. The elf clutched her stomach, her body shrinking on itself as they watched helplessly.

Rowan shut her eyes again, wishing she could drown

out the sounds, sprinting through her internal forest and screaming for her phoenix. *Help! We can't stop it. We need you. Please.*

A flash of gold that momentarily blinded her. The rushing of wings and roar of fire.

And then the area around the pond grew still.

A few uneven sobs echoed out. Someone hyperventilated, perched on hands and knees.

Rowan stumbled back from the shriveled form of the blond elf who had screamed at her, the water and blood utterly drained from her body, pooled around the husk that remained.

She clapped her hand to her mouth, trying not to retch.

Vraise stared at her in horror.

And he wasn't the only one.

From the disparate stations around the pond, offerings glared at Rowan.

Athenza stood with gaze lowered before the pillar of fire, slowly shaking her head.

Wordlessly, Forsythia placed a bouquet of flowers as yellow as her namesake into Rowan's hands. She closed Rowan's fingers around the blossoms and patted the back of Rowan's hand, skipping away from the bedraggled offerings.

Rowan stared, open-mouthed after the little girl.

Tullemaien's voice cracked as they called the remaining offerings back to their side.

The glass of their spectacles had splintered. They raised them to their nose, scoffed, and tucked them away again.

"That . . . was far from what I expected in our first lesson," the fae began. They added their glare to that of the other offerings. If Rowan could have sunk into the earth, she would have.

Their disturbingly wide smile returned. "I hope you will remember *that*"—the fae waved their arms, the gesture taking in the whole of the pond and its surroundings—"the next time you decide to show off."

"I didn't—"

Distant whistles sounded and figures clad in gold sprinted toward the offerings.

"I said remember," the fae warned. They turned away from Rowan. "Those of you who are able, gather on the knoll at midday," Tullemaien called.

The offering who'd been flung from the darkness, the dried body of the blond elf, the petrified offering of earth, and the two skeletal piles of ash remained behind as the offerings stumbled away from the pond area.

Tears blurred Rowan's eyes. They couldn't believe that she was responsible for such a tragedy, that she would wield the elements in such a fashion.

As she huddled behind Athenza in the line for the midday meal within the Druidess's towers, a rotten apple core struck her shoulder.

Angry whispers followed her and the druid as they passed between the tables. After they settled along the edge of the dining area, those nearest by lifted their trays and relocated elsewhere.

Vraise was nowhere to be seen.

It was exactly like the conclave had been, only worse.

CHAPTER TWENTY
ROWAN

The unreality of the morning's lesson cast its pall over Rowan and Athenza's lunch.

She couldn't bring herself to eat. At her mentor's orders, she forced down water and two cups of tea.

"I don't know what happened back there, but it wasn't your fault," Athenza said for the fifth time. "Maybe we were set up? A foul enchantment placed in the pillars?"

Rowan shook her head, not wanting to engage with Athenza's constant search for a conspiracy.

They were offerings. The Pentacle had brought them here to die in a series of magical trials. The morning's disaster was exactly what they all should have expected.

What she should have known would transpire when she tried to revive her magic.

Rowan hugged her arms around her waist. It was an impossible dream, proving her worth to the hearttree.

Not even a full day here, and she had blood on her hands and wasn't sure how it had gotten there.

In a blur of greens and the blue of the sky overhead, Rowan dutifully followed after Athenza to the assigned gathering place for the offerings on their way to meet the imbuers.

She hovered at the edge of the group, easily enough done as no one wanted to linger near her.

"What exactly are imbuers?" Orella asked as a wearily cheerful Professor Tullemaien attempted to rouse the group's spirits by saying that the petrified offering might be revived within the month if the healers could work out the precise enchantment that had ripped out of the pillar.

"A fair question but, before we see for ourselves, I may have been hasty in my accusations earlier." Tullemaien gestured for Rowan to come forward.

She refused.

"As you wish," Tullemaien forced, the singsong of their voice returned. "Upon reflection, I realized that such a magical display was impossible for one of you to manage and so can only conclude there was an imbalance within the elements of the training temple. It has been several moons since it was put to use," the professor explained.

The offerings exchanged uneasy glances amongst one another, but Rowan knew it was too late to salvage her reputation among them. How distant her visions of unity and shared effort already seemed.

"And no one cared to check before we used them?" Vraise asked. He had drifted back to Rowan's side. The muscle along his jaw pulsed unevenly and he tried to catch her eye.

Tullemaien simply smiled in answer as if by sheer wishing, the morning's unpleasantness might be washed away.

"Are we still going to see the imbuers?" Orella asked, angling herself toward the center of the group.

Athenza pinched the bridge of her nose, her way of staving off a coming headache.

"Right you are," Tullemaien said. "Follow me."

Professor Tullemaien was either less connected to reality or still caught in the trauma of the morning. They pointed out a few locations of note as they led the offerings across the academy grounds, the cheerfulness with which they had started the lesson that morning returned even though a third of the students had already been carted away to the healers and a few others were deceased.

"And here we approach the imbuers themselves, some of our most interesting recruits. Artists, really, with an aptitude for magic but, more importantly, with transference."

Rowan caught Athenza's eye. Her mentor had raised an eyebrow. For the first time since their arrival in the Academia Magica, even Athenza was intrigued.

Rowan's spirits revived slightly as Tullemaien led the remnants of the cohort around the far edges of the Pentacle's grounds to a series of rounded huts built into the shade of the wall bordering Delmoir.

On the far side of the huts were open-air market

stalls with chairs and small tables arranged in a line, almost like the groomer's station back in the conclave.

Bright colors adorned the huts themselves with varying designs and artistic styles mingled across them.

"Welcome, all," said an elf with pink-and-purple braids, wearing a wrapped tank and flowing pants as she emerged from one of the huts. She used a damp towel to wipe paint from her hands and looked over the offerings. "Fewer of you than we were expecting."

"Not to worry there," Tullemaien added quickly. "Please, begin your tour."

"Not so much a tour really as introductions." The elf turned and called back toward the huts, giving Rowan the chance to study the intricate patterns of tattoos that resembled stained glass that lined the elf's arms and torso.

Lightly muscled curves rippled beneath the elf's tattoos. She caught Rowan's eye, her own gaze sweeping and appreciative as well.

Rowan shifted her grasp of the daffodils she was still holding—a sign of friendship from the silent little girl who had absented herself from the afternoon's tour. Perhaps it was for the best, Rowan thought. Their work was clearly too dangerous for a child to partake in.

The emergence of the figures from the huts only served to confirm her suspicions. The elves, fae, and one human who stepped out of the structures were nearly as disheveled as the offerings, though they were covered with soot, paint, and ink rather than blood and dirt.

"Right," the elf continued. "It will be our responsibility to help you internalize the elements themselves.

We're artists by trade, but we're all students of the art of transference."

The offerings looked between themselves, still uncertain of what the collaboration between them and the artists would entail.

"You may have seen magical tattoos before," Tullemaien added. "This is a similar practice. It will prevent tragedies like we experienced this morning, granting you more individualized control over the elements—"

A piercing scream shot out of the open-air market stall on the far side of the artists' huts, interrupting Tullemaien's reassurances.

Several cohort members joined Rowan in sprinting over to see what was the matter. It concerned her that the alluring artist she'd been speaking to had merely cast her gaze away rather than following.

The scream echoed out again as Rowan, Vraise, and the others made it to the stall's edges.

"Make. It. STOP!" an artist cried, clenching their forearm to their chest. He reared back, his body writhing in pain. Sweat beaded his pale brow and pooled along his hairline.

Two other artists abandoned their canvasses and knelt in the straw at the elf's sides. As he writhed, Rowan caught a glimpse of a silver, tube-shaped device with a needlelike quill on the end.

Suddenly what Tullemaien had said about transference and artists made sense—the Pentacle had recruited artists who imbued magic tattoos—that was how they would impart the offerings with magic, in imitation of the marks the titans were said to have given to their champions.

"Seth!" one of the artists clutching the elf's shoulder cried. "You have to let go!"

Seth's scream answered.

The elf's knuckles were white, clenched tightly around the silver implement.

Rowan darted forward and knelt in the straw beside the two artists.

"He can't let it go," the second artist said.

"And we can't touch it," the first added, nodding to the tattooing needle in Seth's hand.

In near enough proximity to the artist, waves of magical energies pelted off him. The hairs along Rowan's arms stood on end. "What's wrong with the needle?"

The elf writhing on the ground shouted in pain, making his companions wince.

"Someone didn't discharge it. The elements have redoubled. Air and fire—"

Rowan didn't need to hear anything more. She dropped her bouquet of daffodils and shoved her fingers through the straw, as deep into the earth as they could go, grounding herself. With her other hand she reached out and latched hold of the metal device, willing its energetic charge to flow through her and into the ground.

The lightning charged through her, causing her hair to stand on end.

And just as she willed it to, it shot into the ground, dispersing beneath the earth.

The sound of a fading wind rustled past as the last of the trapped energy fell out of the metallic device.

Rowan and the artist both slumped forward. She lay on her back, watching the gentle drift of the clouds overhead.

The artist rolled over, coughing and still cradling his arm.

Vraise hurried forward, checking on Rowan, a gleam of concern returned to his eyes. He smoothed her hair, restraining it back into its braid as best he could.

As the artist sighed and lifted his head, Vraise slipped away again.

The whole of the cohort stared at Rowan and the imbuer. He pushed his hair back from his forehead. His straight black locks immediately fell back into his eyes. "Sethavian Sallis, at your service," he rasped, watching Rowan intently.

His black shirt had gaped open, revealing a series of intricate tattoos across his chest. The artist gave a tiny bow at the waist, granting Rowan a momentary glimpse of the tattoos' continuing pattern down his ribcage. He paused to cough again as he did so. "And I owe you a lifedebt." Sethavian held out his hand, watching Rowan expectantly.

"I'm sure that won't be—"

Athenza's cane poked Rowan's hip from behind.

Rowan sighed and took the artist's hand. "A lifedebt it is."

He grinned—a heart-lifting sideways flash that brightened the gold of his eyes and settled onto the grass. "Run along, you lot," the artist called, waving his hand. "Our practice will continue tomorrow."

The other artists scurried away from Sethavian who

Rowan now realized was the artists' instructor in much the same fashion that Tullemaien was hers. The imbuer with pink-and-purple hair doubled back, returning the daffodils to Rowan's care.

She smiled down at the bright yellow flowers.

A shadow fell over Rowan, the artist, and the blossoms and she turned back to find her own professor hovering behind her shoulder, frowning. "How did you know that tapping into the energy of the earth would work?" Tullemaien asked.

It was the first time she'd seen them hold an expression that wasn't a smile.

Rowan shook her head. "I didn't."

The professor struggled, opening and closing their mouth a few times before they spoke. Finally, they sighed. "I apologize for blaming you earlier. It seems your instincts have served you well."

She nodded to her instructor, outwardly accepting their apology regardless of her feelings toward the fae in fact. "Will our lessons resume tomorrow?"

Tullemaien gave a small, tight smile, their cheerful demeanor finally fractured enough to begin to reveal something more genuine underneath. "Tomorrow you'll be working with elemental specialists, those whose study has prepared them for work with a particular element and allowed them mastery."

For the first time, the elemental adept they had presented themselves as surfaced. With a confident gleam in their eye, they added, "You and the other students focusing on water will be traveling to meet your expert, actually." A genuine smile emerged. "One of the merfolk will be waiting for you in a lagoon just off the Circle Sea."

Rowan gasped, scarcely able to contain her own enthusiasm at such a prospect. After all the tales she'd heard of the ocean, finally being able to see it would make the strangeness of her time in the academy more than worth it.

"Go with your friends and rest," Seth said from beside Rowan. "Once you've had a chance to settle in, we will return to the debt you are due."

"I'm not sure they'd call themselves friends," Rowan mumbled.

That sideways grin answered her. "Not yet, but they will."

Rowan thanked Seth and did as he bid. Her mind was still spinning as she, Vraise, Athenza, and the other offerings who hadn't been sent to the Healer's towers gathered for dinner in the gardens outside the Druidess's dining hall that evening.

This time they clumped together instead of disparately. Bonded by the events of the day, even Orella warmed slightly to Rowan, giving her a small nod rather than glaring.

Viridian joined at Rowan's side, a plate of rare meat piled before her on the table. She snatched at the individual pieces gently and then chomped them down. *"How fares your adventure, room-friend?"* Viridian asked.

Rowan shook her head. "I really don't know how to describe it."

The daimon chuckled inside Rowan's mind. *"Then you are settling in and adapting already."*

She tried to accept Viridian's assurance, tried not to see the corpses laid out from that morning, an echo of the graves she'd passed on their way in. Rowan had been right about how much the offerings would need one another.

Not even the most optimistic among them could dare to believe their trials were about to get easier.

CHAPTER TWENTY-ONE

MARCON

THE ROAD TO RESPITE

The city of Respite was still three-days' march away when the first curls of smoke appeared over the peaks of the Meridienne Mountains. Marcon's gut seized. He would have known the acrid smolder of Alessandra's foot soldiers anywhere, even before he'd spent an interminably long fighting day surrounded by their undead reek in the Luz's foolhardy campaign to reclaim Sanctuary.

A full day and two nights had passed since then, and he still couldn't dispel the sweet rot of decay from his nose.

Such an attack should have been impossible. Respite was too well defended. Every training maneuver he'd ever studied or practiced was founded upon that simple fact.

The city's generals had confirmed it—Alessandra had spent her forces defending Sanctuary and in her campaign across the Glade of Shadows. She didn't have the troops to defend Sanctuary, burn the forest, and advance her chokehold against the Cities United.

Yet the black smoke against the pale blue sky protested what they had been told.

They were wrong. The generals were mistaken.

He coughed against the haze from the battle that still clung to his lungs.

Respite is under attack.

Marcon pushed his way through the stumbling ranks toward his commander. The soldiers jogged with their heads hung low. Their ranks were a third the size they had been when they set out from Respite. Half had perished in the battle, and the injured had been kept behind, Vateri among them. Cole had fought to remain by his side, but the field commander had ordered the cavalry to stay and defend the rear of their forces from a counterattack by the undead who remained behind the walls of Sanctuary.

Like the rest of the weary, desperate soldiers around him, Marcon wished the Luz's leadership had been more mindful of such a possibility before they left Respite.

Rezza hadn't waited for full clearance from Silver-sword before ordering her unit's retreat, and others among the infantry had joined them. She'd roused all who were able-bodied and marched them back through the middle of the night toward Respite.

What the repercussions in the city would be upon their return, if there was a city to return to—this might be one of Commander Rezza's last nights breathing the free, fresh air.

The failed battle to reclaim Sanctuary already felt far removed for Marcon, his chance of promotion all but forgotten.

Vateri had been the first to say her name aloud. "What of Lorieannan?"

All other thoughts bordered on incoherence. Thinking of an entire city endangered, a city of the living, not the dead, was more than he could fathom. Those he'd left behind in Respite. Lorieannan, Joane, Abbot, all outside the city's walls—he could wrap his mind around that, though he saw no way in which their defenses had held. His stomach churned at how he'd left things with Lorieannan, his frustration, even the sense of freedom he'd felt at leaving her behind.

Let her be there, and I'll make it right, he prayed to whichever gods would listen. He had nothing to bargain with, nothing to give. Was it possible she had retreated in time and found Garreth? Abbot and Joane wouldn't leave the children, and children did not flee quickly.

Anger rose alongside blame. *The generals promised she would be safe.*

A pale elven woman sprinted up the mountainside toward them. She wore the brown leathers of the scouts, those positioned between the warfronts and the city centers. Those of elevated birth deemed too important— or too weak—to fight.

Soldiers grumbled as they moved aside. A sea of what had once been white and gold, now stained with soot and ash, parted.

Marcon quickened his pace. *Tell me I'm mistaken.* He had to hear. Had to know.

"Commander!" the elf cried.

From the center of their ranks, the commander slid off her horse. "Aye?" Rezza answered.

The scout doubled over in front of the cavalry. She pressed her hand against her chest, trying to catch her breath. "The horde's pressed against the walls of the city. They're fighting them back from within, but we're cut off." She straightened, her narrow frame curved back, and shook her head. "It's the largest force I've ever seen."

Marcon's blood ran cold. The rumor along the battle lines had been one thing—confirmation from a scout with news of the front was another. Murmurs and shouts rushed down the ranks. Voices rose, and several soldiers crumpled to their knees.

How had the generals missed such a large portion of Alessandra's forces? Left them unaccounted for?

All hope that the midnight missive had been mistaken, that it was some sort of trap or ploy to force the Luz to retreat was lost.

Rezza raised her sword overhead and silence fell. "The latest intelligence is worse than we feared. Hidden forces have attacked our city. We must fight through them to defend Respite," the commander yelled. As an alarmed murmur ran through the exhausted soldiers, she turned back to the scout. "The rear forces of the Luz remain outside Sanctuary." She tugged her stallion forward and held out the reins. "Go there and alert those who remained to the severity of the attack, whatever it takes."

Alessandra's soldiers worked too swiftly. They were

without remorse. He would never reach Lorieannan before Respite fell.

The stallion pawed the rocky earth as the elf swung up onto his back. She snapped the reins and they cantered off. The scout would ride till the horse collapsed, and then her run would begin anew.

"Soldiers of the Light!" Rezza shouted.

Marcon clamped his arm against his chest and stood tall. He barked out a cry of attention. Five hundred of his fellow soldiers did the same. Their shout echoed across the mountains.

"Ilona has spared us for this," the commander cried. "For Respite, we fight!"

Marcon bellowed, the sound grating against the scratches the smoke had carved along his throat.

His heartbeat set the pounding drum, and the soldiers sprinted down the mountain. The swelling of his knee, the scrape along his back faded from his mind. He wouldn't stop until he reached Lorieannan's side.

Every soldier around him had someone in the city they loved.

This time, there would be no surrender. No defeat.

THREE DAYS LATER

The rolling fields that stretched out from the city walls had been scorched. In the hills outside Sanctuary, Marcon had seen the devastation Alessandra's fires had wrought.

But they had not been the hills he'd known all his life.

His knees shook from their days of sprinting through the jagged mountain paths of the Meridiennes. Dozens of his fellow soldiers had crumpled beneath the strain. But he had to get back.

The city he'd sworn to protect—his friends, Loriean-nan, they were waiting for him.

Leaping over crevasses and darting along trails on his charge down the mountainside, Marcon remembered all the instances in which Lorieannan had begged him to find another way, another path. Her prodding had ebbed and flowed around her own desires, worse when he enlisted and at times of increased strife. All his life, he'd wanted nothing more than to join the Luz, the Army of Light, whose soldiers had found him after his parents had died in battle, who had taken him to the hillside vineyard beyond the city gates.

For a few hours, he had held on to the dream of joining the battalion, a position his bravery and a pinch of cleverness had won. And all of that was about to fall away again.

"How else am I supposed to protect you?" he'd shouted at the turn of the season after their first few months in their small apartment. His chest constricted at the memory even now. "And how are we to live? Were we to linger forever on Abbot's farm?" The merchants and residents strolling through the market nearby fired glances over their shoulders, but no one intervened. After decades of war, they understood.

That last afternoon when he'd left—their final argument haunted him even now. He'd thought they had reached an understanding as time passed. His position afforded them a small, street-level apartment only a few blocks from Lorieannan's favorite market. Every other day, she worked for the laundress, pressing linens and washing rugs for those whose ranks were higher than he'd yet achieved. "One day," he'd promised near the end of their first year, pressing a kiss to her temple as he rubbed the knot from her shoulder after a day's washing.

Lorieannan hadn't said anything, had only nodded. He'd taken that as acceptance enough.

She tried her hand at keeping a garden in the tiny plot of dirt beside the front stoop. After a few months, she left the laundress and went to help the widow down the street who watched over several children too young to help their parents in their day's labor. She began to sprinkle comments into their conversations, talking always of little ones.

Marcon had nothing to say to these remarks. He spent the mornings training in the barracks within the walls. After they broke their fast at midday, he studied their enemies' ranks and the foul creatures who lurked along their battle lines. Other afternoons, he tracked the wide network of spies and informants used by both Alessandra and the Cities. The two declared sides spent the greatest reserves of their secret forces in the Emeraude and Lis-Maen.

The titans had upheld the Cities in their conflict against the betrayer goddess for centuries, but Sanctuary's fall twenty years before had brought the unending battles to a head. The titans began to retreat, to abandon those they'd sworn to protect. Alessandra's power swelled.

His afternoon studies had convinced him of the surest way to break the stalemate: whoever convinced the mages, witches, and whatever other magic-casters lived in the wilds of their world to join their side would win the war.

Since childhood, he had been told that there was not a corner of Eldura untouched by war. As a soldier, he had learned the truth of this. Now war had come to his city.

His stomach twisted as the three walls of Respite came fully into view. Pillars of smoke rose from the Inner Ring. The clang and drum of battle echoed against the base of the mountains.

An open plain full of scattered clumps of vultura and wraiths stood between them and the outer walls of Respite.

The soldiers around him broke ranks. They bellowed with swords raised, flying with limping, uneven gaits toward the city far below.

Marcon echoed their cry. Captain Rezza thundered past on the mare she'd taken from one of her lieutenants who could ride no more.

Blood ran down the horse's legs.

The mare would not see another battle.

Marcon ignored the shooting pains in his shins that jolted up into his hips. The wound along his back still ached from a blow he'd sustained during the fighting in Sanctuary.

Ash and smoke obscured the winding roads that led

into the city. Where small homes and farms had been, only rubble remained.

An explosion of rock burst out from the Inner Wall, near Garreth's forge.

Marcon took a roundabout path to the city's outskirts, his feet finding the way to the vineyard of his youth, where he and Lorieannan had smiled at one another and picked grapes in the sun. Not even the skeletons of the vines survived.

He slaughtered the few vultura who lay in wait between him and his destination. Somehow, the city still clung to life.

Marcon fell to his knees when he reached the doors of the barn. Splinters of charred bone stuck out of the wise oak beside the barn, twenty feet above the ground. Around the tree's base lay the half-decayed bodies of children and a smattering of limbs torn from their tiny frames.

Something had picked through the children's ashen remains.

He dry-heaved into the ash. It scattered beneath his ragged breath. Broken bones lay beneath the slate-dust heaps.

The forces had slaughtered the living and retreated.

Marcon's arms shook as he pushed himself up to his feet. *Lorieannan.* He had to find her.

A low groan echoed out of the black-scarred barn. Marcon raised his sword over his shoulder and crept nearer. "Abbot?" he called. "Joane?"

The groaning ceased, replaced by a slow clacking sound, bones against wood.

Marcon wrapped his gloved hand around the loosened barn door and slowly tugged it open. Charred flakes fell onto the earth from the burned wood. He steeled his stomach, unsure of what he would find inside the barn, a place that had been a refuge on many a sweltering afternoon as an adolescent. Joane had once caught him and Lorieannan together there and whapped him over the head with the arm of her rake. "Abbot?"

A thin shadow shifted in the back of the barn. Marcon drew back from the door and tightened his grip around his longsword.

Whatever moved inside echoed the creak of the door. Muffled footsteps rolled through ash and charred hay.

The red, mottled skin of a burned human leg flexed into a hazy beam of sunlight. Gaunt muscles rippled beneath the torn flesh.

Marcon's stomach heaved again as the vultura's smell reached him, rotted bowels and burned hair. The threadbare ties of an apron clung to the creature's waist —aside from the char and blood, it perfectly matched the style of apron preferred by his adoptive mother.

A second shadow, the clacking one, mirrored the first's movements. Marcon rolled his feet back through the ash. His gaze darted between the two creatures. They would not wait long to strike.

The second vultura hobbled closer out of the darkness. It careened side to side as it walked. One of its skeletal feet was missing.

Marcon shifted his weight to his back foot as he turned to the side. He would need to kill them before he could continue toward the city, so they wouldn't infect an unwitting victim and add to Alessandra's army.

Shredded black leather draped in a circle around the second vultura's scalp. It was all that remained of Abbot's biretta.

"Ilona forgive me," Marcon sighed under his breath.

Abbot's bloodstained maw shot open, exposing two broken rows of teeth. Marcon's adoptive father sprang for his throat.

His soldier's instincts overwhelmed the restraint of his heart. With two decisive swings, he severed Abbot's head from his body and bifurcated his torso. Joane screeched and lunged forward as though some lingering part of her knew what Marcon had just done.

He swung his sword forward and caught her in the chest. Joane's mouth slackened and she screamed again but continued to drag her corpse forward, her bulging eyes fixed on his throat.

Marcon's injured shoulder burned as he whipped the blade through the side of her chest. He swung the sword back and severed the screeching jaw from her skull, driving through the thin, exposed muscle of her shoulder.

The woman who had raised him crumpled beside her husband. Marcon's legs shook beneath him, and he fell to his knees. "I am sorry." He gagged on the words. "I failed you."

His gaze swept the ashen landscape, searching for some small sign of hope. But he had seen Alessandra's devastation before. He would find no hope here.

Marcon ground his teeth together. No hope. No help.

With a cry, he swung his sword over his shoulder and drove it into the earth. "By the blood of my parents," he screamed at the sky, "by the souls of those who took me in, this I swear—I will not rest until you meet your end." He gasped for breath. Soot choked his throat. "If any hear me, meet me here. Enable my vow."

He slumped over his sword and rested his forehead against the pommel. No answer came from above or below.

Marcon pushed himself up on shaking legs. He stumbled away from the horrors of the barn, the destroyed vineyards, and dragged himself toward the city's outer wall. Toward Lorieannan and the small apartment they'd shared. The life he thought he'd left behind.

CHAPTER TWENTY-TWO
MARCON

Shouts rose from the city walls. Columns of smoke twisted toward the sky, congregating together in a hulking cloud that obscured the blue overhead. No matter how many rains fell upon Respite in the days thereafter, the devastation of this day could never be washed clean.

He fought his way away from the farm. The streets were largely deserted. The vultura who remained had been turned by Alessandra's forces and left to intercept the soldiers of the Luz on the return.

There had been a few moments in his days away where he had imagined Lorieannan rushing to the barracks to apologize for questioning him, questioning the Luz, what he fought for.

But in the light of Alessandra's flames, he could not dismiss the rightness of Lorieannan's fears. She had seen what he deliberately ignored.

Screeches erupted from the rays of light behind him. Closer by, the shadows stirred.

With a heavy sigh, Marcon pulled his sword free from its sheath. Its silver gleam caught the aura of the light.

"*Ree ree ree!*" A half-burned body burst forth from the ashen remains of a small structure—what had once been the home of the herbalist—at the end of his street. The herbalist's head had fallen back at an unnatural angle. She twisted to the side, one eye stacked atop the other. Blood gurgled up from her throat as she repeated her squeal. Her slashed vocal cords scraped like grinding metal and gears.

Two sure strides carried Marcon forward. He swung into the herbalist's lunge. His sword carved through the matted remains of her hair. Gore sprayed across the ash-strewn cobbles as he yanked his sword free from her skull and sundered her head from her body. A final strike bifurcated her torso. Her legs fell opposite her sunken chest cavity. The missing skin along her jawline, torn free from the remains of her face, indicated where the infecting bite had struck.

Marcon strode on. He had trained to face the undead, the favored foot soldiers of the betrayer goddess. He had killed fellow soldiers who had been turned by her hordes.

But all of that death—true death, not her false animations—had been in service of protecting civilians. Of protecting his home.

Marcon's knees shuddered beneath him as he passed the low stone wall that ran along the dirt lane outside the one-room house he and Lorieannan shared. Around him, all was still. The few remaining blades of grass brushed against the sides of his boots as he limped toward their home.

He had to find her. Each step carried him closer to what he feared to see. Imagined phantasms leaped toward him from the sooty remains of their small yard.

If she had been here when they attacked, there was no hope that she had survived.

The door to their house hung loose and leaning, torn free from its top hinge.

He had hung that door, three years ago. Abbot had stood behind him as he knocked the hinges into place, Lorieannan at his side.

Marcon's thoughts narrowed to the next breath, the next moment. Could he find a single reason to hope? His were the only footprints in the ash—had she escaped into the protection of the city?

"Lorieannan," Marcon called as he approached the door. His throat swelled with all that he could not say, apologies he would never have the chance to make. *I have not loved you as I ought. And I know not when what we had fell away. But I swear to you, if given the chance, I will make it right.*

A low moan rippled out from the house. Marcon's heart leaped in his chest and he tightened his grip on his sword. With a trick of the fading fires all around him, tongues of flame seemed to flash up the length of his raised blade.

He blinked to clear his gaze again. "Lorieannan," he repeated. The hope he'd tried to squelch—the hope of a madman—clung to her name. For a moment he was sixteen again, breathless beneath the twin gaze of the moons, Lorieannan smiling beneath him, their bodies entwined.

Through the door, a gray shard of dappled light shone on a fallen roof beam. A crumpled shape, clad in dark blue, lay crushed beneath the beam.

Marcon shouted and sprang forward. *Crushed by our own apartment—*

Behind his head, the length of his sword caught flame. He bellowed again and drove the sword into the beam. *He could free her. If only—*

A broken snarl shot from the corner of the cabin behind him. Before he could turn about, the hidden creature jumped on Marcon's back. The force of its attack drove him forward. He dropped his sword as he spun, desperate to keep the exposed skin of his neck free from its gnashing jaws.

Marcon landed beside the pinned form of a young woman. Half of her leg was missing, and flecks of blood and crumbs of flesh littered the wooden floor. *Too small to be Lorieannan. One of the older children in her care.*

He threw his weight to the side, his chest in the air. From the shadows, the creature leaped toward him again. He knew the pale blue fabric, dotted with lopsided flowers Lorieannan had attempted to add to the linen.

With a cry that could have rent his throat in two, Marcon leaned back on his elbows and drove the heels of his boots into Lorieannan's lunging form. Her jaw snapped, lolling to the side, and she shrieked as she careened backward.

Marcon lunged for his flame-covered sword. Smoke

and fire from its blade licked over the fallen beam. He seized the hilt; it was strangely cool in his grasp.

He gritted his teeth as he pivoted over the beam, avoiding the worst of the flames. Lorieannan screamed again—like she had when she'd broken her leg falling off her horse. Everything in him longed to help her, and yet his body would not heed his call and move toward her.

I can't do it. Not again. Not to you.

And yet his hands curled around the grip of his sword. *You must*, the soldier inside him insisted.

Without glancing over his shoulder, Marcon dove free from his burning house. He stood a better chance of survival—he would not think against *what*—in the open.

Lorieannan's fingernails scrabbled against the wooden floor as she clawed her way forward after him.

Outside, he stopped short, extending his sword in a shaking hand to hold Lorieannan at bay as he gazed up at a silver-blue airship emerging from the choking smoke. Soot streaked the shining hull of the ship, marring its opalescent surface and iridescent scales. *An airship from the Luz.* The scout Commander Rezza had sent back to the force gathered before Sanctuary must have been successful.

Four sets of tri-part wings, blue-white as a winter sky, stretched around the ship's hull, two above and two below. The mecho-alchemists had forged living tissue as strong as a dragon's hide and light as a butterfly's wings. Its delicate veins lent the appearance of stained glass that rippled in time to the ship's corebeat.

The ship that had settled the truce upon the battle-field of Sanctuary following that first day's fight.

The airship that carried Field Commander Silversword.

A dwarf with thick blond braids leaned out of the hovering airship, her hand outstretched toward him. A brilliant white light blazed out of the center of her chest. "You'll need to jump," she yelled.

Marcon glanced back at Lorieannan's hunched form. His chest tightened. He couldn't leave her here to forage among the dead. He couldn't leave her here alone.

Lorieannan's broken jaw ground back and forth. She yelped and rushed toward him. Her arms swung low at her sides.

"Steady on!" the dwarf cried. Over Marcon's shoulder, the light intensified and narrowed into a beam. The dwarf grunted, and the beam struck the earth. Ash and soil burst free in its wake. The ray of light carved a path toward Lorieannan. It struck her in the chest, too quickly for her to even make a sound.

"No!" Marcon shouted. He fell to his knees, his arm extended out toward her. Flecks of light trailed like embers onto the ash-covered earth.

A dark fog coated the edge of his vision. Vaguely, insistent puffs of wind beat against his back.

The light-embers faded to nothing. Lorieannan was gone.

A small, strong hand gripped his shoulder. "Up you get," the voice he'd heard before said.

Marcon turned. The blond-haired dwarf was at his eye-level. Her large brown eyes glanced from him back to his sword. The flames he had imagined had faded back into the blade.

The dwarf extended her hand to help him rise.

Marcon cleared his throat and squared his jaw. The golden necklace upon the dwarf's chest glowed softer now. At the end of the chain hung a depiction of Ilona, the titan of light, her arms extended overhead with a glowing orb between her hands. "Lightbringer," Marcon said with a bow of his head. "Field Commander."

The tragedy of the day, the series of losses—he could not internalize that he was speaking to *the* Tali Silversword.

A bolt of heat shot up his arm as he clasped his hand around the field commander's. Marcon winced and glanced down. The heat radiated from beneath his bracer, blazing along his forearm. A faint orange glow peeked out from the leather. It had the same aura as the lightbringer's necklace.

The dwarf's eyes widened, and she took a step back. "Get on the ship," she said quickly. "Hurry."

Marcon frowned down at his arm—Where was the glow coming from? And the flames he thought he had seen along his sword?—but he pushed himself up off the ground and strode to the airship as she had commanded. He ducked beneath the rolling hide-door the dwarf had leaned out of to offer him aid. The hull's interior was cramped and bright. With a low hum, the iridescent paneling in front of him shook. Scales rippled off its surface and formed a second, pale-purple seat where there had been only a blank wall before.

From the pilot's seat, a fae with dark blue skin stared at him. Her piercing purple gaze was so dark as to be almost black. "For you," she said with a nod at the seat that had materialized.

He turned and sat as the fae had ordered, and the dwarf slipped inside behind him. The field commander sat on the chair opposite, and the hide-door rolled shut behind her. More scales rippled and hummed around its opening—the skin-like hull mending itself and sealing them safely inside.

Marcon's stomach lifted toward his chest as the soft, rapid beat of the wings lifted them off the ground. The ashen remains of his and Lorieannan's home grew smaller beneath them as the airship glided away toward the city center. In the distance, more shadows gathered over the mountains, and the burning city of Respite spread out beneath their ship. Through the iridescent scales, he could see both the earth and sky all around him, everything overcast by a faint lavender glow. How the pilots adjusted to such sights, he would never understand.

The pulsing heat along his forearm drew his attention back to more immediate concerns. Marcon grabbed the strap of his bracer, preparing to lift it free.

"Don't!" Silversword urged. She caught his hand fast in her fist. "Not yet." Her eyes flashed toward the airship's pilot. "Wait until we land."

The burning sank deeper into the muscles of his arm. He would have remembered sustaining an injury. And if one of the vultura had bitten him, the change would have already begun. Whatever it was, perhaps the biting pain was a blessing, something to distract him from what had transpired in his city. From those he and the Field Commander had just killed.

"As you have already gathered, I'm Field Commander Tali Silversword," the dwarf said as she settled back into her seat.

Marcon's mouth hung open as he nodded. "Yes. I saw your blast of light in the Second Battle, just a few days ago."

The dwarf smiled. "And am I correct in asserting that you are the soldier who orchestrated the rescue of the Blazing Battalion?"

"I, umm . . ." Words failed him. "I did not act alone, Field Commander."

"That's not how we heard it," the fae pilot shot back.

"Enough, Rafferty," the dwarf commanded. A ring of golden light flashed from her irises.

The pilot rolled her eyes and turned back around. She pressed her middle finger against the wide panel in front of her, and the airship tipped forward, descending toward the garrison at the center of Respite.

Three bodies, each clad in golden armor and long red capes, curved upside down atop the iron-spiked walls that surrounded the military fortress in the center of the city. Impaled by their own garrison. Marcon gaped again. "The generals . . ."

Across from him, Silversword shrugged. "I suppose they thought their death would be faster in their own hands than one devised by the rage of the city." She ran her thumb across her lips. "We'll see if the fourth agrees with them or not."

Marcon tucked a stray lock of hair behind his ear. It

had fallen free from the thin leather tie at the back of his head. His heart should go out to the generals and their families, should have extended to Commander Rezza and the others who had trudged through the mountains by his side to save their city—how many had survived what was waiting for them in the outer wards and how many had joined the already unfathomable number of the fallen of Respite? But over and over again, he saw Lorieannan's twisted, undead form. And the beam of light that had rendered her into nothingness. "I am sorry, Lorieannan," he mumbled under his breath. Such a short time before, he'd thought he'd had his greatest victory to date. He'd protected his friends. Gained a promotion.

How wrong he had been.

He had failed those he'd sworn to protect. Joane. Abbot. The woman he had loved in childhood and abandoned just before her death. He had failed them all.

CHAPTER TWENTY-THREE
YVAYNE

THE EMERAUDE

Yvayne sank back against one of the ancient oaks of the great Emeraude Forest, the hopelessness of her task settling like a fur cloak upon her shoulders—too heavy for her liking.

Almost two decades had passed since she'd last traveled through the covens' territories for more than a brief conference with the grand matron. After her failure to rescue a young witch gifted in the revival of spirits twenty years before, she had been hesitant to involve herself again.

But then missive after missive had arrived, magical owls of varying shades sent via a thread-loop of portals from Vaxis's position in the Glade of Shadows, through the Brightlands, to Yvayne's hidden library within the Emeraude.

Tipping her head back against the bark, Yvayne clenched and released her jaw as she reread Vaxis's missive, the news from the Glade of Shadows increasingly grim.

How much longer could they even refer to the ancient forest by its given name?

The fae forced an exhale through her nostrils.

The Glade was not the only place where the lore-keepers' efforts were falling apart.

Two decades before, she had found the spirit-witch and had succeeded in discovering how Lilia's soul might be recalled from Astralei.

The ritual had come at a great cost—the life of the Oracle and that of her friend, Kailena, the one who brought Lilia, reborn, into the world. Though her informants hadn't been able to reveal the full particulars of what had transpired, Yvayne knew that the current Oracle had murdered her mother, the former Oracle, and taken her place as one of the Five. Officially, the Academia Magica had not said much of the transition of power, only that there would not be mourning ceremonies held as old gave way to new.

From the little Yvayne had been able to glean, the Sorceress had determined that the former Oracle betrayed the Pentacle's cause with her secrecy, her determination to revive Verdigris's magic whatever the cost. It was the same mission the Sorceress herself had been pursuing, but where Yvayne and the former Oracle sought to bring back a soul that might save their world, the Sorceress had sought to forge the perfect, elemental warrior, then an army of them, so she might stand against the power of the Cities. Her elemental army would have been able to counter the champions and make Lis-Maen the military equal to the Cities United.

Together, Yvayne and the former Oracle had set about a rival project to the Sorceress's aim. Neither the Oracle nor Yvayne had believed the Sorceress's professed motivations that her Hexblade force would protect Lis-Maen's independence from the Cities' warmongering.

Yvayne and the Oracle's approach had been quite different. Rather than accumulating a pile of bodies that the Sorceress called "offerings" in her attempts to imbue the raw elements into the individuals she'd selected, their own creation of the hexblade entailed the recalling of Lilia's soul from Astralei.

Their quest had claimed the Oracle's life, the spirit-witch's, and Kailena's. After, the Sorceress entrenched her power at which point Kailena's partner, Andeus, thought it best to sever ties between Yvayne and himself to protect his and Kailena's daughter. Yvayne understood the prudence of this and the sense of betrayal that ran as an undercurrent beneath Andeus's decision. He would have adored any child Kailena bore, and he would have preferred maintaining his family rather than sacrificing a treasured few to salvage the fate of the world.

Yvayne pressed her fingernails into her palms. As usual, she remained after everyone else had fallen.

Though in this case, her lone survivor narrative did not hold. Andeus and the child had remained hidden from the Sorceress's plots as far as her spies had been able to tell. Rowan, Kailena and Andeus had called her. The one reborn, Lilia made new, a spark of Verdigris returned.

Yvayne sighed as she returned a final time to the end of Vaxis's letter, the one she would have to burn shortly in case one of her many enemies had broken through her defenses and succeeded in scrying on her. *Find the one who can revive spirits*, the message read. *The grand-daughter of the one who helped us before. I am sending a champion of earth to you through the weave before I retreat to the Academia Magica's Archives for a while. Without inter-vention, the champion of earth is not long for this world.*

The spirit-witch who had helped Yvayne discover how they might recall Lilia's soul had taken shelter in one of the smaller covens within the Emeraude alongside her daughter, Teresa. The coven had made short work of sacrificing their ally to the forest and expelled Yvayne and Vaxis before they could rescue the girl. Vaxis tried to cheer herself with reminding Yvayne that it was not an absolute certainty that Teresa had been given to the forest as well. The only information they could be sure of was that Teresa, too, had borne a daughter who would be raised as a nameless within the coven until she came of age.

The fracturing of their world was making Yvayne's work increasingly difficult. How were the lorekeepers to preserve the secrets Alessandra was determined to erase if they were excluded from the very societies whose magical secrets needed protection due to fears of the dark goddess's reprisal?

Not for the first time, Yvayne scoffed at the short-sightedness of the Sorceress and her lackeys, the same for the grand matrons. Did they truly believe that the path of neutrality would preserve their societies? That

Alessandra would not devour their lands and peoples the moment the whim took her, just as she had the Glade of Shadows?

Yvayne lowered the parchment from Vaxis to the flames. *Let me find a way to protect Rowan and the nameless witch from such a fate*, she thought to the distant memory of her great-grandmother, the vanished titan, Verdigris. Had Yvayne been able to consult her own mother and had her mother retained her right mind, she might have known what to do. But such a path had been cut off long ago, when her mother banished Yvayne to preserve their people's memory.

If the answers dwelled in her homeland, the place of her creation, she would never find them. No, the path before her would have to be one of her own design.

She wouldn't again fail those she'd sworn to protect. Rowan and the nameless spirit-witch would not be the next in the long line of those Yvayne had lost.

Yvayne pushed herself off the tree and settled her light pack over her shoulders. It would take time to comb through the Emeraude and retrace steps twenty years old, but she would find the nameless spirit-witch and save her from the coven repeating their cruel sacrifice a third time.

The survival of the lorekeepers and a possible champion of earth depended upon her success.

She would see it done.

CHAPTER TWENTY-FOUR
ROWAN

Four offerings out of two dozen. Lost during their first training session.

Because she awakened the elemental pillars and unleashed chaos into the academy's ordered practice grounds.

It was Rowan's first thought upon waking. She shifted to roll out of bed, accidentally disturbing Majestyk's curled form over her shins.

The dracat rose, arching her back into a deep stretch.

"Ouch," Rowan cried as the creature's claws pierced through the worn down of the quilt and into her skin.

Majestyk simply yawned in reply, showing off her tiny, perfectly pointed teeth.

"Would your creature like to be aired today?" Viridian asked, emitting a wide yawn of her own.

Rowan grinned at the daimon. She never could have lived alongside one of the ancient dire wolves in her forest home of Willow Glen. The rope passageways weren't wide enough to accommodate a creature of

Viridian's size. "If she'll go with you, that sounds like a great activity for her today."

She turned back to the dracat. "Don't fly too far off, and come when Viridian tells you."

Rowan winced as Majestyk's answering prickles worked their way up her legs before the dracat tossed herself from Rowan's bunk and curled up in the center of the bed Viridian had just vacated, purring at the surrounding warmth the daimon left behind.

"Aside from Miscreant, what does your day entail?"

"A few small tasks and a trip to the archives." Viridian's teal gaze met Rowan's. *"Worry not about me, room-friend."*

She answered with a hesitant smile. At times Viridian's demeanor made it difficult to tell if she was prying into the dire wolf's affairs or if she was simply a being of few personal details.

And then she remembered. *Merfolk.*

Rowan's eyes brightened, and she scurried along the top of her bed to gather her garments for the day and change out of her sleeping clothes. She braided her hair back into a twist at the nape of her neck and threw her legs over the side of the bed to don her boots.

In just a few short hours from now, she might catch her first glimpse of the sea.

Vraise had already departed for the dining area when Rowan met Athenza outside her room. The druid seemed a little tired from the day before but not worryingly so.

As they trailed along the winding garden paths, Athenza's clicking cane one of the few similarities from her life in the forest, Rowan tried not to think about their first training session. She tugged on a strand of hair that had fallen out of the braided knot she'd fashioned that morning, twirling it around her finger as she attempted pleasantries with Athenza.

But keeping her mind from the disaster wasn't working.

The conversation fell away the moment she and Athenza arrived. Curls of steam rose from the teacups held by the remaining eighteen offerings outside Athenza and herself.

Despite saving the lead imbuer artisan the afternoon before, Rowan knew better than to count on the other offerings trusting her.

"There you are," Vraise said brightly. He waved them over, a pot of water and pinches of tea leaves already prepared for them.

"Wonderful, wonderful," a familiar voice cried from just beyond the garden walls. Tullemaien had elected to meet the offerings in the garden dining area rather than the training arena surrounding the pond.

Rowan's stomach churned at the knowledge of why that was. One of the other offerings of darkness had whispered the evening before about how the groundskeepers were struggling to remove the gore from the tree where the darkness had ejected one of the offerings.

At the sight of their teacher, the energy around the offerings grew more unstable, nerves and anxiety sparking all around them.

"As you all know, today you'll be pursuing your individualized assignments and getting to know your elements with your group members." Tullemaien asked each group to gather with their respective members so they could deliver the assignments more easily.

"Now, for the students of the element of fire," their instructor said with a nod to Athenza and Orella, "you will proceed to the dungeons, er, under-floors beneath the Oracle's towers where you will find a captive fire mephit and an apprentice who will oversee your training."

Orella's hand shot into the air. "That cannot be safe!"

"We're *offerings*," Vraise murmured under his breath beside Rowan.

She glanced over, surprised to find her companion already aggravated by their fellow offering.

Vraise shook his head when Rowan met his gaze. "I'll tell you later."

Athenza, too, looked surprised by the announcement. Her brow furrowed but she shook off her alarm. The druid straightened, drawing her shoulders back. "Lack of safety and *deadly* are not the same," she said loudly enough for the remaining offerings to hear. "Like Rowan pointed out to us last night, we stand a better chance working together than we do apart."

There were a few grumbled protests—Rowan's popularity remained low.

"She was complaining about you before you arrived," Vraise whispered to Rowan. "It seemed like she was trying to stoke the others' fear more than anything else."

"What a lovely sentiment," Tullemaien answered Athenza with a wide, easy smile.

Such constant cheerful gawping eventually ruined the effect, Rowan thought to herself. She simply nodded to Vraise's confession. It wasn't as though she could blame Orella for being suspicious of her or the others for doubting whether they would be safe with her nearby.

"Do you want to succeed in joining the six elements or not?" Athenza had challenged a particularly aggravated offering to the element of earth the evening before. "If you think the Pentacle will let you go before the task is complete, think again."

Tullemaien ended the gathering with a clap of their hands and dismissed each of the groups, sending Rowan, Vraise, and Forsythia off to the stables to retrieve their mounts. Their guide would meet them there.

Forsythia came to stand at Rowan's side and made a complicated series of gestures with her hands. "Oh," Rowan sighed, having never learned the language of signs.

Vraise slid in beside her, grinning, and signed back to the young elf who brightened immediately. "She says she likes you," Vraise translated. "And she's hoping for help with her cervidae. Her brother says they're too big for her to ride by herself."

"I would love to," Rowan answered, with Vraise's help. "Who's her brother?" she asked as they set off toward the pens.

Vraise frowned at Forsythia's answer, making what Rowan assumed to be a series of clarifying gestures. The elf laughed. "She says it's a secret, but that we'll find out when it's time."

Rowan shrugged. "Can't argue with that, I suppose." Their young charge skipped ahead, stealing handfuls of blue-purple phlox and mixing them with sprigs of ivy.

"She seems entirely too young to be an offering, don't you think?"

Her companion nodded, avoiding Rowan's gaze. "It made me think of what we learned from Samara about the recruitment ban from our conclave that wasn't enforced elsewhere." He bit his lower lip. "Yesterday was . . . more than I thought it would be. I knew it would be dangerous, but I can't believe they were so, well—"

"Careless," Rowan answered. "Like our lives don't matter to them."

"Exactly," Vraise agreed. "Which is why I think Athenza is right. We should forge ahead and figure out a sustainable path on our own. Learn from each other, share elemental knowledge."

Rowan nodded, the weight of the weeks ahead resettling over her heart. She had a promise to keep, a chosen destiny to fulfill. What was the Pentacle holding over everyone else that made them stay?

There was a gekkering cry of delight from the cervidae pens as Rowan, Vraise, and Forsythia approached.

Gardenia rushed up to the fence, prancing in delight at their reunion.

Rowan hurried over, climbing onto the lowest railing of the fence to accept the cervidae's greeting. Gardenia nipped playfully at the stray strands of Rowan's hair.

Pulling back from the creature, Rowan checked to see how she was faring after her relocation, whether she was missing her herd. A few of the cervidae's vines along her antlers were drooping, but the keepers assured Rowan that it was simply part of Gardenia's adjustment to the sunny environment as opposed to the shaded forest.

Rowan threw her arms around the cervidae when they were side by side, breathing in the heat of her fur. "There's someone I want you to meet," Rowan said, holding the fox-deer's dark brown gaze. "And Majestyk sends her regards of course."

Gardenia made a snuffling noise as she investigated the young elf, taking particular interest in the top of Forsythia's head, which made her giggle.

Checking with Vraise, she made sure her charge was ready. Rowan mounted first, and Vraise handed Forsythia up. It took a bit more conversation between the two of them before Rowan could get across that Forsythia should not clench tightly to the cervidae's short fur, but eventually the girl relaxed enough to enjoy her raised position.

Forsythia brought her hands together in what Rowan had learned was a signal of readiness. Just in time, their guide appeared. She rode a dark brown mare that had to be cajoled into proximity to the cervidae but who eventually found her stride.

The Pentacle had assigned them an adept of the Druidess with small, pinched features and a cautious demeanor who would lead them to a cove where they would learn the ways of the element of water. Tulle-maien had been sparse on the specifics, but Rowan hoped the location would grant her a clear view of the sea.

As the four of them rode out, Rowan drummed her fingertips against her thumb in silent cadence to a song

Paupa used to sing to her, trying to shove the memory of the fourth offering assigned to water from her mind. For the first time in her life, she might catch a glimpse of the ocean. Instead of the offering, she tried to imagine what the Circle Sea was like, the body of water that surrounded her homeland and figured prominently in her father's stories. How was it that waves could whisper when rapids never made such a gentle susurrus?

She fell back into the easy rhythm of riding Gardenia, the cervidae quickly adjusting to bearing two riders rather than one. With Vraise's help, she told the young elf that the fox-deer shared a name for a flower just like she did. Forsythia giggled at this new revelation and leaned forward to Gardenia.

"Is the route far to the seaside?" Rowan asked their guide.

The adept shook her head. "Perhaps you misunderstood—I am taking you to the lagoon."

Rowan waited to see if there would be more but the guide had already turned back around and urged her mount ahead. "Am I missing something?" she asked Vraise.

His answering smile came quickly. "Undoubtedly, though I am as well."

Her hope that their route might take them through Delmoir was quickly dashed as the guide veered away from the Sorceress's tower, opting for a road that led beyond the gates, leaving the Pentacle's towers and those of the city behind them.

She had hoped that a return to the forest might bring a sense of relief, but this part of the forest was strange to her. The answer why came through absence rather than presence. "There's no birdsong," she murmured to Vraise.

Gardenia, too, sensed something amiss. The cervidae's ears flicked about to the sides. Her long tail twitched. Gardenia's tongue flitted forward, tasting the air.

Just as Rowan was about to call out to their guide for answers, the cervidae gave a sharp, shrill cry. She raised her neck and adopted a light prance to her footsteps, hurrying forward. Ahead of them, the adept's mare whinnied and quickened her pace also, anticipation rippling from Rowan to Gardenia to the mare.

The sound of running water broke the silence between the trees. Rowan sucked in a breath, trying to prepare herself for a sight she had only imagined before.

She and Forsythia leaned forward to help push the low-hanging branches out of Gardenia's path. The rush of water ahead sounded more like the constant burble and hiss of a waterfall than Rowan had imagined for waves.

Following the adept, they rounded a bend and emerged onto a rocky outcropping overlooking the lagoon.

Rowan's lips parted and she stared across the opening within the forest. The source of the sound was immediately apparent, though how it occurred, Rowan couldn't yet understand.

The outcropping looked out over a bare, rocky area that had once held the wide mouth of the river. Only a few small patches of moss remained along the rocks nearest the trees. The rest bore the bleached remains of moss and flakes of lichen.

There was a waterfall winding out from the river that carved through the forest which was the source of the low roar she'd heard, but rather than emptying into a river basin, it poured itself into a giant orb rather like those Paupa had designed for the treetops of Willow Glen. Water poured out of one side of the orb through a lip that let out onto a second orb, this one with a lower, wider mouth. The second, in turn, emptied into a third smaller orb which splashed water over its sides and onto the rocks beneath.

"This isn't a natural lagoon at all," Rowan said, turning back to Vraise. Her shoulders drooped. This was nothing like the trip to the ocean she'd been imagining.

Though the orbs were of an impressive size, together even larger than the stretch of the council tree back in Willow Glen, how was it enough space for the merfolk to thrive within?

The image of the petrified offering to earth flashed back before her eyes. *They never promised they'd help us thrive.* But wasn't that precisely what it would take to bear the six elements in balance?

Vraise turned toward their guide. "How do they, umm..."

"The merfolk have everything they need," she said with chin raised. "As soon as you are ready, you are to approach and commune with the element of water. I will remain nearby until sundown at which point I will return to the academy."

Vraise frowned as he turned back toward Rowan. She

hadn't missed how the adept neglected to include the three of them in her return plans. Had their introduction to the Pentacle gone differently, Rowan might have thought that the adept was trying to give them an encouraging sense of their own ability to remain behind and study at their leisure. She knew better than to believe that was the case.

The adept set about ignoring them, and no merfolk popped out of the orbs to wave hello and provide instructions.

"I don't see how they're going to come to us," Rowan said, studying the artificial environs. Had the merfolk even opted to come here, or had the Pentacle forced them? Or was it some sort of twisted trail toward a seemingly promising end, like the quest to be an elemental bearer was proving itself to be?

With years of experience climbing into the treetops of Willow Glen, it was a relatively simple task for her to chart her way along the rocks, into the basin, and across to the other side where a second rocky ledge aligned with the tops of the two taller orbs.

Vraise and Forsythia followed along behind her at a slower pace, with Rowan occasionally offering guidance to the two of them when they lost track of the path she'd originally taken.

One of Paupa's most impactful lessons had been the afternoon he spent teaching her to balance the dual energies of the orbs of light, managing its tension with the darkness. There wasn't an energetic glow of other elements within the water, but that wasn't atypical of the physical energies.

A film of algae covered over the insides of the open orbs, structured almost like a tulip first spreading its petals in spring. As she got closer, the shadows of rocks and water fronds emerged behind the algae curtain. Tendrils of seaweed waved at the shifting of the water.

A dash of movement within the second orb caught Rowan's attention as she neared the base of the opposite rocky ledge. "I think I saw one," she called back to Vraise as loudly as she dared.

The adept didn't glance in their direction. She had settled against the opposite wall, a giant tome open upon her lap instead.

The shape might have been finlike. It had been too indistinct to tell, especially at the depths of the orb pool.

This near to the three of them, the hairs along Rowan's arms stood on end, and the back of her neck prickled. There was a palpable energy to the orbs. Maybe that was what they were meant to attend to.

Whatever she'd seen didn't return to her line of sight. Rowan climbed the wall of rock up to the second ledge. "Maybe you should stay within the riverbed until I can get a closer look," she called down to Vraise. The elf who had first left the conclave by her side would never have surrendered the opportunity for magical advancement to her, but their days through the forest and their arrival had brought out a side of him Rowan would never have anticipated.

She hefted herself onto the second ledge which was narrower than the first. Apart from the wall of rock opposite her, the change in height completely trans-formed her surroundings. Large, verdant fronds poked their left tips out of the orb. The sound of the water was gentler up here, more like a large brook than the pounding of a waterfall.

From the water itself, she could almost believe she heard singing.

Rowan's pulse jumped. *Why* hadn't she thought to study siren lore last night?

Her phoenix's golden eyes flashed open in the back of her mind in the same moment her inner voice helpfully reminded her about the scene of chaos and death she had accidentally played a central role within.

With the phoenix watching from behind her eyes, Rowan crept forward, allowing herself to feel in tune with the watery environment. Actual attunement with the element of water would require more from her, but this was a start.

Rowan knelt by the side of the water. The ferns arched overhead, shielding her from the warmth of the summer sun.

She held out her hand over the water.

"It seems you're making great progress," a woman's voice said.

Rowan's heart quickened at the sound. The voice was impossibly melodic, like stepping away into a dream-melody—the sound of the forest breeze and the lull of a river all at once. In Paupa's stories, she remembered, it would have been described as the voice of the sea, but Rowan had never been.

This lagoon was the closest she would get for a while yet.

"Uh, thank you?" It seemed rude not to answer,

though an inarticulate reply could be worse than saying nothing at all.

A melodic laugh replied, perfectly striking the dream-notes of an arpeggio which did little more than to puzzle Rowan further.

You're here to commune with the element of water, she scolded herself. Without thinking further about it, Rowan pressed her palm to the taut surface of the water, testing its give, noting the way that it pressed back against her, embracing and resisting her all at once.

A shadow moved beneath the water near her. On the opposite side of the orb, a distant splash. Vraise called her name.

And a blue hand that matched the shade of the autumn sky sprang out of the water, snatched her wrist, and tugged her in.

CHAPTER TWENTY-FIVE
MARCON

The fae airship pilot wove through the curling black smoke that rose along the outskirts of Respite. Tiny dots below them showed either survivors or vultura—it was impossible to discern which from this height.

"How were you able to find me?" Marcon wondered aloud, gazing out over the city.

The field commander had settled back into her seat, her head leaned back against the iridescent wall of the airship. She closed her eyes and smiled, tapping the amulet that hung at the center of her chest, the sign of Ilona. "Let's just say I had a strong sense of where someone needing my help might be."

"Because of—"

Silversword's eyes shot open and she shook her head.

Marcon frowned. He didn't understand.

The dwarf shifted her gaze to stare at his forearm, a finger raised to her lips. "Take us within the palace grounds as quickly as possible, Rafferty," the field commander snapped at her pilot. She met his gaze once more, her expression a mask.

Whatever she had to explain, Silversword didn't want the pilot to witness it. Marcon stared out over his city, a numbness settling over him. The burn along his forearm still ached, but it paled in comparison to the pressure rising in his throat at what he had witnessed, what he had done. There would be time for his questions when they landed.

To calm himself, Marcon directed his thoughts to the airship itself—the lower positioning of the fae's seat with a long board covered in dials. It was even more complex than the measurement tools employed by the alchemists in their experiments. He'd ridden in an airship a few times during training, but they had been more enclosed, without seats that could appear at the pilot's will.

The fae did as Silversword ordered and directed the ship beyond the inner walls and past the barracks, all the way to the central district of Respite that held the nobles' homes alongside the dwellings of the political advisers, generals, and the Secret Council of the Cities United.

Marcon's heart rose into his throat as they landed. He had never even stepped foot on palace grounds before, much less landed in the open-air gardens inlaid along one side of the roof where airships could take off and land.

"If you'll come with me," Silversword said to him with a nod of her head. "Rafferty, stable the ship then find Stozdak and bring him to me."

His spirit lifted at the familiar name. "The blacksmith's son?" He fell into easy step beside her as they crossed the open-air tunnels built along the ramparts and strode toward the upper story of the palace.

"Oh, you know him?" The dwarf seemed pleased by this news.

Marcon hesitated in his reply—did Garreth know that his son was so closely connected to Tali Silversword? He cleared his throat as she raised an eyebrow, waiting. "Err, yes, Field Commander. I was a year or two ahead of him in the academy and am acquainted with his father."

She betrayed no reaction to Marcon's mention of Garreth, which he wasn't sure how to read. There were a great many people in the city, he imagined, who disliked Silversword. Garreth had always been careful in his speaking out against her, never one to engage in idle gossip, but neither was he a man to encourage his son to blindly follow the promises of power. The blacksmith had always stopped himself before going so far as to spew what the Luz would consider to be treason, but he might need to be more careful if his son had the ear of Silversword herself, which would elevate Garreth's position as well, even if he didn't want it.

"Excellent," Silversword said. "I'll be tasking him with helping you feel comfortable here, at least until we've had a chance to get your training under way."

"My training?"

Marcon stopped a few paces behind Silversword who had turned her attention to the guards stationed at the end of the ramparts.

The two guards bowed low and held open a pair of reinforced wooden doors for Silversword and Marcon.

The interior hallways bore enormous shining windows, casting just as much light into the upper palace floors as the open-air passageways.

A flurry of attendants seemed to be lying in wait for her arrival. Their livery suggested different roles within the palace—some associated with the Luz, others the battalion specifically, one or two from Beacon, and one bearing the black crossed keys of the Secret Council.

"Later," she told this final attendant, quickly dismissing most of them as Marcon rejoined at her side.

The attendant for the Secret Council melted back into the shadows, and another pair of guards opened a new set of double doors for Silversword and Marcon.

She held her hands out on either side as she entered the room, a confident bounce in her step. "Welcome to my Command Central, Colabra."

The middle of the room held a raised dais with a desk and tall chair. Maps lined the sides of the chamber with a few open and spread across a low, long table. The entire back wall looked out over the walls of Respite.

Sunlight glinted off the impaled body of one of the generals who dangled off the wall, visible through the window. In the distance, groups of people amassed in the streets.

Marcon's pulse jumped. "Are you expecting unrest, Field Commander?" He hadn't thought through the implications of the city's near-catastrophe, the scores of survivors dealing with loss and heartbreak exactly like he was. And they'd had days to stew in it rather than being fresh arrived and battle weary.

He was a soldier, not a strategist, but seeing the

mobs, a dark vision of his city's future flashed before his eyes.

"I assure you that you're quite safe here, Captain."

Marcon shook his head. She'd misunderstood him and was unaware of his true rank—his promotion had been mentioned but never finalized, and that was before the city had nearly been sacked by a surprise attack from Alessandra's forces.

"Let us speak of what occurred on the outskirts. The power that, even now, is flooding your veins." She spun away from the windows, her eyes flashing as she studied him. For a moment, the dwarf glowered at him like she was a predator and he was the prey, despite her head only coming to his waist, her sword only the length of his forearm.

"Do you know why I asked you to keep silent in the airship? It is a state you will have to acclimate yourself to from this point forward."

The amulet around her neck had obliterated Lorieannan with very little effort. Hells, it had eliminated an entire horde of vultura.

Marcon shook his head. He'd understood the signal to hold his questions clearly enough, but magic? In that, too, she had to be mistaken.

The predatory air about the dwarf shifted, and the controlled air of command returned to her features. She gestured for him to be seated before her desk.

As he did, Silversword slid into her chair and, with a wave of her hand, raised it into the air so that she could meet the level of his gaze behind her desk. "I understand that you will need time to work through this news for yourself," she began. "It is fortunate that I was the first to find you as I can help in your time of need."

"Time of need?" Marcon's thoughts kept sticking. He was here, within the Palace of Respite, home of the generals and the Secret Council that ruled over all the Cities United, speaking to Field Commander Silversword, a champion of light.

"Becoming a champion is difficult at any time and has been more so after the last twenty years following the Secrecy Act."

"Secrecy Act?" He had to find some way of processing what she was telling him outside of simply repeating everything she said. But she wasn't making any sense.

Marcon steeled himself and started again. "I am not a champion any more than I am a captain, Field Commander."

"Is that so?" A golden glow flared behind her eyes again, but it did not carry the irritation it had toward the pilot. Instead, it seemed almost . . . curious.

"The flame that appeared along your blade—did you not see it?"

"I imagined it," Marcon corrected. He stiffened when he realized he'd forgotten his place.

Silversword chuckled to herself. "Denial is a natural response to the situation. I have seen it before."

Slowly, Marcon shook his head. "I am having diffi-culty believing—"

"That you are a champion of fire? Selected by Ignis himself?"

Marcon swallowed. He couldn't be a champion of fire. There hadn't been a new champion in years—the titans had stopped appointing them, leaving Silversword as one of the last active champions who served in the actual defense of the Cities. The rest had died or moved to less visible positions.

"Ignis chose well," she continued, either unbothered by his confusion or too busy trying to organize the saving of Respite to slow down enough for him to catch up. "Titans forgive me for saying as much, but I believe he would be hard-pressed to find someone more worthy."

"I . . ." Marcon cleared his throat. "Thank you, Field Commander Silversword." He bowed his head as seemed a proper show of deference. "If you'll forgive me, I am afraid I still don't understand. The champions—they are no more. How is this possible?"

A knock sounded against the door as a few aides and a medico gathered outside. Silversword glared at the interruption. "Leave us," she ordered.

The aides responded immediately, but she had to snap at the medico a second time. "Leave or your life is forfeit."

The man repressed a shrill shriek and rushed to follow the aides down the marble-tiled hall.

Silversword rose, crossed her office, and bolted shut the door. Once that was done, she tucked her hands behind her back and strolled toward the row of windows overlooking the city. Despite her short stature, her every movement radiated strength.

The crowds had only grown in size in the interim. The red flags of guards were beginning to form up in opposition to them.

His stomach churned. Alessandra would get her wish

if matters deteriorated. They would turn on one another and tear Respite apart from the inside.

Marcon clenched his jaw and directed his attention away from the windows. His arm still burned. Without waiting for the field commander's permission, he withdrew the bracer from his arm. The burning intensified the moment his skin was exposed to the air.

A mess of swirls and runes had been branded onto his skin, bright red and swollen. Among the markings, he recognized the sigil of the titan of fire. The mark of Ignis.

"Impossible," he murmured.

"Is it?" Silversword challenged, amusement sparking in her eyes.

He turned back to the sigil and gently traced his fingertip over the lines. It burned to the touch, internally and, Marcon winced, singed his fingertip as well.

Jerking his hand away, he watched, eyes wide, as the burn healed itself.

Was this truly the newest in a series of impossible circumstances coming true? Or had he been bitten by Lorieannan back in the field and was hallucinating now as Alessandra's foul magic won his mind over to her dark purposes? He had never considered the possibility that the vultura were thinking beings, their senses confused. Was that what was happening to him?

He shook his head. Too unlikely.

Marcon had never dreamed of setting foot inside the Palace of Respite. He would have settled for fighting within a unit controlled by Field Commander Silversword, though such an attack had been less auspicious than he'd hoped—one in two soldiers wouldn't return from the battlefield, and with so many of their number transformed into vultura, Sanctuary was well and truly lost.

No one would be so foolhardy—egotistical, Garreth would have said—as to try to liberate it again. The city would be known as Reckoning from that day forward.

"I will not bore you with the particulars, Captain Colabra—"

Marcon's pulse stuttered at the title Silversword repeated, especially in the context of his future as a champion. Could such things be true?

"Your confusion is justified." She continued on, ignoring his gasp of surprise. "Suffice to say, after the First Battle of Sanctuary, the leaders of the Cities United and I had a difficult choice to make. It was clear that, if matters had continued forward unchanged, the enemy would eliminate the champions one by one." Silversword positioned herself perfectly between two of the columned window frames, staring out over the city, shoulders rolled back, hands still clasped.

"We had to act and quickly, so a secret resolution was passed." She spun about, and Marcon straightened in his seat, his eyes wide as he stared down to meet her gaze. "We resolved that for the good of all Eldura, champions who were not instantly recognizable, like myself, would go into hiding, using their titans-appointed magic in controlled, special operations units rather than within large military units so that if and when the enemy sensed their magic, loss of life could be minimized."

Marcon could barely internalize what she was

saying, so incompatible was this truth from the lie he'd grown up believing nearly his entire life.

Alessandra hadn't succeeded in eliminating all the champions. They were still alive but in hiding.

And he was one of them.

Silversword's eyes narrowed as she sized him up. "You should know, Colabra, that there are rules regulating our behavior and identity as champions. Rules that, if broken, the consequences will be severe."

Beyond her, the mobs coalesced. Clouds of dust rose in the streets as they rushed forward.

Panic gripped his throat.

True innocents, veterans like Garreth, the few soldiers who remained behind—people who were angry and frightened were facing off against the city watch who had sworn to protect them.

A few distant explosions sounded through the thick glass. Plumes of dust rose in their wake, blocking the chaos of the streets from view.

"Captain—" Silversword's voice was sharp.

Marcon straightened in his chair, forcing himself to attend closely to her words. "You are saying other champions exist."

The dwarf nodded, a single bob of her chin.

"They are in hiding or working within small, secretive units."

Another nod.

"Are there other champions of fire?"

Her mouth quirked upward into a smirk. "For your safety, Captain, I can neither confirm nor deny such a possibility. I can only specify that it is in your best interests to avoid seeking out fellow champions, regardless of their magical inclination. A gathering of two, such as the pairing of you and me in this moment, is, from what we've gleaned, a sustainable collection of magical power in one place. More than two—" The field commander of the Luz shook her head. "It leads to death, and at mass scale. It must be avoided at all costs."

Silversword's following answers were similarly evasive. Her answers grew more satisfactory and concrete as Marcon asked specifically about his own future. "What role do you envision for me as a new champion of fire?"

His mind rebelled at the words, but he held firm.

The field commander's smirk returned. "The manner of your appointment as a champion of fire has opened up some intriguing possibilities for your next steps within the Luz. I understand that you wish to join the Blazing Battalion, is that correct?"

Marcon assented, his pulse racing once more.

"I understand as well that two others of your cohort survived the Second Battle and are making their way back to Respite with all haste."

Marcon's breath caught—*Cole and Vateri*. He couldn't imagine how they would take the fall of the outskirts, the unrest within the city. Lorieannan's passing. But if he still had them, he might be able to weather the rest.

"There may be others as yet unaccounted for, but my sources say that two of those closest to you, a newly appointed Lieutenant Cole and Lieutenant Vateri comported themselves with both wisdom and bravery in the battle."

Marcon could not help the sigh of relief that swept his body. He lowered his head into his hands and breathed deeply, trying to compose himself. Lorieannan was lost to him—his throat constricted—but his friends had survived.

Her smile evened out. "Having loyal companions by your side in the days to come is of the utmost importance. Entrust your identity to them, no one else, so you have someone to confide in, two someones with ears to the ground to ascertain if rumors start to circulate about your abilities so you can either be relocated or those suspecting your gifting can be removed."

Warning bells sounded distantly in Marcon's mind, but they would have to wait. There was too much of dire import in the field commander's immediate information. He could tell Vateri and Cole. It wasn't clear to him how they would take the news, but he could confess it all the same.

"I will have the three of you work toward a transfer to the Blazing Battalion. You will still have to earn such a place, you must understand. Alongside the battalion qualifying training, you will complete training with me until I can be confident in your ability to control your gifting."

That predatory gleam returned to her gaze. "Secrecy is paramount, Captain." Silversword's gaze flickered to the wall of maps. "I think this will work out well for all involved. It will bring a great deal of peace to my mind to know that one loyal to me is stationed within the battalion's ranks. Just as they will benefit from having a champion of fire in their midst."

Marcon frowned at this but said nothing.

Silversword's attention was diverted, and his hesitation passed without remark. "Now." She clapped her small hands together, a startling echo bursting about the spacious room.

"Leave your armor here with me for cleaning. My staff will affix your promoted rank to the pauldrons of your fighting suit. After we've had you fitted for new dress leathers, send them to my aides and we'll do the same."

Another strange request, but maybe it was meant as a favor, something to set him more at ease as he settled into his advanced position alongside his secret identity. "Err, yes . . ." Marcon's cheeks heated as he searched the office for a space where he might change.

"Ah, this way." Silversword gestured, leading him down the hall where he found a side room with changing screen and a fresh set of clothing, almost as though it had been lying in wait for him. A servant waited outside the door with hands clasped at their hips.

The field commander gave her leave and the servant stepped away to give him a chance to change.

With his dominant sword hand, Marcon unbuckled the other bracer, starting from near his elbow and releasing the three straps down to his wrist. He placed it on the floor next to the first bracer he'd removed, the one that hid his champion's mark.

He forced a roll of his shoulders as he removed the leather from the cloth binding beneath then set about removing the cloth. Marcon held out both his forearms, staring down at them. One red and angry, the other marked with dirt and a few pale pink burns.

Marcon lowered his off-sword arm and studied the mark again. Most of the arcane runes he couldn't read. They formed a diamond-like shape around the edges and outlined a fractal with six branches leading toward the center, where he found a mark he had known his entire life. A shield and a tongue of fire—the sign of Ignis, borne by the Blazing Battalion, the fiercest fighters of the Luz. The force that, in generations past, had been led by one of Ignis's chosen, a champion of fire.

Precisely who he was now.

But rather than lead their ranks, he would keep secret his power and identity among them.

Marcon forced his jaw to unclench, turning his attention to the ritual of stripping off his armor, taking stock of his body, his muscles. He would need to visit the medicos and see one of the trainers about a new stretching regimen so his knee would heal quickly.

Ash, grime, and blood coated his body. He hoped there was a tub in the room the attendant would take him to.

The tunic was a similar design to what he'd seen in sketches of the wrapped shirts of the trainees dispatched to Delmoir, which was curious enough. The pants were nearer to those adopted by soldiers of Respite and Beacon, though far too short at the ankles.

The explosions outside had grown more constant, the dust thicker. To this, the aide paid no mind, just as Silversword had seemed uncaring. Instead, the aide bowed her head to a second aide who lingered behind to collect his armor and have it cleaned.

"The field commander will have fresh clothes that are the correct size sent to your quarters and provide for your friends as well," the aide promised with a wide grin as she led him through unfamiliar hallways to his room within one of the interior halls of the palace. "Expect their arrival on the morrow."

She opened the door of a modest chamber with a bed and a copper tub. The aide lingered for a moment, showing him how to work the tap, and assuring him that she would return within the hour with refreshment. "Make yourself comfortable, Captain."

CHAPTER TWENTY-SIX
ROWAN

Rowan's cry of surprise reverberated all around her in a muted echo carried by bubbles along the inky interior of the water. She tried to yank her hand back from her mermaid captor, but the scaled blue fingers held her fast.

She kicked and writhed, struggling to free herself. *I'm sorry*—she thought at the mermaid whose dark hair rippled in thick waves behind her head. *Let me go.*

The mermaid's fin stretched back past Rowan's feet, fanning out in shades of amethyst and sapphire laced with thin strips of pale lichen green.

When her wriggling did nothing to free her, Rowan lashed out with her foot and weakly struck the fin. She mistimed the mermaid's powerful fin strokes and failed to make solid contact.

The mermaid glanced back at her—eyes twin black pools almost like the offering's had been the day before. Rowan jolted at the memory, another burst of bubbles escaping from her mouth in her desperation to get away.

A haunting melody tugged at the edges of her consciousness. Rowan hummed loudly beneath the water, trying to block it out.

A second, harmonizing voice joined the first.

Rowan whirled around, trying to find the second mermaid, spotting her just in time before she joined in the circular strokes of the first, twirling around and around the inside of the orb's pool.

She had been right to suspect the orb of being too small to contain merfolk. In a matter of four or five swipes of their tails, the mermaids could circumnavigate the entirety of their territory.

Her lungs began to burn, and she was no closer to freeing herself.

Rowan reached up and scratched at the arm holding her. When that failed to produce an effect, she jabbed her hand against the edges of the scales. Rowan yelped as the sharply pointed tips sliced her thumb. A bloom of blood swirled behind her in the water.

A shrill, melodic note answered her attack, and the second mermaid closed the space between them.

Their voices melded perfectly together, climbing and dropping across scales that fell outside the patterns of music Rowan had heard in the conclave. In spite of her panic, the music began to soothe her.

"*Help me!*" she demanded of her phoenix.

The bird simply trilled in answer.

"*If they bewitch us, we will both drown.*"

The phoenix trilled again, and the mermaids' song faltered. They stopped swimming, tilting their heads and studying Rowan instead.

Rowan seized whatever opportunity the phoenix had given her and kneed one of the mermaids' wrists, freeing her hand.

She twisted out of the grasp of the other and began kicking madly for the surface.

A third phoenix trill, this one sounding more bored than anything else, reignited the mermaids' song.

The first shot up toward her and seized Rowan's torso and arms, squeezing her tight. The second was more gentle, bobbing behind Rowan and cupping her hands over Rowan's eyes and holding Rowan's head against her scaled breast.

"What did you just do?" she screamed at the bird.

The phoenix squawked back. The golden glow of its eyes communicated one word. *Stop.*

Rowan sighed, releasing a final flurry of bubbles from between her lips. Dark dots were beginning to prick at the corners of her vision, patching over the blue from the mermaid's hands.

She relaxed into the mermaids' grasp and let their songs take her over.

There was no getting away from them in their own environment. Either the phoenix was trying to help, or it had a death wish that would minimize their suffering.

The mermaids' harmonies filled her senses, trickling over her body as smoothly as the water. It caressed the hills and valleys of her muscles. Brushed languidly over her lips. Grasped her throat.

Rowan stilled her struggle, and a third figure joined the other two bodies that held her fast.

The presence was great, near-eternal. Impossibly wide-reaching. Unfathomable.

Salt, sand, and sun filled her senses. From deep beyond the water of the pool—in a watery expanse that defied the workings of time and space, the third figure neared. Two giant pairs of eyes opened, each set layered over the other, the scales around them blue, depths purest silver—*Thalyssa*—her phoenix said in a pulse of recognition.

Rowan relaxed further, her shock at the impossibility of seeing one of the titans, of a titan *noticing* her, over-ridden by the irresistible tide of the figure she was facing.

The darkness thickened in the corners of her eyes. As she gave herself over to the water, to the creatures and mistress of the deep, it told her about itself through a series of flashes—giant swaths of ice as far as the eye could see, the riotous crash of a wave, the gentle burble of a brook, water pouring out of a hole in a leaky well bucket.

A final bubble broke from her nose as the images came faster and faster. A ripple within a puddle between stones, the glimmer of precious rocks catching in the sunlight beneath river rapids, the drum of rain along thatched roofs in a forest settlement built along the ground rather than in the branches.

On and on the images came, and Rowan sank back into the embrace of her captors.

In a flash, the second mermaid removed her hands from Rowan's eyes. The interior of the orb was trans-formed—impossibly bright colors illuminated between sun and sea. An entire community of merfolk lounged upon the rocks, tending to their pet seals, braiding seaweed tendrils into their hair.

The rocks were carefully pointed, like the tips of a crown. The mermaids hummed at this—somehow they sensed her thoughts now. In a vision that swirled past her senses, they catapulted her deeper into the water, holding fast upon the manes of the seawolves—daimon like Viridian but with fins and great sweeping tails.

They pulled her into the deep, into a city captured in story but that no land-dweller she'd met had ever visited —the kingdom of the merfolk, Nepta. From a distance, they gave her a bright view of their vast city's towers beneath the water. It was grander than the varied rooftops she'd seen of Delmoir, different levels of the city spiraling out and up.

The sense of floating, of being tugged through the water, ascending this time, yanked her from the vision.

A garbled cry and Rowan opened her eyes to find Vraise beside her, shouting and kicking at the mermaids.

They warbled their rebuff. One released Rowan's arm and seized Vraise instead. Rowan's head bobbed on her shoulders, and the mermaid shot toward the surface. Her momentum was so great that she pulled Rowan in an arcing leap from the water, depositing her onto the giant, wide bed of a fern.

Vraise sputtered, groaning from the edge of the pool, arms resting along its curved mouth. He coughed up water and rubbed the back of his head.

Rowan turned, hacking up a lungful of water herself, her mind spinning at what she'd just witnessed.

From the upper pool, two beautiful scaled heads

with giant eyes watched her, heads tilted as she recovered, as she gulped in air.

They opened their mouths and sang to her, the sound less resonant than it was beneath the water. When they sang, the pools transformed, returning to the brilliant blues with pinks, purples, and greens she had seen beneath the surface.

When they stopped, the mar of algae and artificial nature of their trapped abode returned.

They retained a connection to their titan regardless of the prison the Pentacle had made for them.

Rowan sighed, brushing her hair back, a last cough sputtering out of her chest.

"Now you see in part, phoenix-keeper." The perfect melody of the voice reverberated within her mind and made the hairs along her back and arms stand on end.

"Water carries life and transformation. It shapes itself to its vessel. Gives being to the imagination."

Four scaled hands clacked their nails against the sides of the orb before they shoved away from the side, arcing back with twin splashes into the water.

Rowan stared after them, mouth fully ajar.

"What in the hells was that?" Vraise cried. "What just happened?"

Before Rowan could answer him, their young elven charge sprinted up the rocks past Rowan and Vraise. "Forsythia, wait!" Rowan cried. She flailed against the bed of ferns, slipping and sliding along their leafy surfaces.

Vraise shouted for the child as well, shoving himself out of the water, his vest and tunic plastered to his skin and boots squelching from where he'd dived in to save Rowan.

Forsythia cheerfully ignored them, balanced upon the rocky ledge, and plunged her head beneath the water, her little hands gripping the sides.

A pure song echoed out across the largest of the three orb bowls, and two alto voices answered.

The tall rays of the sun illuminated the center of the pool where the two mermaids held hands and spun in a circle, their free hands extended up toward the elven child.

Rowan and Vraise reached her at the same time, hovering on either side of her slim shoulders.

"She seems happy," Rowan said.

"How is she . . . She doesn't speak."

Another refrain passed between the mermaids and the little elf. The two women in the water caught their arms around each other's shoulders, their heads bowed as the song's final note rang out.

Forsythia tossed her head back from the water, her dark hair sending a small wave out from her, splashing across Vraise's face.

He squinted shut his eyes and huffed.

The elven girl covered her hands over her mouth, her eyes alight with mischief.

Rowan reacted too slowly to prevent her own chuckle from escaping through her lips.

Vraise pushed the droplets from his eyes and glared between Forsythia and Rowan. "Do you think this is funny?" His hands formed a complex series of gestures again that Rowan assumed echoed the question in a way the child could understand it.

Forsythia nodded, sparking a second wave of laughter from Rowan and more frustrated grumbling from Vraise.

The child's shoulders dipped side to side, as though the melody was still reverberating within her mind. She turned and reached out for Rowan's hand and led her back down to the second pool of water.

She stopped in the center of the rocks and turned back for Vraise who was watching the pair of them with hands on his hips.

When he met Rowan's gaze he softened, shook his head, and ambled after them. "You really should look more flustered after nearly drowning," he said as he rejoined Forsythia and Rowan.

The young elf was picking bits of algae out of her hair.

"And you shouldn't scare me like that," he told Forsythia who only smiled in reply.

The three of them settled into a spot in the sun. Rowan stripped out of her tunic and boots, and Vraise did the same. They draped them over the rocks, and she recounted what she had seen beneath the water.

They tried various activities to commune again with the element of water. Just like she'd known what needed to occur the day before, Rowan's stomach twisted with the knowledge that they would have to touch the pools again before they could fully understand Thalyssa's element.

As the sun drew low in the sky, she and Vraise

decided there was nothing for it and returned to the edge of the pool. He hefted Forsythia onto his hip so she could balance as well.

The moment their hands all touched the surface of the water, the mermaids leaped out of the upper pool and into theirs.

Forsythia signed frantically to Vraise who shook his head. "It's dangerous."

"What is she saying?"

His jaw clenched as he looked between the child and the water. "She says they have something to tell us before we depart."

"Maybe we can just stick our heads in this time?"

"I hope so. I almost drowned trying to save you from the same before."

It made sense the mermaids would ask them to reenter the water. Her hair had finally dried.

The three of them took a deep breath and stuck their heads back into the water, Rowan holding onto Forsythia to help her balance.

The voices surrounded them again.

Rowan wasn't entirely shocked to find the mermaids suddenly appearing within arm's reach when she opened her eyes under the water.

Vraise exhaled in surprise, a flurry of bubbles separating them from the figures.

Like before but much more quickly this time, the thought-waves from the mermaids struck Rowan. *"You care for one of our young ones marooned on the land. Protect her, and we will see your first imbuing delivered."*

Forsythia sang back, and Vraise stared openly at the mermaid.

She grinned back at him, batted scaled eyelids, and shoved a wall of water to splash against them and drive the three of them back over the side, soaking Vraise from head to toe again.

Forsythia fell back onto the rocks behind them, hands draped over her stomach, shoulders shaking with silent laughter.

***

The three of them spent an hour on a sunny rock, allowing their garments to dry again before climbing out of the lagoon and riding back to the academy. As they lounged in companionable quiet, Rowan's head spun from the mermaid's declaration of Forsythia as one of their own—how was such a thing possible? She was no closer to understanding the larger implications when the three of them climbed back up to the opposite wall of rock to ride out and report their day's lessons to Tullemaien.

They bore almost identical rings of water around their shoulders from their drenched hair, with Vraise's curls more disheveled than Rowan had ever seen them.

She mounted Gardenia and settled the merchild trapped on land on the riding blanket before her. Vraise swung up onto his cervidae and fell into the middle position behind their guide.

Something about the lagoon nipped at the base of Rowan's neck as she turned away and began to direct

Gardenia into the woods. For a moment they stopped, and she turned back.

Along the top of the waterfall, silhouetted against the setting sun, she could almost have convinced herself that a great winged figure had been watching over her, the bat-like wings pointing toward one another like a crown overhead.

She squinted to see closer, but the figure was no longer there. It was a tree with a strange growth habit, nothing more.

Rowan tapped the cervidae's sides with her feet. Gardenia huffed through her nose and followed after the mare, leaving the lagoon and her imagined sighting of the guardian behind.

CHAPTER TWENTY-SEVEN

THE NAMELESS WITCH

THE EMERAUDE

Deep within the evergreen boughs of the Emeraude, near the thick, twisting bands of the Iclyee where the river runs north, a young witch sat in the center of her hut, staring at a shard of glass. The shard had been dropped by a caravan that passed within a league of her coven. She found it two suncycles ago, roving through the trees, in practice preparation for the Ceremony of Naming.

The ceremony she was finally old enough for.

Within the glass, the witch saw a ghost—not like the spirits that spoke to her, unseen, within the deep recesses of the forest. More the ghost of a false memory, for in the glass, the witch glimpsed her childhood imaginings of the mother who she only knew through a few scant stories, recounted by a friend.

The previous herbalist Baba Mae had told her enough times that they looked alike that she couldn't see anything else within the mirror fragment. Pale, olive-toned skin with a slight flush from the chill that whistled through the gaps in the sticks that made the outside of her hut—gaps she would need to mend before winter.

By winter, she would be no more, or she would have a name.

Above the spangle of freckles atop her flushed cheeks and below the black sheets of her hair, two bright blue orbs shone. Tiny flecks of copper and gold winked from within the azure spheres. A blue so bright strangers will think you blind, Baba Mae liked to say.

Not blind. Just nameless.

The witch sighed as she tucked a thick strand of hair behind the delicate point of her part-elven ears. Her mother had been a half-elf, her father human, which made her neither, really—almost as unknowable as being a nameless.

It was by the goodness of the coven's hearts that she and her mother had been allowed to live at all, the breathing elders had told her all her life.

The nonbreathing elders, the trees, were never so blunt nor so cruel.

The witch leaned forward and exhaled onto the glass, polishing it with a bunched corner of her mother's threadbare shawl so as not to cut her wrist upon the mirror's sharp edges. Beyond her looks, the shawl was the last remnant she had of her mother.

"I'm finally old enough," she told her reflection. The nameless witch stared back at her. Apprehensive, that was the word for her expression.

"I'm as ready as I know how to be," she added. This

year, she would prove herself to her coven and join their ranks as a true member. By the start of the harvest season, she would have a name.

From within the center of the coven's settlement, the chimes signaling the matron's call rang out. *Finally*. The matron would announce that the Ceremony of Naming was near at hand, giving the nameless witches a fortnight to prepare so that they might prove themselves to the matron and their coven.

The witch gasped and scrambled to her feet, ducking outside her hut and rushing to the center of her forest home. This was the start of what she'd been waiting for —training for—for years.

She was one of the first to arrive and took her position along the outskirts of the concentric circles of logs, lingering as near as she dared to the gap in the coven's circle around the matron's pedestal where the renge would assemble. They were the huntresses and cervidae riders who provided for and protected the coven from without.

It was her dearest wish to join their number upon her naming day.

Two weeks and she might.

And she would have a name.

The murmurings of the coven rose and rippled around her as more and more assembled to hear the matron's announcement. The other nameless fidgeted with their tunics. One chewed on a loose strand of hair.

Just before the matron's arrival, the renge emerged from the shadows of the trees and filed into their shoulder-to-shoulder rows, filling in the open space of the gathering, their gazes fixed as one upon the matron's empty chair. The witch knew a few among their number, had been a couple of years behind them in school. They held their shoulders back now, like their leaders. Two of them wore quivers of arrows strapped to their backs. The witch's eyes widened. *Cervidae riders, at such a young age.* The position she coveted above all others within the ranks of the renge.

If the matron could only see how hard she'd worked, how much she desired to earn her place among them, she would strive tirelessly to prove her worth. To give back to the coven.

Anything beyond giving her spirit to the forest and being no more.

She dug her bare toes into the dirt while she waited for the matron to appear and initiate the fortnight countdown to the ceremony, careful not to crinkle any fallen leaves with her feet lest the noise draw unwanted attention. Her only true friend in the coven, Baba Mae, had passed two winters ago. She'd spoken to a few peers and her tutors since then, but with the matron waddling up toward the central platform, it was dangerous for her to draw negative attention toward herself.

The matron was the one who would decide, ultimately, whether she received a name.

Silence fell upon the coven as the matron emerged into the center of the circle, with the only whispers passed upon the voices of the trees. The witch echoed the posture of the cervidae riders and raised her head high, pretending she bore a quiver of arrows as well.

Her imagining held until the matron's cloudy eyes

swept the gathering and she shrank in on herself, leaning out of sight behind those seated in front of her. Other nameless and a few who, like her, trespassed upon the generosity of the coven by virtue of their existence, lingered along the edges of the gathering.

It would not do to draw the matron's ire, and with each passing year, such a possibility grew more likely for even slight infractions.

This matron had held her position of power the whole of the witch's life and had taken over the role from her own mother, much like the Oracle of the Pentacle was said to—only the witches of the Emeraude would never eat another witch's eyes.

To open the gathering and call the witches and silent spirits to order, the matron raised short, wrinkled arms toward the forest canopy and began her speech, calling in the harvest season. "The Ceremony of Naming began long, long ago, back when the Emeraude Forest still resembled her name. Countless armies have marched beneath the ancient boughs since then, stripping gems and minerals from the earth and maiming the living totems of our ancestors, the beings who stretch between earth and sky."

All around the young witch, the named members of the coven nodded.

She bit her lip and glanced up at the dark green of the nearby trees. To her, the Emeraude still resembled the most beautiful emerald she could imagine, even though she'd never seen one in actuality. How could a gemstone that resembled the green of the trees be more green or beautiful than the living ancients who protected the witches and supported the other forest life?

So near to her own possible naming, another part of the matron's speech confused her. What did the external world have to do with their coven when these forces they spoke of—cities—with buildings and rocks where trees should be were so impossibly far away?

There were outside forces near at hand—she knew this well. Her shoulders tightened. The settlement where her father had come from, for instance. One of two outsiders rumored to be connected to her mother. The other was not a human but a fae and had been the one to beg the coven to take in and shelter her grandmother and her mother in the decades before.

Baba Mae had said the fae was best not spoken of. The fae had failed to save the witch's grandmother and mother and had been expelled from the coven. No one beyond Baba Mae had ever mentioned the fae to the witch, but she held on to the memory of Baba Mae's tales in her dark moments, when the fear of what might be pressed too close and blotted out all light.

'Unaccountably angry,' the herbalist had said. And then she'd hugged the tiny witch to her chest and allowed her to cry.

Coven life was hard enough. It was much worse as a nameless alone.

The matron had continued her speech while the young witch's mental fingers combed through the delicate fronds of her past. "The forest goddesses punished the covens for failing to protect their home from outside forces. She sent raiding bands who pillaged and burned."

Murmurs of agreement followed this declaration. More than one named witch nearby cast a sour glance at the nameless witch. Her father was rumored to belong to one such band. He too had tried to save her mother from the spirit harvest.

The young witch swallowed down the wish that he would do the same for her if she failed in the ceremony. She tightened her fists. She would *not*.

"We understood the missives of the goddesses," the matron continued. "The tribulations of the outside world are not our concern. That is why two decades ago, beneath the guidance of myself and at the instruction of the Great Coven, we did as the goddesses bade and withdrew deeper between the trees. From our new position, we made a vow to the goddesses. We swore to protect our homes and to hold that aim above all others."

Several among the conclave gripped their athames at this reminder, raising the ceremonial blades overhead. Others dipped their fingers into jars of sacred water, pulled from the meeting of the rivers by the Great Coven's home further north and sprinkled the water about themselves.

The members of the renge raised two fingers to their lips, signaling the sacred silence of the hunt.

The nameless witch sighed as the matron's speech neared its end.

"In spite of our failings, pieces of the old remain true," she pronounced. They all knew this part of her speech by heart—it hadn't changed in the twenty years of her rule. "We remain, here, hidden inside this forest.

The Emeraude is our birthright and we, hers, whether the changing limbs interspersed with the evergreen are bare or blossom-laden.

"Traders seeking our wisdom—those who pass through but never remain. They bring gifts to our home. Their ships bring rare herbs from Lis-Maen. Others carry fine teas from the south, harvested in the rolling fields that stand between here and Palais. They climb the hillsides, into the mountain peaks, and descend again into the vast reaches of our forest."

The young witch held her breath. This was the part of the speech she'd been waiting for. The part that opened the coven for new members. For the granting of names. She grasped her arms and hugged them against her ribs to restrain her excitement.

"Each naming, we strive to return the forest to her former state. When all is as the goddess wills, the Emeraude will return to the way she was made. And we, the faithful, will ascend into the power we were destined to command."

With that, the matron dismissed the coven, and the young witch joined in the struggle among her peers, preparing herself for what was to come—the Ceremony of Naming with the first harvest of the suncycle.

Every summer for as long as she could remember, she had heard the story of the witches' connection to the Emeraude, their sacred task in righting the forest following outside influence. And every summer for the past few years, she had hoped that a miracle might occur and she would be named early. Such a miracle had not come to pass, and this year was the first in which she was truly old enough for such an honor to be bestowed upon her.

It was also the first year in which she was old enough to be a spirit harvest. Like her mother had been, and her grandmother before her.

As the changing leaves deepened in color overhead, as the coven built the fires to celebrate the first harvest, the gentle swell of heat before the cooling autumnal breezes, the elders reminded the nameless why they were without a name to call.

It was not yet time, but soon would be.

Again and again she had heard those words.

Soon. Soon. Soon.

She narrowed her eyes as she scampered back toward her hut, depositing her shawl before starting on her foraging for the day's needs and to prepare what she could before the ceremony that was exactly one fortnight away.

This time next year, *soon* would mean only a day or two between hunts with the renge.

This time next suncycle, she would have a name.

The matron's speech opened fourteen days and thirteen nights of fluttering activity in which the nameless among the coven who were of age could prepare for the Ceremony of Naming.

Each day she would rise at dawn and walk barefoot to the edge of the Iclyee where she wandered after depositing her mother's shawl back at her hut. She paused, looking over the gaps in the sticks, the holes in the patches of mud that had been worn through by the spring rains.

There would be time after she'd prepared for the Ceremony of Naming to tend to such matters, and that was only if they didn't immediately relocate her into the shared huts of the renge.

Her mind whirled at the possibility. Imagine, not living alone.

The next morning, thoughts of named friends calling out to her carried the witch down to the river. She cast her smile upon the familiar water, the earth cool under her feet. The young witch crouched, hand balanced upon a nearby tree as she dipped her toes forward. The cold bite of the rushing water pricked her skin. She settled down upon the bank, her feet immersed in the water. The burbling rapids soothed the frayed edges of her spirit.

My mother was a spirit-vessel, she thought to the waters.

It was the fate she hoped to avoid above all others.

However great the honor the witches claimed such a sentence was, she wanted to remain in her body. Not be sent as a spirit to renew and protect the forest.

This hope, the river knew. "That is not so dark as it seems, little one," the water replied.

She shivered when she caught the river's voice. The Iclyee was one of a few spirits who whispered the thrilling edge of a name in her ear as it addressed her. The witch wiped the end of her nose, a rounded ball of cold against the back of her hand. A chill had swept through the coven in the night, and her scant hut on the edge of the settlement struggled to keep out the harsh wind.

I want to be something else, she told the waters. The coven had sacrificed her mother's energy, her body, her being. And still they said it was not enough. Still they needed more. *I want to live. To continue to be.*

"Hmm," the water rumbled. "We asked to remain ourselves at the dawn of the worlds. The goddesses gave us each other instead."

An honor, her coven would have said. But all the river's water was allowed to return. It continued to babble and breathe.

It had not had its throat slashed. Its blood given unto the earth.

Its voice never to be heard by its daughter again.

Her lips trembled as she thought over what might happen during the Ceremony of Naming. The dreaded answer the matron might give if she failed to prove herself, failed to show them how valuable she could be.

One evening, a week before the ceremony, she watched the new wrinkled herbalist grind the river-wet sage beneath the worn stone of her pestle. The witch and the other nameless had gathered outside her hut for their weekly lesson.

The syrupy gurgle of the herbalist's concoction wafted scents of spring-melt and soft mint with each circular grind. The scent reminded the witch of the herbalist who had been her friend, who had passed on.

This herbalist's voice quavered as she spoke, "Those who don't belong, who would cause us harm, don't make it far, even if they try to flee the forest. The maera see to that." The pointed ends of the old woman's filed teeth glinted in the firelight as her eyes rested on the semi-circle of upturned faces.

The herbalist spared no more than a glance for the witch before moving on. This was the way it had always been.

This herbalist was one of the few who passed on to a second life within the coven, having served the renge before beginning a second study when the embedded mark of the crow already pressed at the corners of her eyes. Though she'd studied with the witch's friend, none of the friend's warmth had passed on to the new herbalist.

Her training had occurred at a time when the forest was leaner than it was now, a few years before. But even then, the coven sacrificed so the herbalist could live on among them. Most of the elderly who did not pass into the matron's confidence were not so lucky.

The best chance for such a second life was joining the renge, the band of fierce witches trained in hunting, combat, and the seeing arts. They slipped as shadows between the trees or rode the coven's herd of cervidae after their prey. They left offerings for the maera to keep their greedy appetites away from the coven and worked closely with the remaining daimon pack who roamed at the base of the mountains. The Emeraude had been the home of the daimon before the goddesses sent the witches here.

From an early age, the witch had learned to fear and respect all who called the forest home. If she could find a way to prove her worth to the Emeraude, the forest would find a way to let her stay.

The night before the naming, the dark moons rose, an auspicious conjunction, the matron had declared, a sign that even the oldest coven members had witnessed only once in this lifetime, about twenty years before.

She sat outside for a long time that night. Star-stories glimmered down at her, winking in turn behind the veil of thin clouds.

To take part in the Ceremony of Naming, after reaching the proper age, each nameless presented the matron with a tea of her own creation, a gift in exchange for a name. With a name, a witch became part of the coven. With a name, a witch gained a family and responsibilities to share.

The witch had selected her tea carefully, a unique blend that came from the southern fields best known for their wisdom and seeing properties. She blended the leaves with chamomile, purple ausplind, and a single sprig of lavender and rested the mortar on three fresh leaves—one of bay, one of sage, and one from the rowan tree that leaned out over the river.

With this offering, the matron would see that she was rooted within the coven even though she'd grown up alone. "Each of these I have tended from root to leaf," she longed to say, "just as the coven has raised me." But the offerings were silent.

She still remembered the first time Baba Mae had taken her to see the river and pointed her gnarled finger at the spindly lean of the rowan tree. "Your mother planted that tree the night before you were born," the elder healer had said. "Though they gave her to the forest shortly thereafter, I still see much of her in you."

Baba Mae had told her that her mother possessed the same bright blue eyes, raven-black hair, and olive-toned skin.

How much of her life had she spent trying to prove the resemblance stopped at the surface?

A few of the nameless had begun to follow their mothers in their daily tasks in the weeks leading up to the ceremony. The one with straight brown hair had pressed ink into her fingertips and dribbled three dots onto the end of her nose to show her readiness to join the scribes.

But the nameless witch had no mother to follow.

The night of the ceremony, they gathered in the sacred clearing with the twin shadow moons overhead. Each of the nameless bowed before the matron. She sipped thrice from their cup of tea and pronounced the name the spirits gave her, the one whispered by the earth and the ancestors in the trees.

For three fortnights before the ceremony, the nameless had vied to be the first to present their tea to the matron. The first selection's tea would retain the purest flavor, that of its strongest intent, rather than growing bitter as the ceremony progressed. Name after name proceeded before her.

The witch with the straight brown hair, the matron

sent to join the scribes. Two others joined the renge. One the matron appointed as an apprentice to the new herbalist.

Nameless and motherless, the witch was the last to approach the antlered throne.

Her hands shook as she placed the simple tray on the wooden platform at the matron's feet. Some of the other nameless, especially those whose ancestors had been matrons themselves, possessed heirloom trays, carved with the runes of destiny, foretelling their line's future and recounting their honorable past. Later generations had inlaid the runes with silver or turquoise. Hers was a planed sheaf of bark.

The only past she could claim was that of an outsider and of a spirit sacrifice—both fates ended the same, with the spill of blood upon the earth. Spirit living on, body no more.

She'd held her breath as she took in the other details upon her fellow namelesses' trays. Some held an ivory spoon or jade cup. One had a kettle forged from bronze and polished to shining.

Her own scrounging and scavenging, over the course of years, had allowed her to purchase from a traveling merchant a cracked brass kettle which she curled up next to each night to keep it safe. Beside the kettle, she'd placed a small plate she'd braided from dried spindles of rosemary. On top of the plate was a cup she had spent three great-moons hollowing from the fallen limb of the old oak to ensure no splinters remained.

Her hands clenched into fists as she placed the tray before the matron's wrinkle-squinted eyes. Did the matron know that a few of the coins that had paid for the purchase of the kettle she'd found in her mother's leaning hut when the healers judged her old enough to live on her own? Baba Mae had said that the coins were a gift from her father, a highlander who had begged her mother to run away with him before her own Ceremony of Naming.

What might have happened had her mother assented? Would the souls of the ancestors have risen from their tree trunk graves to prevent her flight? The despiriting ceremony had granted her mother six additional moons, a boon no other vessel had ever had. Her mother was the first spirit-vessel to be with child at the time of her appointment. The coven had to choose whether to sacrifice them both at once or to grant the young, unborn witch a trial as a nameless. They had called themselves merciful, waiting to see if her mother's spirit might be enough to slake the Emeraude's thirst.

Had her mother seen the time to bring her daughter into the world as a blessing? Or did that cast a darker pall over her death, her spirit sent to satiate the dark heart of the Emeraude alone?

The witch stepped back from the matron's feet, her head lowered until she was a respectful distance away. Her palms started to sweat.

All the eyes of the coven turned to the elderly woman perched upon the throne.

The matron opened her palm, and her helper poured the tea.

The matron swirled the wooden cup beneath her nose, wafting the thin stream of steam from the cup into her nostrils. An hour had passed, and the water was only just warmer than the chill of the air that came with twilight. The matron's face betrayed no emotion as she raised the cup to her lips.

I am brave enough to serve the renge, she promised the spirits of the forest. *I will fight honorably and defend you from those who would bring harm.*

The matron stretched her arm out toward the trees, bidding the ancestors nearer. She returned the cup to her lips and sipped again.

If not the renge, then place me with the healers, she asked the spirits as the matron swallowed her second sip. *Allow me to repay them for helping me as a child.*

The matron smacked her lips and placed both hands around the cup for her final draft. As she tipped the dregs of the wooden vessel into her mouth, her eyes rolled in the back of her head. She arched her shoulders against the throne. The liquid wave crested in her chest, and she reared forward. Her eyes flared open, bright yellow now, instead of the brown of damp wood. "Daughter of Teresa," the matron sighed, "the one who fought her fate . . ."

The young witch's heart thudded in the hollow of her chest, the war drum whose beat had followed her every step.

"I have a name for you." The matron's wide, toothy grin had none of a renard's warmth or a daimon's wisdom. She was the mountain lion incarnate, salivating over cornered prey.

Only a few of the coven witches swayed back and forth, like autumn leaves caressed by a cold breeze. The others stared at her, a lone nameless, trapped in the center of their ring. Their eyes were empty reflections of the storied stars above.

No, no, no.

To them, she could never have earned a different fate.

"Tess-sina," the matron hissed.

A shudder rippled over the assembled crowd. A few of the elders gasped. The kindest of the nameless, those who would navigate the ceremony in a future summer's end, raised their hands to cover their mouths.

Named for her mother, the harvested one, whose identity burned only in its extinguishing for the soul of the forest.

And for victory. When the third candle was blown out —her grandmother, her mother, and now her—the line was no more. There would be no further sacrifice. Their imposition on the forest, their position as outsiders, would end.

The matron raised her head to take in the coven surrounding them.

Far, far away, the river roared.

"My sisters and daughters," the matron called as, above, the treetops writhed and whispered, "my mother's sins from decades ago will this night be undone." With shaking arms, the matron pushed herself up from her antlered throne. She pointed a gnarled finger at Tess-sina's chest as the old herbalist, Baba Mae, had done to show her the rowan tree so long ago. "Some thought it a mercy to grant additional moons for this child to be born, but the spirits have not agreed. The spirits show us an altogether different truth, one I declare to you now— We've no need of pollution from beyond our borders, no invasive streaks of mercy for those who do not to our forest belong. There is but one path forward, one way to right the past wrong."

Ravens croaked within Tess-sina's mind. *So this was why.* Her hands twitched. *You only pretended to offer shelter to one not your own. To a woman and her daughter and her daughter's daughter who came from outside.*

You meant to make an example of us instead.

To harvest us to the forest.

For our spirits to serve the Emeraude.

The matron's screech shot out across the clearing, her hands raised to the cloudy sky. "Our forest will grow strong again," she cried. "With the third gone, a tripart harvest served over years and in blood, we shall renew the spirit of our woods. And then, the Emeraude revived, the goddesses' blessings shall once again be ours!"

The witches screamed, their hands and faces upturned to the closed eyes of the moon goddesses high above. Others stomped their feet, alerting the spirits who slithered across the earth below. The time for their sacrifice had come.

"Arise, Emeraude," the seers shouted, "arise!"

Tess-sina's legs shook.

The winnowers grinned as they swept their scythes in front of their chests. They began to chant the spirit-severing song.

This was the dark side of the renge, the sacred task Tess-ina tried to forget was theirs to carry out.

They would be the ones to harvest her spirit for the forest.

The ones to end her line.

The matron nodded at Shadda, the leader of the

renge, one who was both a cervidae rider and a winnower.

The warrior's curved blade sighed as she pulled it free from her sheath. Their energy, their power, hummed as one.

"No," Tess-sina whispered. After all she had done, all she had tried to be.

They would tear her spirit from her body and give her corpse to the ancestor trees.

Spirit-harvest. A feeding, deepening, of the magic of the forest.

Shadda would slit her throat and spill her blood upon the ground, like her predecessor had done to her mother Teresa, the harvested one.

The Emeraude was hungry, vengeful, and in need.

Tess-sina's thigh muscles twinged. She glanced at the surrounding circle of witches. They pressed shoulder to shoulder together.

She could never run free.

A raindrop plinked down into the empty cup of tea the matron had cast aside. It looked like a pine cone shed by the evergreens. Shadda twirled her blade in her hand and stomped across the clearing.

The coven's pounding feet raced with Tess-sina's heart.

"This won't be enough," she shouted at the matron. But the wide panther's smile continued to shine.

From deep within the forest, a raven croaked.

And then another.

For a moment, the stomping faltered.

The patter of raindrops tiptoed closer, tiny stones

running across the Emeraude's hair. The rain's stream trickled down from the leaves and sprinkled across the clearing like a warm spray of blood.

The warrior wiped the water over her face, rubbing the water spirits' blessings into her skin. "By the light of the day and the dark of the moons"—Shadda murmured the renge's prayer of sacrifice as she advanced—"over mother earth and her lover, the dancing air . . ."

Whooshing wind rose overhead, buffeting the splay of branches.

Tess-sina backed away, her feet slipping on a soggy patch of leaves.

The warrior shouted to be heard by the spirits over the howling wind. "By fire's bite and water's power, we release thee to the void, into the forgotten embrace of nature's bower."

Lightning crackled as Shadda hefted the shining curve of her blade overhead.

Tess-sina cried out.

And the thunderous form of a shadow-spirit with wide raven's wings burst into the space between them.

The impact drove the warrior from her feet and sent Tess-sina skidding over the damp carpet of fallen, dirt-colored leaves.

The raven spirit did not fly alone. Darting shadows flooded the clearing, swooping upon the driving waves of the rain. They dove from the treetops into the water-logged earth, the ground shaking as they struck against the foundation of root and rock below.

Witches screamed as they fled through the forest, abandoning the press of their circle. The sweeping storm of ravens pursued them into the trees. The witches' shouts echoed through the dark.

The matron bellowed, her hunched body erect before her throne. Her fingertips writhed as she bid the ancestors' spirits to spring forth from the trees and defend her. "Enact the Emeraude's will!" she ordered her warrior.

Shadda rose to her feet and tossed back the long, golden locks of her hair. The warrior froze as the winged silhouette of a woman strode forth from the trees, barreling straight toward the place where the giant raven had appeared.

Tess-sina's lips fell open. The Emeraude's spirit-protectors were said to be women with wings, the fallen warriors of old who would one day rise in answer to the forest's call.

A second flash of lightning crackled overhead. Tess-sina gasped. This was no spirit. A sepia-skinned fae strode into the clearing. She pulled taut the longbow in her hands. Upon her back, slate-colored wings fluttered as a mist in the night.

Shadda halted, halfway between Tess-sina and the fae. She turned to the matron.

And in her doubt, the warrior sealed her own fate.

The fae glanced at Tess-sina. Lavender irises glowed. "Run," she breathed. In a single fluid motion, she turned her bow from Shadda to the matron and loosed the arrow she held.

Tess-sina sprinted toward the cover of the trees.

With her second footfall, the arrow found its mark. Tess-sina glanced back. The arrow creaked through the ancient body, thudding to a stop as the indigo fletching met the bone of the matron's chest. Thick torrents of blood pooled over wrinkled skin, soaking the elder's cloak.

Shadda's cry rent the trees. Branches tumbled free. Tess-sina dodged one's grasping fall and slid clear of a second.

Ahead of her, the river called.

Three shadow ravens flitted to her side. They burst against the raining limbs. Tess-sina raised her arm, shielding her face from the splintered spray.

She leaped over fallen limbs as the ravens coalesced around her. The cries of her coven faded as the thunderous voice of the river bid her back to its earthen banks.

The rowan tree bowed in the storm. One of her branches broke free and pitched into the water.

"This way," a whispered voice, one she'd never heard before, murmured inside her mind. *"Follow the rowan and find your destiny."*

Tess-sina leaped past her mother's tree and plunged into the icy waters below. The rushing cold pounded against her ears. Life and memory pulsed and rolled all around her. The spirits pressed against her lungs as the current dragged her to the water's surface.

She gasped for breath, tugging her head free from the churning rapids. A path of winding dark rolled over rocks and forest ahead of her, rumbling deeper into the heart of the Emeraude.

Battered and bruised from the worn, hidden teeth of the Iclyee, Tess-sina swam for the shallows and dragged herself ashore. Water streamed from the sodden wool of her dress. Her thin leather boots—pulled out and polished for the ceremony—squelched in the sand as she sank onto the riverbank.

Wafting waves of energy and the persistent beat of wings approached. Tess-sina tilted her head back.

The fae archer clamped her wings tight together and plummeted onto the sand beside her, fist, foot, and knee striking at once. She bent her head toward Tess-sina's. Dark blue braids fell free from her shoulder. Up close, a pattern of tattoos covered her skin, the same slate as her wings covering over the sepia glow. The markings were druidic or some other ancient form of magic, Tess-sina wasn't sure.

A single shadow raven, the same size as the tree dwellers she had known all her life, flapped down onto the sand in front of her. The bird croaked and tilted its head.

The fae raised her eyebrow at the spirit familiar. "He wants to know your name," the archer said as she turned back to Tess-sina. "What is it?"

Her breath hitched in her throat. *Teresa*, her mother's name. Little one, the river had whispered. Harvest and victory, the matron had called her.

She took the fae's proffered hand and pulled herself up to her feet. Her lips twisted into a smirk as her spirit supplied the name—the calling—she had long been without. "Tessina," she answered. A name reclaimed for the lost spirits of her mother and grandmother, and from their broken legacy, a new path opened before her.

Rather than being the harvested, as her mother had been named, she would be the harvester, winnower, caretaker. Instead of cutting down those who were lost, sacrificing those who did not fit, and expelling those who carried reminders of strangeness and an outside world in their veins, she would be their spirit-beacon in the darkness. To protect them, she would be a harvester of those who winnowed the souls of innocents.

A new legacy. A new name.

CHAPTER TWENTY-EIGHT

MARCON

Marcon collapsed onto the narrow bed in the stone room where Field Commander Silversword's attendant had led him, his knees finally giving out beneath the strain of the last several days.

Beyond the windows of his chamber, smoke still choked the skies, curling and black. Mercifully, he couldn't see the city streets from here, only the orderly rows of the barracks.

"We're lucky the city didn't fall," he'd overheard Silversword tell the pilot.

Marcon slumped forward, catching his forehead with his hands. *Lucky.* As though he hadn't just slain the reanimated corpses of the couple who'd raised him after his parents had died fighting for the Luz. As though the field commander whose strategy had failed to recapture Sanctuary—who had been in charge of the battle that had made him an orphan and had called for the march to Sanctuary in the first place—hadn't just torched the woman he'd thought at one time he would spend the rest of his life with in a beam of supernatural light.

Failure, failure, failure. The word spun around and around Marcon's mind.

How was he to face Vateri and Cole? Were they experiencing the same? Did they even know yet what they were returning to?

And how would they take his news that he was a champion of fire? Would they even believe him, or would it take his lessons with the field commander for them to take him at his word?

Wearily he slumped back, allowing his arms to flop down onto his thighs. He couldn't imagine Garreth's reaction to his special lessons with Silversword, and he had no idea how to tell the blacksmith who had become like a father to him that he would be studying with a woman Garreth considered an enemy.

But the battle of Sanctuary had shown him the true stakes of the larger fight for Eldura. Marcon tensed his jaw, knowing what had to be done but not wanting to do it.

There would be no turning back from his vow of vengeance. No reversal of the promise he'd made. And no release from the bond that he'd sworn.

He groaned as he sank deeper into the mattress. The bed frame creaked as he did so—most likely designed for light-footed aides and not well-muscled soldiers. *Champions,* he corrected himself.

Silversword had dodged his questions about the other champions, insisting that he needed rest, all would be explained in time. Was he the only champion of fire that remained?

A soft knock sounded against his door. "Pardon, sir, err, Captain? Your dinner was ready early." The voice was shy and apologetic, one that, in other circumstances, Marcon might have gone out of his way to help feel at ease.

But for now he only had the strength to rise from his horizontal posture and press himself up to standing, the muscles along his calves cramping as he shuffled forward to take the proffered tray.

His eyes grew heavy as he limped back toward the bed. Food, bath, sleep, he promised himself.

"I've brought you some towels as well," the servant said, padding in after Marcon and setting the towels on a stool by the bath. "Will you need a medico's attention tonight?"

"No." Marcon regretted the gruffness of his tone but couldn't bring himself to apologize to the frightened aide.

"I'll leave the altered clothing outside for you," the aide promised before scurrying away.

He dropped onto the edge of the bed again, shoulders hunched.

It was all too much.

Lorieannan. Joane and Abbot. A champion.

Marcon's throat tightened. When he looked at the tray of food, he felt sick.

Maybe just a bath, then, and he'd see about the rest later.

Turning the tap, he twisted his wrist and tugged against the sigil newly burned onto his arm.

Yet another scar to serve as a reminder of his failure of his city, of those he'd sworn to protect.

Marcon's shoulders tightened as he sank into the heated water of the tub, even in this small way refusing to allow him to relax until he'd uncovered some way to begin to make right what he'd done. Worse, what he'd failed to do.

He leaned back against the edge of the copper tub. "I don't know," he murmured, lifting his arm out of the water and studying the runes. A normal burn would be sensitive to the water's heat, but this one didn't burn. It found the heat soothing instead.

Marcon propped his arm along the side of the tub and closed his eyes. Against the back of his eyelids, he could have sworn the faint light of embers glowed within his sigil.

His vow to the titan of fire.

TALI

The first champion of fire in years, Tali thought to herself as she marched past her office toward her private quarters, shoulders back and head high.

The loss of the generals upon the ramparts was unfortunate. The fourth general had perished just before her conference with the new champion. His loyal guards had barricaded him in his office, but they hadn't been suspicious enough of the runner sent up from the kitchens with food and drink for the panicked general.

A crash from inside the chamber had seen the guards wrenching open what they'd nailed shut. A pool of vomit and blood was already crusting before the general's corpse, his lips the dark purple of a bruise.

Tali shook her head. The loss of Respite's leaders was nothing she and the secret council couldn't handle.

She'd have to make an appearance before the crowds, rally their hope, make a speech about togetherness in a time of loss.

As ordered, one of her spies was waiting outside her prayer chamber.

"Did you get the armor?"

The spy gave a single nod of her head. She was of the number who had given their tongues in a show of their commitment to secrecy. Though Tali wasn't one to encourage such antics, she appreciated the demonstration of devotion.

"Preserve every drop of blood you can. Not all of it will be his, but some will be."

The blood of a champion of fire was precisely the bargaining chip she needed to secure the next stage in her plan. She would divide it between the Cities' alchemists and devise an offering of the rest to Alessandra's servants to buy the Luz more time to organize themselves after their embarrassing defeat in Sanctuary.

Or so it would seem to their enemies.

The spy bowed and scurried off to do as she was bid.

Tali lingered at the door to her private sanctuary, a room enclosed deep within her rooms where no light could penetrate so she might prove to Ilona her own dedication. There were two champions who were growing unruly, struggling to keep secret their identities within their special units. That was what the messenger from the Secret Council had whispered to her with the new champion of fire only a few feet away.

Marcon was more composed than most of the rest. And already loyal to her, which was a boon as well.

The report had indicated that there were strange surges of power afflicting the two champions, making their power unwieldy. One champion of air, the other of darkness.

Tali lifted her amulet into her hand, staring down at the golden sun inlaid with opal. The excuse smacked of weakness. And there was no room for weakness in the rise of the Cities United.

She dropped the necklace and forced a slow exhale before slipping into her chamber to perform ablutions and attempt yet another prayer to Ilona. Maybe this time the titan would hear her and answer?

But whether she did or not, Tali had a new way to prove her loyalty, a new weapon within the Cities' arsenal with which to win the forgiveness of her titan. The blood of a champion of fire, distilled into alchemists' fire.

The perfect weapon to take down the forest peoples if they continued to resist the Cities' alliance.

And the perfect weapon to wield against the commoners of Respite if they could not manage to calm themselves and accept the loss of the outskirts, those who contributed little, who had been a plague upon

Respite's resources in a time of war. No one necessary had been lost.

The alchemists' fire, fueled by the last champion of fire was, after all, precisely what Alessandra was using to scorch the Glade of Shadows, ridding Eldura of the dryads and their judgmental resistance to the wheels of progress.

Too like our enemy? Tali's smirk widened, remembering the Druidess's accusation the last time the Cities had met with the Pentacle. *You have no idea.*

CHAPTER TWENTY-NINE

TESSINA

"So who are you?" Tessina cocked her head as she stared up at the fae.

"Yvayne."

She bit her lips together, waiting for more. Perhaps the fae carried a great deal of weight behind her name too. Three heartbeats passed. A respectful enough stretch of time. "Do you often drop in on Ceremonies of Naming?"

The fae grinned. "No. But this one was special."

That was one way to describe it. "Did you know my grandmother?"

Yvayne shook her head. "Why would you think so?"

Baba Mae's urging toward secrecy tugged at her sleeve, but if this was the fae she'd heard about, the one who had tried to save her mother and grandmother, she had to know. "I heard about a fae who tried to help them."

The fae brushed the sand off her hands, avoiding Tessina's gaze. "I was, and I owe a great debt to them."

She sighed. "I am sorry I could not do more." Without a glance back, Yvayne began walking deeper into the forest.

Tessina scrambled to follow after her. "Is that how you knew to appear? Did you come to help me?" She held the sopping fabric of her dress off her hips to keep pace with Yvayne. The fae was going somewhere in a hurry. Or she always walked purposefully. Probably that. But her question had to be answered. "*Why* did you rescue me?"

Yvayne scanned side to side as she strode through the forest. Her long legs easily carried her over branches and brambles Tessina had to dodge or struggle over.

"Your old coven is mistaken in what they believe will revive the forest. It won't be a sacrifice, as I tried to tell them before." The fae was careful when she spoke, her accent a whispered memory from somewhere deep within.

Yvayne scowled at a crooked beech tree and changed her direction, angling further away from the river. "With half the titans absent and the champions scattered—"

"I thought the champions were dead."

Yvayne stopped. A beam of green-hued sunlight fell across her lavender eyes. "No, Tessina," she murmured, "but they are in hiding. You are going to help me convince them to return."

With that declaration made, the fae returned to her rapid walk through the forest.

"Wait, what do you mean?" Eldura hadn't witnessed the epic and impossible deeds of the champions since before she was born. So many had perished in the battles to the north, in the fallen city now known as Reckoning.

"That city was the best of our world," Baba Mae had told her as a child. "The High Matron, in her wisdom, left before the final battles when the city fell. She returned to protect the Emeraude and those who dwell within it. In so doing, she severed any ties between our fate and that of the Cities."

Tessina released the spirit-memory into the trees and with it, the tangled unknowns of her past. Yvayne's motivations. The coven's sacrifice of her mother and grandmother. Her own near-death.

The memory fluttered away. Tessina exhaled, her burden lighter without so many internal brambles to bear.

To her surprise, a fevered fluttering sound emerged from the woods in the direction she'd sent the thoughts. Weaving through the tangled branches of the deep forest, a spectral raven cawed and flapped closer, landing on her shoulder. Its spirit-form shimmered in the growing twilight.

Tessina smiled at it and continued. She'd met similar manifestations of her imagination before. They were friends.

She hurried to catch up to Yvayne and tried to find the loose thread she might unravel to understand the fae's logic. Even if Yvayne knew where the few remaining champions were—if any of them had survived—why would they listen to her, a former nameless?

For three days, Tessina followed Yvayne through the woods. Her muscles ached from her escape in the river and her struggle to keep pace with the fae.

The Emeraude grew darker as they walked. The great pines and spruce stared down. At times, the teachings from her coven pressed out of the trees' bark and threatened to overwhelm her, as though the trees knew the sacrifice she should have been.

No, she thought back to their intrusions. Their teachings were false. She would find a new way forward.

The raven spirit remained upon her shoulder as they traveled. On the second day with her new companion, she had begun to whisper her questions to it. Each time she did, the spirits swirled at the raven's heart and its feathers darkened.

Yvayne slowed as they approached the trunk of a sprawling elm tree.

Tessina gasped. A young woman in a brown cloak sat huddled against the bark.

Bodies were this still only in death.

Yvayne nodded at the figure. "Bring her back."

It was the first the fae had spoken all day.

"What?" Surely she had misheard. Such powers were beyond—

"Bring her back," Yvayne repeated.

Tessina tiptoed closer. "But . . ." The girl's white eyes stared blankly out into the woods. "Yvayne, she is gone."

The fae shifted her weight onto her hip. "Your grandmother held the magic I am asking for. She knew how to use it. The coven killed your mother far before her time. I know your bloodline, even if your inheritance was stolen from you. I sense their magic. It is my suspicion that the matron did too, which is why she feared you. You asked me why I rescued you. Beyond my debt to them, it was for this. To rescue her." She nodded toward the woman draped against the tree. "Call her back."

The trembling rose again, the same sense Tessina had carried each day in her coven. She had escaped one death, one expulsion already. What would happen to her if she couldn't wield the magic Yvayne believed she possessed? "I don't understand what you are asking of me."

"Do you not?" Yvayne's shout echoed through the trees. The forest fell silent. Its shadows grew longer. They reached toward the fae. Yvayne pointed at the raven on her shoulder, her sepia and slate arm shaking. "Have you resurrected him yet? Whispered enough spirit-power to revive the raven who materialized from the ghosts of the forest?"

Tessina blanched. Yvayne wasn't making sense. She couldn't restore Elevray from spirit into a fully embodied form, could she?

Tessina stopped herself from arguing with the fae. No one in her coven had ever noticed one of her spirit-friends, though none had stayed by her side as long as the raven had. "Elevray," she murmured to the raven, "where does your spirit live?"

The raven had lost his spectral appearance. His feathers were darker than the new moon. He turned a glimmering black eye toward her.

Tessina repeated the question in her head, rehearsing the many times she had heard the coven witches ask it of the other nameless. The answer was always the same. "With our ancestors," the nameless would say, "at the roots of the Emeraude or hovering in the branches."

At the time, she had been unable to answer this question. Her ancestors' spirits—or at least those of her mother and grandmother—had been devoured in service to the Emeraude.

But perhaps that had been the answer all along. "You're saying my ancestors' spirits weren't extinguished. They live on in another plane?" She squinted at Yvayne.

The fae shook her head. "You have more ancestors than those lost to the Emeraude." She nodded at the body leaned against the elm, a guardian tree of the passageway to death. "A select few of them possessed a gift to awaken spirits that lingered nearby. That was the magic your grandmother held in memory. She passed it to you through blood."

The trees resumed their whispering, and Tessina relaxed. The world was strange, eerie, without their thoughts and melodies.

"H-how did they do it?"

Yvayne scrunched her lips together. "A fair question. And one I cannot answer. It is something you must remember. It is not something you can be taught."

Tessina wrapped her arms around her waist and sank down on the forest floor. Yvayne's demands divided her within herself. On one side, she wanted this magical heritage, what would have seemed impossible to her only a few days before. But on the other, it made her feel the way she had as a nameless, like she was nothing more than a convenience, something to use, and not a being.

The fae turned her feet toward the body. "This girl bears Gaia's mark," she said finally. "The sigil of earth. It marks her as a champion of earth. If you wish for anyone who might be able to reawaken the forest, *all* of the forests, you need look no further."

Tessina did care about the Emeraude. The trees, her mother's rowan, the river—they had looked after her. "But they do not sleep!" Her eyes shot up toward Yvayne. "The trees, I hear them. They are speaking now!" How could the fae not hear?

Her long eyebrows flashed. "That is what I was counting on." Yvayne crossed her arms and stared down at Tessina.

The witch chewed on her bottom lip and turned back to the girl slumped against the tree. "I will try," Tessina whispered.

Yvayne nodded. "I will give you space to work."

After the fae had disappeared between the trees, Tessina crawled closer to the girl. Fallen pine needles pricked the palms of her hands.

Up close, she could make out the faded pattern of bark across the girl's skin. What she had taken to be the shadows brought on by death were simply the natural shading that covered her body.

The girl was a dryad.

"I don't know exactly how to help you," Tessina said. She glanced over her shoulders at the nearby trees. "I have never brought someone back to life before. Maybe you haven't either."

The trees and Elevray watched her. How was she supposed to remember something she had never known?

"Yvayne said that I helped Elevray come back to himself, or helped his spirit to return. She thinks I can do the same for you." Tessina reached out for the girl's hand. Her skin was rough and cold to Tessina's touch. "But all I did for Elevray was to tell him things about my forest and to ask him questions about his life." She sighed. "Yvayne has told me some sad things about you. I didn't realize she was talking about someone specific at first, or that anyone could have survived such destruction."

On their long walk through the forest together, Yvayne had told her the story of a forest very much like the Emeraude, a forest that would soon be no more.

"It is called the Glade of Shadows," the fae had said. "Our enemy is burning it and destroying those who dwell within. It is the sort of fate the matrons have been trying to stave off, though they are not going about it wisely. Soon, the Glade will be no more."

Tessina spoke long into the night. She leaned against the girl's tree and retold the stories she had made up about her parents and their romance, how her mother had rescued a highlander who lost his way in the woods. How desperately he had loved her mother, and how he would have loved Tessina too. She spoke of the Ceremony of Naming and how lonely she had been growing up in the Emeraude.

"This part of the forest doesn't seem so bad," she remarked to the dryad and Elevray. The crickets chirruped around them, and the two crescent moons glowed overhead. Already, the smaller carved a sickle across the sky, while the larger was still thin as an eyelash.

The small hours crept past. An owl hooted overhead, the carrier of wisdom. "I don't know what to do," she murmured to the nighttime sentinel. "I don't know how to awaken one who sleeps. She walks in dreams I cannot reach."

CHAPTER THIRTY

ROWAN

After they returned from the lagoon, over dinner with the other offerings, Vraise inspired everyone to engage in a late-night study session in the archives. "There's a great deal we need to learn about our elements, not to mention any previous records of those who attempted something like what we've been assigned."

Like his fathers' position within the conclave, Vraise was becoming the de facto leader of the offerings, which kept him in close proximity to Orella who wished to influence the others as well.

The pattern of investigation and study spread across the next several days—mermaids by day, archives by night.

While the others preferred to work within the dark library with its flickering candles, Rowan preferred to take her reading outside, with one of her father's orbs perched on her shoulder, leaning back against Viridian's side for warmth to hold off the chill that draped over the academy grounds after twilight.

Most nights she only read for a short while, preferring to let her mind wander as she sat with Viridian, stroking her hand along Majestyk's fur as the dracat purred on her lap.

Rowan's study with the element of water was coming along quickly with the mermaids' help. She and Vraise had decided not to tell Tullemaien about Forsythia's proclivity for the water, and Vraise had helpfully agreed to take an hour each afternoon as they took a break from the water to help Rowan learn the child's signs while Forsythia played with the mermaids.

As Rowan's command over the water grew, she could sense the bodies of water all around her, the element's whisper from a distant fountain, its stretch to fill rows of cups in the dining areas.

Vraise's study was slower than hers. He kept getting preoccupied by the nature of their plight rather than surrendering to the task at hand.

At the close of their first week in the Academia Magica, Vraise returned from the nighttime study session elated by the connection he had made with one of the archivists, a fae named Vaxis who had taken great interest in their work, one who was newly arrived in the academy. "She gave me several histories of Lis-Maen to study so I can try to uncover where this instability in the elements is coming from. Is it from the titans, or is it due to something else?"

From Paupa's stories, Rowan already knew several possible culprits for the imbalance of energies—the

Pentacle's removal of the hearttrees from their wild holdings to a centralized glade save the willow hearttree she would pledge her services to protect once she was ready. The centralizing of power by the Pentacle, turning the forest peoples to a reverence for their rule rather than a more open worship of the titans and the old gods could be responsible as well.

"If the answer is in there"—Rowan nodded at the giant tome Vraise clutched to his chest—"and you're able to find it in time to affect our studies, what will that do for us?"

Her companion frowned. "Besides hopefully prevent us from dying?"

The question-answer was so simple, Rowan couldn't stop herself from grinning in reply. "Yes, besides that."

Vraise bunched his lips together, considering. "I suppose I've started to see things differently away from our conclave and now that I'm spending more time with you." He glanced between her and Viridian, with a brief flash of a smile for Majestyk watching him with beady, yellow-green eyes on Rowan's lap.

She meowed at the attention and slunk over to Vraise, rubbing herself along his shins in her attempt to woo his arms away from the book.

"I see things on a grander scale now. Maybe some of that is thanks to the Pentacle's faith in us." Vraise sighed. "I guess what I'm wondering is what would happen if we were able to rebalance the elements? Yes, maybe we can do that as offerings when we're successful, but what if the ripple effects of our efforts branch out further? Across the whole of Lis-Maen. What might that mean?"

Rowan nodded, the question reverberating deep in her chest. "I don't know," she admitted, "but I'm relieved we have someone so clever asking the question."

She popped up and caught her arm around Vraise's shoulder. "Come on, let's get some tea and you can tell me all about your new fae friend."

Viridian padded along after them, her fur catching the glimmering shadows of the moons overhead.

A few days later, Tullemaien accompanied the three of them to the lagoon. The mermaids refused to surface, but Rowan demonstrated what she had learned from them.

To impress the fae, she called forth a duplicate of their figure to walk along the water, tapping into the water's power to make the imagination into solid form. Tullemaien was particularly delighted by this trick and dabbed at the corners of their eye with the handkerchief pulled from their vest pocket. "Most thoughtful, Offering Rowan, most thoughtful."

She did not care for the title of "Offering" affixed to their names, but Tullemaien insisted upon the formality in recognizing their "success," an exception to their previous pattern of referring to the offerings collectively as "students" rather than the sacrifices they truly were in the academy's eyes.

Following her demonstration, the fae declared that she was ready to receive her first elemental marking and that rather than reporting to the lagoon on the morrow, she should visit the imbuer who would be waiting for her. "You're in luck too," Tullemaien assured her. "This early in the process, Seth won't be busy. He's particularly skilled at the water marks."

The next morning she dutifully accompanied Vraise and Forsythia to the cervidae pens and reassured Gardenia that they would ride together again soon. Then, there was little left to do but cross the grounds and return to Seth's open-air station.

The elf was waiting for her, his expression somber.

Rowan attempted to engage him in pleasantries, though such efforts had never been a strong suit of hers.

"Let's go ahead and get started," Seth said after a few failed attempts at light conversation. He instructed her to sit in the central chair that bore the right angle for their work together. "I warned you that this would hurt," the elf reminded her.

Rowan pointed out the tattooed vines that trailed down her left arm, the greens and browns that reminded her of her trips into the treetops and helped her feel connected to the magic her mother had added to Paupa's orbs of light.

Seth's lips thinned as he adjusted his gloves and reached over for the metal device holding the distillation of the element of water she'd received from the merfolk and the needle that would imbue it into her skin. "We advise thighs first so the magic isn't directly next to your heart," the imbuer said ominously.

She sighed and untied the ankle bindings of the right leg of her pants, tugging the fabric up to her hip and revealing the long line of her leg before leaning back onto the padded chair. "If you are trying to make me nervous, I am determined that you will not succeed," Rowan said, only partially to stave off the very feeling she was denying. "I'm ready when you are."

"It is not my intention to make you nervous," Seth murmured, squatting down beside her so he could level his gaze with hers. "But it *is* my intention for you to know how serious the exchange you're about to take part in is."

She saw them then, the deaths that hovered behind the dark depths of Seth's gaze. "Do you blame yourself?" Rowan couldn't help but ask.

"Not for what you think, but yes." He nodded to her thigh and knelt on a blanket on the earth beside her. "Close your eyes, try to relax, and think about the water."

The imbuing hurt at first, just like he'd promised, but over time, the cadence of Seth's voice lulled Rowan just like an afternoon float with the mermaids. When the eyes of Thalyssa flashed before her awareness again, Seth gasped as though he saw it too. "Focus," he urged, an edge of panic in his voice. Rowan wasn't sure which of the two of them he was correcting.

As he neared the end of the design, the pain worsened. Sharp stings began shooting down her legs, along her hips. Her right foot went numb. "Seth?" Rowan murmured. She wished that Tullemaien hadn't prevented anyone from being present for this first imbuing, not even Majestyk who would have slept through the entire thing but would have soothed her regardless.

"This part's always the hardest," the imbuer

groaned. Beads of sweat poured down his temples. His hands shook, muscles straining, knuckles white.

"Why?" Rowan couldn't keep the whine of fear from her voice.

"The elements." Seth spoke through gritted teeth. "Don't want. To be. Contained." He hunched over, leaning onto the needle device, teeth clenched, practically drilling into her skin. "Focus, Rowan."

Her breathing quickened. She was underwater again.

"Rowan."

She couldn't breathe.

Seth called to her, his voice muffled by watery surroundings.

The black dots returned.

She was losing control. The water was going to overwhelm her.

And a pair of golden eyes opened, blotting out her awareness of anything else.

Rowan gasped in a breath, and Seth sighed beside her. "Almost there," he promised.

She dug her hands into the wooden arms of the chair, forced her body back against the wooden planks beneath the padding, reveling in the discomfort that meant she was here, not drowning.

Thank you, she sent to the bearer of the eyes. In the moment she hadn't been sure if it was Lucien or her phoenix.

She smiled to herself, realizing that she hadn't been as alone as she'd felt. Someone had been watching over her, protecting her all along.

CHAPTER THIRTY-ONE

MARCON

That night, Marcon dreamed of a woman with flaming red hair, an elf he was pursuing through a thick, overgrown forest. The dew on the undergrowth smeared damp shadows along his breeches, made his tunic cling to his skin. Pine needles and leaf spines pressed into the bare soles of his feet.

He pursued her every step, as though he'd been chasing her all his life, through this very forest, one they'd returned to again and again. Though he'd never seen her before, had never witnessed anything so lush and green, even at the heights of summer in the vineyard, he remembered meeting her here. She'd held him at arrow point, a curious collection of animals gathered around her.

His vision narrowed, the world condensing to flashes of her, his pulse racing in his throat at the memory of pressing her against the rough bark of a tree, his fingers tangled in her hair, bare legs wrapped around him.

"*Lilia,*" he'd murmured.

"Hugh," she'd breathed back.

The scent of roses carried him up a hill. She darted just out of sight, her hair swishing loose over her shoulders, showing him the way.

Marcon awoke with a start, beads of sweat covering his chest, panic gripping his throat as he found himself apart from her forest and in an unknown stone room.

The sigil on his forearm glowed faintly against the gloom, a comforting touch of warmth within his surroundings.

You're in the Palace of Respite, Marcon reminded himself. *You don't know any red-haired elves.*

His stomach twisted as fragments of the dream came back to him.

Lorieannan had been killed in front of him only the day before. Well, she'd been killed before that by a vultura. The undead remains of her had been pulverized into ash by a champion of light was more accurate.

Marcon clutched his stomach. He was going to be sick. *It's just a dream*, he told himself. *You have nothing to feel guilty for.* He couldn't have helped it. Besides, it wasn't real. It was just the compiled trauma of the last several days—the battle, the sprint down the mountains, the fight for Respite. Becoming a champion of fire. Of course he was having weird dreams.

A knock sounded against his door. "Come in," he called, his voice hoarse.

A familiar figure opened the door with a grin. "Colabra." Garreth's son, Patrick crossed his arms as he leaned in the doorway. "I must say, I was surprised by the order I received from the field commander this morning to fetch you. So you're finally coming around?"

"I, err, yes." Marcon hadn't expected to run into Patrick here, though he remembered Garreth complaining before they deployed for Sanctuary about his son being roped into Silversword's inner circle and forgetting everything he'd learned at his parents' knees. It seemed so long ago now that Patrick had asked for him, Cole, and Vateri to help with morale on Silversword's behalf before the battle to reclaim Sanctuary. "She got me out of a tough spot yesterday."

Marcon rubbed the back of his neck as his friend lingered in the doorway. Silversword had sworn him to secrecy about his identity as a champion—threatened his life was more accurate—but he hadn't had time to come up with a believable explanation for why he'd gone from someone who listened to the blacksmith's complaints about Silversword while fiercely defending the leaders of the Luz who had led them all into folly to now being in her good graces.

"You'll have to tell me about it this afternoon after we meet our new instructor?"

He frowned and asked what Patrick meant.

"Oh." The half-orc was equally confused. "I thought —" He cleared his throat. "Not to spoil anything, but I believe you and I, alongside your friends, are being recruited as part of a special partnership between the Battalion and Silversword's personal circle." Patrick beamed as he relayed this information.

He waited outside the room while Marcon prepared for the day.

Marcon found the better-fitting clothes as promised. He glanced down at his sigil of Ignis as he dressed. The sigil had calmed as he slept, its fevered glow fading. It still more closely resembled a brand than a soldier's tattoo, but given the many markings common across the Luz, it might go unremarked upon.

A half hour later, Marcon had just as much trouble believing he'd been chosen for this special collaboration when Silversword repeated as much to him, smiling as she dismissed Patrick. When they were alone, her expression grew more serious. "I have barely slept while preparing your training regimen. Given the circumstances and various threats from abroad and within, yours will be the most intense training I've overseen." She inclined her head to him. "You will have to trust me, but given your background as a soldier, your bravery upon the battlefield, I know you have what it takes."

Marcon thanked the dwarf, his thoughts leaping ahead to what this training might entail while she described some of the unrest within Respite's streets.

Still disoriented by his dreams and the new sigil upon his arm, Marcon had trouble following Silversword's concerns about the riots of the previous days intensifying into outright coups on behalf of the common people.

"We'll have to work your training around street patrols, I'm afraid," Silversword added. "It shouldn't take long to break the back of this rebellion and get the city back in line."

"I hadn't realized matters were so serious," Marcon added, alarmed by the direction the conversation had taken, the quick turn to military rule following the attack though, without the generals and given the violence of the mobs who had burned several shops in the night, he supposed he understood.

The soldiers of the Luz had been trained to fight the undead, not calm pedestrians. Silversword outlined the additional training sessions she'd laid out for him—history lessons with one of the masters, an arena training every three days or so with her where he could practice wielding the fire as needed while maintaining his anonymity.

While she spoke, a nameless servant placed a platter of eggs and cured meats before him and a second brought a pitcher of water and a pot of true coffee—not accelerant.

As she had the day before, Silversword began to pace by the windows, always scanning the skyline of Respite. When they became more familiar with one another, Marcon planned to ask what she was looking for.

Once he'd finished, Silversword strode away from her position by the windows to posture before the map of their world affixed to the wall, tiny flags signifying the movement and location of troops.

Marcon followed her, trying to settle his mind upon the present moment, the words of his field commander. His fellow champion.

"It will not surprise you to learn that I have spies everywhere," she said without turning about for confirmation. "And you know already of the troublesome resistance posed by those in Lis-Maen to our efforts at uniting our forces with theirs." She reached up and tapped Lis-Maen's central position on the map. A wave of black markers had stretched across the forested landscape behind the island nation—Alessandra's forces advancing across the Glade of Shadows.

There were only a few green flags remaining across the entire swath of conquered continent.

A similar cluster of black markers hovered over what had once been Sanctuary. A cluster they'd failed to unmoor.

For the first time, it struck him how Lis-Maen resembled a shield, one that, under the banner of the Cities United, might be raised in defense of the grander cities like Respite, Beacon, Bastion.

Turned against them, it was a shield their enemy bore—one that would allow any number of foul creatures to be only an airship's ride from their shores.

Silversword turned to face him, her hands tucked behind her back, much like they had been on his first meeting with her. "I have great hopes for the advances you might make in your training, Colabra. Ambitions as well, for what it will mean to have a champion of fire so near at hand. I'd like to speak with you about what your first mission will be, when your training here is complete and matters in the city are . . . in hand."

A jumbled stammer of gratitude and doubt crowded Marcon's mind, thankfully preventing him from immediately answering his commanding officer. "You honor me, Field Commander," Marcon said, bowing his head. "What would you have me do?"

Though Silversword used different words, in her broad view of the battles unfolding all around them, his first assignment was to enact the vengeance he had sworn to exact, the vengeance that had allowed the flame of Ignis to answer him. Choose him. Set him apart from the rest. The field commander identified a target for these aims, one Marcon would never have picked on his own.

"When the time comes, I'd like for you and an ally to infiltrate the Academia Magica and uncover what the Pentacle is plotting. My spies who have survived their surveillance return troubling reports, news of magical experiments with catastrophic repercussions for the whole of our world." A dangerous fire burned behind the dwarf's gaze. It wasn't a desire for vengeance Marcon saw smoldering there. It was hatred.

"And these experiments?"

"They are elemental in nature. Manipulations of the alchemists' sacred work and blasphemous transgressions against the titans' power." Silversword clutched her amulet in her small fist. "This will be a multistep mission. On your first deployment, you'll pose as a soldier on leave, seeking to visit more of our war-torn world while away from the front lines."

Marcon nodded. A simple enough assignment, and a motivation he'd heard similar instances of in his years of service. Many soldiers traveled during times of reprieve, though rarely did they venture outside the protection of the Cities.

If the Academia Magica was truly threatening the titans and the Cities, he would find out what he could and put a stop to it, but the dwarf's fervor made him uneasy. He'd seen a similar reaction from young recruits in training, those who struggled in wielding weapons who, rather than turning their attentions toward their true talents, lashed out at those with a natural gift for sword, shield, and bow. If jealousy was driving the field commander, what was it she was jealous of?

The dwarf leveled her gaze with his. "This won't be your only trip there, so you will need to take your time. You're to spend the interim preparing and learning their customs. Once you're there, we will need accuracy. Insight." She scowled. "These are discoveries my spies thus far have lacked." Silversword shook her head and continued, "I believe what we need is someone with elemental sensitivities. Maybe you will see what they cannot. You're to ingratiate yourself with someone within the inner ranks of the Academia Magica, someone who might have access to information we would otherwise miss. Someone adjacent to their centers of power."

Surely there were countless figures who would suit such a description. "And what exactly am I looking to uncover, Field Commander?" The particularities of his mission were still vague to him. What would his "elemental sensitivities" allow him to do that her spies could not? He was not an alchemist, familiar with elemental experimentation and transmutation.

The corner of her lip upturned, alighting the banked coals behind her gaze. "I have reason to believe they are working on a weapon, something connected to the elements entrusted to the Cities by the titans." Her scowl returned. "They claim such a gifting belongs to them, embedded within the 'innate magic' of their lands or some such nonsense." Silversword waved her hand as though she could brush away the notion and banish it, forever, from her presence.

"You want me to find an elemental weapon they're working on in secret?" He refrained from adding that he was meant to be on leave during such an assignment, complicating the ruse still further.

"Eventually, yes, and you are to tell no one beyond myself of such a discovery." Her mouth thinned into a line. "Until I can reaffirm the loyalties of the Secret Council, especially in the generals' absence, this matter is to be treated with the utmost delicacy."

"Yes, Field Commander," Marcon answered. He must have missed the concerns with the Secret Council while she was lecturing earlier.

"I'll make sure you're ready, before you set out. We'll need the city to be at peace. I understand the people's anger following the attack, I do," Silversword said, more like she was trying to appease Marcon rather than herself. She confided in him that she thought there might be an enemy spy within the ranks of Respite's leadership, possibly even among the members of the Secret Council who had expertly orchestrated the near-disaster that had befallen the city in the army's absence. "We'll root them out and any followers they have," she assured Marcon, dismissing him.

He had no response for such concerns. For himself, his feelings about what had happened to his city went far beyond anger. He suspected that was the case for most of Respite's residents as well. They had every right to feel betrayed.

Rising from his chair, his thoughts turned to his first

mission coming up at the end of his training, when he could control his fire. It would be nice to get away for a while. Perhaps he could convince the field commander to allow Cole and Vateri to accompany him. She had mentioned one companion. Would a second so greatly stretch their ruse?

"We'll begin your official training on the morrow, Colabra," Silversword said to his back, catching him at the door. "You'll be on street patrols in the morning, and the following night, you'll meet me here. We'll descend to the dungeons for you to train without being detected."

He took the tomes she had assigned him, *The History of the Champions of Eldura: Fall to Present Day Volumes I-IV* back with him to his rooms.

They were books one had to stand to read, Marcon thought to himself, surveying their bulk and frowning at their musty odor that overpowered the entirety of his small room.

"We learn from the past to avoid repeating mistakes," Marcon repeated the field commander's words as he flipped through the first few pages of Volume II. His eyes grew heavy five pages in, the exhaustion of battle and his strange night's sleep compounding to make the dry text a more formidable foe than was reasonable.

Another knock called him from his brief study. "Captain Colabra?"

Marcon grinned. He was already growing used to his promotion. Vateri would soon accuse him of his chest being permanently swollen.

"Your friends have returned, sir. I'm to take you to them and your new barracks."

All thought of the coming days of training, of the possibility of calling upon the element of fire or soothing concerned citizens in the streets faded. He hadn't realized how badly he needed to see them before now.

Marcon's shoulders relaxed as he repeated the aide's words to himself. *My friends have returned. They are well. Safe.*

Alive.

He dropped the book he'd been perusing and sprinted down the hall, darting ahead of the palace guide assigned to assist him, impatient to reunite with the two people dearest to him.

The sounds of their bickering reached him first, Vateri reprimanding Cole for an incorrect address of an officer from an unfamiliar unit.

"Can that truly be your concern after what we just witnessed in the streets?"

"Of course it can," Vateri shot back. "Military decorum organizes the entirety of our—" She stopped short as Marcon jogged into view.

His smile fell the moment he saw them. Cole with a bandage over his brow, Vateri with her arm in a sling.

And the heavy news he had to confess to them.

"Marcon?" Vateri's voice was so high-pitched he could scarcely register it.

He pitched forward, catching his hands on his knees. It was too much.

A scramble of footsteps and they were there by his side. Vateri murmured soothing phrases and huffed at

Cole to be more helpful while his friend stood planted in place just within arm's reach, stammering and unsure of what to do.

Marcon exhaled slowly. They'd made it back together.

He rose, his eyes misting as he gazed upon both of them. They were lucky, to have all three survived. "I can't believe—"

Vateri launched herself into his arms and tugged Cole with her. They embraced, and Marcon's throat grew thick again.

Perhaps he might survive the coming weeks after all.

The next hour saw the trio out of the palace walls and ensconced instead within the Dracat's Grin. The barkeep was relieved to see anyone out and about given the unrest in other parts of the city. "Few enough of you'uns came back," he said with a nod to the three soldiers, "and the cityfolk knows we're a soldiers' bar."

"For which we're incredibly grateful," Marcon said, clapping the barkeep on the shoulder.

"I didn't know you were burned," Cole said with a frown, looking at the underside of Marcon's forearm. "What happened?"

Curse these tight sleeves that he had to keep rolled up over his elbows so he could move. Marcon tried to shake off his friend's question before the barkeep took notice.

"We'll take our regular corner booth," Vateri said loudly, interrupting Cole's protests at Marcon's attempted deflection.

"Anywhere you like, missy," he said with a wink,

waddling into the back to fetch some day-old bread and butter on the house.

"Cole," Vateri scolded the moment they had all huddled into their booth.

"We just sat down," he protested. "How am I already in trouble with you?"

"*Obviously* Marcon has lots to tell us and is trying to keep secrets and you're spilling them like your beer is frothing over!"

"How is that obvious?"

"Friends," Marcon interjected quietly.

Vateri's expression was already grave. Cole looked back and forth between the two of them, confusion creased between his brows.

With a heavy sigh, Marcon told them about his return to Respite, charging down the hillsides, the vineyard, Lorieannan. Tears wobbled at the base of Vateri's eyes as his voice cracked.

"The field commander killed her?" Cole whispered. "With a ray of light?"

Marcon nodded.

"How did the field commander know to come save you?" Vateri added.

"We should have been there," Cole said at the same time. Their eyes met.

"It's actually good, err, maybe, that you weren't beside me for this one." Marcon wetted his lips, the sigil on his arm beginning to heat. He tucked his arm under the table and shifted in his seat in case the barkeep came back sooner than expected.

He told them about his vow of vengeance, being chosen by Ignis, becoming a champion of fire.

His friends' jaws dropped. Cole's looked like it might never return to its rightful place again.

"So, do you have magic powers now?"

Vateri punched Cole's arm and then turned eagerly to Marcon, waiting for the answer.

He inclined his head. "I think so. The field commander is going to teach me. And, well, she swore me to secrecy besides the two of you, so we'll have to come up with something else to tell the rest of our unit." Marcon sat up taller, relieved to be coming upon the piece of good news they could all enjoy without any hesitation. "Our unit in the Blazing Battalion."

Vateri's screech of delight brought the barkeep running out from the back wielding a butcher knife, ready to defend the bar from an unruly mob. "Are things truly so bad in the rest of the city?" she wondered aloud.

"I'm not entirely sure," Marcon said. "I've been cooped up in the palace, waiting for the two of you."

Their conversation ebbed between anticipation and grief, gratitude and anger as the night thickened outside.

The next day, their patrols of Respite's streets would begin, followed by Marcon's lessons with Field Commander Silversword while the three of them trained to join the Blazing Battalion. But for tonight, he was relieved to be reunited with his friends.

CHAPTER THIRTY-TWO
ROWAN

The other offerings had been deeply curious about Rowan's imbuing, asking her endless questions about the process, the pain. Some of them had never had tattoos done before, which made them even more nervous for what to expect from Seth and his team.

One by one, they each received their first elemental sigil. One had to be taken to the Healer immediately—one of the offerings to air, who reacted to their sigil poorly, their chest filling with air until one of their lungs burst, their ribs cracked.

Their imbuer hadn't fared much better. Seth sent her into Delmoir with a friend for two weeks to recover. "The first one you lose is the hardest," he'd confessed to Rowan.

She wanted to ask how many it had been for him but knew better than to try and find out.

Near the end of Rowan's first fortnight in the Academia Magica, one of the offerings dedicated to the element of earth disappeared. Rumors swirled among the remaining offerings as to what had occurred. Had she run away? Been taken by one of the Faces? Somehow absorbed by the element of earth?

The offering who had been petrified during the first day's trial was only just well enough to rejoin the others. The earth offerings were more insular than the other groups. They were each taken by Tullemaien in for questioning with the Sorceress. They emerged pale and even more reserved than they had been. Rowan wasn't sure whether they had been tortured or if the Sorceress was frightening enough on her own to provoke such a reaction.

She fell into a fitful sleep, mulling over the plans the others had whispered about their own thoughts of running away.

A scream woke her in the middle of the night. "What was that?" Rowan cried.

On her lap, Majestyk hissed awake, the scales sticking out along her spine and tail.

"Something outside," Viridian answered, immediately alert.

Rowan's stomach curled—somehow she knew she needed to see what had occurred.

"I'll come with you," Viridian said. *"It is best to not face the Pentacle's shadows on your own."*

They rushed down the stairs, Vraise and Orella close on their heels. Athenza had risen as well and leaned against the frame of her door. "Tell me what happens," she made Rowan promise.

Rowan was the first out the door, the others just

behind her. Across the field beyond their dormitory, a dark silhouette wandered closer, moaning to itself as it moved.

The figure was slumped, with odd shapes hanging off itself. Had it moved more slowly, she might have thought it was one of the Cities' vultura that had somehow crossed the Circle Sea and landed upon their shores.

"It's one of the offerings," Orella murmured. "One of earth, I believe. Hullo—" she called, waving to the figure.

"Get down!" Viridian growled. The daimon seized Rowan's tunic and tugged her back, huddling overtop of her as the figure rounded toward the sound.

She peeked through Viridian's legs.

An eerie laugh rippled out of its chest. "Yo-ou!" it groaned. The figure stretched out its hands just as the clouds sped away overhead, revealing the mismatched phases of the moons. And an offering tangled in choking vines before them.

Orella screamed, and the vines shot out from the figure's arms, slithering at impossible speed over the earth toward the four of them.

"Make her stop!" Rowan ordered Vraise. The noise was clearly agitating the figure.

Viridian was already dragging Rowan into shelter behind one of the elegantly shaped topiaries nestled within the confines of the garden.

Vraise leaped into action, caught his hand around Orella's mouth, and dragged her aside as well.

With a mumbled groan of outrage, the figure continued its ambling walk toward them.

The reason for the off gait became clear in the moonlight—sticklike growths stuck out of the figure's legs and one of its shoulders, as well as from behind its head.

Rowan's stomach heaved. Not sticks but bone, grown out of the flesh and in a branching structure.

She recognized the offering who had just received the sigil of earth two days before from the golden curls of her hair, the one who had disappeared.

"We have to do something," Rowan whispered to Viridian.

"Shall you kill her or shall I?"

Rowan's chest tightened. Her phoenix, lingering in the recesses of her mind, watched on, golden eyes gleaming, waiting to see what she would do.

She rubbed her hand along the tattoo for the element of water recently inked across her thigh.

Seth had warned her the mark would hurt.

She thought he had meant in the imbuing of the element through a needle, a mark that would gradually heal. But she had failed to realize the ways in which her opting into the Pentacle's magic would continue to bring her pain.

Rowan placed her hand on Viridian's chest, the touch answer enough for the wolf. *I will.*

Viridian rubbed her head along Rowan's arm to reassure her.

She steeled herself and strode forward, stepping into the open archway, lit by the glowing moons overhead, in plain sight of the returned offering. She hadn't run away, like they'd thought. The offering had been taken by the element of earth.

The possessed offering—Rowan shuddered as she

put the two together—rumbled in recognition, turning toward her.

She remembered the lesson she'd received from the mermaids, the way that water allows itself to fill any receptacle. It flows, moves, allowing other energies to be the one to invite it. And that saving of its energy is what led to its deadliest potential.

The potential she would need to eliminate the offering twisted by the power of the earth and turned against them.

Rowan thought back to Vraise's theory from the archives, to the kind fae he'd met there who helped with their research. Maybe the elements of the Pentacle had become more unstable after three of the titans abandoned Eldura.

She wasn't sure that the why mattered very much.

Rowan stepped forward again, away from the stone of the arch. She raised her hands in a protective stance, challenging the offering.

"I'll be right nearby if you need me."

There wasn't time for her to answer Viridian.

The offering's garbled cry rang out again, and it ambled forward, arms extended.

The vines that had taken over the body shot forward, whipping and slithering over the earth.

Be like the water. Be like the water.

Her muscles stiffened, but Rowan refused to flee.

She let the vines take her instead.

Rowan screamed as the whipping vine caught around her ankle, stinging her flesh. It yanked her toward the figure. Vraise's cry echoed out distantly behind her.

The vines lashed around her wrists, one around her neck. They tugged her across the grass.

She tried to force her body to relax to no avail. The vines tightened around her neck and Rowan gagged.

Long grasses whipped across her face, scratching her skin and tangling in her hair.

The vines pulled her straight into the torso of the offering, knocking its breath from its chest. Rowan choked around the vines—her objective finally possible.

She wriggled against their tangling grasp, muscles straining, and caught hold of the offering's throat. Rowan pressed her opposite hand against the still-swollen side of her thigh where Seth had imbued the sigil of water several days before.

Ignoring the vines that lashed at her arms, across her neck, she squeezed the offering's throat and called upon the water in the offering's ruined body.

For a moment nothing happened.

She closed her eyes, relaxing into the vines' hold, the lash around her neck tightening further. *Flow*, Rowan ordered.

A bead of sweat answered her command, trickling from the offering's skin onto her hand. Another and another did the same.

Rowan cast her order again, turning her mind to floodwaters, a rushing river, the vision she carried of the sea she'd never seen.

The water from the offering's body began to pool

over her skin. A slight trickle at first, but it quickly grew into a stream.

The offering choked, and the vines screeched, writhing as they turned black. The water pouring forth from the offering's lips turned darker, her blood pooling out.

As Rowan's balance swayed, the figure fell to the ground, blood leaking out of her skin.

Dark specks dotted the corners of Rowan's vision.

A growl sounded behind her, a giant shape closing in, and then the figure fell still.

Rowan rolled over, coughing and choking. She clawed at her throat, trying to get the desiccated vines to release her.

Viridian snarled as she snapped hold of the vines around Rowan, rending the offering's arm from her body with a rapid snap of bone.

The daimon postured over Rowan, a low growl prickling deep within her chest in case any other threats decided to interpose themselves nearby.

Rowan crawled away from the body, its dark shape occupying too much of her vision. The wet warmth of rot filled her nostrils.

The branches made of bone that stuck out of the offering's body shone white beneath the moons.

Viridian growled again as a new figure rushed toward them.

Rowan rested back against the wolf, trying to prepare herself for whatever was coming for them next.

Tullemaien appeared in the corner of her eye,

running with arms akimbo toward her and Viridian. They skidded to a stop, breath wheezing. "I heard . . . Oh." Their expression turned, and they withdrew a handkerchief from their breast pocket. The salt mingled with the scent of decaying earth was a lot to take in.

"They called me too late it seems," Tullemaien said, their voice constricted. The nasal tone suggested they'd plugged their nose with the kerchief. "You fared well for yourselves."

The expert in energy looked between them, inclining their head to Viridian. "I don't believe we've been introduced."

The daimon stared back at Tullemaien. Unlike when she'd spoken with Rowan and her companions, she didn't open her psychic channel to include Rowan in the conversation. Or she simply wasn't answering Tullemaien at all.

"Right, err, Rowan. A word?" The instructor waved her over to the shadowy garden wall. "I know better than to ask you whether or not this was provoked."

"The crumbled stone around us and wide spread of vines should answer that for you."

"Yes," Tullemaien mused. "Simply trying to do my duty is all."

Rowan knew why Viridian had chosen not to answer the instructor if that was the choice the wolf had made. "You wanted to speak to me?"

"Yes, well—" Tullemaien cleared their throat. "This is monstrously uncomfortable."

Interesting choice of words.

"Our colleague here, umm . . ." Tullemaien turned toward the body, keeping their nose covered. Vraise was quietly conferring with Orella in the opposite corner of the gardens. Her shoulders were shaking. Viridian stared down the instructor who gave a sharp "yeep!" as they caught the daimon's eye.

Tullemaien cleared their throat. "Unfortunately, it seems that our friend was on their way beyond the walls of the Pentacle when the transformation overtook them. A most dire undercurrent in the magic that, but the populace must be protected."

Rowan narrowed her eyes. "What are you talking around? Speak plainly."

Tullemaien dropped their handkerchief. Their eyes were shining, and their lower lip trembled. "In an earlier round of offerings, after the first few students tried to flee and had to be hunted down, the Faces ordered an additional enchantment to be placed in the magic without the imbuers' knowledge, or so I understand. The test proved tonight that the efforts were a success."

"I still don't—"

"Anyone who tries to flee will be overtaken by the imbued element *by design*," Tullemaien said quickly, nearly choking on the final words.

Rowan's lips parted, and then the instructor's words sank in. She stepped away, her knees bending—a great, warm presence caught her from behind, steadying her. Holding her up.

"Are you saying we cannot leave?" Rowan's voice was small, shrill.

But loud enough for Vraise and Orella to hear. He took the other offering by the hand and led her nearer.

"You cannot be serious," Rowan said, recovering herself.

Tullemaien was shivering, their hand clutched to their throat. "Please," they gasped.

Rowan stomped forward. The feigned weakness made her sick.

"Room-friend."

Viridian had caught the end of her tunic between her front teeth, restraining her from seizing the energetic specialist. *"They will kill Tullemaien if they say anything more. They have shared as much as they are able—what the Pentacle deems warning enough to save your life. Their voice will choke them to death if they say anything further."*

The fae's head was lowered, gentle sobs shaking their shoulders as had beset Orella a few moments before.

They held up a small glass vial from their neck. It held the dark of a cave, infinitely deep, pulling her nearer despite its small size.

Rowan hugged her hands around her waist, stopping herself from lurching forward. "You'll see to the burial?"

Tullemaien nodded.

The four of them began to trudge away.

"Rowan," Tullemaien called.

She stopped but did not turn back.

"You've been assigned to the element of earth next. Th-they want to make sure it's stable."

She forced a deep breath. Was the Pentacle listening

at every turn? Did they have a death wish for each of the offerings? Or just for her after her accident the first day and the blood vow she'd made?

Rowan nodded, once, indicating that she'd heard. She hurried to catch up to Viridian and followed the daimon inside.

CHAPTER THIRTY-THREE
MARCON

Marcon arose with the dawn, his gaze immediately landing upon the fresh armor placed at the foot of his bunk. Cole and Vateri had received their new pieces as well. There hadn't been time after their visit to the Dracat's Grin for them to explore their new barracks or meet the others who would be stationed here before being deployed to various battalion outposts.

The wooden door of their shared room creaked open as someone padded out into the hall. An orange beam fell across the chest of his new leather armor—designed to be worn in urban environments, with a few metal plates for additional protection.

The insignia of the Blazing Battalion, the mote of flame upon a shield, had been burned into the chest of the armor. The orange light wavered as the hall crystal shifted its internal light, giving the illusion that the flame within the shield was dancing.

Marcon smiled to himself and placed his hand on the

sigil of fire that covered his forearm. Would his titan be watching over his training, curious to see the potential of his newly chosen champion? The sigil warmed as if in answer.

He leaped out of bed and donned his armor, ready to begin his first day as a soldier of the battalion.

Marcon held his shoulders back, stood taller. Despite all the loss, the struggle, the rampant death, this, at least, felt right.

Patrick was stationed down the hall from Marcon, Vateri, and Cole. He was waiting for Marcon as he emerged in his new leathers, similarly decked out himself though he curiously bore the insignias of both the Luz and the Battalion upon his armor.

"Stozdak." He nodded to Patrick. "I think you remember Cole. Vateri." He reintroduced his friends to Patrick—though he'd spoken with them before the battle for Sanctuary, it had been years since they'd all been in training together. Patrick had advanced into the advisory branches of the military working as an aide while the three of them remained within the fighting units.

"I do." Patrick inclined his head to Cole, and his eyes brightened as they landed upon the elf. "I understand that you have a penchant for military history," he said, speaking only to her and gesturing that they should follow him down the hall.

Vateri warmly reciprocated Patrick's interest, much to Cole's irritation. The closeness Marcon had sensed between his friends outside of Sanctuary had cooled somewhat. He suspected they were just as overwhelmed as he was with what had become of their city not to mention his new position as a champion.

"I hate to interrupt," Cole interjected a few minutes later, "but are you going to tell us where we're heading?"

"Of course." Patrick seemed utterly oblivious to Cole's irritated tone.

Vateri frowned at Cole who smirked in response.

"The field commander has requested the three of you specifically. There's been more unrest in the night. She's seeing to the calming of Respite personally."

They stepped out of the barracks and filed toward the palace. The unrest Patrick spoke of was immediately apparent. The choking scent of ash lingered in the air.

"As such, she'll need protection," Patrick continued. "I hope I don't need to impress upon you the importance and the honor of such an appointment."

Cole's irritation returned at the half-orc's tone while Vateri's eyes widened, immediately settling into the gravity of their new positions.

"How exactly is she setting about this increase of peace?" Marcon asked to break the tension and prevent Patrick from continuing to condescend to Cole who was short-tempered already this morning. He wished he'd paid better attention the day before as she'd told him her concerns of the aftermath of the attack against the city.

"We're to offer protection while she makes speeches at designated positions around Respite," Patrick answered simply.

Cole groaned. "*Guard* duty? You cannot be serious. We did that *years* ago. Remember that one guy with the poofy hair we had to protect, Marcon?" Cole chortled.

"The crowds hated him. His speeches were absolutely terrible. No wonder he lost the council vote. This one day, someone lobbed a tomato—"

Patrick halted and spun back, passion blazing in his eyes. "I asked before but now the answer is clear to me that I *do* in fact need to impress upon you the importance of our mission today. If someone were to hit the field commander with a *tomato*, as you so blithely recount, it would not only signify an attack against the rightful rulership of Respite but of the entirety of the Luz, the Secret Council, and the Cities United. It will mean their head." He let the words hang between them for effect. "And possibly ours as well."

The half-orc spun on the toes of his boots and quickened his pace, leading them toward the dense cluster of guards stationed around a team of biomechos dressed in full battle gear pulling a narrow wooden platform behind them. The pennants of the Luz and of Respite fluttered from the vertical poles of the platform.

Marcon immediately sensed the shortcomings of the rolling platform's design. Either they didn't intend for it to go very far into the city, or they planned to force individual neighborhoods to lower their laundry lines so the platform might pass.

The connection to previous instances of "guard duty," as Cole called it, fell away as soon as the full retinue came into view. Row upon row of soldiers in black leathers with masks that partially or entirely covered their faces stood at attention. Their weapons consisted of curved swords, crossbows, and throwing daggers, with only a few masked soldiers who, like him, wielded two-handed swords. "They're armed for street combat," Marcon murmured to Cole.

His friend's jaw twitched. "Are we a peacekeeping force or the tools of a tyrant?"

Marcon ran his tongue over his teeth, not trusting himself with the answer, especially with so many guards nearby.

"Take a mask," Patrick said, pointing to a table at the edge of the gathering area.

He'd finally gone far enough to provoke Vateri's concern. "Why would we wear masks?"

"It helps promote a unified front. The citizens of Respite see the different branches of military protection gathered together as one, and it inspires them to want to join alongside us instead of resisting and protesting while we rebuild." Patrick shook his head. "Their ring-leaders claim that the military leadership knew about the vultura and did nothing. We all know how impossible a claim that is."

At Vateri's side, Cole rolled his shoulders back, glaring at Patrick. They were almost exactly matched in height, both posturing to look down on the other. "The masks help to frighten them, you mean."

Patrick's patience finally frayed. "What would you have her do?" he seethed, the words coming through clenched teeth. "Orphans died in the fires set in the night. People are already grieving. There was a stampede in the market, and former soldiers are charging war widows for protection—astronomical sums they cannot possibly afford, all because they're frightened. The people *need* a show of strength. And if that frightens them, then so be it."

He breathed quickly, forcing himself to calm. "We were all at the battle to reclaim Sanctuary. We saw what can happen under Alessandra's reign."

The half-orc met each of their gazes in turn. "They should be frightened. I know I am." With that, he snatched a mask from the table and stomped away.

Vateri turned toward them, worrying her lower lip between her teeth. "Are you afraid?"

Cole held her gaze. "No." He forced a smile for the elf's benefit, and Marcon did the same. "We've nothing to be afraid of. We're a peacekeeping force, just like Patrick said."

They selected masks for the lower half of their faces, as Patrick had, and filed into line.

"Colabra, good," Silversword's voice rang out as they searched for their places. She was wearing full battle plate, the polished armor shining in the low morning light. "Leave the black-coats to the edges. The three of you will be stationed near me."

Vateri and Cole were rendered speechless in the field commander's presence. They both stared at him with wide eyes. Cole's gaze darted toward Marcon's covered wrist as though he hadn't fully internalized what Marcon had told them the night before. He was a champion of fire.

And this was his first mission in Ignis's name.

"Here's your commanding officer now, Sergeant Isadora," Silversword announced, leaving them in the hands of the woman in blue armor Marcon had met in the battle of Sanctuary. The raven that had accompanied her during the battle was nowhere to be seen, but the warrior was otherwise exactly as Marcon had remembered—quizzically amiable, especially for a soldier.

Isadora grinned when she saw Marcon and greeted him warmly, extending her hand for his and introducing herself to Cole and Vateri. "Major Barton is anxious for me to get the three of you ready to be deployed to the front, particularly his new captain." Light danced behind her eyes at the mention of her partner.

A flare of warmth spread along Marcon's forearm from his sigil, like it was equally pleased by his promotion to captain.

"This is a strange urban mission and one I believe we'll be repeating until matters in the city calm," Isadora explained. "There are five squares the field commander will be rotating between for speeches to rally the people. Any troublemakers are to be dealt with swiftly."

"Dealt with?" Cole clarified.

Isadora dropped her gaze. "Apprehended and then brought to justice."

Marcon's lips parted but before he could protest, the sergeant's gaze snapped up to meet his. Quickly, she shook her head. "Our numbers should provoke peaceful dealings. If they do not, act swiftly for the safety of all involved."

Her tone was difficult for him to read. Marcon wanted to believe she was just as concerned about what they were being asked to do as he was, but he also sensed her hesitation to counter their orders.

At Silversword's signal, the large force marched out,

winding through the narrow city streets like a large serpent along a dry creek bed.

Most of the citizens of Respite hovered behind windows or peeked out of cracked doors as the procession passed them. The large caravan had to stop for the laundry lines, as Marcon had suspected. Whoever had designed it had clearly never stepped outside of the Inner Wall of Respite to see how people in the outer rings lived.

The field commander gave two brief speeches to somber crowds ringed in by guards at their first two stations. The people looked more like refugees than the citizens Marcon had seen before his deployment. They listened to the speech with heads bowed. He wondered whether they attended willingly or if those who were idle nearby had been forced into attendance by the black-coats.

A sharp tension hung in the air of the third square. This one was more open than the other two, with a far larger, more engaged crowd. Angry shouts rose up over the din. Those gathered glared at the amassed forces, the black-coats who stood shoulder to shoulder around Silversword's platform.

Vateri clutched Marcon's elbow. "This doesn't feel right."

Marcon shook his head. "No. It doesn't."

Cole shifted to stand closer on Vateri's other side. Their new sergeant stood at attention behind them.

A great drum pulled by one of the biomechos rang out across the courtyard, ordering silence.

Silversword cleared her throat and marched forward

from the back of the platform. "Good people of Respite," she began, her voice magically amplified by a clear screen placed before her, designed by the windcallers, the alchemists who studied the magic of the titan of air. "We thank you for gathering today to celebrate the resilience of our city, our determination as a people to come back together, to prove to our enemy our bravery in our survival, that though we have lost many, we are stronger now than we have ever been."

"Like hells we are," someone jeered from the back of the crowd.

"You sacrificed those trapped outside the walls like they were cattle!" another cried.

"These black-coats locked them outside to bleed and burn!"

At that, the crowd grew more restless. They began to shove one another. The collective fear that had befouled the air ever since he'd returned sharpened into something else. Anger.

Marcon turned back to Isadora. "This is a bad idea. We need to get the field commander away from the people. Find a different way to appease them."

A bright blue light shone in her gaze, one Marcon hadn't noticed before. "We have our orders, Captain."

"These people are going to get hurt," he shot back.

Almost to prove his point, a faint whizzing sound crested through the air, ending as the object splatted against the back of the platform.

Silence fell over the crowd.

A splattered egg had smeared the polished wood of the platform.

Marcon's jaw tensed and he turned back toward the crowd, but something about the egg compelled his gaze.

The white of the egg ran forward despite the even planks of the platform. His blood ran cold. The egg had landed upon a square cut into the base of the platform, one in a line of four.

Trap doors.

His eyes widened in horror, and he turned to face Isadora straight on. "This was never about peace, was it?"

Fury tightened her jaw, but she wasn't looking at Marcon. She was staring at the short form of the field commander whose armor made her a blinding target, almost a provocation to those who had lost everything, the singular figure upon whom they might hang all their frustration and despair.

"No, Colabra," she murmured. "Welcome to the field commander's service."

Silversword raised her voice and called the people to order, resuming her speech as though nothing was amiss which only served to incense the crowd more. When another burst of shouting rang out, her temper cracked. "There is no room for lies or false accusations within our city as we rebuild," she cried. "Violators will be punished."

"Told you so!" one citizen cried.

"It's exactly as they said!" yelled another.

A flurry of projectiles arced toward the stage, spattering near the dwarf.

One egg sailed straight toward her head.

Silversword raised the shield built into her armor and caught the splatter against it.

Marcon held his breath.

The field commander stood frozen with arm raised, staring down at the podium where the scroll with her notes lay unfurled. When she raised her head again, her eyes were the same brilliant white that they'd been when she blasted Lorieannan with her necklace.

But now they were surrounded by hundreds of innocents.

"The example begins now," she growled, her voice low enough that only the surrounding soldiers would hear her. With glowing eyes, she surveyed the crowd. "Bring the rabble to me!"

Isadora gave the signal. "Go."

Vateri stood rooted in place. Cole grabbed her arm. "Come on," he urged.

Marcon shoved his way through the crowd. The panicked citizens of Respite pressed closer to one another as cries rang out among them. The anger had ebbed, and fear returned.

"Gah!" Silversword screamed as a rotten vegetable splattered across her shield. "Enough!"

Marcon had spied one of the perpetrators earlier and struggled through the panicked crowd toward them.

Back on the platform, Silversword had thrown aside all disguise of decorum and seized her pendant of Ilona instead. Her eyes rolled back in her head as she murmured a prayer in what must have been the elemental tongue, though it made the hair along the back of Marcon's neck raise.

She leveled her gaze from the podium at the perpetrators while her black-coats slunk like poison toward where they'd been. Her eyes were orbs of pure white, utterly horrifying to look upon.

The vegetable-throwers blanched. They opened their mouths to scream. Marcon kept shoving his way through—

And a beam of burning white light shot out of Silversword's pointed finger at the figures. She turned them instantly to ash.

Pure chaos erupted then. Children's cries rent the air. Distantly, he caught Vateri's shout.

A woman screamed as she was knocked down, her arm trampled.

Marcon sprang forward and hoisted her off the ground. The woman, in her panic, wrenched back, elbowing him in the face. His nose broke with a sharp crack and tears flooded his eyes.

"Clear the area!" Cole shouted.

Marcon twisted about, trying to get his bearings in the crowd. Panicked figures crashed into him. There were too many in the square with too few routes of escape.

Whose idea had this speech been?

His hair stood on end again, a telltale prickle against his skin, and the field commander released another blast, this time coming from her amulet.

Her eyes were still white, her mouth twisted into a sickly grin as she cast her burning beam across the crowd, only making the panic worse.

People shoved one another, entire families knocked

down in the street, innocents trampled in their haste to escape.

Marcon searched the chaos for Vateri, struggling to keep his own footing in the crowd. His sigil burned on his arm. Silversword had lost control of her element—there was no other explanation.

"Hunt them down," Silversword growled to her elite troops. "Kill them all."

Time slowed around him as the sigil on his arm burned brighter. Almost against his will, Marcon turned back toward the dwarf, wanting to answer her burning light with his own fire.

A tall figure in blue crashed into his side, knocking him against a building.

Marcon struggled, finding Isadora before him and holding himself back from a strike just in time. "This is madness," he shouted to be heard above the crowd.

"They deserve to see the truth," she replied, her eyes bright with a meaning he couldn't decipher. "And we have our own role to fulfill."

The phantom end of a knife pierced Marcon's ribs as her words sank into his chest. She couldn't mean that—years of work to join the battalion couldn't coalesce in him being turned against innocents, made to hunt grieving civilians through the streets of Respite.

"Make your arrest, Captain," Isadora ordered him. "Choose your moment with care."

As before, he could only make out part of her meaning.

A man darted past them, one of those Marcon recognized from the speech, one who had armed himself with rotten vegetables.

Marcon tore after the man, sprinting through narrow streets, dodging carts at the ends of alleys.

When he charged around one corner, the man was waiting for him. He swung his fist and collided with Marcon's face for the second time that day. Though Marcon's eyes watered, he caught the man's hand between his and crushed his wrist, the bones snapping beneath his grasp.

The man screamed, writhing, and Marcon wrenched his arm behind his back, his other hand catching the man by the neck and driving him forward. The perpetrator was thin with deep shadows beneath his eyes. "She killed them," the man sobbed as they drew back toward the square. His legs were giving out beneath him, and Marcon had to drag him forward. "My wife and my baby. A second on the way."

He doubled over, sobbing. "I was at work. They barred the gates." The man stopped trying to walk.

Two black-coats appeared at Marcon's sides and seized the man by the shoulders. "You're monsters," the man said, his dark brown gaze finding Marcon's. "You may look different from the undead she sent, but you're just as heartless. Monsters all the same."

CHAPTER THIRTY-FOUR
MARCON

Just like he'd feared, the platforms were gallows. By the time Marcon dragged himself back to his station by the platform, Vateri was balancing an injured Cole on her shoulder in line for the attentions of the medicos.

Marcon stood in line behind her, wiping the blood from beneath his nose.

Monster, the man's voice rang out in his mind.

Was that what Lorieannan would have called him too?

A second line formed beside the gallows, supervised by the soldiers in black. He'd lost track of Isadora in the fighting.

For some reason, Marcon's thoughts drifted to his friend, the blacksmith, a fight he'd had with his son Patrick about the field commander shortly after Patrick had been appointed into her service.

"You put entirely too much faith in one with such an

extensive command and so many deaths upon her ledger," Garreth had said.

Patrick had scoffed as though this was just the newest in a series of foolish notions from his father, someone Marcon found to be a source of infinite wisdom. "You would say that about anyone in command."

"I was there, Patrick, there when her weakness as a leader cost the souls of a city." Garreth gestured to his right leg and the injury he had sustained while the forces of the Cities United had been unified under Field Commander Silversword in the First Battle of Sanctuary.

What did it mean that her promotion had come after the Order of Secrecy for the champions? The order that prevented those like himself from stepping forward to aid the people of the Cities?

Garreth was right—there were visible injuries from her faulty leadership then. His leg had never fully healed and continued to cause him pain. The invisible injuries were worse—Marcon rubbed his chest, the empty place where the memories of his own parents should have been.

Had the routing of the Luz in the Second Battle been Silversword's fault? She carried herself with confidence, ordering the first four of the huddled mass of innocents standing with arms bound, heads bowed by the gallows to be placed on the platforms.

Marcon looked away, his shoulders tensed against the inevitable swish and tightening of rope he knew he would hear. Cries of fear, begging, rang out from the corral of people rounded up.

He couldn't prevent himself from looking for the man he'd arrested. The man slumped in a corner, one of his eyes blackening where he'd been struck by a soldier. He held himself stiffly, likely in a great deal of pain from where Marcon had broken his wrist.

Marcon's breathing quickened.

"Do it," Silversword called.

The platforms creaked. The bodies dropped.

"A captain I see." Garreth's growl was rough. The smith wiped his hands on a towel, the forge cold behind him. He ground his teeth together, his short tusks protruding into his upper lip before he reconsidered whatever he'd been about to say. Garreth was not one to waste words.

The half-orc waved Marcon around the back and flung open the door of his living quarters positioned behind the forge. Even with his limp, Garreth carried himself like a soldier—aware. Almost coiled. He was nearly as tall as Marcon, his work as a blacksmith keeping his chest and shoulders strong.

Garreth's home was one of Marcon's favorite places in all of Respite, a refuge he'd escaped to many times. The smith kept his quarters tidy, with a few delicate pieces of décor scattered about, ones his wife had selected years ago. Garreth couldn't bear to throw them out.

On instinct, Marcon had wound his way to the forge after his first disastrous day under Silversword's command. Cole was sleeping off his sprained ankle so they could begin combat training in the morning, and Vateri had holed up in the library, trying to cauterize the events of the day that they would have to repeat on the morrow. He was desperate to speak to someone he could trust, someone without ulterior motives. Garreth would care what was happening to both the people of Respite and the city's soldiers.

Garreth waited until Marcon had shut the door firmly behind him before he spoke, ambling through the entry passage and toward the kitchen so Marcon would have room to enter. "Shall I watch what I say about Silversword like I have to do with my son?"

Marcon frowned. "Things didn't improve with Patrick after the defeat at Sanctuary?" He didn't know how to tell Garreth about the round-ups, the executions. The role he had played in the murder of innocents.

"Heh. Boy won't even call it a defeat, much less an arse-whooping trick and brilliant turn of strategy on Alessandra's behalf, feeding the Luz an impossibly tempting morsel about the dragon's absence. I'm sure the dwarf was salivating at the prospect of salvaging her reputation after the defeat twenty years ago."

The half-orc continued to huff to himself as he hobbled over to his armchair. "Help yourself, and one for me," the half-orc called, gesturing over to the kitchen at the corner of his living quarters behind the forge.

Marcon thought over Garreth's words and the layered insinuations within them as he drew the corked, dark green bottle out of the ice box and poured a glass of chilled red for Garreth and a half-pour for himself.

Matters between the half-orc and his son had been difficult since Garreth's wife's passing. Patrick's promotion into Tali Silversword's ranks hadn't helped matters. No matter what Garreth said or what he had experienced, Patrick's faith in his field commander had never wavered. Marcon hadn't sought Patrick out after the morning's executions. Would they be enough for Patrick's devotion to yield?

"You're awfully quiet," the half-orc observed. "Anything you want to tell me about? They mistreating you?"

Marcon hadn't fully thought through his visit, the necessity of keeping his secret about being a champion from his friend, how Garreth might expel him in disgust once he revealed what he'd done.

He downed his wine and refilled his glass, topping off Garreth's as well. Tongue loosened, Marcon recounted the whole story, leaving out only his appointment as a champion of fire and the sigil pulsing beneath the armor.

The sigil had burned all through the morning but calmed in his friend's presence, like it found a kindred spirit in the blacksmith's moods.

Garreth listened with jaw tight, expression grim. "You're certain you've never seen the elf before?"

Marcon sat back in surprise. "Of all the things I've just said, that's the one that stands out? A figure in a dream?" He'd mentioned the haunting familiarity and left the more amorous details unsaid.

The half-orc chuckled. "My wife was part elf, if you recall. Poor lad takes more after me, though I like to think he has her spirit, always wanting to go his own way. So yes, a beautiful dream-elf guardian-fae-angel—whatever you want to call her, did catch my notice."

He rubbed his hands through his hair and sighed. He couldn't tell Garreth the truth about his new identity, so he couldn't ask the smith whether the elf in the dream might somehow be connected to Ignis or his path as a champion.

"I can see you're overwhelmed right now," Garreth said, changing the subject. "Do one thing for me." He met Marcon's gaze. "Trust Isadora. She'll see you through."

After the horrors of the morning of marching and then chasing through the city streets, the shocked cry of the prisoners as the platforms fell beneath their feet, Marcon was relieved to find himself by the river in the forest, the sunlight glinting on the opposite riverbank.

In his dreams the night before, he'd chased her through the forest, but this time she was still.

The elf sat by the waterside with her knees drawn into her chest, her head tucked against them.

Marcon stopped at the edge of the tree line, the ferns tickling his ankles. Was she upset? Lost in contemplation? In pain?

"You found me." The muffled voice rose from the elven woman and as a whisper through the trees all around him.

He tilted his head to the side. "Is it me you've been

running from?" She seemed different from when she'd let him chase her before, more like she was in danger. Fleeing something he couldn't perceive.

She looked up at him then, the ghost of a smile on her face. "What do you think?" Behind her green eyes, she seemed to hint at the other memories with her that had haunted him in his sleep and upon waking, memories that weren't his own—the bob of her throat beneath his lips, her whimpered delight at his touch. The roll of her hips as she straddled him and threw her head back, his thumb between her legs and his other hand palming her breast.

"I would say no," Marcon said with a shrug, striding casually forward with a great deal more ease than he could have imagined doing were she actually here before him.

On the off-chance the elf was connected to his sigil, he had prepared for what to do if their paths crossed. His first step would be figuring out who she was and why she was appearing in his dreams. He had pushed away the guilt of the woman not being Lorieannan, though when Cole asked who he was daydreaming about and Vateri chided Cole, the guilt blazed anew.

"What are you running from then?" Marcon asked.

The elf shook her head. "Not for you to worry about."

He took a few steps closer. Her eyelashes were impossibly long, stretching up to the red arches of her eyebrows. He'd never seen anything as brilliantly green as her eyes, the effect made more dramatic for the gold and copper flecks trapped within the peridot pools. "Are you here to tell me something, then?" He crossed his arms over his chest. "Did Ignis send you?"

"Should I have something to tell you?" The elf plucked a long-stemmed blue flower from the grass and began denuding it of its petals. *Periwinkle*, his mind supplied when he couldn't place the blooms.

This dream figure definitely didn't know about the hunts through the city streets and the fervor of the field commander.

The elf ran her hand down the length of her thigh, and the river beyond her quickened its flow.

He wasn't getting anywhere with his questions. Time to try a different tack.

Marcon steeled himself and lowered to his knees in the clumps of grass by her side. She had wisely perched on a rock by the river, so her clothing wasn't absorbing water like his was. "My dreams of you carry echoes of more than me chasing you through the forest."

He swallowed, finding his nerve again, and brought to mind one of his dream flashes that had been impossible to forget after it appeared before him. She was perched on his lap, her bare legs wrapped around his back, the sheet tangled around the two of them. The feel of her—Marcon's arousal grew kneeling beside her.

Her pupils dilated, and her lips parted. She turned toward him, placed her hand on his chest. "I have memories of you too." The elf smirked and fluttered her eyes closed. Visions of the two of them together washed over him—her kneeling before him, nude, his back pressed against a wall. A second memory interrupted the first, him slamming shut the door of an inn that was somehow located within a tree, clutching her to his chest. She was giggling, a red cloak over her head, her finger pressed to his lips. The images grew too fast for him to follow them, all he knew was a burning need to hold her now before she slipped from his grasp again.

Marcon reached out for her in turn. He wrapped his hand around her shoulder, lowering it toward her waist, drawing her nearer to him.

A growl echoed out from the forest behind her. A pair of impossibly large, yellow glowing eyes glared out from between the trees. They flared at catching Marcon by her side, threatening him away.

He released her and rose to his feet, his hand drifting to the sword hilt that had appeared, strapped along his back. Anger flared bright through his chest, replacing the longing that she had awakened within him. Though he knew it wasn't possible, it felt like he knew her. Had known her for years.

What sort of creature are you, monster? Marcon thought toward the menacing presence. It lurked beyond the cover of the trees, more shadow than man. *Are you what she's been running from?*

The creature was one of strong will, but it would not emerge where he could see.

You can only find her in sleep, it taunted, the voice a menacing growl that echoed within his mind.

Marcon withdrew his sword from its sheath, poised over the elf, ready to strike at the beast the moment it emerged.

The brush of long wings scraped along the forest floor. A winged beast then.

And you? Marcon shot back. Her haunting his dreams didn't mean the creature could find her while she was awake. Was she imprisoned somewhere? Trapped in the beast's lair perhaps?

I know her more deeply than a brute like you could ever dream, the beast answered, a noble lilt layering honey over the rough stone of the voice.

Marcon closed his mind to the creature's threats, blocking out its shadowy, winged form and the darkness it cast upon the forest.

He knelt at the elf's side instead, peering into her eyes. Marcon tucked a bright red strand of hair behind her ear, savoring the delicacy of its pointed tip. "I'm trying to help you, if that's what you need."

The vexing creature raised an eyebrow, challenge flashing behind her eyes. "What makes you think it's *me* who needs *your* help?"

CHAPTER THIRTY-FIVE

MARCON

Marcon did his best to follow Garreth's advice and, after a morning of horrors back on patrol, spent his afternoon in a blessedly distracting training session with Sergeant Isadora who drove Marcon, Cole, Vateri, and Patrick particularly hard.

Sweat dripped from Marcon's brow, stinging his eyes, but he couldn't deny how much the exertion helped. He went a few extra rounds with the sergeant, amazed by her prowess with the blade. The fighting seemed to soothe the element of fire on his arm.

She dismissed them all for dinner. "Colabra," she called as they filed out of the outdoor training arena, "remember to find the field commander after dinner. She'll be at the lowest of the lower rings. Part of captain training," she added for Vateri and Cole's benefit.

He forced himself to swallow his dinner, his appetite gone.

Whenever he thought of Silversword, he pictured bodies swinging in the breeze. Screams in the street.

But years of dutifully following orders did not vanish so easily. And Silversword was the only one who could train him to call at will upon his sigil of fire so he could actually use his position as a champion for the good of the Cities.

He picked at his meal, eating enough to avoid raising Vateri's suspicions, and met Silversword outside the lowest of the training rings on the outskirts of the Luz's holdings within the city.

"Good, you're here."

Silversword held out her hand and gestured for Marcon to proceed ahead of her into the arena.

His stomach dropped the moment he opened the door. Something was deeply wrong. It was more an amphitheater than arena, with rows built into the architecture, the earth dug out and carted beyond the city walls. At the center of the arena below, two metal poles stuck out of the sand. Chains hung from them. One of her masked knights in black stood at attention behind the pillars. Opposite them was a stone plinth.

"Colabra."

He turned back, Silversword posturing on the stairs above Marcon, hands on her hips, looking down on him thanks to the steep slope of the stair.

"You want to be a champion of fire? A true wielder of Ignis's flames?"

Marcon tightened his jaw and nodded, once.

"To survive in our world as a champion means that your control never falters. Most days, your control does not waver. I see that. But the day Ignis chose you, your control had slipped. We need to rectify that. Starting with rage."

She held her hands out toward the two pillars. "Remove your armor and shirt and place your sword on the plinth. Then stand between the poles."

He glanced back at the arena. The masked man in black held a long whip down by his side. Its tip coiled in the sand like a snake. "You cannot be serious."

Silversword raised her chin. "I am. We do not have the luxury of time, and so we will lean upon what some might call extreme measures in order to protect you from what awaits in the world beyond these walls."

"You mean to strike me with that whip." He wasn't sure what the effect of saying the words out loud would be, but he hoped Silversword would sense their insanity.

"My man will. *I* will be gauging your control of your emotions."

Marcon shook his head. He'd performed strange, dangerous, and humiliating tasks all in the name of bearing the badge of the Luz, now the Battalion. But this was too far.

"Utter your refusal, and I will bring one of your friends down here in your place, and you can practice your control in that way." Silversword snapped her fingers, and a line of armed guards began to march around the top of the arena. Black masks shielded their identities.

Cole had told him that Silversword's recruitment of her new peacekeeping force was going remarkably well among Respite's citizens. The food rations were less severe for those employed by the city. The competition to draw within Silversword's orbit would grow fierce as her hold on Respite tightened.

Marcon clenched his teeth. He swallowed his objection. There was no way he would subject Cole or Vateri to the torment she'd picked out to test him, to provoke his titan into answering. To force Marcon to control the blaze of his flames.

He turned on his heel and marched down the steps, doing as the champion of light had ordered. With a clamped jaw, he turned his bare back on the burly man covered in black from head to toe and faced his sword.

The man's footsteps whispered across the sands. He fastened Marcon to the pillars.

Silversword took her time crossing the arena's sand and positioned herself across from Marcon.

"On my signal."

His heart thundered within his chest. *She cannot be serious.*

The bite of metal against his wrists suggested that she was.

Ignis? Ignis. He tried again to call his titan, but he had never heard the titan's voice, had only felt his answer when Marcon unleashed his wrath, when he swore his revenge.

The voice he was growing to despise spoke a single word. "Begin."

His muscles flared in protest with the first strike. With the second, hatred filled his eyes and he glowered at his supposed trainer who watched him with lips slightly parted, as though she was merely curious at how he would respond.

By the time blood dripped steadily from his back onto the sand, pattering softly against the silent press of the large interior room buried beneath the training grounds, he could take it no more.

Marcon cried out, rage clawing out of his throat. His sword ignited.

Across from him, Silversword clapped her hands. *Clapped.*

He might kill her.

"Now, Captain, rein it in."

The whip cracked again and Marcon reared back. He sent flames rushing out from his arms up the pillars, heating the iron until it burned molten red.

Silversword had to shout to be heard. "We will stop either when you collapse or when you learn to control the fire."

It was the former. Marcon didn't know how long he hung between the pillars. His legs gave out far before he could staunch the flames.

Beads of black dotted the edges of his vision.

Dark shapes carried him to a cot in an underground room.

He couldn't grasp his surroundings, how he was meant to survive such torment.

He let the darkness carry him away and awoke in a wooden structure suspended in ancient trees. A fire crackled in a small stone furnace. Balls of light clacked happily on tracks suspended from the ceiling overhead.

"Where am I?" Marcon murmured.

"What a strange question to ask in your condition."

Marcon gasped—he knew that voice. He turned to

find her and growled in pain at the flare of fire along his back with the movement.

"It's called a refractory. And it would be better for you to hold still." The elf from his dreams padded nearer. She wasn't sprinting from him through the forest this time nor were they making love against the trees. The sight of her made the back of his mouth dry. She wore a covering of leaves and vines over her chest, a short skirt over her hips, with decorative vines along one calf, but the rest of her was utterly bare.

There was a strange mark tattooed along her leg, its patterning almost reminding him of scales.

She clucked her tongue at him, her tone oddly playful. Familiar. "I thought I told you not to move."

"I, err—" It was hard for him to focus on her words, to focus on anything beyond the golden glow of her skin and the burning along his back. "Apologies, miss," Marcon said, finally remembering the manners instilled in him in childhood. Joane would be most displeased at his gawping.

"Miss?" The elf tittered at his formal address. She returned and knelt beside him, placing a clay mug full of a bitter-smelling tea beside him.

"Lilia, then?"

She frowned and shook her head. "It is an old name and no longer mine."

Marcon rubbed his jaw. He was not "Hugh" as he had been in the earlier dream, so it made sense that she was not Lilia either. But guessing a name seemed an unnecessarily complex and lengthy process. "Is there something else I should call you?"

She smirked in answer. "Drink that." She rose, drifting past him and running her hand over his chest as she did so.

Her touch raised pebbled marks across his chest and sent a pulse of heat low, shooting through him despite the pain.

"If you won't tell me, I'll have to invent something myself." He affected as much ease as he could muster.

Her mood shifted as she stepped behind him. In a thicker accent than he usually noticed, she cursed under her breath looking at the marks along his back.

Marcon suddenly stiffened. She couldn't see him like this. True, he wasn't as much of a raging mess as he'd been back in the arena, but this wasn't the image of him he wanted her to carry.

"Whoever did this to you, I hope you've uncovered a creative way to dismember them. I have a few ideas if you need suggestions."

For some reason, her sudden turn to violence made him laugh which quickly resulted in a groan as the movement rippled over his ruined back.

"Alright, alright," the beautiful elf soothed. A few stray strands of dark red hair fell from her loose braid and tickled his shoulder as she knelt behind him. "This will take a moment, but you'll be entirely well soon enough."

Warm fingertips balanced against the backs of his shoulders, and she chanted in a low cadence, the words utterly unknown to him, but they cast a soothing heat over his skin, nothing like the burn of Ignis's fire when he lost control. His skin knit back together. The tension in his muscles eased. "There," she whispered, grazing her lips over his shoulder as she rose from behind him.

He had to clamp his jaw to hold back a moan, so different from the ones that had clawed their way out of him before. The sound tugged him from his dream, returned him to the stone room they'd dragged him to.

Marcon reached behind, tracing where her lips had been. There was no pain along his back. His wounds were healed.

A few days later, Silversword ordered his return to the arena. The torture masquerading as training continued. Cole and Vateri were too distressed by the horrors of the hunts through the city to pester Marcon about his nighttime lessons and why every few nights, he had to sleep away from them.

After the second beating, Marcon asked the woman again if Ignis had sent her. After the fourth, she climbed onto his lap, straddling his hips. His back burned but even in spite of that, he thought his heart might burst out of his chest at the close press of her body. She tilted her head at his repeated question. "Why would your titan send me when he could cast fiery retribution onto whoever is doing this to you?" An internal fire flared behind her bright green eyes. "I know that I would, if I wielded flames the way you do." The glint deepened, like she was imagining calling upon the full might of the element of fire. "There are other things I'd do with the gifts I have."

"You're dangerous, aren't you, Wildfire?" The nickname slipped out, but the moment Marcon uttered it, he sensed it fit. She leaned fully into him then, setting his skin aflame.

"Yes," she whispered against the taut tendons of his neck. "That I am."

Night after night, he thought of her when the lash struck his skin, knowing, somehow that she would be there to mend him again. He preferred chasing her through the woods and the flashes of memories of what happened when he caught her, though he'd never lived out one of those moments. *One day*, Marcon promised himself as the lash rent through skin and muscle and struck bone. He clenched his jaw, the pain so great he blacked out.

Sometimes as the strikes came, Marcon knew he deserved them. They were a payment for what he'd failed to do for those he left behind when he went to Sanctuary. Revenge from Lorieannan's ghost for his abandonment, for the elf who haunted his dreams. Recompense for the innocents he chased through the streets, who couldn't outrun him for long. Who he brought to Silversword's gallows to hang for sedition and dissent.

And other times, he wondered if Silversword lingered on the opposite side of the arena on the off chance his titan answered and he broke free. The field commander wielded the noose over the people of Respite just as her hired torturers wielded the whip over Marcon.

He refused to yield to any taunts, any perception of weakness. Thus far, he'd managed to stay her hand toward his friends, the vulnerability she'd sensed, had somehow known about before they'd even met. When he considered stopping trying, giving up before she was satisfied at his humiliation, he remembered her threat to tie up Vateri or Cole and see if he was able to more fully control the flames then.

Slowly, he gained a handle over the fire. He could make the flames flare and then cease. Three weeks into the whippings, and he could limp along to the stone room with the cot where Wildfire awaited him in his dreams.

She emerged from within the confines of her refractory, the strange wooden structure built into the side of a tree, usually appearing behind him which prevented him from witnessing whatever magic brought her into his dreams. She seemed unconcerned with such matters, responding to any questions with a furrowed brow before she slipped away to make him a soothing tea and, upon returning, murmured unfamiliar words that knit his wounds back together.

When she was done, he asked her to teach him the enchantments. She showed him more basic healing instead, how to soak bandages in sorghum bark and water overnight so they would soothe wounds, how to make a poultice from different herbs depending on what he would find in the environment around him.

Without fail when he woke, his wounds were healed. Silversword said it was a side-effect of their connection to their titans and didn't question him about the miraculous healing. It was the one way in which Marcon felt Ignis might be protecting him. He couldn't help but sense that the titan had connected Marcon's fate to the elf's somehow, if she was even real.

Ignis allowed Marcon to peek beyond the shadows that haunted him and glimpse a different life, what was waiting after the nightmare in Respite had ended. When he would no longer have to round up civilians incapable of defending themselves.

Each time he returned to the arena at Silversword's bidding, the blood had been cleaned, the sand replaced.

At the beginning of his fourth week of training, Marcon's fire failed to appear when he called it, the whip hot against his back.

Silversword's eyes flashed in concern that she tried to hide. One of the other soldiers had arrested a child that morning. A boy of seven. Eight. His mother had been in the crowd. Marcon hadn't been able to eat all day. Vateri was inconsolable.

"Focus!" Silversword screeched at him. "Again," she ordered her torturer.

Marcon dropped his head. This would never be over. No true champion of fire would stoop to *this* to learn to wield their flame.

At Silversword's command, the whip stopped. She called his name.

Marcon clenched his jaw and raised his head.

The champion of light glared at him from across the sand. "Perhaps, just this once, we'll stop early." The cold white light flared in her eyes. "Fail again, and I will tie up your friends. Remember that they don't have your fortitude."

He darted away from his tormentor the moment his wrists were free, snapped up his armor and fled. Marcon dumped his belongings in his bunk room and threw on his cloak. What did it mean that the fire hadn't come?

His thoughts raced. He couldn't tell Vateri. Cole would never forgive him if something happened to her. Patrick sang the field commander's praises at every opportunity.

With a sigh, Marcon knew exactly where to go.

He tucked his hood over his head and pulled the cloak about his shoulders, determined to escape the training grounds before Silversword could change her mind.

His feet knew the way to the blacksmith's shop. Marcon banged on the door, desperation tight at his throat.

A gruff call and the point of a sword answered him. "Lad," Garreth scolded, "I thought you were the law." The blacksmith sighed and beckoned Marcon within.

The latest whipping was beginning to catch up to him, and Marcon regretted his haste in coming here. His cloak was probably stuck to his wounds, and he couldn't tell Garreth the truth of who he was. He'd only confessed that he was part of an elite training unit Silversword was preparing for herself.

Marcon's head spun, and he collapsed onto one of Garreth's chairs. He stared up at the half-orc, utterly lost for words.

His friend looked him over in silence for a minute, maybe longer. "What in the burning *hells* are they doing to you, son?" Garreth was shaking—Marcon had never seen him so angry, not even the week before when Patrick had revealed that he would be the personal protector of Field Commander Silversword. He'd warned his father to be cautious of what he said from that point forward. "Don't think I'll protect you."

The words still rang in Marcon's ears. Was that what Ignis was trying to tell him now? Was the titan powerless to help beyond the ministrations of the dream elf? Or did he not care enough to intervene beyond healing Marcon's wounds and freeing Silversword to torment him all over again.

"You know I cannot tell you that," Marcon answered.

The half-orc's jaw tightened. "That wretch has already sent my son from me. Do not tell me she has her claws into you too."

His lips parted. Words utterly failed him. He dropped his head into his hands, the weight of what he was being asked to bear overwhelming him.

"Alright, lad, steady on, now." Garreth limped over to the ice box and popped the cork on one of his bottles of chilled red.

A second cork popped and he dragged himself back. A shining brown liquid for Marcon, the red for himself. "I was too hasty with you, it seems," Garreth said. The half-orc downed a swallow of wine and ran his tongue over his teeth. "She's the one harming you, isn't she?"

Marcon's throat tightened and tears prickled his eyes. *Tears*. As though the whippings to provoke his internal fire weren't enough.

Silversword said she did it to bring out his rage. Did she know how far beyond it he was?

Marcon ran his hands through his hair. Parts of it were already standing on end, and his scraping only made it worse. "I really don't know how much I can say." Patrick's warning hovered between them. "It's dangerous enough for you already."

"Mmhmm," Garreth agreed. "And more dangerous still not to know." He shook his head. "I'll not lose you, lad. Not to this. Tell me."

Marcon dropped his head again, but he did as Garreth asked. He answered the questions he could about the masked man with the whip, explained when the sessions happened, where they fit in his training regimen. Garreth didn't press him as to why Silversword had singled him out in this way.

"Your friends, do they know?"

"No," Marcon rasped. "She's made the threat too clear, against Vateri especially." He held Garreth's gaze. *To your son too*, when she wasn't threatening his two closest companions.

A single nod at the end of his tale. Garreth reached out and clasped Marcon's wrist. He met the dark forest of the half-orc's eyes. "Do you trust me?"

Marcon's throat bobbed. "Yes." The confession might have been the most frightened he'd ever felt.

"Good. Turn your mind from it. Tell me of something else." They struggled to speak of more cheerful topics, though there were a few motes of light within the city. Marcon could tell by the heat in the house how Garreth's business had increased by night and day, his mandatory contributions to the military patrols of Respite fueling the underground industry he was a part of. He was arming the people of Respite for their resistance.

And though Marcon knew he was part of their oppressors, not their saviors, he was glad of that small fact. Respite deserved better than the leader who'd claimed them.

CHAPTER THIRTY-SIX

QUINDYTHIAS

BASTION

The late summer rains had washed the clinging yellow pollen from the courtyards across the city of Bastion, "golden week," as the city's residents called it, marking the transition from summer to autumn.

Quindythias Darkstrider stepped outside of his family home, stack of books and scrawled sheafs of parchment in hand. Finally, after weeks of being trapped indoors with his aging parents and the endlessly nosy waitstaff, he could make some real progress on his studies. The first of the qualifying exams were less than a week away.

"You'll begin in law before transitioning into the lower echelons of the political circle and then make a name for yourself in the field of diplomacy," his father had been telling him since he was a lad. Dutifully, he had followed each step laid out for him. It was the Darkstrider way.

The tests before him were to be the first true challenge to his mettle. Quindythias smiled to himself. They'd said that about university as well, and look how easy that had been for him.

He wiped a few stray leaves from a side table by his favorite chair in the courtyard, ensuring no hint of moisture remained beneath them before placing his books and pages down. Over the months of his preparations, with a slight break for the summer pollens, Quindythias had slowly accumulated each of the side tables from across the courtyard around his studying chair. A "bookish constellation of furniture" his sister Calixta liked to tease him.

The thought of his sister sparked a pang inside his chest. She should have returned by now—three weeks, nothing more, she'd promised.

Quindythias fussed about the courtyard, straightening chairs and cushions. The restlessness that had plagued him for days remained, even though he was finally outdoors.

He stared off the courtyard balcony, the vague shimmer of the Circle Sea far below, at the base of the terraced rows of Bastion's cityscape.

For almost ten years, he'd been preparing for these qualifying exams. Yet his worry over his sister kept plaguing him.

Less than six weeks before, the sea had taken his sister away, part of the Cities United's grand strategy to recover the lost city of Sanctuary. A "strategic nightmare," the most daring of his military strategy professors had called it.

Secretly, Quindythias had agreed, though given his family's position among the ruling class, he could not voice such dissent aloud.

He couldn't blame the Circle Sea though. Rather than stranding his sister among the alarmingly optimistic army of the Luz in Respite, the sea had seen her returned.

A month ago now, she'd made it back to Bastion. They'd had one afternoon of hushed conversation, her gaze still haunted by the horrors of the sea, before an urgent missive bearing the seal of Field Commander Silversword reached their home.

Respite had nearly fallen, his sister said, and there was a pressing mission of protection that her specific training prepared her for.

Before Calixta had even unpacked, she was gathering her things again. "I'm sorry Quindy," she had said, her expression ashen. "This is not a task I can refuse."

"But you promised you would be here through the exams." In the decade that he'd been preparing to complete his exams to pass from pupil into the ranks of the apprentice lawmakers, his sister had been working her way up in the ranks of Bastion's army. She'd achieved captain in record time, but such a feat still shouldn't have put her within the notice of the field commander.

There was something she wasn't telling him.

In part because of his father's urging and in part due to his concern for her, he'd taken a few extra courses in military strategy. Calixta's path had veered a few years before from the norms of promotion. More secret missions followed. More nights separate than together.

"I swear I will be there to support you through your exams," she had promised. Though he tried to project confidence, something about the qualifying exams made Quindythias's stomach curl.

He had a brilliant mind for strategy, his instructors had told him over and over again. That same praise had begun to fall flat with the feeling of dread that came over him around the qualifying exams.

A cold wind picked up and dashed across the court-yard, scattering pages and leaves. "Drat!" Quindythias dashed about, snatching up the pages and huffing at their disordered state.

His sister was the only one who knew how to talk him out of his dark moods, his states of worry. At her urging, he had faced the feelings that closed his throat, that caused his heart to race. "The fear should be specific or it's not worth engaging with," she'd told him before shipping out for Respite.

Before word reached his parents that the soldiers were being routed back to Bastion due to unnavigable storms, he had finally put words to the looming dread—his exams signified an unalterable shift in his life direc-tion. A point after which, his world would never be the same.

Worry for his sister continued to grow as he tried and failed to turn his mind to his studies. The exams were only two days away.

His mother caught him pacing along the banister rather than burying his nose in his books like he was supposed to be doing. "You know how seriously your sister takes her post," his mother soothed when he slowed enough to share his concerns for Calixta's safety. "It's only an outpost assignment. Don't let her pride in her small accomplishments divert you from yours."

Quindythias choked on the reply he'd been preparing, a fight he and Calixta had shared clawing forward from the archives of his memory. "You have no idea what it's like for me!" Calixta had screamed, tears brightening the dark hazel of her eyes and carving a single trail down the warm brown of her skin. "They favor you. They always have. And what was left for me in return? What other option do I have to prove myself?"

By design, there was no other option. One path of honor among the Darkstriders. One way forward. He'd denied his parents' favoritism and the pain it caused his sister, the reckless edge it gave her, and then his mother put it perfectly into words, confessing the opposite side of the pain his sister had held back from him for so long.

The pain that had sent her into the army in the first place.

"Mother. Calixta's accomplishments are simply different from yours and father's. From what mine will be."

She huffed in reply. "We are *Darkstriders*, Quindythias." Pride blazed gold behind her eyes. "We do not follow the whims of uneducated military commanders. *We* are the ones who put the ideas in their heads and make them feel as though they are in control."

His mother squeezed her hand into a fist. "*Never* forget who truly holds the power in this world. In this city and beyond. Your sister has. I did not think you so foolish."

Calixta's red-rimmed eyes shot across his vision once more. He choked back the rebuttal he was desperate to shout at his mother. *It's your fault she's not here to help me! Everything we've worked for is in peril because of you!*

But the dread had never gripped him so tightly before. Calixta needed him. Her desperation to prove herself had put her into harm's way.

A flicker of calculation crossed his mother's expression. He was delaying too long in his answer.

Quindythias forced a sigh and dropped his head. "You are right, Mother." He spun on his heel and returned to his books, piling them onto his lap.

She raised an eyebrow, waiting to see if he would argue more but he did not.

Senator Darkstrider patted him on the shoulder before slipping back into the house.

Quindythias's hands shook as he held himself still, knowing she would be watching him. *Tonight,* he promised himself. After they'd turned in, he would make his escape and find Calixta.

As darkness fell over the city of Bastion, Quindythias made good on his promise. He waited until the voices of his parents and their consort had faded into the recesses of their hall before sneaking out of his own suite and into the smaller set of rooms belonging to Calixta.

The disparity between the two made his stomach churn. How had he not realized before? He did not blame the waitstaff for failing to keep fresh flowers in his sisters' rooms, but did they need to neglect the plants too? Where he possessed an arresting view of the distant terraced cliffs of Bastion, including the Halls of Rule and all their grandeur, Calixta's rooms opened to the side gardens and the walls of the neighbor's home.

He ground his teeth and dedicated himself to his search. Somewhere here, his sister had tucked away the pieces of her commission papers that she hadn't had to burn. Upon them, he'd find a coded signal telling her where she should be.

Quindythias smirked as he pulled open her desk drawer and discovered a thin scroll, the bottom edge bearing the field commander's seal ripped off.

He'd never told his sister or his parents that he had been the one to devise the military code used by Bastion's strategists.

"Silversword herself called it nigh-unbreakable," his dissident professor had said, raising an eyebrow.

True, he had allowed the professor to take most of the credit—a failed attempt to woo his instructor with his brilliance during the embarrassingly long crush he'd harbored for the man, but such infatuation was paying off now.

He scanned the missive. He knew the code by heart and didn't need to consult the codex he'd devised for those less sharp-witted.

Protection. The Highlands. Our continued existence depends upon your success.

"Small accomplishment, Mother?" he imagined retorting back in their conversation that afternoon.

They could have that fight when he returned.

He'd see everything arranged with his instructors and let the Darkstrider family name pull some weight in a helpful way for once.

His fear for his sister clamped around his neck like a vice. He wasn't going to let it go unanswered.

In short order, Quindythias had packed a travel satchel for himself and donned his sturdiest boots for the task. He brushed his fingertips over the robes that would be his following his exams, kept on hand to remind him of his inevitable future. He would return in time, and despite what their parents would say, he had spent enough time in his studies.

His mind and his predetermined fate would be far better served by locating Calixta in the mountains and returning her home. There was a grand celebration planned to toast his success which she would not want to miss.

With a map rolled into his pocket and compass dangling from his hip, Quindythias set out from his family home, the stars guiding him overhead. Toward Calixta and their meeting with destiny.

CHAPTER THIRTY-SEVEN
ROWAN

Dread curdled Rowan's stomach as she awoke early the next morning, the sight of the bones beneath the moons still bright behind her eyes.

Over the morning tea, the other offerings ignored her. Rowan glared at Orella. She was the only one of the four of them who would have told the others what had happened and cast Rowan in a murderous light in her account.

At the end of tea, Tullemaien appeared, their outward demeanor cheerful, though dark shadows hung below their eyes, magnified by their spectacles. The offerings avoided their instructor's gaze as well, causing Tullemaien to stammer through sending everyone off to their various training areas. "Those of you advancing to your second element, hold back, if you please."

Forsythia fell into step beside Vraise. She glanced over her shoulder as he led her away back to the mermaids' enclosure. Vraise and Rowan had talked over ways to postpone the young elf's imbuing, though it involved Vraise deliberately slowing his own growth in affinity.

Rowan waved to the young elf who grinned at the attention and skipped off, excited to return to the lagoon.

Alongside Athenza and Orella, Rowan lingered by Tullemaien's side. At first, Rowan thought Athenza also blamed Orella for the continued cold reception Rowan was receiving, but watching the two of them side by side, it seemed as though something else was amiss with the two offerings to the element of fire. Orella's cheeks were flushed, her hair limp. Athenza kept wiping at her brow as though she was feverish too.

"Wonderful," Tullemaien beamed, appraising their charges. "For next assignments, the two of you will be studying the element of air." The specialist regarded Athenza and Orella over their spectacles. Only the slightest furrow in their brow indicated that they'd noticed anything amiss in their health, especially the similarity of their symptoms.

"And Rowan, as this is your second element and, well, given the state of the remaining students of the earth . . ." Their pause held space for the offering that Rowan had desiccated the night before and the one who had been turned to stone during their first training session. Though the healers had reversed the petrification, the offering was making little progress in affinity with the element of earth.

No wonder the other offerings were trying to distance themselves from her.

Tullemaien cleared their throat. "Yes, well, suffice to

say, we've made a slight adjustment to your training area." They gestured toward the edge of the Druidess's holdings near the wall. The path the specialist indicated grew more wild as it approached a dilapidated greenhouse that was overgrown and neglected in sharp contrast to the rest of the academy's careful landscaping.

She followed the trail, freezing when rushing footsteps sounded behind her. Rowan spun about, releasing a panicked breath when she found that it was Majestyk and Viridian hot on her tail.

"Athenza said you might need companionship, roomfriend," Viridian thought to Rowan.

"Thank you," Rowan murmured. She hadn't realized how on edge she had been as she prepared to take on the element of earth alone. Majestyk opted to stay on Viridian's shoulder instead of Rowan's, though Rowan couldn't really blame her for that.

Whispers darted out of the shadows as the three of them tiptoed closer to the greenhouse.

Rowan jumped, nearly calling out as a strange shadow crossed her path. She laughed, shaking her head as she backed away from the shape and found an overgrown topiary threatening her from the shadows. "Quite fearsome," Rowan said, inclining her head to the stag.

With a trill of mightiness, Majestyk launched herself from Viridian's shoulder and paraded into the greenhouse. Her tail stuck straight up in the air, curved slightly to one side as she marched forward, the posture she adopted while hunting.

"Your creature has discovered a threat," Viridian observed.

"Let's support her mission," Rowan whispered back. It was becoming increasingly clear that Tullemaien had sent her here to get her out of the way while they figured out a true assignment for her to practice with the element of earth.

"Majestyk?" Rowan called as she pulled open the creaking door of the greenhouse. The whispering was louder in here, but it no longer sounded sinister. It was a blend between the voice of the wind and the chirruping of birds.

At the end of the first aisle, Majestyk was hopping up and down before a pot, hissing and spitting.

"Ha ha!" a tiny voice cried.

A cloud of dirt exploded from the pot, spattering over Majestyk's face as a sticklike creature with a flowered hat upon its head popped out of the soil and threw a tiny clod of dirt in the dracat's face.

"We awaken, my brethren!" the mandrake bellowed. "Our time of action has arrived!"

Three more mandrakes burst out of their pots. Some were as thin as the first while others had round bellies and squat legs.

They attacked Majestyk with their clods of dirt until the dracat yowled in frustration and fluttered in angry retreat, back to Rowan's side.

To prove her bravery before the tiny creatures, Majestyk perched in Rowan's hair, hissing loudly.

"Rouse the others!" the first mandrake cried.

Chaos descended upon the gardens all around them, with mandrakes popping out of the soil, screaming in victory, and arming themselves with pointy twigs stolen from plants nearby.

Rowan snatched Majestyk from atop her head before the dracat's claws lodged in her scalp and tucked the creature into her chest. "What have you done, Miscreant?" she giggled.

"*They're so small,*" Viridian observed, lifting a paw out of the way as two mandrakes rushed past, chasing a third and trying to force it to don a flower hat. "*However shall we escape them?*"

She laughed again at the daimon's feigned woe. "I think it best we play along," Rowan added, raising her voice to be heard over their cries.

"*You'll never get them back into their pots,*" Viridian answered.

"True, but what are they trying to do?"

The mandrakes were rushing back and forth along the greenhouse floor. They had all successfully placed flowers atop their heads, though several wore the petal hats upside down, which blocked their ability to see their surroundings.

One rotund mandrake rushed headlong into a table leg and had to be guided to a resting area by its friends.

The injury to one of their own seemed to rally them, and the mandrakes stacked their twig-shaped bodies on top of one another, swinging along the rafters of the greenhouse toward one of the walls.

"*They're searching for the tools, room-friend,*" Viridian warned.

"Why would they—gah!" Rowan stumbled back, grabbing onto Majestyk who hissed in protest as a team of four mandrakes seized a pair of garden shears and rushed past.

Rather than aiming for Rowan's ankles, they trumpeted the others to the cause and raced for the door. "The tyranny of the topiaries has tormented us for long enough!" they screeched in the earthen tongue. "It ends today!"

Dozens of mandrakes descended upon the overgrown topiaries lining the garden walks outside. They hacked and slashed at the figures, bellowing victoriously each time they beheaded an ivy lion or a stag made from bushes.

Viridian burst out of the opposite side of the greenhouse doors, and their gazes met. *"Athenza was right about you needing protection, room-friend."* Her teal eyes glistened.

"Don't you dare—" Rowan said, a grin pricking at the corner of her lip for the first time in days.

The daimon sank back onto her haunches and raised her nose to the sky, her laughter a mix of barking cries as they looked upon the mandrakes' subjugation of the plant life that had encroached upon their greenhouse.

Tiny giggles burst out of Rowan's throat as she spied a trio of mandrakes bashing a severed deer head made of leaves with a hand-sized spade.

Fearsome creatures indeed, these wielders of the earth.

With tears in her eyes, Rowan rushed to Viridian's side and settled down with the wolf, Majestyk curled up angrily in her lap.

As the afternoon light stretched over the garden area,

all but the most energetic mandrakes grew tired of subjugating the shrubbery and collapsed into piles of their own, their loud snores the sighing of wind through autumn leaves.

"What is the Pentacle going to do with you now, room-friend?"

Rowan grinned, looking out at the newest chaos she had unleashed since her arrival. Besides the topiaries and Majestyk's pride, no one had gotten hurt this time.

"I'm sure they'll sentence me to some sort of clean-up."

"Maybe the mandrakes will name you their queen, and you can rule over them from this day forward."

The dozen remaining stick creatures who had not succumbed to sleep cackled as they chased one another through the trees, the patter of their feet like that of squirrels over the greenhouse gables.

"Will you rule by my side then?" She sank back into the cushion of Viridian's fur.

"Of course, room-friend. I will be your chief aide. And Majestyk can be in charge of public relations."

Majestyk's spines poofed out as the giggling mandrakes rushed past them again.

Rowan began to wind a crown of vines for the dracat's use, something that would distinguish her among their new stick-bodied kin. "I'm worried Athenza is getting sick," she murmured to Viridian. "She seems feverish and withdrawn."

The wolf hummed her agreement, shifting her posture slightly to better accommodate Rowan against her fur. *"The fire is a challenge, room-friend. But with you to help her, she will adapt to it in time."*

"I hope you're right," Rowan sighed. She couldn't lose anyone else. Not again.

CHAPTER THIRTY-EIGHT
TESSINA

There was no use.

Tessina wandered away from the elm and the still body of the dryad, the former champion of earth. If only Gaia had not left with two of the other titans as Yvayne had said. If only she had not turned her back on her champion, on the peoples of the forests. The priestesses who rode through the Emeraude had said that their titan abandoned this plane to protect her own. Were those of the forests not her people too? Did they truly matter so little?

She lay down in the field of autumn hyacinths, a late-blooming variety unique to the Emeraude and her chilly summers. The bright spring of their perfume wafted over her—a promise between the seasonal goddesses. The flowers had emerged, peeking chutes that stretched out of the earth and opened their violet eyes to the sun. After the first frosts, their bulbs would nestle beneath the covering of earth, and the ghosts of these blossoms would drift through the heavy winter air.

The growing spirit-sense had shifted her relationship with time. How was she supposed to recall what was in her soul to remember?

Tessina trailed her fingertips over the soft, star-faced blossoms. Who were these ancestors Yvayne was so certain she would remember? Where had they come from before they found their way to the Emeraude?

Could she call their spirits back to her?

She jolted awake at a gentle shaking of her shoulder. Tessina jumped at the closeness of the wide lavender eyes of the fae. "I haven't done it," she said before Yvayne could speak.

Yvayne leaned back on her heels. "I know you have not. You have two days more before her spirit passes to Astralei."

"And if I do not—"

"We have lost another champion of earth." Yvayne's face betrayed none of the emotions Tessina sensed swirling far beneath her gray-brown skin. The fae kept careful watch over her thoughts as well. Was she angry? Disappointed? Tessina couldn't tell.

"What would that mean?" Tessina whispered. Were there no other champions of earth left? This dryad was the last of her kind?

Yvayne shook her head and rose. Though she did not look at her feet as she moved back from Tessina, the hyacinths dodged her steps and exhaled their pollen into the air. "Those in a position of utter weakness count down to the very last of what they have. They depend too greatly upon these few. But that is not the place we are in. Not just yet."

Yvayne stared down at the purple blossoms. Each flower offered the apology Tessina couldn't find the words to say. Perhaps the flowers could succeed where Tessina had not.

The fae sighed. "Many have come before you. I have to believe others will arise after. Or else we have little hope. My allies and I have done what we can over the years. I had planned for you to help increase our ranks. As I said, I believe it is time for the champions to emerge from their hiding. We have little enough time as it is."

For the past three days, Yvayne had made off-handed remarks like this, as though she expected Tessina to understand her meaning. She knew that Yvayne belonged to a secret order of some kind, but their number and aims remained murky to her.

"Will you tell me about this order of yours?"

The fae squinted at Tessina. Her gaze flashed over to the dryad and back. "As you wish."

Yvayne wove a story of a hidden group spread across the planes of life, a group called the lorekeepers. They entrusted pieces of themselves and what they had learned to others, hoping that the wisdom of the ages and sacred magics would carry on.

"There are many sacred objects and artifacts that belong to our order," Yvayne said. "Our numbers have always been small. Long before your birth, as mechanomancy in its earliest stage was first taking hold across Eldura, we realized that we would have to choose the direction of our records. Magic was changing so quickly. And as more peoples spread across the planes of life, history quickened its pace to match. Was it our task to catalog the evolution of magic through the ages, or was it ours to record the transpiration of events, to ensure the memory of what has occurred and what has yet to be lives on?"

Tessina remembered that in the witches' tales, the mechanomancers had turned to forbidden magics—the animating of the dead, the manipulation of spirits—forsaking the sacred paths carved by the titans and watched over by the goddesses and gods. For their heresy, they had fallen out of time as the stores of their magic came to an end. What had seemed more likely, to her nameless eyes, was that the mechanomancers, much like her mother and grandmother, had represented something outside the covens of the Emeraude's power to control, and for that, the covens had condemned them. There were times in past ages when the Emeraude and Lis-Maen had vied for power, and the matrons had proclaimed druidcraft a "nonsanctioned" magic. How much more so for magic they could not wield?

The mechanomancers left vast graveyards of glimmering machines in their wake as they shrank back across the lands of Eldura, their numbers dwindling to almost nothing. The denizens of Lis-Maen had seen the promise of these abandoned mechanical creatures. They enchanted the plants of the forest and breathed new life into the metallic herds. Travelers said that the creatures served the city of Delmoir still, and that their living creations could be seen flying overhead in regions where the trees did not obstruct the sky. This was a wonder she had never witnessed.

"How did you decide?" Tessina asked.

The fae smiled. "We consulted our ledgers stashed across the great libraries. Magic flows like the element of water. It changes, and yet it returns. But what has transpired in our world is more like the earth. That is what we pledged to keep and to remember."

All her life Tessina had heard tales of the Emeraude's sacred library, the loretree, a great sweeping oak whose branches and leaves were made of books and scrolls, a living, written history of the forest and her people. Once after Baba Mae's passing, she had foolishly asked if the nameless were written in the books. She missed hearing stories about her mother, and she thought she might learn more about her and what had brought her family to the Emeraude. "Of course not," her herbalism tutor had scoffed. "Books and scrolls are for those who do something of note, and the greatest feat a nameless can hope to accomplish is the attainment of a name and service to the coven."

But Yvayne spoke of having searched for her, of believing in her inherent spirit magic. Tessina sighed. She could awaken ravens but not dryads.

Elevray croaked in the branches overhead. Would awakening a raven count as deed enough for recording? Maybe in a library kept by ravens. Perhaps they had a secret store of knowledge too.

If the lorekeepers kept such extensive records, they could be the ones to help her recover her ancestors' magic and to understand what brought her family beneath these soul-hungry trees.

No longer would she limit herself and her power to the strands of the coven's sanctions. Whatever these other out-of-reach magics were, a thread of their power flowed through her veins. And with Yvayne's help, as a lorekeeper, she would learn to use it.

The evening of the final day before the dryad's passing on to Astralei spread liquid twilight across the sky. Tessina couldn't bear to meet the fae's eyes, and she had stopped her whisperings to the dryad. All she could do now was build a fire whose spirit would send the dryad on her way.

She placed soothing herbs and protective charms around the fire's base. The dryad could carry their power on with her if she wished.

The moons rose, and the stars glimmered overhead. How many funeral pyres would they see this evening? How many spirits would they call into their storied depths?

Yvayne sat with arms clasped lightly around her knees. The light from the flames danced over the sepia hues of her skin and caught upon the silver and charcoal of her tattooed markings. Light and shadow reached the still form of the dryad behind them where she rested against the elm.

After a long silence, Yvayne began to speak, but her words did not seem to be addressed to Tessina, sounding more like a recitation, a spell from a dream. "The shadows that stir among the trees, that grow like parasitic vines through the trunks of the forest—it has happened before."

The fae closed her eyes, and the smoke curls from the fire stopped their rise. Instead, they spread out across the camp, hovering in the shape of a vast forest. "The Glade of Shadows was home to the dryads. They sheltered among the trees, added their ancestral harmonies to the treesong, all as Lyric had intended for it to be."

Tessina knew this story, in part. Yvayne had added to it, on their way through the forest. Had she known then that she was leading Tessina toward a fallen dryad? The witch smiled sadly and wiped a tear from her cheek. Of course she had.

Yvayne sighed and opened her eyes. "But this idyllic age was not long for our world. As Alessandra's power settled across the first cities, the lands we now know as Scourge, she turned her eyes outward toward the rest of Eldura. And her gaze landed upon the Glade of Shadows. Though she has conquered other lands since, claiming the city of Sanctuary for her own, something about the Glade held her attention, her hunger.

"So much elemental power, dryads, druids, and fae who paid homage to Pandora, one of two prime goddesses—the true goddess of darkness—and to Nyx, the titan of darkness, rested beneath those trees. These seekers had retained a semblance of the prime goddess Pandora before she slipped away from the known spaces of our worlds. A glimmer of her magic lived on beneath the Glade, an aspect who dwelled on as a great shadow in their woods. Alessandra longed to turn this loyalty toward herself. She believed that if she could wield such magic, had her servants such power, there would be no land she could not conquer, nothing she could not devour."

Tessina drew shallow breaths, not wanting to disrupt the cadence of Yvayne's tale. The matrons had blamed the Cities' thievery for the plague of shadows that had fallen upon the Emeraude. They had said nothing of a stretch of Alessandra's might.

"The betrayer goddess hopes to repeat her past deeds, that when she has finished burning the Glade of Shadows, strengthened as she will be, she can then claim the Emeraude and Lis-Maen, Bastion, Beacon, Respite, all for her own. But there is a reason we look to the Glade of Shadows for the next chapter in our tale." Yvayne leaned closer. "The dryads resisted, Tessina. The few who survive resist still. Many gave their souls to the forest, that it might have the strength to linger on. Others banded together around their druid allies, slipping into the secret groves and joining the ranks of the fierce warriors of the Sapphire Circle. Still more thought it best that they be the ones to survive, and that with them, in their hearts, this remnant of Pandora's magic would find a new start."

The fae rose and turned back toward the dryad. She held her arms out at her side. "It is for this that you continued on, Declane, dryad-daughter, wielder of the element of earth, chosen by Gaia."

Tessina sucked in a sharp breath as verdant runes shuddered to life from the forest all around them. Their lights pooled, condensed, and formed themselves into the shapes of the creatures of the forest—an antlered muridae scampered after a feather-tailed hare. Bright green squirrels chased each other around Yvayne's feet. The silver and gray of Yvayne's markings shone as well. Their glow darkened the indigo of her hair.

"You understand more than most the magical lure of the shadow, the shade we need to bear the light. You know what it is to hold Gaia's gleam through day and night."

A second tear trickled down Tessina's cheek as she watched the fae work her reviving spell. This was what Yvayne had called her to, the craft she had asked Tessina to work. Recalling the soul of a raven was one thing—she had known the melody of his story and, singing it, could perceive the verse.

Here was the key to the lorekeepers' workings, to their stores of memory and ancient tomes.

A sliver of recollection from her ancestors broke free across her mind. There, she saw a great green dragon reared back, observing her. Behind him, a silver tree, larger than any she'd ever seen. Branches grew from the dragon's horns, and vines curled off the scales of his back. His claws were wrinkled as tree trunks, the peeling texture of maple and the dense grooves of the oak. The dragon sighed and exhaled stories, centuries of knowledge over two figures— a man with curved dragon's horns and a woman with flowing onyx hair, standing side by side, hands clasped.

"You must remember," Yvayne had said. She was asking the same of the dryad now.

Souls had to know who they were in order to return. And it was the job of the lorekeepers to be ready to remind them when they forgot.

It was a deepening of the vow she'd made when taking her name.

The spirits she would call to herself, those she would beckon forth—some were outcast in body. Others were outcast in soul.

Tessina shot to her feet as the spirit-memory vanished and followed Yvayne. She whispered a spell to her ancestors and lent her might to the fae's casting the only way she knew how. Shadowy tendrils slipped free from Tessina's fingers. The forest spirits answered her call. They slithered out of the tree trunks in the form of twirling dryads, of brave riders of the renge.

The spirits drew the green-glowing creatures to them. They stood vigil over the dryad as she slept.

With a glance back at Yvayne, one of the squirrels darted forward. It paused, paw extended, beside the dryad's leg. The fae nodded, and with a chittering bark, the squirrel pressed its paw onto the dryad's knee.

The forest held its breath.

And the dryad—Declane—champion of earth, breathed in deeply and opened her eyes.

"Yes!" Tessina squealed. She rushed forward to the dryad's side. The forest spirits faded back into the trees, and the verdant creatures scampered off, disappearing among the fallen leaves. Tessina took the dryad's hand in hers. "Yvayne, she brought you back."

Moonstone eyes took her in and then stared over Tessina's shoulder.

Yvayne had crumpled over onto the earth. Tessina cried out and ran back to her.

The fae pressed her hand against her chest. "You remembered," she panted.

Tessina shook her head. "No. *You* did. You called the memories back."

Beyond them, the dryad smiled placidly at the trees. She curled her fingers, and fresh green leaves sprouted where nails would normally be.

Yvayne allowed Tessina to help her over to the base of the elm tree.

The fae reclined against the elm as Declane had before. "I must ask much of you both in the days to come," she said with eyes closed. Her hands rested over her abdomen. "A false light grows stronger and casts its foul gleam across our world. I have not yet determined its source. But if we can get to the library, we can determine where it is most likely to strike."

Tessina glanced from Yvayne to Declane and back. What did it mean, a false light?

Yvayne smiled as though she could feel Tessina's gaze. "There are two things I must show you, spirit-witch. And then you will be ready to set out on your own."

CHAPTER THIRTY-NINE
MARCON

Marcon's visit to Garreth had lifted his spirits, somehow letting him believe that change was on the horizon.

He blocked out the faces of those who gathered at the field commander's daily speeches. The riots had all but died out, her campaign to break the people's spirit succeeding.

In the afternoons, he exhausted himself in training with Isadora. Her experience was extensive, and she incorporated magic and battle tactics into their training sessions, opening his mind to what the life of a soldier could be.

But then the nighttime champion training would call him back, every few days, to the underground arena with Silversword. He was determined that her threat to Cole and Vateri would never come to pass.

His fire blazed to life at the crack of the whip. Marcon harnessed his will, calling it back. "Good," Silversword yelled. "Again."

Before he could protest, his tormentor struck him anew. His flames immediately answered. He wouldn't have the strength to suppress them a second time. Not with the anger so close to the surface, his tormentors so near.

Garreth was right, as were the rebels she couldn't catch, the ones who affixed posters to the city walls at night, decrying the tyranny that had befallen Respite. Silversword was the problem. She had to be stopped.

"What are you doing?" The voice of Marcon's other trainer, Isadora, the one who was kind and fair, whose eyes never shone a deathly white, rang out across the sands of the training arena, bouncing off the empty stands beyond them.

Marcon tightened his jaw, dropped his head. He winced the moment he did so, the movement tugging at the stinging marks laced across his back.

The humiliation every third night was bad enough. Tied between two metal poles, his sword just out of reach, the chains that bound him a constant taunt.

No one was supposed to see him like this. Weak. Uncontrolled. Broken.

If only he could freely channel the fire as he had upon the field when he made his vow of vengeance. He would smite Silversword from the sand.

The whip rang out again, and Marcon jolted. Shame stung at his eyes.

Isadora wouldn't want to train with someone who subjected himself to this. Would the revelation of his secret identity as a champion of fire throw him out of the battalion?

"Stop." Silversword called, her small arms crossed over her chest on the opposite side of the arena. His tormentor, the man in the black hood, stilled his hand.

She met Isadora's gaze across the sand, the cold white light flashing. "I warned you not to get involved," Silversword warned. "I am doing what is necessary. He must learn to control the flames."

"What you are doing is cruel and unnatural," Isadora snapped. Her boots clanked as she took the stairs several at a time, landing with a thud into the sand behind Marcon. "If I catch even a *whiff* of you doing this again, Andrak," she growled to Marcon's torturer, a man he'd never learned the name of even after all these beatings, "your drowned body will be so unrecognizable that neither your mother nor your sister will ever be able to claim your corpse."

The sand shifted as the masked man shuffled back.

"Your father would poke out his eyes in shame at what you've become," she added.

Keys jangled, and Isadora snatched them from Andrak's hand. "Get out," she growled.

The black-coat didn't hesitate to obey her.

Hearing the fleeing footsteps, Marcon was able to calm himself down enough to douse the flames.

"I am sorry I didn't realize sooner what she was doing, Colabra," Isadora murmured when she came to stand at Marcon's side. She supported his weight as best she could and removed the shackles from his wrists. "I'll have someone retrieve your armor. This will never happen again. You'll train with me instead."

"But—"

"Silversword is not the only champion," Isadora murmured. "And the titans have no desire for their chosen to be treated in this way."

Each step away from the arena made the lacerations along his back burn in protest. He refused to glance back at Silversword.

"She's going to be furious," he told Isadora as she brought him to her quarters and began tending to his wounds. "How did you know to find me?"

Her blue eyes sparkled. "We have a mutual friend. He thought you might need help."

Marcon started to ask if their mutual friend was Garreth, but Isadora shushed him.

"She is likely still listening. Champion rule number one—trust your instincts."

His chest tightened, and Marcon dropped his head again, at a loss for what to say.

"I'm looking forward to training you, Colabra. Get some rest. We begin on the morrow."

***

Gray light and the tinge of ash greeted Marcon as he and his companions found their places around Silversword's newest rolling platform. This one had been reinforced with metal as the citizens of Respite had burned a few of the others.

They returned to the third square where Marcon had made his first arrest, the energy uneasy, just as it had been then. Isadora had been keeping her distance from him all morning. If that was part of the lesson he was meant to understand, he wasn't sure it was working.

Silversword launched into her new speech, one that congratulated the people of Respite on uprooting those who would cause them harm, those whose interests ran counter to their own and to the cause of the Cities United.

"Death to tyrants!" A voice rang out over Silversword's.

The champion of light grew deathly still.

"I said we would begin our training today," Isadora murmured, suddenly at Marcon's side.

He turned to meet her gaze, his pulse jumping at the steely determination he found there.

"Lesson number two, know when to take a stand." And with that, she slipped away, disappearing into the crowd.

"Not again," Cole murmured, his face pale as he looked out over those assembled.

"Respite deserves freedom, not control," a second voice called.

"This city deserves to be taken care of," Silversword shot back, drowning them out. "Give up your ringleaders, or we will execute twenty citizens a day until they're found."

Her eyes flashed, and that same white glow filled her gaze.

"Enough, Silversword!" A third figure called from within the crowd, a woman's voice this time.

A voice they knew.

"Titans," Vateri squealed beside him.

The crowd parted around Sergeant Isadora who stood tall in the center of the square, openly opposing Silversword's power while in her battle armor.

A cruel laugh echoed out from the platform. "You're more foolish than I bargained for," Silversword barked.

She clasped her hand around the necklace and aimed the beam of white light straight at the figure in blue.

"No!" Marcon shouted, but it was already too late.

The blast struck Isadora head on.

And Isadora conjured a shimmering blue shield of water to protect herself from the light.

Marcon's lips parted. He had managed to coat his weapon and chains in fire, but he hadn't come anywhere close to creating a shield of flames for himself, one that could have protected him from the lash.

This whole time, he'd been training not with one champion, but two.

"Look what you've done!" Silversword bellowed. The entirety of her fury focused on Isadora. Bolts of lightning flickered across the sky above the square. "Round them all up," Silversword shouted. "No one leaves alive."

The people of Respite screamed, their panic a living beast unleashed within the square.

Isadora ground her teeth, her feet planted firmly to withstand the onslaught. Pillars of steam rose off her shield.

The warriors clad in black slipped away from the platform and darted across the emptying square, pursuing the innocents and cutting them down.

The implications of Silversword's command flared in Marcon's chest.

She was ordering the death of innocents to protect the champions' secrets.

"No! You cannot!" he cried.

Eyes of purest blue flashed from Silversword to Marcon's face, and twin, disembodied hands made of water grasped his ankles, soaking his boots.

Isadora diverted her attention only for a moment, stopping him from darting forward to intervene.

"What're you—" Cole cried.

A woman's sharp scream rang out and immediately fell silent as a black-coat cut her down, pursuing those beyond her.

"I warned you," Silversword bellowed at Isadora. "I made it clear what the consequence of disobedience would be."

"You've lost your way," the champion of water shouted back. "You cannot blame the people for their lack of trust, nor can you hide the truth of who we are."

"Do not tell me what I can and cannot do!" A second, lower voice echoed alongside Silversword's—the magic of its command reverberated across the courtyard, freezing Marcon, Vateri, and Cole in place.

The force of the second voice sent Isadora shooting back, sliding along the cobblestones of the courtyard.

The field commander stomped down her platform, dragging her shortsword behind her, cape billowing off her shoulders. "I knew better than to trust you. She warned me against it." The lightning continued to crackle, arcing down and turning those trying to flee into ash. "Thaylssa was and always has been a traitor. And you, the last of her champions, the weakest, most disappointing of all."

The second voice continued to batter Isadora, shoving her in a huddled mass along the street.

"Champion of Fire!" Silversword bellowed.

Marcon's eyes widened as the voice seized him, breaking the hold of the watery hands at his ankles and tugging him closer against his will.

"Bear witness!"

With sword pointed forward and necklace clasped in hand, Silversword aimed her will at the champion of water.

Isadora gulped. Fear widened her eyes, cast tears down her cheeks. "No, please," she begged. She tried to stand. "Anything but—"

She reared back, screaming, her legs twisting at an unnatural angle.

Vateri and Cole seized Marcon's arms, trying to hold him in place but sliding along instead.

The three of them gasped as they saw what Silversword had done to Isadora.

Her feet had turned pure, crystal blue, stationary upon the courtyard stones.

"No!"

A loud, maniacal laugh rang out from Silversword. "This is the price of your betrayal. Your breaking of your sacred oath."

Isadora screamed, her body writhing in pain. The strange blue crystal trailed along her fingers, turning them rigid, shining like glass.

Vateri sobbed openly, no longer resisting and

allowing herself to be dragged alongside Marcon instead. "I can't watch this."

"What's happening?" Cole cried.

"Are you watching, Colabra?" Silversword shouted back. "*This* is what transpires when someone breaks their vow of secrecy. Their soul is *forfeit!*" She spat the last word as though Isadora was the most disgusting creature she had ever seen.

As though Isadora was the one who had ordered the deaths of hundreds of innocents to protect a secret they deserved to know.

Their bodies would hang along the streets and from the palace ramparts by morning. The city would look as though Alessandra had conquered them after all.

Vateri had told him accounts she and Patrick had uncovered of such measures being taken before, in the earliest days of the Secret Council. He'd only hoped the cooperation of the Cities United would have moved past such steps by now.

Isadora continued to scream as the crystal spread over her body. Her features crumpled in pain, no longer able to writhe. Marcon sensed that the crystal was starting to restrict her movements, weighing down parts of her body in unnatural ways.

On and on she screamed, the pain too great for her to withstand.

The stealing of her soul.

He could not move or turn away. It took all his willpower to even blink.

Remember. The single word, whispered just below his ear before it vanished.

A final sob, and Isadora's voice fell silent. The crystal had crept over her neck, thieving her voice.

Her face was the last to solidify, the face that Major Barton had gazed upon with such adoration.

Silversword lorded over the capsized crystalline figure, Isadora's body contorted in pain and preserved.

The field commander breathed heavily and finally lowered her sword.

The moment she did, the spell over Marcon released.

Cole and Vateri stumbled to a halt by his sides.

A single breath and swish of her long braid brought Silversword to her full height.

She spun back to face the three of them. Her eyes had returned to normal, though the ghostly white glow lingered about her face. "This day you bear witness," the champion of light panted. "From the Fall of the First Age, such magic has existed. Fail your friend"—she cast her eyes upon Cole and Vateri before looking back at Marcon —"fail *me*, and this will be the consequence."

Vateri was shaking. A single sob escaped her throat, and she pressed her head into Cole's chest.

"Be ready at dawn," Silversword called before stomping away.

A troop of black-coats followed in her wake. One pulled a body-sized cart. Two others hovered by Isadora's statue.

Marcon couldn't wait around to see what they did with her crystalized corpse.

"Go back to the barracks," Marcon said to his friends. His voice was low, shaky. He was surprised he was able to talk at all. "Speak to no one." He met Cole's gaze. "Get her in the baths if that will help. There's something I must do."

Cole swallowed hard but nodded. He bent to murmur in Vateri's ear and led her away. She gazed back at him as they departed.

There was one man in all of Respite who had suspected the truth of Silversword's nature. One man who had warned him what happens when you lay down in a bed of snakes.

Marcon slid away from the black-clad soldiers and, as soon as he was away from the square, flicked his hood up over his head.

He couldn't ignore the trails of blood that meandered through the streets of Respite. He knew they marked every alleyway that led away from the square.

The people's spirit wouldn't take much more of this. *He* couldn't take much more of this.

Marcon dodged in and out of shadows, checking for tails. He finally allowed himself to breathe when he knocked upon the blacksmith's door.

The solid wood creaked open. A meaty hand grabbed his shirt and yanked him inside.

CHAPTER FORTY

QUINDYTHIAS

"Calixta?" Quindythias called, scrambling over the rocky edifice. Surely this was the place the missive had indicated? For the umpteenth time over the last three days, he regretted not donning gloves for his traversal of the mountain slopes. And his dress boots were doing no favors for his ankles as he tried to navigate the difficult terrain.

Wild winds howled all around him, tugging at his hair, his clothes. He slipped on a ledge, cursing under his breath as he tore another hole in his trousers. They were beyond mending now.

Three days. He'd missed the first of his exams. His mother had likely dispatched members of the rulers' guard after him, a private security firm kept apart from the dictates of the Cities United in case a coup threatened the ruling families. "Merely a security measure until peace can be restored," his father had always said when Calixta provoked an argument with them about the private military force.

"It cannot be a marker of disloyalty to defend your own," his mother always added.

Despite the bitter conditions and his own soreness, Quindythias smiled at the memory. He would say as much back to her when he and Calixta returned.

But beneath his smile, the dread swam forward once more.

Quindythias tipped his waterskin up, wetting his parched throat and careful to conserve the remaining liquid. He had been lucky thus far in his travels, not knowing how to pace himself across the rocky terrain.

Beneath the dread, another surety pushed toward the surface. He was getting closer.

The afternoon sun slunk behind the distant mountain peaks. He uncovered a narrow path, snaking over the terrain and leading to an ancient outpost, carved into the mountain itself before the Fall of the First Age.

Victory. He had found her.

Quindythias adjusted the straps of his pack and hurried over the mountains, only a slight catch in his ankle to slow him down.

"Calixta!" he called as he neared the end of the narrow mountain pass. He'd expected to have encountered soldiers by now, those stationed at his sister's side to help defend whatever crucially significant artifact or territory the field commander had determined was worth risking his sister's life and those of her unit.

"Calix—" His shout fell into silence as he crested the rise and looked out over the valley his sister had been sent by Field Commander Silversword and the Rulers' Council of Bastion to protect.

A narrow ray of sun fell across the ancient watchtower.

No one stood within its circle of stone.

Quindythias scanned the valley, and his breath seized.

Rotting corpses dotted the landscape—elves, humans, ghouls, and dezra mingled together. His stomach churned as he recognized the bright blue fletching of the arrows poking out of the ghouls. *Calixta's arrows.* She'd recruited every aviculturalist and fancier Bastion-wide into her efforts to acquire as many bright blue feathers as possible.

"You have a signature, brother," Calixta had said when he asked after the pile of feathers that littered the courtyard as she prepared her arrows in the weeks before her first deployment into the highlands a few years before. She'd nodded to the jeweled brooch he wore pinned to his wide lapel, gifted to him by their grandmother, an all-seeing eye associated with the Darkstrider house in generations past. She'd spread her arms wide, indicating the feathers, arrows, and the tufts of down that trailed like fresh-fallen snow over the flagstones. "This is mine."

No, no, no, no, no.

Calixta was here.

She has to be here.

The impossible thoughts jumbled together in his mind. Where was his sister in the midst of all this death?

Before he'd even realized what was happening, Quindythias was already halfway across the field. He broke into a run.

The watchtower. If he could just get to the watchtower—

He arrived, breathless. The scene before him knocked its carnage-dripping fist into his gut and he stumbled back.

What he had taken for dark rock made into the circular base of the watchtower before was pale gray stone soaked in blood.

The bodies were piled higher here—soldiers wearing the pale blue of Bastion. The mangled corpses of ghouls, some with their eyes missing, others with strange burns across their skin.

The hill beyond the watchtower bore scores more bodies and more sapphire-fletched arrows than he could have imagined his sister shooting in a year much less in the few weeks she'd been gone.

Hands clutched against his stomach, he searched the ruined tower. He couldn't locate Calixta and yet he had to find her.

"Cali—" he murmured, his breath catching on the final syllable of her nickname and exhaling it to drift upon the wind.

He forced himself forward, carefully stepping between the draped bodies, his gaze leaping along the perimeter for a sign of her dark curls, the pale blue of her armor.

His vision snagged on a cluster of sapphire feathers. They rested in a quiver, bundled together. He'd know the tight curls and slender neck of the figure beneath the arrows anywhere.

And she was lying perfectly still.

A dozen paces away, Quindythias's body froze—he longed to run toward his sister, but what he would find when he did—

A shadow shifted beside Calixta. There was another fallen soldier, this one wearing deep purples and blacks, strange colors.

The shadow knelt behind the second fallen soldier. A dark hood covered its head and shielded its face.

It lingered beside his sister.

"Get away from her!" Quindythias screamed. Without thinking, he withdrew the pen blade from his waistcoat and chucked it at the intruder hunched by Calixta's stationary form.

The figure ducked, his blade whizzing by, over their head.

"Gah!" Quindythias shouted, leaping over the earthen mounds arranged in a circle in the center of the watchtower—*soldiers' biers*—he thought absently, and charged toward the figure.

Was it a ghoul come to devour his sister's flesh following a battle? Everyone knew how Alessandra fed her titans-cursed army with the very carrion her endless machines of war created—part of her never-ending quest to diminish the Planes of Life into nothingness.

It didn't matter what manner of beast Alessandra had sent. He'd beat them with his bare hands to keep them from his sister if he had to.

The figure shot up as his penknife clattered against the pillar behind them. It fell onto the blood-drenched stone and then tipped over the edge of the watchtower, bouncing down the far side of moss-covered rocks as it plummeted off the mountainside.

He'd do precisely the same to the ghoul dressed in a cloak. Quindythias bellowed in rage as he rushed toward the figure, his hands outstretched.

A ghastly scream echoed out from behind the hood. Not the scream of one who devoured flesh.

The scream of one who's lost the love of their life.

Quindythias was too enraged to care, too desperate to reach Calixta's side and save her.

Whoever the cloaked figure was, they couldn't wish her well or they would have saved her by now.

He leaped over the final bier and the cloaked being rose to meet him.

The figure crashed into him at full speed, sending the pair of them careening to the ground. "Who in all the *hells* are *you*?" she spat, hands clenched around Quindythias's throat.

He sputtered and gagged—never in all his years of studying to practice law had he been seized by the neck and restrained. He had imagined a few intimate partners performing something similar, but the execution fell far short of the reality he'd envisioned.

"-in-d-th-s," he gagged.

His attacker had dark, blue-hued skin and impossibly long ears. *Fae not elf*, he realized as spots began to pool at the corners of his eyes.

Not a ghoul either.

Then why was she here?

She seemed to have a similar revelation about him as she released his throat a moment later.

Quindythias rolled onto his side, choking and coughing.

"Rafferty," the fae said, her alto voice full of smoke, a hint of Shadowlands heritage lingering in her speech.

He lifted a hand from the rocks up by his shoulder. "Quindythias." With a groan, he pushed himself up to standing.

The twist in his ankle was worse, but it didn't matter. He dragged it behind him, limping toward his sister. He had to see her.

The fae sprang up beside him, blocking his path. "Where are you—"

Quindythias set his jaw and shoved her aside. "My sister," he answered, rushing to Calixta's side.

With the fae out of the way, he leaped over the final piles of bodies separating them. "Cali—" Quindythias whispered as he sank to the ground next to the figure the fae had been draped beside.

Blood, there was so much blood.

"Calixta . . ." he murmured. His hands were shaking as he reached out for her.

His sister was impossibly still as he took hold of her shoulders and rolled her toward his lap, trying to cradle her, help her somehow.

Her quiver of arrows padded her back as he nestled her head in his arms.

Black-fletched arrows littered her front. *Titans* how many times had they shot her?

Her arm flopped to the side and her neck rolled back as he pulled her closer.

"Ahh!" Quindythias cried as her head fell back, widening a slit along her throat.

Someone's blade had carved through her, side to side, ensuring her death.

"No!" Quindythias sobbed out, crumpling over his sister. He squeezed her tighter against his chest, his cries shaking them both. "Why!"

There was one soldier from Bastion for every dozen of their enemy, and still she had prevailed over so many before they fell. It looked as though they all had—universal slaughter along all sides. Why did Calixta and her defenders not fall back with the odds so stacked against them?

He looked up from her body, searching the site. Why hadn't the council sent an airship to aid them? Such a brutal assault—

"Did you know?" the fae asked from beside him. She'd knelt next to the corpse in black and purple, the armor similar to Calixta's, only the sign of Nyx—two crossed black daggers—upon the shoulder was different.

Calixta bore the sign of Atamos on the shoulder of her armor, three feathers drifting down through the air.

Strange. She usually bore the sign of Bastion.

"Leave us alone!" Quindythias screamed. He didn't know who this fae was or why she was here. It didn't matter. His sister was gone.

Quindythias fumbled at the pouch by his side, withdrawing the healing potion he'd found in one of her drawers before making his trek into the mountains.

"That won't help her," the raspy voice added.

"I said leave us be," Quindythias seethed. He barely

recognized his own voice for the growl burbling up within it.

He propped Calixta's head and shoulders with his elbow, holding her like he had in the portrait their mother had commissioned when they were little—both elven babies with overlarge heads, the sketch posed as they had been too close in age for him to actually be large enough to support her.

Twins, they'd been called often enough through their schooling, given how unusual it was for elven children to have siblings, much less ones so close in age.

He forced himself to study her face. Familiar features were creased in pain. Frozen that way in death.

"Why!" he cried again.

Quindythias bent down to hug his sister into his chest. As he reached to grasp her, his hand brushed against the arm she'd clasped to her chest, held in place by the arrow wounds.

The touch burned.

He frowned, glancing down at her arm.

A pale blue glow radiated from her skin.

Quindythias tucked his fingers around his sister's hand and drew her arm back, careful to not hurt her or jar the arrows that littered her stomach and chest.

He winced as the burning sensation returned. It grew until he thought his arm might be on fire.

All around them, the wind's howl roared across the bare mountainside, rustling the cloaks of the fallen who lay scattered across the stone.

His arm was glowing with that same blue.

It emanated from beneath his sister's bracer.

"What is this?" Quindythias groaned through clenched teeth. Hating himself for disturbing her, he unfastened the bracer from around Calixta's arm.

Along her arm, that same sigil of three feathers falling was surrounded by an intricate series of lines, including the ancient symbol of the element of air, but there were other shapes, even a few runes, within the pattern as well.

His throat swelled.

No. It wasn't possible.

"Look," the fae ordered. She nodded at his arm.

The pale blue emanated out from beneath his sleeve.

Quindythias unbuckled his tunic sleeve, the last of his traveling clothes that hadn't ripped.

The triangle with three lines and the three feathers of Atamos marred the dark skin of his arm, raised welts that glowed blue in the falling light.

"What just happened?" Quindythias croaked, staring in disbelief at his arm.

Rafferty rubbed her hand along her thigh, grimacing as she did so. "The same thing happened to me when I tried to rouse Aubryn. When I moved her, Aubryn's arm pressed upon my leg. The mark transferred. She did not wake."

Quindythias shook his head. "But it's impossible."

The fae merely gazed back at him.

"Impossible," he repeated. "The champions faded out of existence after half the titans left. And Calixta couldn't have been . . ." The words died on his tongue and Quindythias choked back a sob.

Nothing made more sense to him than Atamos, the Titan of Air no less, choosing his sister.

The emotion turned to lead in his throat and Quindythias clenched his jaw, trying to hold it in.

No use.

He reared back, throat and chest raised toward the sky. "Why didn't you protect her?" he demanded of the low, smoke-hued clouds rushing past overhead. "She kept your cursed secret from me, and for what?"

Quindythias's shoulders slumped, and he nearly collapsed onto the stone beneath him, his body hunched over the person who was dearest in the world to him. His breaths rose and fell in a too-quick panting.

Rafferty grasped his shoulder. "Breathe," the fae urged. "Nice and slow." She gestured for him to follow her own breathing pattern and Quindythias shut his eyes, allowing the sound of her breath to guide him and stave off his panic.

A deadened calm took its place. "Please tell me you know more," he murmured, grasping at this last thread of hope. If Rafferty's fallen partner had been able to confide in her, if he could make some sense of the sacrifice that had been made of his sister, he might stand a chance, eventually, of making sense of the sigil that had been branded onto his arm.

The mark that designated him a champion, chosen by Atamos, the titan of air.

"I know more than I should," the fae answered. "And I know how dangerous it will be for us if she finds us here."

CHAPTER FORTY-ONE
ROWAN

A few weeks later, Rowan fought the urge to clasp her hand to the crusted green and blood of the sigil of earth along her arm. Seth had imbued the intricate flowers and whorls into her skin following her success at forging peace with the mandrakes. With Viridian and Majestyk's help, they had reorganized the gardens, bringing a sense of wildness and grandeur to the rundown greenhouses. The mandrakes had a complex social structure but had appointed Rowan to an advisory role and were planning a conquest of other garden areas.

Tullemaien had been particularly impressed with the way she supported the mandrakes in their own cause, saying that was an important part of becoming one with an element—recognizing that each element had a will of its own. They were more than simply tools to be used.

Her second imbuing had been more cheerful than the first, not just because Rowan knew what to expect, but something was lighter about the imbuer himself, a weight that had pressed upon his shoulders at least momentarily lifted.

Her levity had abated somewhat upon her return to the dormitories where a concerned Vraise paced up and down the hall, alternating his attentions between Orella's room and Athenza's while waiting on one of the Healer's apprentices. In Rowan's absence, the two offerings had both developed severe fevers. And another offering, one who had been blinded by a blast from the element of light, was also struggling to recover.

When the apprentices arrived, they ushered Rowan and Vraise away, starting with a magical scan of Orella. The pair of them retreated to Athenza's room, where Vraise told them of his latest discoveries. "Orella said that they took the stricken light offering to the Healer's towers this morning," Vraise confided. He shook his head. "I had to leave when the apprentice she'd called arrived, seeing about her fever."

He glanced over at Rowan to see if she was still going to tease him over the Healer's apprentices' immediate fascination with the "brave outlander." Were she less worried about Athenza, Rowan might have, especially because the apprentices went out of their way to avoid Rowan, as though she carried about her the pall of death which, given the lingering reputation of her first lesson despite saving Seth afterward, she supposed was true.

The apprentice was coming to check on Athenza's fever after she had tended to Orella.

"They're not optimistic," Vraise murmured, his thoughts returning to the offering struggling to contain the light that had blinded her.

Athenza shrugged this off. "They did invite us to be offerings, and here we are," she said.

When she grimaced again and clutched her stomach, Vraise and Rowan shared a look. With a tiny shake of his head, Vraise stopped Rowan from asking Athenza more about whatever was plaguing her.

Rowan settled Athenza's blanket over her shoulders, not even disagreeing when Athenza insisted that she'd be well the moment she could shake this cursed fever. "I know you're worried about me," Athenza said, patting Rowan's hand and calming a little. "But don't you be. After this would-be mage prods at me, I'll close my eyes for a spell, dream of our forest again, and all will be well."

Rowan slipped out into the hall, her stomach in knots over whatever it was that Athenza was concealing.

Vraise was waiting for her when she emerged. "What do you think is really going on with her? Orella isn't saying much either."

Rowan shook her head. "She's clearly not well, but she won't tell me what's wrong."

They took turns lingering outside Athenza's and Orella's doors while the apprentices tended to them inside. While Rowan was out fetching broth from the cooks, the apprentices conferred with Vraise. He was pale when she returned.

"What. Did. They. Say?" Rowan repeated.

He wetted his lips and reached out for her hand, clasping it in his. "Take a walk with me."

They held their silence on their trek down to the

garden and Vraise found one of their favorite benches, the one near the nymph playing in the water.

The debris from Rowan's rogue mandrakes still littered the garden area. She'd be receiving glares from the Druidess's acolytes for weeks if not longer.

Vraise turned toward Rowan, positioning himself so he didn't have to squint into the slanting afternoon sun. "I didn't want to tell you the full truth where Athenza and Orella might overhear," he confessed. "It's worse, actually, than what we feared." His lips thinned as he swallowed. "They said their symptoms are acting as though they're being burned from the inside out." He turned his head away, tears brightening his eyes. "The magic flowing through them is healing them to some extent, but the burns come too quickly. The fire is scorching faster than their bodies can heal, creating scars and burns at once, with the two feeding off one another."

Rowan gripped the stone bench, driving the rock into the soft pad of her palm.

Vraise's hands tightened into fists. "I didn't want to tell Athenza. You've both been so kind to me after . . . after we were raised apart." He shook his head. "I was raised to believe you were my rival would be more accurate. And Athenza was my fathers' example of who not to be, of what failing to serve the conclave looked like."

Vraise's shoulders slumped, and his gaze fell to the severed shrubbery head of a cervidae, the antlers ringed in flowers rather like Gardenia's. Her mandrake army had left no survivors.

"I can't believe how wrong they were." Vraise's lips trembled. "And I don't know how to make it right." He met Rowan's gaze as a tear trickled down his cheek. "The apprentices don't know how to help them."

---

on't know how to help them. Being burned from the inside out.

The proclamation of doom hovered like a choking shadow just behind Rowan's throat as she fled the walled garden and sprinted for the wild patch she'd been tending near the wall.

From the inside out. Nothing they can do.

Vraise had called out to her as she leaped up from the bench and darted away. But she didn't stop. She couldn't linger within sight of the hall any longer.

Rowan's jaw tightened as she ran. *You didn't have to come here. You volunteered in order to stay with me.*

How was she always bringing about death?

She couldn't return to the hall. Couldn't bear the press of the stone, the weight of unmoving wooden floors rather than the gentle shifting of the trees. Vraise's cry of protest still lingering in her ears, she had flown to the overgrown garden plot that reminded her of Paupa's garden in the refractory. The grass was patchy, not receiving as much sun as would allow it to thrive.

Rowan ran her palms over the earth, calling forth the wildflowers she remembered from the forest as a child, their colors and shapes mingling in memory to the point that she wasn't sure whether the pictures she still held were of naturally occurring flowers or not.

She focused on the blossoms in a failing attempt to

keep her mind from turning toward Athenza's ailing state upon the bed in her room. Before her eyes, blisters had formed beneath the druid's skin. Her fever that had first appeared a few weeks ago, over the course of the afternoon, growing increasingly severe.

And if the apprentices' estimations were right, her mentor wouldn't be getting better. She and Vraise had overheard their conversation in the corridor. The blindness that had fallen upon the offering trying to bear the sigil of light had spread from her eyes, taking her hearing, her sense of taste.

Within the Healer's towers, the offering lay flat on her back, unmoving, her breath only just stirring her chest.

"By all accounts she'll be the next to go," one of the apprentices had said, jolting back as she rounded a corner and met Rowan's glare.

She knew it wasn't the apprentice's fault their numbers dwindled by the day.

What had she been expecting, coming here? That the academy would blithely aid her in growing her magic for the good of Lis-Maen, with no thought to its own ends and designs?

The Pentacle's answer had been etched into the stone fountain built into the living wall of the Sorceress's towers—*Knowledge is opportunity. Magic is might. For them both, together, there is always a cost.*

Rowan shook her head. How different such a belief was from how she'd grown up, taught to tap into the magic of the living world around her.

But such magic was dwindling. She narrowed her

gaze, seeking to draw more energy up from the earth into the wildflowers she was calling into being. Just out of reach, a different patch of grass was withering away. The energy was no longer boundless, especially not here.

The chirruping of the birds quieted. Unusual.

A long, stretching shadow covered Rowan and the blossoms she was tending, disrupting her thoughts. She stilled as the warmth of the late summer sun left her skin, and her breath caught as the shadow twisted—two curved points reached off the figure's shoulders. The fanged points of wings.

Lucien.

Rowan turned back over her shoulder. The chirruping chorus remained silent. She stifled a gasp, gazing up at the impossibly tall, winged man who seemed to trail an umbral cloak of fog behind his every step as though he commanded the forest mists. Lucien pressed the points of his fingers together and touched his joined thumbs to his lips.

Rowan mirrored the signal, a greeting for the dawn.

The guardian raised an eyebrow, studying her. "You're not like the others with their books and their practicums. Why is that?"

Other than possibly glimpsing him by the lagoon, she hadn't seen him since she'd arrived in the Pentacle weeks ago, when he'd spoken up on her behalf and secretly added his blood to hers during her vow with the Sorceress and Oracle. Why had he chosen to seek her out now?

"I don't think the answers I'm looking for have been

transcribed. Why else would the Pentacle have brought me here?"

The guardian's eyebrow raised. "I can think of several reasons, quite easily. Try again."

Athenza's warning to keep her distance from Lucien trickled back toward her. But the guardian had sought her out, and Athenza was too feverish to rise from her bed. "Before the Pentacle took an active interest in my home conclave and pushed dissidents like my father out of power on the council, he used to take me on trips through the woods to practice magic. He wanted me to understand the world around me and my part in it. After their intervention, he made sure I knew how to protect myself."

The scarlet wildflower with the moons-white center she'd just called forth out of the earth bobbed on a soft breeze. Diminutive in size, it would be a simple enough flower for someone else to overlook, not knowing that the flower's petals sparked the fire in one's blood, adding heat to magics such as that of the earth that were more readily at hand. Being impaled by a spiked vine would be painful enough. How much better for the vines to burn as they ensnared the caster's attacker.

The towering figure arched his brow. "There was something more though, wasn't there?"

Perhaps the guardian knew about the flower's properties. The memory of Paupa's garden patch overwhelmed Rowan's senses. Bobbing, mingling colors. The scent of rich, sun-warmed earth. She clenched her teeth and turned away. It was more than she would share with a stranger.

And how quickly it had all fallen away.

"Do you want to know why I spoke up on your behalf, the day we met?"

Rowan bit her lip, her hands hovering over the flowers.

Lucien's gaze heated the back of her neck, willed her to turn around.

"I do."

A shift in the energy behind her pulled Rowan back. The guardian was smiling. Despite the sharpness of his elongated canines, the sight was surprisingly bright, completely transforming his appearance.

She understood now how he'd been able to secure his position with the Oracle and the Sorceress. It wasn't just his power as a guardian. He wielded charm over them as well.

"There is a difference between allies and tools," Lucien said. The smile twisted into a smirk as Rowan met his gaze. "We can cover that later in your training."

He softened as he studied her. Lucien slid closer to where Rowan knelt among the grasses. His voice dropped an octave. "In my role as a sacred protector of this plane, I have seen fear manipulate the minds of those who would rule." He held her gaze, the sun bringing out more of the golds of his eyes rather than the over-bright yellows. "In the worst instances, this fear causes paranoia for it also exposes a truth."

She tilted her head to the side. There was something oddly alluring about the guardian, the contrasting shadows of his features. "And what truth is that?"

Lucien gestured to the flowers before her. "You are

more powerful than they can ever dream of being. And they will never feel easy allowing you to reach your full potential. But your potential is precisely where you can achieve all you've ever dreamed of and more." His voice dropped conspiratorially. "Precisely where you can uncover what you need to save your friend."

Rowan stiffened. "How do you know about that?"

"I saw what happened to the previous offerings, while you were still securely tucked away from their sight in your forest. You passed their graves on your route here. Do you think it was by accident they asked their agent to guide you past the burying field? An agent who, upon bringing them an offering with more raw power than they could have ever dreamed, they sent to her death to fight along the front lines of the failing battle for the Glade of Shadows?"

Her words failed her. *Samara.* Another name on her ledger. How many more could she be responsible for? "Magic is dangerous if you can't control it," Rowan countered. "My first lesson—"

"In your first lesson you awakened six elements that had lain dormant through the entirety of the last round of offerings. And then the *elements* fed upon those who were unworthy."

Her mouth still hung ajar. "The elements . . . wait. The *last* round of offerings? How many have there been?"

Lucien's eyebrow raised again. "You didn't think you were only part of the *second* did you?" He held Rowan's gaze. "They will not stop, but they are too frightened to be successful." He ran his tongue over his teeth, looking away. "When I sensed you, I had to intervene. Their trial *is* important. It needs to succeed."

The memory of dried blood on the back of her hand fluttered across Rowan's memory. "Is that why—"

He raised a finger to his lips and bowed his head. "Magic comes down to belief, sparrow. And your belief in its potential is far greater than most. But you will not reach what is meant for you if you're kept inhibited by those who hope and fear what you might become, those who would prevent you from rivaling their power."

Lucien's edifice of calm flickered. Something else raged beneath his aura of measured control. "In their wisdom, they tell themselves, they aren't so nearsighted as to cut off a future source of power at its stalk, before it has a chance to grow."

Without realizing it, Rowan had risen and slid closer to the guardian's side while he spoke, the way the Circle Sea responded to the moons. He was enormously tall, over seven feet, the tips of his wings even taller.

"But between their fear and that of their pupils, they will hold you back from becoming what and who you must be." Lucien brushed a lock of her hair back from her face.

A shiver ran down Rowan's spine, but she didn't falter. "And what is that?"

The grin that had alighted upon his dark gray lips before shone from behind his eyes instead. "Why don't you tell me?"

Words her father had told her over and over drifted back to her then. "The magic is yours already," she repeated, lowering her gaze and finding herself transported back to their patch of flowers on the outskirts of Willow Glen. "It's not a gift bestowed by the Five Faces. It's been with you since you were born."

Rowan balled her hands into fists. "He believed the magic of Verdigris passed on to her daughters, that her sacrifice, followed by Lyric's was the only one we would ever have to pay."

"We?" Lucien murmured. His hand still hovered near Rowan's face. He dropped it.

"The druids of the wilds." Paupa had taught her the old ways from before the Quadrate added the Druidess as the fifth Face to appease and then subdue the conclaves, binding their magic to the Pentacle's will by shifting the living magic of the earth of Lis-Maen itself.

"He used to say that they enact the same weakening they swear revenge upon the Cities for." Beside Paupa, Athenza had mumbled her agreement while she tended her herbs.

His golden eyes glowed. "Then perhaps it is time we let your training take on its own course, outside the limitations of the Pentacle. Would you like to tap into this wild magic at its source?"

"I can't." The answer came without thought. Perhaps the guardian didn't fully understand. Rowan gestured to the stone walls that bound in the gardens. Even within their own walls, the Pentacle's hold over the soil of Delmoir kept her magic restricted. Single flowers, she could grow, maybe a couple at a time with an extension of her will. But true wild magic had ebbed with each year.

Her phoenix stirred within her chest, cooing softly.

Lucien held out his hand. "Let me help you."

Rowan hesitated. The thought of untainted soil beneath her fingertips squeezed against her ribcage as though her phoenix had bound her in its wings.

"I know you aren't afraid."

She shook her head and returned to her study of the guardian. "I'm trying to work out why you'd want to help me."

Lucien placed long, taloned fingers against his chest. "You don't think it's something I do out of an innate, charitable goodness?"

His wings sprang open from his back, unfurling, giant and bat-like with spines even sharper than his talon fingernails.

Rowan stumbled back, eyes wide. "Not really, no."

Lucien's grin returned. "Maybe I've had enough of their stifling too." His golden eyes turned molten. "Maybe I want to see some true wild magic. Maybe I want to be *surprised* for the first time in an age." He closed the distance between them, his wings bobbing gently with each step and held out his hand once more. "Are you ready?"

She slid her hand into his, and Lucien tugged Rowan into his chest, wrapping his arms around her. "It's much faster if we fly."

CHAPTER FORTY-TWO
QUINDYTHIAS

"We don't need to go far," Rafferty assured him, exasperation poking through the deep, raspy grief of her tone. "We missed them by less than a day, I'd guess. Which means we'll know soon enough if I'm right. Come on."

Rafferty's assurance of their peril and her refusal to fully explain until they were further from the watchtower eventually urged Quindythias away from Calixta.

"I'll be back," he murmured, smoothing the soft curls at her hairline. Her forehead was cold.

He hunched over again, tears blurring his eyes.

"It will be for naught if you die as well," Rafferty grumbled, tugging at Quindythias's elbow and pulling him after her higher into the peaks.

They made a small fire to thaw their hands—one they could easily stamp out if given cause—and hunkered in the crags of the mountainside.

"I have spent the last several years working for Field Commander Tali Silversword," Rafferty began. "I was her airship captain. My partner, Aubryn, was from the army of Vestige. She was naturally suspicious of Silversword, but we were able to form an attachment regardless."

Shadows stretched across Rafferty's face as she leaned away from the fire. "During a battle beyond the borders of Vestige, something happened. Aubryn began to draw away from me." Rafferty told him how her elven partner, who had always been so suspicious of the dwarf, had entered into a training program with her instead.

"The more they trained together, the more fearful and secretive Aubryn became. Eventually I had to confront her—either she could tell me what was wrong, or we wouldn't be together anymore." The line of the fae's narrow jaw hardened. "The next day she was sent out here. Silversword began planning another battle to recapture Sanctuary. And I thought that was the end of it."

"But it wasn't?" Quindythias whispered.

She agreed. "It wasn't." Rafferty told him how her feelings toward Silversword grew more complicated during the failing fight for Sanctuary though she tried to hide it. "I don't know if you heard how the Luz were routed and the wave of death that beset those outside the walls of Respite?"

Quindythias bit his lower lip. "I heard about it."

Rafferty nodded. "It was hard to ignore. Harder to see, not to mention the unrest that followed." She swallowed thickly. "The people turned against the Luz almost immediately. Silversword added her own troops to the city watch. I couldn't help but think how if she hadn't sent Aubryn away, she would have been one of the ones marching about, antagonizing the people she swore to protect."

His parents' assurances about the private security they and the other rulers kept flared in the back of Quindythias's mind. How different were their contingencies than what Silversword had unleashed in Respite?

But the disparate threads of Rafferty's story weren't aligning for him. "I still don't understand how you figured out that Aubryn was a champion."

"Ah. That." Rafferty dropped her voice. "There was a soldier Silversword helped save during the final hours of the battle for the outer walls of Respite, as the vultura were clearing out and leaving the city's undead to devour one another and the retreating soldiers." The fae's dark eyes met his own. "She ordered the airship toward him. He wielded fire along the length of his sword—not alchemists' fire either. Pure flames. Silversword blasted the vultura attacking him, and as soon as she pulled him into the airship, she became possessive, protective, exactly what she had done with Aubryn."

Rafferty explained how she had been suspicious of the repetition in treatment. She had snooped through the soldier's rooms and found little beyond a few of his garments and disparate pieces of armor. But still, Silversword hovered over him differently than she had anyone in a long time. "I thought my search was over until Silversword ordered an execution of an officer in Respite. Turned her into a crystal, somehow." Rafferty shook her head. "The whole thing seemed like a show for the man she'd saved. I recognized him, even in a mask, but I couldn't work out what he had in common with Aubryn."

The fae shuddered. "Even reflecting on it now, I think I understand why they didn't tell us. What Silversword did in Respite—" Rafferty's shoulders sagged. "Don't blame your sister."

Quindythias narrowed his gaze, searching the dark hills for answers he didn't know how to read in the landscape. He wouldn't be holding Calixta to account for this. "Keep going," Quindythias urged.

"Right. In the aftermath of the execution, I knew I had to get away. And then I remembered a strange reaction Aubryn had during one of our fights." Her voice thickened. "She glanced to a corner of her room where there was a plant in a basket. I snuck back there in the dead of night, dug through it, a-and—"

Rafferty's gaze dropped and she hugged her arms around her waist, trying to compose herself. "I found a bundle of letters. Some scraps of notes, all bound together." Her lower lip trembled. "They were addressed to me. In them, she told me the truth of how Nyx had chosen her, made her a champion. Silversword bound her from telling me about her new role. But she hadn't made the oath binding enough to prevent her from writing to me about it." The fae's shoulders slumped. "That was why Silversword was so possessive. She's collecting and training champions while outwardly saying she's one of the last."

As soon as Rafferty learned the truth, the fae had taken one of the old airships from the base and flown across the Circle Sea, asking around until she found the most likely outpost that Aubryn had been sent to. "I arrived only a little while before you. Too late to help her. To apologize."

The fae placed her face in her hands, and silence stretched between them.

Had Calixta done something similar for him? Attempted to tell him of her secret role as a champion? Quindythias's lips thinned as he thought back, trying to recall a sign, a secret look. Nothing. Had he missed it? Or had she been forced into a similar oath like Aubryn?

Their fire died as night descended. Rafferty said they should wait up and keep watch, though he still wasn't sure what they were waiting for.

He picked up one of the pieces of kindling and began snapping it into small pieces. His mind had been whirring, years of military strategy mapping possible courses across his consciousness.

What would happen across the Cities United if the populace knew the champions were alive and well and living in secret?

Outcry. Chaos. A great deal of danger for those in power. But after the dust had settled?

They might have the swell of courage needed to finally win the war.

"Someone needs to intervene. Force Silversword's hand. Keeping quiet isn't working." He would have thought that tears would rise in his sister's absence. But with the press of night, anger blossomed behind his eyes instead. "It isn't right that no one will know what they died for. That they had to keep their magic a secret."

He stared out over the natural lookout point set into

the mountains far above Bastion, part of the ancient network of watchtowers designed to protect the city from an enemy erased from history. *What brought you here, dearest? What did you die trying to defend?*

Rafferty's voice rose over the crackle of the embers, bringing Quindythias back to himself. "What do you propose we do?" She met his gaze, brilliant lilac sparks shimmering behind her dark eyes.

Quindythias grinned. The path of obedience he had walked all his life had led to the death of his sister. To her not being able to confide in him her greatest secret. The secret that had led to her death.

They needed to carve a new way forward, doing something he had never done before. The answer itself was simple. "Rebel."

A gust of wind picked up from behind him, rustling his cloak and darting over the remnants of their fire, sending a tower of sparks up overhead.

If he wasn't mistaken, the shadows around them increased as well.

What would the people do with a swelling of magic, a sign of the titans' return? He couldn't let the question go.

The years of training in strategy and politics would serve him on this road. There had to be sympathizers in Bastion, those who were ready to start anew, build an age free of war, steeped in magic instead. He and Rafferty had both hope and rage on their side. Who could stop them?

Quindythias closed his eyes and tilted his face up toward the sky overhead. He exhaled slowly. *I'll never forgive you for taking her from me,* he thought to Atamos, the titan of air. *But I will allow your power to flow through my veins if we can reverse the tides of this age and punish those who sent my sister here to perish.*

A howling wind cut through the distant mountainsides, whipping through the camp with its biting chill.

I'll take that as a yes. Quindythias straightened, attuning his senses to the tremors in the air all around them.

There was a great deal for him and Rafferty to learn. He smirked at that. How fortunate that he'd been training to pursue life as a scholar and politico. Though the magic would be new, the route to mastery was one he already knew how to walk.

"We return to the city at first light," he told Rafferty, pulling her out of the deep shadows of her own smothering cloud of grief and schemes. "We'll find a place to hide you away. Begin our training in secret."

She nodded, exhaustion weighing down her shoulders.

"Get some rest," Quindythias soothed. "I'll take first watch."

His mind darted ahead, charting the possible courses before them.

A day was coming, soon, when he would make them all pay. The marquis and marchioness who ruled over the military. Bastion's rulers who might have known the secret of the champions' existence and kept it to themselves. And, most of all, the Secret Council of the Cities United who had ordered his sister into hiding in the first place.

The same council that had sent her here, to her death.

He had one clue as to their membership already, one thread to tug and unravel the whole. The one known member of their ranks.

Tali Silversword.

CHAPTER FORTY-THREE

QUINDYTHIAS

In the middle of the night, a distant flutter of wind roused Quindythias from his uneasy slumber.

The wind prodded at him. Provoked him.

He sat up tall. Something wasn't right.

"Rafferty," he whispered, rousing the fae from her sleep.

The emotions that crossed her face beneath the moonlight tightened in his chest—confusion, hope, pain, resolve.

He had to remind himself that his sister was gone.

A great chasm yawned open within him.

Whatever was drawing closer might be the first in a series of sacrifices to try to soothe it.

Or carve it open wider.

Quindythias pressed his finger to his lips and gestured for Rafferty to follow him out of the cover of the rocks along the peak to look down upon the valley.

The fae murmured low in an unfamiliar tongue behind him.

He pressed his hand to his mouth to hold back his surprise as shadows thickened around them, so dense they could have been ensnaring vines.

Rafferty's dark eyes reflected the glow of the moons overhead. The shadows clung to her hands and trailed from her fingertips like blood from the claws of a forest creature in a faery tale.

What would an equivalent power of air be?

His fingertips tingled at the thought.

The disturbance upon the air materialized before them—an airship, hovering at the side of the watchtower.

Rafferty hissed as the ship emerged from the darkness, its cloaking mechanism removed as its doors opened. "I know that vessel," Rafferty said. Her jaw tightened as she stared at the airship.

"How?"

Rafferty forced herself to still. She had begun to shake beside him. "Because I used to fly it. It's one of hers."

The airship's wings disturbed the grasses and stirred the bodies along the ancient watchtower site.

Any winged creature might have departed with whatever artifact Calixta and Aubryn had been sent to protect, he realized, his musings the night before about the lack of tracks from the field of battle sounding ridiculous to his bleary-eyed self.

Four figures crept across the watchtower, their voices swallowed by the distance.

His stomach grew queasy again, followed by a swell

of rage, at the thought of the disturbance to Calixta's resting place.

She should be in the family plot, laid to rest with our ancestors, he thought at first.

But Calixta hadn't wanted that, had thrown aside every entreaty his parents had made in that regard.

This couldn't have been what his sister wanted instead—grave robbers sneaking about the site where she'd drawn her last breath.

He and Rafferty crept closer, the caution of their movements torn between their desire to know what was happening to their loved ones and their fear of being caught by Silversword's forces.

Quindythias closed his eyes and willed the wind to draw toward them. *Bring me their voices.*

He gasped as Atamos answered.

"You sure these are them?" The airship captain's voice was rough. They spoke without care for being overheard.

Quindythias shook with unspent rage. Rafferty clasped her hand around his arm, holding him back.

"Have to be. They have the marks."

His hands closed into fists as he realized how they would have determined such a fact.

He and Rafferty hadn't covered back over the elemental sigils. Would the figures realize his mistake or continue on as though nothing was amiss?

Quindythias glared at the airship. Could he fell it from here with a gust of wind or somehow rend it from the sky?

He wasn't sure how to tell if he had such an ability,

but his internal drive toward self-preservation stopped him. Calixta and Aubryn had died for something. *Or been sent into an ambush*—his years of military strategy supplied.

Quindythias's jaw clenched as several bursts of wind whipped over the mountains. Exhaustion tugged at his body, behind his eyes, yet there was no alleviating his rage.

He and Rafferty had to survive to ensure the sacrifice he didn't fully understand meant *something*. However hard she was to reach, he'd make sure the field commander answered for whatever order had led Calixta and Aubryn to that watchtower.

The robbers carried Calixta's and Aubryn's bodies aboard and zipped away into the night.

The ship paused a few hundred feet from the cliff. Before it disappeared, it lobbed balls of fire over the battlefield, scorching the corpses and burning whatever evidence might have remained of what Calixta and Aubryn had died protecting.

Rafferty held onto his wrist so tightly he knew it would bruise, but he didn't stop her. The swell of shadows around them became so thick he couldn't see the side of the mountain any longer.

As the inferno raged, the ship turned and vanished from sight. Quindythias released his pent-up rage with a shout.

An impossibly strong gust of wind rushed down from the peak, doubling the conflagration set along the corpses.

He fell to his knees, spots of black dotting his vision.

Quindythias awoke with his head cushioned by his pack as dawn pricked over the sky.

"I think you may have overdone it," Rafferty said, peering at him.

Quindythias winced and rubbed the side of his head. There was a coppery tang to his mouth and dried blood beneath his nose. "So it would seem."

The fire had died out in the night. He and Rafferty stumbled down the mountainside to search through the ashes for anything the midnight thieves might have missed. He found himself drawn to the plinth in the center of the stone watchtower, but even after searching it for hours, he couldn't determine the site's significance. Alessandra's agents flying off with the prize made more sense.

Just before midday, Rafferty broke the silence of their searching. "Will it be a problem, do you think, that the power of their sigils passed to us? Will they be able to tell?"

Quindythias smiled, the pieces of a plan slowly trickling into place. The trick was not to rush such things. Allow your enemy to fall into a carefully laid trap. "I certainly hope so," he answered. It might serve their ends and speed their timeline, if Silversword was looking for them. She couldn't very well keep the champions a secret and uncover two of them in hiding, could she? "What do you know about this new champion of fire?"

A distant caw caught on the air before Rafferty could

reply. The sound made Quindythias's teeth rattle. Goosepimples rose along his arms and down his neck.

A dark shape, and then several appeared against the gray sky.

"Dezra," he and Rafferty murmured as one.

They glanced at one another and sprinted back the way they'd come.

The hybrid creatures were one of Alessandra's most prized and most depraved creations. Perfect hunters, used to wipe out entire populations throughout Eldura's history.

They helped each other over the rocks, clawing their way to the top as the creatures landed upon the watchtower's ruined pillars, croaking and cawing to one another.

"We have to get away from them," Rafferty said, eyes wide. "If they catch our scent—"

He nodded, understanding. Their tenure as champions would be impossibly short-lived.

"Can you run?" Rafferty asked.

Quindythias's lips quirked at her question. "I can. And one day, when our revenge is complete, I'll fly."

THE UNDYING GROVE

Rowan's heart drummed in her ears as Lucien cradled her against his chest. She stared out over the breadth of the Academia Magica, their towers, the turrets of the walls, the distant shapes of Delmoir beyond, and the barest hint of the glittering blue of the sea.

"Wait!" she flailed in Lucien's arms, remembering the offering of earth's return. The way the element had possessed her senses, taken over her body.

Lucien's nostrils flared. "Easy, sparrow. You are still learning to fly." He tightened his grasp around her legs and arms.

"They enchanted the elements—"

The guardian smirked and dropped his gaze to meet hers. There were flecks of deep brown and a ring of black in his eyes that she hadn't noticed before.

Rowan's pulse jumped. Though there was something terrifying about him, the guardian was strangely beautiful as well.

"Do you control the imbuing of water within your being, or do they?" So faintly she could have convinced herself she was imagining it, Lucien's talons traced the outer curve of her thigh where her sigil of water pulsed, its energy flowing through her veins.

Before she could answer, he trailed his thumb down her sleeve over the sigil of earth. "And the earth? Is that yours or theirs?"

"M-mine." He smelled of damp stone and smoke, a heady masculine musk that reminded her of incense in a cave swirling through and blurring her senses.

Lucien's smirk returned and he nodded his chin toward their destination. A dense patch of forest beyond the Pentacle's holdings. "Where we're going sparrow, they won't be able to touch you."

His promise danced in his golden eyes and Lucien's powerful wingbeats carried them beyond the Academia Magica's walls.

As soon as they emerged from the academy's boundaries, leaving behind the cliffs that surrounded the lagoon, a new pulse of ancient energy caught Rowan's attention.

She stiffened in Lucien's arms, searching the forest.

Blearily, her phoenix opened its eyes.

In the distance, one copse of trees towered over the rest.

Rowan's breath caught, and her phoenix squawked

in her chest. One tree of each type—ash, oak, hawthorn, maple, pine, birch—her thoughts skipped and jumped, counting them all.

All save willow.

"You're taking me to the Undying Grove," Rowan murmured.

The guardian smiled. "We need to be somewhere it's safe for you to unleash who you truly are."

His wings carried them nearer, and Rowan's thoughts darted ahead. "Are the stories about it true?" She raised her voice to be heard over the wind.

"Which stories have you heard?"

Rowan repeated the rumors she'd learned back in Willow Glen, the legends she'd encountered on her paupa's knee—each Druidess, through the ages, gave up her heart near the close of her life and entrusted it into a hearttree. In turn, the hearttrees protected the whole of Lis-Maen, preserving the druids' ancient magic, their living heritage.

"Paupa said that the spread of hearttrees across Lis-Maen started to provoke the other forest mages, particularly as the Quadrate gained power. Alessandra's agents pursued the trees' protectors, rooting them out one by one. In part to protect our ancient knowledge and to allow other magics the chance to grow, they relocated all the hearttrees save one to within the Undying Grove."

The oak tree towered over the rest, her branches spread wide in a sweeping embrace that beckoned Rowan nearer. She couldn't believe she was about to enter one of the most sacred places in the world.

Lucien nodded. "And that was when the Quadrate expanded to include those of a wilder persuasion, like yourself. From there, the Pentacle was born." He smirked, a glint of mischief in his eye. "It was one of my better ideas."

Rowan gasped, staring up at the guardian. "It was your idea to form the Pentacle?" Her muscles stiffened, and she wondered, not for the first time, if she'd been too hasty in accepting his aid.

The guardian shook his head. "It was my intention to save the druids." He caught his finger beneath her chin and raised her gaze to his. "Forming an alliance those like the Sorceress could understand was the most expeditious way I could ensure my aims."

She frowned, puzzling through this newest in a series of revelations.

"Tell me, sparrow," Lucien purred as he circled over the clearing at the center of the Undying Grove, "what are *your* aims here?"

The various pulses of life of the sacred site reminded Rowan of her and Paupa's trip to the edges of the heart-tree's territory so many years ago. Her heart lifted in her chest, and the scents of the earth swirled through her senses, spring rain and autumn breezes mingled together.

He landed and placed her gently on the ground. A soft hum filled the air around her, lulled her breath the moment she touched the earth. Time slowed, her burdens lightened.

She could lie. She could try to conceal the truth, but

Lucien had found her. He was trying to help. Rowan looked from one tree to the next, holding herself back from pressing her palm into the heart of each of them. "My friend is sick," she murmured. "She may be dying." Rowan told Lucien about Athenza's troubling symptoms, how she didn't know what to do to heal her. To help.

"I'm afraid I'll have to choose between saving Athenza and pursuing my vow to the Pentacle, learning to wield the six." She already knew what Athenza would say—that Rowan should remain focused on the elements like they'd planned. But however certain the healers were that there was nothing to be done, she couldn't accept powerlessness. Not when so much potential remained unexplored—if only she knew where to start, where the true problem lay.

"Separated from its source, doesn't magic come at a cost?" Rowan's voice caught, and she turned back toward the guardian to find him watching her intently. The blaze of his eyes froze her breath. No one ever looked at her that way. As though she was something precious he longed to cradle and devour.

Lucien held her gaze, calculation etched over even the small tilt of his chin, the twitch of his eye. "That can be true, I suppose." The gold in his eyes intensified as she slid closer. His body was rigid, towering over her.

Rowan's pulse skipped as she drew nearer. The wet stone and musk of his scent washed over her—at once a beckoning darkness, like Nyx's embrace, and the yawning maw of a portal into the depths of the Shadowlands from which she would never escape. "True in what circumstance?"

The faintest twinge at the corner of his mouth said he was intrigued by her questioning. "There are always limitations to an individual's power. You have seen this for yourself in your training, have you not?"

With her nod, he continued, "Some find themselves quickly overwhelmed by even the barest answering flicker of power, like the unfortunates who were there for your first lesson when you awakened the slumbering elements and the titans saw them culled."

A chill swept Rowan's spine. Lucien spoke of them like it wasn't only inevitable they had perished. It was good.

"Others, though—" The glint in his eyes said what he did not—these others. *You. Me.* "Others have to search far and wide to even begin to find the limitations of their power." He gestured to the trees around them. "They find ancient sites of sacrifice, pure, wild magic. And they open themselves to its possession." The yellow light she'd first noticed within his gaze the night they met flashed from behind the gold.

Her phoenix ruffled its feathers—warning Lucien off or warming to him, Rowan couldn't tell.

She stopped just out of arm's reach of the guardian. His nostrils flared.

"There is a third possibility, sparrow. One that is nearly as rare as an innate gifting of wild magic." Lucien reached out and tucked a strand of hair behind Rowan's ear with his talon. The scrape of his claw against her skin sent a second shiver down her spine.

Her heart thundered over the shallowness of her breath. "What is it?" she whispered even though they were the only two in the Undying Grove beyond the flora and fauna who dwelled here always.

For a moment, stillness stretched between them, and she could almost have sworn she heard the still-beating hearts of the former Druidesses, tucked away into the hearttrees all around them.

Then the answering glint of molten gold within his eyes, his sign of approval. Interest.

"For those visionary enough to reject even the possibility of limitation, there are routes forward. Secret pathways forged by other trailblazing souls."

Lucien reached beneath his dark tunic and withdrew a crystal pendant, clear as water, dangling on a delicate gold chain that wrapped around the gem and held it in place.

"Do you know what this is?" His tone was half purr, half predatory snarl.

"A necklace," Rowan answered simply. She decided that was preferable to the more obvious *by the fact that you're asking me, no, obviously not.*

A flicker of amusement crossed his face as though he'd read her thoughts. "Have you ever heard of a soul-bond?"

The forest grew still, holding its breath alongside Rowan. The beat of the hearttrees fell silent.

"A binding spell would be the more general term, often facilitated by an artifact created to hold the enchantment—in this case, an amulet of binding."

Despite the shade of the forest, iridescent light danced within the dangling pendant.

"Some believe in recurring souls, those who are

bound to another, even a specific destiny, from the moment they are born if not before." His gaze narrowed at the unspoken truth between them. *I know who your father told you they tried to revive.*

Lilia.

"An amulet of binding is an answer to such a predetermined fate." He held her gaze, waiting to gauge the effect of his words. "It lets those who have returned choose their own fate."

"And if someone is not returned?" She had no memories beyond her own. Whether Paupa and his friends had succeeded in recalling Lilia to the world through Rowan or not, she still had the fate she and her father had chosen, together—to prove herself to the wild hearttree. That was her part in the revival of Verdigris, the one being who could unite Lis-Maen as one people and protect them from would-be allies and proclaimed enemies alike.

Lucien simply smirked, the existential nature of her question of no concern. "That you would ask tells me you have what it takes already."

Rowan wasn't certain what he meant.

Without warning, Lucien lunged forward, trapping Rowan in the darkness of his wings. One arm snapped over her hip, holding her against his legs. With his other hand he seized her throat, grasping her just tightly enough for the protest of her pulse to press back against his touch.

Rowan's jaw clenched. Her phoenix had blazed to life, its golden gaze staring out of her eyes. Were she to release the scream she'd forced herself to catch between her teeth, she feared the phoenix might burst free.

"Do you feel powerful, sparrow?"

Her shoulders tightened, and she pulled her hands into fists. She sensed the flick of the vines hanging from the trees nearby, wriggling at the ends of the branches. They would try to answer her. But would their aid be enough if she called for it?

Lucien bent toward her ear, folding his wings back so she could see the clearing again. The damp musk and living shadow of his scent drowned out all else.

Rowan couldn't bring herself to say no. It was a weakness she wouldn't allow. But neither could she say yes.

"It's all a matter of perspective, you see." The tip of his nose grazed the line of her ear as he lowered toward her. His breath cast a hot breeze through her hair. Lucien's voice dropped dangerously low. It reverberated through Rowan's chest. "To an untrained observer, I hold all the power here between us." His heartbeat was a slow drum to her own fevered, furious pulse.

"But to a very few wise enough to not be blinded only by what they know how to see," he murmured, tightening his grasp on her hip, "they would have the clarity to recognize how impossible it would be for me to let you go even if I wished to." His pointer finger traced the line of her jaw. "And I have no desire to do something so foolish."

Lucien released her hip and carefully spun Rowan away, holding out her arm between them. She was dizzy, fevered by his presence but couldn't pull herself from his grasp. She had to know what he was building toward.

One by one, he unfastened the hooks of her sleeve, rolling it up to reveal the sigil of earth that wrapped around either side of her elbow and stretched up and down her arm. The mirrored flowers Seth had designed for her were her favorite part of the sigil tattoo connecting her to Gaia. Lucien pushed her unbuttoned sleeve up toward her elbow, her bare arm stretched between them.

"Were you to desire a different fate, sparrow, one of your own determination, one that would allow you to save Athenza and fulfill your oath to the Pentacle, I could help you, as I promised to do when I added my blood to yours with the vow the day we met."

"What are you saying?"

With his free hand, he retrieved the amulet of binding from around his neck and held it out toward her. "Bind yourself to me, and I will help you become more powerful than you could have ever dreamed."

"Bind my soul?"

"Soul. Magic." He met her gaze. "What is the difference?"

For all the passion, the desire of his words, Lucien kept his features strangely blank through this request. As though he was asking her to share a cutting from her garden or to separate the roots of a plant for prop-agation.

"And what would you get in return?"

Lucien straightened to his full height but kept his head bowed, gazing at the sigil on her arm. "Aside from the satisfaction we guardians always receive from helping those in our charge"—the telltale glint flashed—"I would gain access to your stores of elemental magic. Together, we'll deepen them which will allow you the power you seek and let you save your friend."

Rowan glanced between the guardian and her sigil. With him so close, she could not sense the wisdom of the trees. Her phoenix was rigid in her mind, unblinking in its study of Lucien.

"I can help you carry the six," Lucien murmured into her neck.

She was still panting, her mind spinning.

"I can help you save your former mentor."

Rowan had no doubt that he was asking—demanding to take Athenza's place. Her body trembled at the elemental energy he'd awakened that was still seeking to find its way out of her being. Her phoenix had been so near.

"Share your power with me," Lucien murmured. Gently, he rolled her sleeve up higher, securing it by her shoulder. He motioned for Rowan to join him on the grass. She settled onto his lap.

"Like this." With the tip of his talon, Lucien carved a line through her skin, tearing through her flesh and unleashing a stream of blood. Threads of bright green wove through the sanguine spill.

He held her gaze as he raised her arm to his mouth. Rowan's thundering heartbeat returned. Her phoenix's feathers trembled—waiting to fly them away, to lash out at Lucien, or flutter in ecstasy, she wasn't sure.

Lucien pressed his lips to her cut and sucked on her

skin, pulling the blood, the magic of the earth into his mouth.

Rowan cried out in pain, writhing and trying to escape his hold.

His arms tightened around her, a vice of iron. Lucien's teeth pierced her skin. Her phoenix screamed.

And then his tongue darted along the soft underside of her arm, tugging a ripple of pleasure after it. Her protest faded from her lips, and she stopped trying to writhe away from him.

Lucien's tongue stroked her flesh again, and her phoenix trembled.

With the third brush, Rowan groaned. Her eyes fluttered back in her head.

A deep growl followed her moan of pleasure. The sense of wings at her back returned.

Lucien ripped his teeth away and wrenched Rowan's arm before her face. She gasped, breathing heavily. Her pulse pounded in her ears, and quivers of anticipation shot across her skin, making every inch of her body thrum with life.

He had added to her sigil of earth—a few broken lines branching off the sigil like roots. Lucien stroked the underside of her arm with his thumb. She shivered in response.

"Imagine what I can do with the six, sparrow," he murmured, his gaze full of dark promise.

Lucien wiped a bead of her blood from the corner of his lip and sucked it off his finger.

She sank back against his chest, suddenly exhausted.

Pointed talons trailed gently along her scalp, tracing

the lines between her intricate braids and brushing the hair that had fallen free during their struggle back into place. "I bound your magic to mine that day," he confessed, his breath hot against the pointed shell of her ear. "Accept the bond, bind yourself to me."

Rowan swallowed her fear, stilled the trembling in her shoulders. She extricated herself from Lucien's lap and turned to face him. "Can you show me what it would mean? So I can understand the binding?"

A dark grin twisted his lips as he gazed up at her. "Sparrow, I thought you'd never ask."

The guardian rose, closing the distance between them once again. Lucien towered over her. He clasped his hands on either side of her face. "Call the elements to bear witness."

"I don't know how."

Lucien shook his head. "I know you do."

She bit her lip, trying to discern what he meant. There was an intensity, a fervor to his request, one she wanted to understand, possibly to match.

During that first day of training, Rowan had awakened the elements, Lucien said. As far as she knew, she had simply reached out to where they lingered nearby.

Can you help me? she asked her phoenix. *We need to know what he means. If he can help us.*

The golden gaze that lived within her mind held hers. Rowan closed her eyes, blocking out Lucien.

The phoenix ruffled its feathers.

Please.

It clacked its beak, and Rowan thought it might ignore her request.

Then her phoenix raised its beak and bellowed at the sky. A rumbling crested over the earth of the grove and wind whipped through the trees. Lightning crackled overhead as storm clouds flocked to cover the clearing.

They broke as soon as they arrived, drenching Rowan and the guardian in their downpour.

Lucien's wings unfurled tentatively to offer her protection from the storm she and her phoenix had called.

Rowan shook her head. She'd done as he'd asked. The elements had answered her call.

He slid his fingertips from around her jaw to perch on either side of her neck. His thumb trailed through the torrents of water on her cheek. "You are magnificent, my sparrow." His molten eyes studied Rowan's face and her stomach fluttered. "Whatever happens, never forget that." The guardian lowered his lips toward hers.

Rowan raised onto her tiptoes, her courage strengthened by the storm. She met his mouth with hers, the rain slicking over her lips, catching in her lashes.

Vicelike hands seized her arms, holding her in place. His lips were soft where they touched, but every other part of him was rigid, the tension of an entire herd of cervidae waiting to begin their hunt.

He drew back, staring down at her, disbelief breaking through his mask. "Sparrow?"

Rowan grinned and thunder rolled overhead, rattling against her chest. For once, she wasn't the only wild thing struggling to control herself. "Guardian."

She fastened her hands in the fabric of his tunic and tugged him back down toward her. Lucien caught his hand in the back of her hair and wrapped his arm around her waist, lifting Rowan off the ground and hugging her against the solid plane of his chest.

From the back of her mind, her phoenix cawed, flapping its flaming wings.

Rowan ignored the bird's cries and let herself be washed away in the guardian's embrace.

CHAPTER FORTY-FIVE

MARCON

"She's gone then," Garreth said, sinking heavily into his chair.

Marcon nodded, his jaw tight. "There's so much I want to ask you." How the blacksmith and Isadora had known one another, if Garreth had been the one to tell her he was in trouble.

"Rule number three," Garreth said, his dark eyes shining.

Marcon held his breath.

Staring back at him were the answers he sought. Garreth raised his glass and waited for Marcon to do the same. "Know when you're being watched and trust your friends to have your back."

The shine in Garreth's gaze intensified, and Marcon felt answering tears prick in his own eyes. A champion of water, training him this whole time. And he'd hardly asked her anything about herself. He'd let a madwoman torture him instead.

They threw back their drinks, and Marcon poured them another.

"Rule four is connected to rule three," Garreth added. "Know that there are more lingering in the shadows than you could ever imagine."

Maybe it was the exhaustion of the day, but Marcon wasn't sure what his friend meant. He sipped the second glass more slowly. "So you're not—"

Garreth coughed into his hand, interrupting Marcon. "I'm a blacksmith, lad. Nothing more, nothing less." He reached over and clasped Marcon's shoulder. "We need to get you back before you're missed. Rest up, and come and tell me what happens after your meeting with Silversword in the morning."

Marcon did as Garreth asked, returning to the barracks to find Vateri curled up on her mattress and Cole playing a card game by candlelight. They didn't speak much, the tension of the day hanging heavy over them.

"She's upset," Cole told Marcon.

"I think we all are."

Cole's jaw tensed. "I'm afraid she's going to separate us."

Marcon nodded at that. "We'll find one another again," he assured his friend.

He climbed up onto the bunk above Vateri, the exhaustion and despair of the day seeping over him.

His dreams captured him, tugging him away to an unfamiliar room in an inn. The red-haired elf writhed on the bed in the center of the room. She moaned, back arched, sighs of pleasure alternating with soft whimpers of pain.

He made to stand, to go to her, but found himself trapped instead. Chained to a chair, his chest bare.

Marcon searched the chamber. A banked fire, worn sitting chair, a small table.

His jaw tightened and he whirled back toward the bed, unreasonable jealousy blazing in his chest. Was someone here with her?

Her breathing quickened as did the pitch of her arousal. The musty rose of her scent enveloped him. Marcon struggled against his bindings, the chains rattling against the back of the chair. The iron gripped him tight, its teeth rough against his skin.

She cried out as a wave of pleasure crested over her, and Marcon swore under his breath. The desire to see the look in her eyes as she came undone overwhelmed him, even if it wasn't by his hand or her own. She gripped the white sheets by her shoulders, her head arched back into her pillow.

Marcon searched the inn again. His chains had been bolted to the floor along with the chair, preventing him from rocking his way free.

He gritted his teeth. Such measures wouldn't prevent him from breaking his way out of his bindings.

Marcon scooted away from the back of the chair, careful to keep a slight tension in the chains so the chair would be able to give beneath them. He drove his elbows into the frame, angling them away from the upright posts and into the cross hatches at the back instead.

With his first strike they rattled. By the third he broke free.

He sprang up from the splintering wood, the chains impossibly falling away as he rushed to the side of the bed.

The elf was panting, gazing up at him. The way her eyes shone he could almost have convinced himself she thought he was responsible for the orgasm she was still coming down from.

She started to sit up, the sheet riding down her chest. The elf reached out for him and caught his hand in hers.

Along the middle of her arm, she bore a half-sleeve tattoo, marked in green. It formed an intricate flower on either side of her elbow that was mesmerizing.

Marcon tilted his head to the side, studying the carefully etched markings. They reminded him of his own sigil when it heated. But as he watched, cruel lines emerged in jagged roots away from the floral pattern.

He jolted. Blood began to pool around the cuts. "Are you alright?" Marcon asked.

She nodded back, though a small line of tears glistened at the base of her eyes.

As he watched, the cuts hardened into scabs, their rust-hued lines a sharp contrast to the deep summer green of her tattoo.

The scabs healed, whitened into scars. And the whole horrible process repeated.

Marcon's jaw tightened, and rage replaced the desire burning in his chest. "Who, in all the miserable hells, is doing this to you?" he growled.

She stared up at him, brilliant green eyes even

brighter than the verdant lines of her tattoo. She didn't react as the scabs turned white again, darkening to green with time.

He couldn't allow it to happen to her a third time. "Wildfire," he demanded.

The elf smiled up at him instead of answering, lips closed, making the already tantalizing pout of her mouth impossible for him to take his eyes from.

Her blood pooled along his hand as the marks stretched further down her arm, and Marcon loosened his grip, a cold pulse of horror that he might have harmed her in her already injured state.

"Answer me."

She smirked instead.

Marcon huffed through his nose. *Titans*, the smell of her. His throat hummed with need. It was only a dream. He could catch her around the neck, press her into the mattress, but not with her hurt. Was she seeking him out? Or was she simply a figment of his imagination?

"Do you need help? Can you tell me where you are?"

"Come and find me," she answered, exactly like she had in his first dream where this torment began.

Someone pounded against the wooden door of the inn, calling for him. She didn't react.

"Help me," Marcon asked, frustration creeping into his voice. He did touch her then, ignoring the fist thumping against their door that tried to draw her away. He brushed his fingertips along the heat of her neck and wrapped his hand in the back of her hair. "Give me a clue, anything."

She leaned toward him, lips soft. Her gaze dropped to his mouth.

Marcon inhaled.

"Colabra!"

He jolted awake.

Patrick held his shoulders, shaking him. "The field commander sent me." He grinned. "I think we've finally reached our deployment assignments."

Marcon blinked back at the half-orc, struggling to tug himself from the threads of his dream. He couldn't help but feel there had been something important for him to understand, something he had missed that she was trying to communicate to him.

"Colabra?" Patrick hovered over him, concern flickering across his expression.

"Give the man a moment," Cole cajoled, shaking his head as he reentered the room, a towel swung low around his waist. "From the sounds he was making, I don't think he expected to wake up to you."

Marcon flushed. Trust Cole to take something important and twist it.

Patrick chuckled at Marcon's expense. "I can see how you'd be disappointed to see me instead of Lorieannan."

Marcon tensed, guilt twisting his stomach. What did it say about him that the woman who kept appearing in his dreams was nothing like the one he'd failed to save?

Cole's glare made Patrick flush in turn, an effect that only deepened as Vateri stomped into the room also clad solely in a towel, her short damp hair dripping rivulets onto the warm brown of her shoulders like a forest in the rain.

The other two men stopped speaking, watching the elf with lips slightly parted.

Marcon shook his head. They'd agreed not to speak of what had happened to Isadora until they were certain they could be away from the field commander's spies, Patrick included.

As he dressed and Vateri and Cole bickered, Marcon saw again the crystalline statue Silversword had turned Isadora into. It was safer, surely, for them to be assigned positions away from her immediate influence, even if she separated them for a short while.

He couldn't shake from his memory the pale white glow of her eyes. There had been something cold about the light shining forth, more the blinding snow of a treacherous mountainside than the flash of light upon water or blaze of a summer sun.

The titans knew what they were doing, Marcon reminded himself as he and Cole trailed behind Patrick and Vateri on their way to the field commander's quarters. Cole was only partially listening to Marcon as they walked and listed, again, where they might be assigned next. He kept glancing at Vateri and looking between her and Patrick.

Marcon kept his smile to himself. He couldn't tease his friend for his infatuation, not when he was harboring one of his own with an elf his mind had invented who began haunting his dreams immediately after he received the sigil of fire from his silent titan.

The barest hint of heat radiated out from the sigil emblazoned onto his forearm, the only way that Ignis communicated with him. The one sign that made him wonder if perhaps the elf was real.

Desire uncoiled low in his stomach as the memory of her moans, her smell, rushed through his senses. The musk of roses and bay leaves, bruised, as though they'd been dropped onto a bed of moss and mussed underfoot.

Marcon rubbed the back of his neck to urge the phantom feeling of her from his hand. The softness of her skin, the invitation of her lips—*It's a dream*, he scolded himself. *And you're a soldier. Pull yourself together.*

He couldn't afford for his mind to wander while before the field commander.

Silversword was a coiled viper, tongue scenting the air, waiting to strike.

CHAPTER FORTY-SIX
MARCON

Marcon let the elf slip from his mind as he and his friends waited to be called before the field commander. It had been an uneasy transition over the last few months, returning to an intimacy with Patrick now that the half-orc had finally decided Marcon wasn't a threat to his ambitions or, as Marcon at least had always suspected to be the case, in competition for his father's affection.

He turned toward Patrick while they waited to be admitted to Silversword's chambers one by one. "I hope that our paths cross again soon," Marcon said, holding out his hand to shake Patrick's.

The half-orc hesitated, those old patterns of competition flickering over his gaze. Patrick sighed and stuck out his hand. "As do I, Colabra."

He nodded to Marcon as the field commander's aide stepped out into the hall and pronounced Patrick's name as the first Silversword would see. The half-orc paused for a moment at Vateri's side and murmured something in her ear before following the aide into the room.

Cole's jaw was clenched tight enough to cut glass.

Marcon cleared his throat and elbowed Cole in the side as Vateri turned about, smiling at the pair of them. "Where do you think we'll be assigned?" she wondered aloud, the same conversation that had been occupying them for weeks.

M arcon was the last of the four to be pulled into Silversword's office.

The dwarf postured before her row of windows, the air of a conqueror about her armored shoulders, thick braid granting her a few additional inches of height with its beaded positioning atop her head.

"You recall one of my first orders, I assume, Captain?"

Marcon inclined his head to the dwarf. He hadn't been in close proximity to her since Isadora's execution and did not relish the nearness now. "I have learned a great deal by your instruction, Field Commander. To which orders specifically do you refer?"

Her slow scheming smile sent a chill down Marcon's spine. He and his friends couldn't be the only ones so unnerved by Silversword, and yet what were they to do about such treasonous thoughts? Matters across Respite had continued to degrade with the soldiers of the Luz openly patrolling the streets by day and spying on Respite's residents by night.

Alessandra's attack should have brought the city

together. He could see now why the vultura had simply drawn back at her command.

The dark goddess was letting Respite devour itself.

"I have set aside a special assignment in a collaboration between the battalion and my office," she continued. Marcon could only imagine how Major Barton had taken such an order. What had Silversword sent to the battalion to explain Isadora's death? Did he know enough to suspect Silversword's hand in the execution of one revealed, in her death, to be a champion of water?

She waited for him to engage.

"And what assignment is that?" Marcon struggled to maintain a neutral tone.

"The one I've been training you for," the dwarf added, evading a simple answer again. The lessons over the last several weeks jumbled in his mind, Silversword's abuse and sharp orders mingling with Isadora's thoughtful instructions.

Was she picturing his death at her hands if he stepped out of her carefully drawn lines?

Silversword stepped up onto the raised platform of her desk and settled onto her tall chair so she might look him in the eyes without having to crane her neck. "As we discussed when you first arrived back from the front, you'll be sent as a spy to infiltrate the Pentacle's ranks and uncover a secret magical working that's leading to attacks against our forces."

Marcon frowned. "I am trained as a soldier, Field Commander." His training had continued in that vein during his months by her side, not to mention the years before.

"Bah." Silversword waved her hand as though his two decades of drills and service were no matter.

Now that she had cinched her control over the Luz, perhaps that was correct.

"You have shown a great deal of spirit in your work for me within the city. Even the way in which you bore witness to a fellow champion's execution—"

Marcon's stomach twisted. Between the hangings of innocents, Isadora's death, and the elf who dwelled in his dreams, he was haunted, waking and sleeping. When Silversword did return him to Barton's command, would he have the guts to confess to the major that he'd been present when Isadora died? What had truly occurred?

Though Barton had seen his potential during the battle for Sanctuary, the major would never forgive him for not trying to save Isadora, even if it would have meant Marcon's death as well.

Silversword balanced her shiny, plate-covered arms atop one another, swinging her feet beneath the gilded lines of her desk. "You are ready for this, Captain."

Marcon's jaw twinged. Readiness wasn't his objection.

"This is the part where you thank me for the special attention," she added, that dangerous flash of white shining within her dark brown eyes.

Would a time come in which he would be similarly afflicted with the musings of his element? Where a swirl of red would drown out the grays and blues of his gaze?

He forced his jaw to loosen as he rose and bowed to his commanding officer. "Thank you, Field Commander Silversword."

Her grin widened at the return to propriety. "I've selected one of your lieutenants to go with you. The elf rather than your brooding friend. She'll blend in better—otherwise you and the scowling one will appear like you belong only within a brothel."

"Excuse me?"

Silversword chuckled to herself. "It's a common enough practice for soldiers on leave. I'm a little surprised you haven't availed yourself of a similar trip already."

Marcon stared back at her, utterly lost for words.

"With the elf at your side, there will be less speculation is all I mean," she clarified. "Your other lieutenant will join Major Barton's forces in the wilds of Lis-Maen. You can act surprised when they both tell you as much shortly. After you've found out whatever this secret weapon they're building is, you'll report back to me, and I'll instruct those waiting in the wilds accordingly."

He bowed to the leader of the Luz and took his leave, grateful to be stepping free of the confines of her office, at least for a few weeks if not longer, depending on the length of their mission in Delmoir.

A soldier turned spy. It didn't sit right with him, just as it hadn't when she'd first proposed the mission.

What was waiting for him in Delmoir that he and Cole would stand out the moment they stepped out of the walls of a brothel? And why deploy soldiers if his discoveries might not result in an attack?

He knew his friends were waiting for him in the Dracat's Grin, but they could wait a little longer.

Marcon's feet took him along the well-trod path to the blacksmith's home.

Garreth received him with a raised eyebrow, his own glass of wine already in hand. "Have a seat," the smith ordered.

He returned with a second glass for Marcon and listened with brow furrowed as Marcon recounted Silversword's orders.

"It is by forging that one becomes a blacksmith," Garreth answered simply.

Marcon took a deep draft of the chilled red wine the half-orc had brought over.

Garreth tipped his glass toward Marcon and did the same.

"You've said as much to me before, even more often to Patrick when he came back from soldiering with a bloody nose. But I'm not sure I'm following you in this particular application."

The blacksmith laughed at the mention of his son, a rare occurrence lately. "The lad needed encouragement, always comparing himself to you who, only twice, came to me with a similar complaint."

Marcon shrugged. "I'm faster than my opponents usually took me for, and after I hit them once, they didn't tend to get back up in a hurry."

"So you are putting it together then."

"No." Marcon shook his head. "This has nothing to do with soldiering, with being part of the battalion. She's asking me to be a spy on those we're supposedly courting as allies."

Garreth snorted into his glass. "Don't let any of the

forest-folk hear you saying that. They'll send you back with leaves sticking out where they don't belong and little else between your ears."

An even more disconcerting warning than he'd bargained for.

The blacksmith took pity on Marcon's confusion. "If you've been listening as you ought to have been—which I know you have, unlike my son—then you know that matters concerning the Cities, *especially* those involving the dwarf, are more complicated than they appear on the surface. So what I'd say is this—perhaps Silversword is showing you precisely the type of smithing she'd ask of you to be counted among her blacksmiths. Are we eye-to-eye now?"

Marcon swallowed and avoided Garreth's gaze. When he put it that way, the whole picture made sense, and he wasn't exactly grateful for the new truth he could see. "And if I refuse?" His voice was so soft, he scarcely recognized it. "If I decide not to be a smith after all?" The knowledge that soldiers would be waiting in the woods for news about a still-peaceful people, about possible allies, disturbed him.

Garreth sighed. "I worry you're romanticizing again, looking for goodness where there's little enough to be found. Don't sacrifice yourself and all you've worked for on principle." He leaned closer, sloshing his wine in his glass as he did so. "Don't be reckless, in other words." The gleam in the blacksmith's eye said that reckless was exactly what he expected Marcon to be. "If what she's looking for is a puppet, why not let her think that's what she's found. Then *you* decide what new information she gleans based on what you find when you get there."

Marcon looked up at that.

"*You* decide the type of smith you are."

He smiled at his friend and raised his glass. "To wise smiths."

Garreth grinned back and angled his glass. "I'll drink to that." He drained the dregs of wine and, with a groan, pushed himself up to his feet. "I know I'll need this for the second half of your news."

Marcon's uneasiness returned. Patrick would be waiting with his friends at the bar, but after his meeting with Silversword, he'd pressed a slip of parchment into Marcon's hands, as though he'd known Marcon would need to speak with the smith before the night was through.

He'd peeked at it on the way here. Silversword was dispatching Patrick with haste to Beacon, departing at dawn. Patrick said he didn't have time to bid his father farewell, a lie neither of them would believe. He wanted to avoid Garreth's reprimands was all.

Marcon tightened his jaw. Both father and son were stubborn, refusing to yield despite what it cost them. He handed the square of parchment over to Garreth, knowing the sign of Ilona shimmering at the top would incense his friend further.

Garreth's shoulders tightened as he read it, snorting at the end.

Marcon sighed as he drained his own glass. "Two 'top priorities' for the field commander. One spy for each?" The word tasted foul on the back of his tongue.

It would be hard enough for the smith to be losing his son to Silversword. Marcon hated the thought of Garreth believing he would be lost as well.

The half-orc surprised him by ambling over and clasping Marcon's shoulder, the gesture relaying strength and forbearance. "One spy. One smith in disguise." He poured the rest of the bottle he'd brought with him into Marcon's glass. "To wise smiths in the shadows," Garreth said, starting the toast this time.

Marcon echoed it, cheered somewhat by his friend's thoughtfulness, by knowing that in this at least, he wasn't entirely alone.

Vateri would be glad of the chance to visit Lis-Maen, though he wasn't sure how she'd take the more under-handed aspects of their mission. Had Silversword explained in full, or was she entrusting that to Marcon?

The more he thought of it, sipping wine with his friend, the more he warmed to his mission. He could be a wise smith in a foreign land, could pretend to be nothing more than a soldier on leave.

It would be a relief to set aside the concerns of Respite for a time, to not be constantly bombarded by the tension in the streets, the threats of rebellion and the executions that followed, always on edge for others and himself.

He could put Isadora's death behind him, the help-lessness that still clutched his throat whenever he shut his eyes and her twisted, blue form filled his vision.

From what he'd heard, Delmoir was a peaceful enough place. Friendly, even, under the right circum-stances. Cole would be put out that he and Vateri were being separated from him, but from the ever-present jealousy between them, he knew Cole would far prefer she be at Marcon's side than Patrick's.

Maybe with distance from Respite, the elf who haunted his dreams would depart as well.

Maybe you'll find someone like her? the treacherous voice in the back of his mind supplied after he departed the smith's and made his way to meet up with his friends.

He shoved the thought aside.

The last thing he needed on his secret mission was to be distracted by a frustratingly alluring, incommunicative elf who made his senses spin.

No. For this task, he would be clear of mind and fully dedicated to his post. He'd worked all his life to join the Blazing Battalion and had become a champion of fire besides. Nothing, not even bright green eyes and flaming red hair, would keep him from realizing his full potential.

Along his forearm, his sigil of fire burned.

A GREAT MANY DANGERS AWAIT IN DELMOIR . . .

Thank you so much for reading *Phoenix Rising*! Rowan and Marcon's journey continues in book two of the Feather & Flame dark epic fantasy series, From the Ashes!

Though Marcon doesn't know it yet, the elf from his dreams awaits in Delmoir. But greater shadows linger beneath the towers of the Academia Magica, with perhaps the most dangerous of all in the form of a guardian who would have the elf bind her magic, her soul, to his.

The stakes increase for Rowan as well—Athenza's life hangs by a thread, and Rowan is the only one capable of harnessing the elements to save her friend's life. What wouldn't she and her phoenix do to rescue her mentor from such a painful fate?

Find out in From the Ashes!

THE SORCERESS'S PLANS ARE AS LONG AS THEY ARE DARK...

Twenty years ago, Yvayne's path crossed with that of Rowan's parents and the former Oracle during the First Battle of Sanctuary.

Uncover the sorceress's secrets in the multi-perspective prequel novella for the *Feather & Flame* dark fantasy series, *Hexblade*. The novella weaves together intrigue and betrayal, where forces war in the shadows to protect their magical legacies. The true questions linger still— which side will emerge victorious? When all that remains is ash, what will emerge from the remnants of the flames?

We have but one spark of hope against the coming press of darkness—the phoenix, harbinger of Verdigris, draws near.

Upon the tangled threads of fate, we all have our part to play.

For the wild magic users of Lis-Maen, there is a single chance at hope, recalling a departed soul, one destined to save their world. But to others, there are much more enticing alternatives even nearer at hand.

For this Sorceress, this momentous occasion signals an opportunity to reclaim the stolen elemental magic. For Yvayne and the lorekeepers, it's a chance to call back a lost soul.

Regardless of which side prevails, one thing is certain: **Intrigue at the Academia Magica awaits.**

JOURNEY DEEPER INTO ELDURA

For character art reveals, fantasy map deep-dives, and all the latest happenings in Eldura, visit bethballbooks.com/join to be part of my newsletter community, the Circle of Story.

If you'd like to support my work and get early access to bonus scenes, visit patreon.com/bethball.

And finally, for special editions, art prints, and exclusive covers, visit bethballbooks.shop.

THE LEGACY OF THE WAR OF THE CHAMPIONS BURNS ON

The world of Eldura sought to hide its champions. But such power can only be buried for so long.

The tale woven between these pages is not the only legend in which Marcon and Quindythias appear. They emerge again in the *Age of Azuria* epic fantasy series, set five thousand years after the events of *Phoenix Rising* and the *Feather & Flame* series.

A runaway noblewoman. A cursed warrior.
And the quest to save their world.
For those with recurring souls, the journey is just beginning.

SHADOWS OF THE PAST LEAVE THEIR TRACE

The careful purveyor might recall mention of a blood experiment upon a line of daimon wolves in Sanctuary's past, when the city-state was still known as the kingdom of Draykemire . . .

This tale involves another fierce and determined heroine, one who finds her way to a backstabbing court during an autumn harvest festival.

And she's not the only one concealing blades.

If you loved the past-life connection between Marcon and Rowan and couldn't resist the brooding charm of a certain guardian, a new adventure awaits in *Phantom*, an epic romantic fantasy with assassins, courtly intrigue, banter, and slow burn.

The dangers of Draykemire are your destiny!

ABOUT THE AUTHOR

Beth Ball is a weaver of words and worlds spinning stories of druidic magic and the power of nature that span the epic fantasy realms of Eldura, Azuria, and beyond. If you enjoy lyrical tales of action and adventure, dragons, were-wolves, fae, wily foxes, and more, then grab your enchanted amulet, flaming longsword, poisoned dagger, or other mystical accessory of choice, and let's start our adventure!

You can find more of Beth's work and the legends of Eldura at bethballbooks.com. And if you're looking for playable, immersive adventures in Beth's Storyverse, visit groveguardianpress.com.

GLOSSARY

The following glossary entries may contain light spoilers for the worldbuilding and characters of Phoenix Rising. *For a more comprehensive list alongside lore and cross-series interconnections, visit bethballbooks.com/glossary.*

WORLDS & PLANES

Planes of Life, *three interconnected planes*, Eldura, Shadowlands, and Brightlands
Negative Planes, origin planes of the negata, realms of the prime goddess Pandora
Elemental Planes, one for each element, ruled over by and encompassing the power of each elemental titan
Astralei, spirit plane

ELEMENTAL TITANS

Ignis, titan of fire

Atamos, titan of air
Ilona, titan of light
Gaia, titan of earth
Thalyssa, titan of water
Nyx, titan of darkness
Verdigris, titan of nature, *destroyed and transformed into the three planes of life*
Izadra, titan of space, *destroyed and transformed into the spirit plane, Astralei*

POLITICAL POWERS AND ORGANIZATIONS OF ELDURA

Alessandra, the dark goddess, power centralized in **Scourge**

Cities United – Respite, Beacon, Sanctuary, Palais, Vestige, Bastion, Verita

The Five Faces of the Pentacle – Sorceress, Oracle, Creatrix, Druidess, Healer; figureheads of the Academia Magica and rulers of the recently centralized peoples of Lis-Maen, including the various druid conclaves

The Witches of the Emeraude – collected into covens, each ruled by a grand matron

Unaffiliated peoples of the **Glade of Shadows**, including the Sapphire Circle (powerful druid conclave) and the dryads

Lorekeepers – collective of secret keepers who slip between borders to preserve the lore, magic, and history of Eldura

DEITIES

Alessandra, "the dark goddess," goddess of negation
Cassandra, goddess of fate, patron deity of the saudad (travelers)
Fenrir, god of wolves, creator of the daimon (great wolves) and Lycan (first humans, progenitors of werewolves)
Lilith, demigoddess and revolutionary figure for the Shadowlands fae, daughter of Arrakis (goddess of spiders) and Nyx
Rasvana, goddess of dragons

FOLKLORIC HEROES

Hugh & Lilia, a Lycan and a fae, respectively; heroes before the Fall of the First Age who sacrificed their love to save their peoples
Daughters of Verdigris, Evelyn (mother of the Shadowlands fae, sometimes referred to as lummenfae or Umbral fae) and grandmother of Yvayne, Enid (mother of the Brightlands fae, sometimes referred to as brightfae) and mother of Lilia, Lyric (mother of druids whose magic transferred to the prime plane)
Ravenna, deposed queen of the Shadowlands who now shelters in hiding

www.ingramcontent.com/pod-product-compliance
Lightning Source LLC
Chambersburg PA
CBHW061533190726
48289CB00004B/1021